The Etiquette of Love

Minerva Spencer
writing as S.M. LAVIOLETTE

CROOKED SIXPENCE BOOKS are published by

CROOKED SIXPENCE PRESS

2 State Road 230

El Prado, NM 87529

Copyright © 2025 Shantal M. LaViolette

All rights reserved. No part of this publication may be reproduced, distributed, or transmitted in any form or by any means, including photocopying, recording, or other electronic or mechanical methods, without the prior written permission of the publisher, except in the case of brief quotations embodied in critical reviews and certain other noncommercial uses permitted by copyright law. For permission requests, write to the publisher, addressed "Attention: Permissions Coordinator," at the address above.

To the extent that the image or images on the cover of this book depict a person or persons, such person or persons are merely models, and are not intended to portray any character or characters featured in the book.

If you purchased this book without a cover you should be aware that this book is stolen property. It was reported as "unsold and destroyed" to the Publisher and neither the Author nor the Publisher has received any payment for this "stripped book."

First printing February 2025

10 9 8 7 6 5 4 3 2 1

Any references to historical events, real people, or real places are used fictitiously. Names, characters, and places are products of the author's imagination.

Printed in the United States of America

Prologue

Torrance Park
1796

"Wake up, Little Bird. Wake up..."

Winifred thought it was a dream—and a grand one, too. It was her brother Piers's voice, and he was the person she loved most in the world. Although Piers had told her never to tell that to Wareham or Nanny because it would hurt their feelings that neither of them was Winifred's favorite.

"Winifred?"

The sound of her name pulled her from her pleasant dream. Piers almost never called her that; it was always Little Bird.

Winifred opened her eyes and blinked. It was dark.

"Is it late, Piers?" she asked, pushing up onto her elbows.

Her brother's teeth flashed in the darkness. "It is so late that it is early, Little Bird."

"Have you come to take me to see the swans again?" The last time Piers had woken her before dawn they had taken a basket of food from Cook and gone to the lake where Piers had shown her the swan's nest and baby swans. But that had been back when Mama and Papa were still alive. Winifred had told her parents all about the swans when she had returned home that day and they had let her eat dinner in the hall that night with the adults—along with Piers and Dicky—and it had been one of the best days of her life.

Those are cygnets, Little Bird, just like you. And one day, you will grow up just as beautiful as those swans. Piers had pointed to the mother bird, who had suddenly decided to cruise toward them at full speed and had then come all the way out of the water to chase them, running and honking and hissing with her head down.

The Etiquette of Love

Piers scooped Winfred up in his arms and ran, both of them laughing at the poor beast's ungainly waddle on land, when she had been so graceful in the water.

Piers shook his head. "No swans tonight, Little Bird."

Winifred's belly clenched at her brother's smile. On the outside it looked like his regular grin, but even she could see beneath it; Piers was *sad*.

"Is something wrong, Piers?"

"I am going away. Tonight."

"Like Mama and Papa?" she asked in a high, terrified voice.

"No, no, hush," he soothed when she could not help the tear that slid down her cheek. "Don't cry—never cry for me, Little Bird!" he said fiercely. "I am not dying like Mama and Papa. I am just going away."

"But you will be back?"

He hesitated, squeezing her hand so hard it hurt, but Winifred didn't complain. "I will be back, but it might take a very, very long time. While you wait for me, do not believe what they say about me, Little Bird. Never believe their lies."

"I won't, Piers. I promise, I would never."

"Do not tell anyone you saw me tonight. This is a secret just between us."

"I won't tell anyone." She was openly crying, no matter how much she tried not to. "Should I light a candle for you—the way you said that sailors' families do—so you can find your way home?"

He gave a laugh that sounded cracked and broken. "You are too little to play with fire."

"Nanny can light it for me."

"Yes, you do that. You have Nanny light one. And one day, it will lead me home again." He took her face in both hands and kissed her forehead. "You are the only thing I will regret leaving behind. I love you, Little Bird."

And then her big brother—her protector and knight and hero and friend and companion, all rolled into one—was gone.

Winifred never told a soul about Piers's visit—not Nanny or even Dicky, the only brother she had left now. She loved Dicky, of course, but he was not Piers. Dicky had changed after Papa and Mama died. He had become the Earl of Wareham, like their Papa had been, and did not play with Winifred the way he used to do.

"Your brother is Wareham now. He is not a boy to be bothered with your childish demands, my lady," Nanny had chided when Winifred asked why Wareham was always so serious.

So, she never told a soul. But every day, she waited for Piers to come home.

Days rolled into weeks and months into years, and still she waited. At first, Nanny put a candle in the window for Winifred, but soon she was old enough to do so herself.

Almost four years had passed when Dicky came to the nursery to see her one day. "I have a surprise for you, Winny." Her brother had lost the shadowed, haunted look he had worn for years after their parents' deaths. He had become the Dicky of her extreme youth, laughing and playing and holding house parties for all his friends in the summer. They had boating and archery contests down at the lake and it was magical. The only thing that could have made her life better was if Piers had been there, too. But she didn't ask Dicky about Piers because it always made him sad—and also a little angry.

"What sort of surprise, Dicky?"

"I have a new sister for you."

"You—you are bringing home a baby?" Winifred asked, so excited she stuttered.

Dicky laughed. "Soon, I hope. By sister, I mean my betrothed, Miss Sophia Telford."

"Oh," Winifred said, unable to hide her disappointment.

But Dicky didn't even notice. Instead, he went back to the door and opened it. A moment later, he led a beautiful woman into the room, his face glowing with pride. "This is Sophia, Winny. Sophia, this is my sister, Winifred."

Winifred curtsied as her governess, Miss Tower, had taught her.

"How charming!" Miss Telford cooed. She was beautiful, like a fairy princess, with blond curls and huge blue eyes. "I am so excited to have a new little sister." She smiled at Winifred, but it never reached her eyes, and it made Winifred shiver; it was not a truly friendly smile.

Things changed in the months after her brother's wedding. At first it was small things, like Winifred not being allowed to eat breakfast with Dicky anymore.

"The breakfast room is for adults, Winifred. You should be up in the nursery with your governess," Sophia had said.

Dicky had been sitting right beside her, and he had smiled and nodded. "You will be more comfortable up there, Winny."

The small things added up quickly into big, unpleasant things.

"You should not call your brother *Dicky*, Winifred," Sophia said one afternoon. This time, it was just the two of them alone together.

"But it is what I have always called him."

The cool look she had begun to dread entered Sophia's jewel-like eyes. "He is Wareham, now and deserves your respect as the earl. You want to show your brother the proper respect, don't you?"

When she put it that way…

Winifred nodded and said, "Yes, Sophia."

The first time she had called her older brother Wareham, he laughed and pulled her plait. "What's this, Winny?" he teased. "Why so formal?"

Sophia had been there at the time. Winifred had seen the watchful look on her sister-in-law's face and the warning glitter in her eyes, so she had just pressed her lips together and smiled.

And she had never called her brother by his pet name again.

When she turned ten, Sophia gave a birthday party for her, although she did not invite Nanny, Miss Tower, or Gilly and Andy, the stablemaster's children. "They are not proper friends, Winifred; they are servants," Sophia explained in the gentle voice Winifred hated. "You should not be playing with the children of servants—you are too grown up now. And soon both Nanny and Miss Tower will be going away."

"Er, Sophia, darling, perhaps now is not the best time to tell Winny about that," Wareham said, coming to stand behind his wife with a pained look on his face.

"Of course it is! Winifred is a big girl."

Winifred looked at her brother.

Wareham flushed; his smile forced. "You get to go away to school next month—won't that be exciting?"

When she did not respond quickly enough, Sophia said, "Of course it will be exciting! You will meet new girls—proper young ladies, not the children of farmers and servants."

"Sophia—" Wareham said in a protesting tone, laughing uncomfortably.

Maybe it was her brother's expression that made Winifred brave, because—for once—she spoke up. "I don't want to go away, Di—Wareham."

"Perhaps we might wait another year?" Wareham said, looking at Sophia.

"But my love, her place has already been reserved."

Wareham had frowned. "Oh, well…"

Winifred had known then that her brother would never, ever take her part.

So, she had gone away to school. And when she came home during the Christmas break, she hated it and was glad she could escape back to school again when the holiday was over.

Everything had changed. Everything.

But Winifred discovered things could always change even more.

When she turned seventeen, Sophia and Wareham once again sat her down.

The Etiquette of Love

Her brother smiled in the uncomfortable way that he now seemed to save just for Winifred.

It was, unsurprisingly, Sophia who spoke for them. "My cousin, the Earl of Sedgewick, has asked Wareham for permission to court you. You recall Sedgewick, don't you Winifred?"

"Yes." The earl had visited the house on numerous occasions but had not paid much attention to Winifred until this last holiday. He was old—older than Wareham—but there was no denying he was dashing and handsome. He smiled and laughed a great deal and there was a glint in his eyes that gave her a strange tingling feeling in her belly. And lower.

Winifred did *not* want to marry him. Or anyone else, for that matter.

Even though she knew it was futile, she turned to Wareham. "I thought I was to go to London next Season?"

Wareham opened his mouth.

"You can hardly expect to engage the interest of a gentleman more respected and adored than my cousin," Sophia said, the glint Winifred loathed had entered the other woman's eyes.

"Darling," Wareham began, his gaze sliding from his wife to Winifred as he sensed the tension between them, maybe for the first time. "Perhaps Winny can make her decision about Sedgewick with more confidence *after* the Season?"

Sophia's beautiful face hardened and Winifred felt a sudden, almost crippling, revulsion at the thought of her brother, once so magnificent, yet again diminished by Sophia's implacable manipulations.

"I am honored by the earl's interest," she quickly said, meeting Sophia's flat, determined gaze with one of her own. "You are correct… as always, Sophia."

Sophia's eyes had glittered with poorly concealed triumph. "He is the Earl of Sedgewick, Winifred. If you marry him, you will be a countess. Just like me." She gave a girlish giggle that made Wareham smile.

Winifred felt nauseated.

A scant month later, she was betrothed. Not only would there be no Season, but Winifred would not return to school for her final semester, either.

"There is no point, now. All the other girls will be envious of your success—marriage without a Season!" Sophia said. And her word was always law.

The evening of her betrothal dinner she lit a candle as she did every night, even though Wareham had years ago told her that Piers had died in a shipwreck. She simply did not believe that was true. As she put the candle in the nursery window, Winifred said her usual prayer for his safe return. And then she prayed for something new.

"I am to be married, Piers. I should be grateful," she whispered, parroting her sister-in-law's words in a hollow voice, mesmerized by the small flame. "Sophia said there is no reason for a grand ceremony in London, so the wedding will take place in the village church. There will be no time to invite my friends as it will take place so soon," she licked her unaccountably dry lips. "Very soon." Her voice broke on the last word. "If you are ever going to come home, Piers, now would be a good time."

But Piers did not come the next day. Or the next. Nor did he return in the weeks and months to come.

Five months, two weeks, and one day after her wedding, Winifred stopped putting candles in the window.

Nor did she ever again pray for her brother's safe return. In fact, she stopped praying altogether.

Because prayers were nothing but hopes that were put into words, and dreams were for children.

Chapter 1

Twelve Years Later
The Duchess of Chorley's Ballroom
London

I want her.

The rogue thought shook Wyndham Fairchild, the Duke of Plimpton, to the core of his generally unshakeable being. It was not the thought itself that stunned him—he had, after all, been interested in the widowed Countess of Sedgewick for several years now—but the fervor of his desire that left him thunderstruck.

If somebody had asked him whether he was even capable of experiencing such fierce emotion—other than pride and duty, of course—he would have scoffed.

And yet there Plimpton stood, in the middle of the Duchess of Chorley's ballroom, lusting *ferociously* for a woman for the first time in decades.

How...piquant.

It was not hubris to say that he never did the pursuing; women always pursued him.

Cecily did not pursue you...

That was true. Cecily was the one and only time Plimpton had lost his sense over a woman. But he had been a lad back then—an utterly different person. A far younger and more trusting person.

In all the years of Plimpton's disastrous marriage—and the few after his wife's death—he had rarely felt more than a spark of interest in any woman. Nothing even approaching the blinding desire that was currently roaring though his body.

He had taken lovers of course, going through the motions and picking and choosing between the numerous feminine lures thrown out to him, but he had only engaged in affairs to satisfy bodily hungers, never any emotional need. Some small part of him had never been able to stop wondering if there was any woman in England who could stir more than a brief lust inside him.

He was not opposed to falling in love—or even falling in lust—he was just incapable of feeling such emotion. Love, at least the sort a man felt for a woman, no longer had any place in his heart. And like a long dead plant, there was no possibility of it ever taking root again.

Twenty years of marriage had seen to that.

The initial, killing frost had been Cecily's loathing for him. His wife's hatred had been sufficient to blacken the stem and leaves, nearly finishing off his ability to love for good.

Then hope, in the form of a child, had revivified it. But watching three children die, one after the other, had not just ripped the fragile plant out by the roots, it had left his heart a wasteland, the soil salted and barren.

Amusement flickered through Plimpton at the dramatic mixed metaphor he had constructed. Or was it a simile? Damned if he knew. He should have paid more attention to his studies when he'd been a schoolboy.

In any case, his thinking—dramatic or not—was off the mark. What he was currently feeling for Lady Winifred Sedgewick was not love or even affection. He wanted, in the crudest and most direct parlance, to lay her out on a bed, strip her bare, and fuck her until her cool, detached assurance burnt away and revealed the sensual creature who dwelt behind her mask.

Why Plimpton believed she was capable of such passion, he did not know. Probably just wishful thinking on his part.

"—up for auction this week, Plimpton. Will you make an offer?"

At the sound of his name, Plimpton reluctantly pulled his gaze from Winifred and turned to Baron Creighton. The other man was staring at him with a questioning look in his protuberant brown eyes.

"Perhaps," Plimpton said evasively, having no clue what Creighton had just asked.

The Etiquette of Love

The baron grunted and nodded. "Yes, I suppose the last thing you need is another pair given your famous grays. They came from your brother, did they not?"

"Yes," he said, vaguely annoyed that he was forced to converse about his brother Simon's bloodstock when all he wanted to do was ponder the sudden flare of emotion that he had just experienced. And the woman who had elicited it. Why the devil was he suddenly so interested in Winifred after all these years?

"But I thought he only set up his stud a few years ago?" Creighton asked.

"That is true. This pair is from my own stables and are among the very first who came from Charger, some years ago."

"Damned fine animal was Charger! No longer studding him, what?"

"No." Simon's oldest stallion was nearing twenty years of age and spent his days grazing and lazing in splendor. Plimpton would not mind such a future, himself.

"Shame, that," Creighton tiresomely maundered. "I offered a fortune for Loki a few months ago, but Simon wouldn't take it."

Plimpton, who had heard all Creighton's grumblings on the subject of Simon's horses before, merely nodded. His younger brother had bred horses for years before joining the army and had resumed the hobby as soon as he had recovered from his war injuries. Since setting up his stud operation two years before Simon had quadrupled the size of his stables. Breeding horses was what made Simon's life worth living.

Or at least it had been until he'd married the widely renown portrait painter, Honoria Keyes. What had begun as a marriage of convenience—orchestrated by Plimpton and rather against the couple's will—had rapidly grown into a love match.

Now that Simon's wife had assured the dukedom's future by providing a son, Plimpton no longer took issue with his brother's time-consuming and expensive hobby. Indeed, he was pleased that Simon appeared to have quit railing against his future as Plimpton's heir and had settled into the life of a happily married country squire.

Plimpton had no intention of dying any time soon, despite his brush with death barely two years before, but he had not been able to rest until he had assured the succession.

He always assumed that when he'd settled that matter, he could finally begin living his own life. But then Plimpton had made a shocking discovery: he *had* no life. At least none outside of the dukedom. He was nothing but a collection of duties and responsibilities.

A duke was what he was. *All* he was.

Oh, he had his family—his mother, his daughter Rebecca, Simon and Honoria and their son Robert—but aside from the Earl of Wareham, Plimpton could claim very few real friends. He had numerous *acquaintances* and there was his mistress, although he had begun to tire of Evangeline's incessant hints about marriage and would need to end the affair soon, a prospect that did not fill him with any particular regret.

He hunted, boxed, fenced, attended his clubs when in London, and socialized at the requisite number of functions, but he took less and less pleasure from all those activities. They were, he realized unhappily, merely ways to fill his time until something better and more fulfilling came along.

Plimpton smiled faintly; evidently lusting over the widowed Countess of Sedgewick was how he was planning to spend his spare time.

Creighton began to yammer about his younger son's latest exploits at Eton and Plimpton allowed his gaze to wander back to Lady Sedgewick.

Sedgewick. Plimpton frowned at the name. Truth be told, he could never think of her by any name other than *Winifred*, his friend Wareham's little sister. He certainly did not care to think of the beautiful woman across the ballroom as the wife of that bloody pervert Sedgewick. The man's death must have been a godsend to her, and Plimpton could comprehend why she had never remarried.

Her brother, however, was not nearly so understanding.

The Etiquette of Love

"All I want is for Winny to remarry," Wareham had whined to Plimpton on more than one occasion. "It's just not natural for a woman to live on her own."

Well, his friend would be delighted when he discovered Plimpton's intentions toward Winifred. Although Wareham would probably punch Plimpton in the face if he could see the things that he was imagining doing to his sister right now.

Plimpton knew his behavior was unseemly and probably attracting unwanted notice, but he could not wrench his gaze away from Winifred. It had been a long, long time since he had truly wanted anything or anyone this badly.

Not since Cecily, the tiresome voice in his head pointed out.

My ancient calf-love for Cecily and my present desire for Winifred are not at all the same.

Indeed, while his ardor for the cool countess ran surprisingly hot, it was not underpinned by the childish infatuation—fine, *obsession*—he had felt for Cecily.

The fact that his feelings for Winifred were so different than what he had once felt for Cecily was not unusual. After all, a man of twenty-one and a man of two-and-forty were so unalike as to be different creatures entirely. Or at least they were in Plimpton's case. Twenty odd years of marriage to a woman who'd hated him was enough to change any man.

He thrust away the unpleasant thought and turned his attention back to Winifred.

And looked right into her eyes. He could not see their color from this distance, but he knew they were a magnificent silvery shade.

Her shapely lips pulled down at the corners and she immediately turned away from him.

Plimpton almost smiled.

She hates you.

Hate was too strong. He thought dislike—with hefty dashes of fear and suspicion—was closer to the truth. Winifred linked Plimpton with her brother, and that was not a positive association given that she hadn't spoken to Wareham in almost eight years.

Plimpton suspected that Winifred would ignore him entirely if not for the fact that his brother Simon had married her good friend and former roommate, Honoria. Only because of that tenuous connection did Winifred tolerated him. Barely.

Her public mask was firmly in place, but Plimpton, also a person who held the world at arms' length, could read her thoughts almost as easily as his own.

Could she see *his* thoughts just as clearly? Was that why she avoided him as if he were a plague-spreading rat? Did she suspect his desire for her and the plans that had rapidly grown out of that desire?

Oh, he would never harm her, of course. But she had certainly been unfortunate when it came to attracting his interest, an interest that went well beyond taking her for a lover. No, whether or not Winifred wished to marry again, she would do so.

She simply did not know it yet.

The fact that she had never given Sedgewick an heir did not matter one whit to Plimpton. He had spent the first two decades of his adult life consumed with the business of an heir. The matter was now settled to his satisfaction.

This time, he would marry to please himself, not because his father had selected his bride and not because he had to get an heir on his wife as quickly as possible. And this time he would get to know his future wife rather than merely worshipping her lovely appearance from afar, as he had done with Cecily.

Not that he didn't intend to enjoy Winifred's beautiful face and body, too.

While Creighton continued to babble and Winifred looked anywhere but at Plimpton, he permitted himself the luxury of enjoying his future wife's person.

She was slightly above average in height and built upon slender rather than Junoesque lines, her bearing as rigidly proud as a queen's. Her face was a delicate oval with even features that were as close to perfection as any he had ever seen. Her stunning visage was crowned by ash blonde hair that had been brutally subdued into a tidy, almost Puritanical, coronet. It was clear from the thickness of the glossy coils that it would reach her hips when unbound.

She was pale—so pale he knew the faint blue veins would be visible beneath the thin skin of her temples if he stood close enough. Such light hair and skin should have been insipid, but she was saved from that by coral pink lips, the upper one so teasingly kittenish that his own mouth watered to nip and suck and kiss it.

That mouth—her upper lip alone—would have been sufficient to fire his erotic imagination, but her unusual silvery-gray eyes put the final seal on his fascination.

Plimpton's attraction to her had been instantaneous at the Earl of Avington's betrothal ball almost two years ago and it had intensified each and every time he had seen her since. It had been bubbling beneath the surface for months. And tonight, it was boiling over with a vengeance.

The last time Plimpton had seen her before Avington's ball had been more than a decade ago, when he had gone to a house party Wareham and his wife had given at their country home, Torrance Park. Plimpton had not visited his friend often after his marriage because he'd actively disliked Lady Wareham, who'd been a manipulative, sly woman.

At the time, Winifred had been home from school and could not have been more than thirteen or fourteen, still a child. She had always been on the periphery of Wareham's life, his nosy, worshipful, pest of a little sister who followed Wareham about like an eager puppy.

At least she had until that last time. Plimpton had been startled by the change in the girl. She had looked nothing like her former ebullient, happy self. She had been…subdued and repressed. Ten minutes in her presence—along with Lady Wareham—had shown him the reason for Winifred's drastic change in personality: the Countess of Wareham did not like her husband's little sister.

Unfortunately, Wareham had been so enamored of his wife that he simply did not notice how matters stood between the countess and Winifred.

It had not been Plimpton's affair, so he had kept his mouth shut. Even now, years later, he did not regret keeping mum. Wareham had been wild about his wife back then and if Plimpton had said anything even slightly critical of the woman that would have marked the end of their friendship. Not until much, much later did Wareham finally understand what he had in his wife. By that time, it had been far too late for him to rescue his relationship with Winifred.

Not surprisingly, the beautiful girl had blossomed into a surpassingly lovely woman, age adding interesting and mysterious shadows and depth to her ravishing features.

Plimpton could not deny that it had first been her stunning appearance that had all but seized him by the throat. But it had been her quiet, dignified reserve that held his attention.

For years, he had heard the young bucks refer to her as the *Ice Countess*. He had to admit the disrespectful sobriquet fit her down to the ground. It wasn't merely her appearance that had earned her that nickname but also the fact that more than a few men had offered for her—not only *carte blanches*, but marriage—and she had rejected them all. Or at least the offers of marriage. Whether she had taken lovers was another matter. And one he did not like to consider.

Wareham had also been aware of the interest his sister created. He had briefly considered putting his foot down and forcing Winifred to move back under his roof after Sedgewick's death. "Good Lord, Plimpton! I can hardly let a girl—for that is all Winny is, regardless that she is a widow—live on her own and make her own decisions. She will bring shame to the family name within a fortnight."

Plimpton *had* spoken then. "If you force your sister to move back into your home, you will lose her forever, Wareham." What he had really wanted to say was that Wareham's shrew of a wife would probably drive Winifred to do something desperate if she were forced to live with them.

The argument that had followed his words had been heated and ugly and convinced him *never* ever to interfere again.

But Wareham had given Winifred her freedom, so he had obviously seen the merit in Plimpton's advice, even if he had not liked it. Their friendship had been so strained by the conversation that Wareham had not spoken to him for almost six months afterward.

The Etiquette of Love

Wareham might have been furious that his sister had taken up teaching at a girl's school, but it had not harmed her reputation. Like Plimpton, the Earl of Wareham had a pristine reputation and such a mild scandal had not tarnished it.

Oh, there was that ancient business about Wareham's illegitimate half-brother Piers Cantrell. But that had occurred so long ago that few people beyond the dozen or so peers who had been at Torrance Park at the time even remembered the scandal.

Plimpton only knew about it because he had been among those who were there. Wareham had long been his closest friend and he had helped him to clean up the mess Cantrell had left behind.

Winny, as Wareham had called his little sister, had been an infant of four or five years at the time. She had been heartbroken when she had learned of Cantrell's disappearance and had wept. A lot.

He saw very little evidence of that sad little girl in the now-haughty countess.

Plimpton suspected the solid veneer of ice she hid behind had begun accreting even back then. It would have thickened considerably during her unfortunate marriage to Sedgewick.

Sedgewick had been a few years older than Plimpton, but he remembered the man well. Even at the age of seventeen, Sedgewick's feet had been firmly planted on the road to dissipation and ruin. Plimpton was hardly a prude when it came to sexual matters, but Sedgewick had engaged in the sort of debauchery that was acceptable only to men like the Earl of Barrymore, who had been the leader of the fast set Sedgewick had run with.

Life with such a man, especially for a lady of discernment and sensibility, was probably enough to put a woman off marriage—and men—for life.

It would be Plimpton's duty to change Winifred's mind on that matter.

He felt a slight smile pull at his lips. No, not just his *duty*; it would also be his pleasure.

***

Winifred gasped when the Duke of Plimpton turned and stared directly at her. She silently cursed herself for even allowing her eyes to wander in his direction.

The blasted man held her gaze like a lodestone and her heart kicked into a gallop before she jerked her eyes away.

Unhappily, her pulse continued to pound even after she broke free. She might have looked away, but the duke had not. She felt his attention even now—the heat that was somehow generated by eyes that were as hard and opaque as granite—her skin uncomfortably hot and prickly beneath her ball gown.

Freddie had been aware of the Duke of Plimpton's interest in her for some time, now. At first, she had believed it was only her chaperone services for his daughter that he wanted. Because launching the Duke of Plimpton's daughter would be such a feather in her cap she had—against her better judgment—decided that she would accept his request to sponsor his daughter. And yet, when it had come time to formalize the agreement, Freddie had lied and told the duke that she was already engaged to help another client.

The sense of relief that had flooded her afterward had convinced her she had made the right decision, no matter how financially foolish it might have been.

But then she had received a letter from her friend, the former Honoria Keyes, who had married Plimpton's brother. Honey had begged Freddie to reconsider—as a favor to her—and so, in a moment of weakness, she had agreed to sponsor Lady Rebecca. Which meant she was now forced to deal with Plimpton not only socially, but on a business footing.

She should have known better; she should have *never* allowed her friend to change her mind. Because something about Plimpton—a man she had known almost all her life, albeit only slightly, had always left her feeling wrong-footed. And the feeling had only become stronger these past few years.

Plimpton had been—and likely still was—her brother Wareham's closest friend and had been around ever since she could remember. Freddie had vague memories of Plimpton as a quiet and serious boy, but he was so much older than her that he had already been a married man when she was still a schoolgirl.

She had not spoken to him for many years before Honey's marriage to Simon had thrown them into the same company. The moment she looked into his opaque gray eyes, she remembered how something about his direct, level gaze had always made her feel vulnerable and exposed, as if he were looking *into* her mind.

That feeling would have been uncomfortable regardless of what she was thinking. But the truth was that her thoughts were almost always about *him* whenever he was in her vicinity. As much as she hated to admit it, there was something about the blasted man that excited—and yes—aroused her.

Her sexuality was something Freddie had done everything in her power to suppress after her brief, miserable marriage. She had become an expert at stifling even the mildest spark of interest before it could lead her into a situation that might afford temporary pleasure but would end in pain and emptiness.

During her years teaching at the Stefani Academy for Young Ladies Freddie was able to hide away from the *ton* and avoid male attention. But all that changed after the school closed and she was forced to sponsor young women into society to earn a living. It did not seem to matter that she held herself aloof from flirtation and never encouraged attention from the opposite sex; she still encountered flashes of lust in men's eyes—married or single—at every *ton* function.

Lust was not the look she saw in Plimpton's gaze. Or at least it was not the whole of it. The duke would not be satisfied with a brief bedding. And not just because her brother was his best friend.

Freddie knew, although she could not say *how*, that lurking behind Plimpton's cold, implacable façade was the intention to make her his wife.

Intellectually, she cringed from that knowledge. But physically...oh, how her body burned for him.

And that reaction terrified her.

Freddie did not want to remarry. Ever. But if she could be tempted into matrimony again, it would most certainly not be by a man who was cold to his core and interested in her only because of her pedigree.

Somehow, she suspected the duke was not accustomed to being told *no*.

Freddie smiled grimly. It would be a new experience for him.

She felt a telltale prickle on the side of her face—the one not facing the duke—and surveyed the ballroom for its source. She had not looked long when her eyes locked with a man across the dance floor. She inhaled sharply. It was that odd, uncomfortable *man*—the one who'd come to the house to collect a valise for Freddie's roommate, Lorelei Fontenot.

Lorelei was a journalist and was evidently investigating a story that required her to be away for an indeterminate period of time. And this man—Mr. Gregg—had served as Lori's messenger for some reason. She remembered him quite clearly because his angular face and sharp eyes were not the sort one forgot. Nor was his arrogant attitude and confident swagger.

But there was something else about him, something she could not quite identify...

Freddie shook the thought away, instead focusing on his presence at a duchess's ball.

It made no sense.

He raised his eyebrows and nodded slightly, his lips curving into a mocking smile, as if he could follow the train of Freddie's thoughts.

For the second time that evening, she hastily broke eye contact.

Although he was clad just like every other gentleman in the room, he was not a member of the *ton*. Freddie was certain of that. He must have crashed the function. Should she say something to—

"Good evening, Lady Sedgewick."

Her head whipped up and she stared at Mr. Gregg in disbelief, giving him her coldest look. "I do not believe we have been introduced."

The Etiquette of Love

"I came to your house to collect Miss Font—"

"I recall the occasion," she cut in icily, employing the sort of tone that usually depressed pretension and sent the offender scurrying in the other direction.

But Mr. Gregg was made of sterner stuff and was only nonplussed by her coldness for a moment before his smile once again slid across his angular face. "Ah, I see."

Freddie did not ask him what it was that he saw because she did not care. The only thing she cared about was his immediate departure.

"By *introduced* you mean something more formal," he went on, as if she were not ignoring his existence and looking at anything else *but* him. "I have offended convention, haven't I?" he persisted. "I'm sorry, I should have remembered that. But it has been a long, long time."

The nerve of the man to stand there yammering.

Freddie had just decided to make her way to the table of refreshments when Gregg's gaze flickered to something over her shoulder and his smile shifted into a sneer.

"Good evening, Winifred."

Freddie's pulse, which had just stopped pounding, sped up again at the sound of her Christian name on Plimpton's tongue—as if he had every right to use it.

It took all her self-control not to whip around and point out that she had not given him the right to use her name. But one did *not* chide a duke, no matter how badly he was behaving.

Unfortunately, one could not ignore a duke, either.

Freddie turned away from one unwanted guest to face another, dropping into a low curtsey before rising to meet Plimpton's cool gray gaze.

"Good evening, Your Grace."

"Will you honor me with this dance?" The duke's eyes flickered over Mr. Gregg—the same look he might give an annoying insect—and then back to her. The gesture, although slight, was so *proprietary* and insulting—as if Mr. Gregg had just made a low offer on the duke's horse—that Freddie's face scalded.

How dare he interfere as if she needed his protection? And as if he had any right to offer it.

Irked, Freddie deliberately turned away from the duke and back to Mr. Gregg.

Rather than appearing offended by the duke's treatment, Gregg's dark brown eyes glinted with amusement.

Foolishly, Freddie had no idea what to say to him now that she had turned back to him. Especially since she had done all she could to drive him away only a moment earlier. What was *wrong* with her? She never behaved so impulsively.

Mr. Gregg dropped a surprisingly graceful bow. "It was good to see you again, my lady." His eyes briefly moved to the duke and then back. "I will call on you… soon. When I do, we can enjoy a long, *private* discussion." And then, to her astonishment, he gave her cheek a light, affectionate flick, as if she were a child.

Freddie stared in disbelieving outrage as he strolled away, not hurrying at all as if he had every right to be in a duchess's ballroom.

"Winifred?"

Freddie gathered her addled wits and turned back to Plimpton. She was about to remind him that she had never invited his use of her name, but the look in his eyes stopped her.

There was a hardness that had not been there before. It told her that he had seen Mr. Gregg's affectionate gesture. And he had not liked it. The last thing she needed was for him to go tattling to Wareham.

"I beg your pardon. Did you say something, Your Grace?" she asked him coolly.

"I asked you to dance."

Oh, yes. That. "You honor me, sir. However," she gestured to the Conroy twins, her charges, who were seated nearby. "I am here in my capacity as chaperone."

The Etiquette of Love

And we both know you did not come across the room to dance, but to interrupt my conversation with Mr. Gregg.

His harsh expression softened slightly, as if she had spoken the last part aloud. "Your charges are quite safe for the moment."

Freddie followed his gaze to where the twins sat with their respective betrotheds as well as Mrs. Conroy, their mother, who hovered near the couples, beaming beatifically.

Even an idiot would not believe that Freddie's presence was necessary. And the duke was no fool.

It surprised her that Plimpton knew whom she was sponsoring, but then he was the sort of man who made it his business to know about, and exert control over, every facet of his world. Freddie had officially become part of that world when she accepted his offer to launch Lady Rebecca.

Lucky, lucky Freddie.

"Come, Winifred." He held out his hand. "One dance." Although his voice was almost too quiet to hear over the din of the ballroom, his tone was that of a man accustomed to being obeyed.

Irked that he had left her with no polite retreat, Freddie set her hand on the sleeve of his black evening coat, which hugged his muscular torso like a second skin.

She gave him her frostiest smile. "I would be honored, Your Grace."

Unlike his glittering, glamorous younger brother, Lord Simon—whose guinea gold curls and hyacinth blue eyes slayed hearts even after the horrific scarring he had endured in the War—the duke was attractive in a far more subtle way.

He lacked his brother's imposing height and was only a few inches above average. His shoulders were pleasingly broad and tapered to trim, powerful hips and he possessed the muscular thighs and calves of an active sportsman. If his legs were too bulky to achieve the lithe silhouette currently fashionable, they were—in Freddie's opinion—far more attractive and masculine and filled out his black pantaloons quite nicely.

His hair was the sort of middling brown that invited no comparisons to mahogany or chestnut and was liberally dusted with gray at the temples. His face was lean and austere, and his lips were finely shaped but severe in repose, with none of Lord Simon's sensual fullness.

Plimpton's most striking feature was his slate-gray eyes. It was not their color that commanded one's attention, but rather their keen intelligence and supreme self-possession. He was a man who was comfortable with the world around him and assured of his place in it. One would never mistake him for anything other than an aristocrat, and he wore his power and exalted status as easily as he wore his skin.

Unfortunately for Freddie there was something about his piercing eyes and confident authority that upset her equilibrium unlike any other man she had ever met.

And she did not like it. Not at all. Freddie was no naïve debutante in her first Season; she knew *exactly* what it was about Plimpton that unnerved her: she was sexually attracted to the duke, regardless of the fact that she mistrusted and disliked him.

The first time she had placed her hand in his and felt his palm rest lightly on her back—at Miles's wedding ball—she had woken up panting and aroused every night for at least a week afterward, her dreams positively infested with the man.

Plimpton had been a widower of scarcely half-a-year back then and it had surprised Freddie that the duke had attended her friend Miles's— the Earl of Avington—ball while still in mourning. But then it was well-known that the duke and his duchess had been estranged for years. Plimpton had probably been celebrating his wife's demise before her body had even been lowered into the ground. Freddie knew that he had not stopped—or even paused—his affair with Viscountess Buckley, his lover at the time.

Lady Buckley, a lovely widow with a lofty pedigree and even loftier expectations, had not been shy about telling all and sundry that Plimpton would marry her when he was out of mourning.

Poor Lady Buckley. Shortly after his wife's death Plimpton had moved on from her and into the arms of another widow, Mrs. Palfrey.

The Etiquette of Love

For all Freddie knew, there might have been others in between the two women; the duke had never stinted himself when it came to sensual pleasure of any sort.

His rampant infidelity was yet another reason to dislike the man, as if the fact that he was her brother's best friend and likely his spy was not enough already.

The music struck up and the duke smoothly led her into the dance.

After a moment, he said, "I never did thank you for changing your mind about sponsoring Lady Rebecca."

"The opportunity you have given me is more than sufficient thanks, Your Grace."

"What was it that made you change your mind?"

As much as she would have liked to stare at his cravat for the entire dance, she forced herself to meet the duke's gaze. And then she lied. "My client was forced to cancel due to a bereavement in the family."

"Ah." The single syllable was enough to let Freddie know that *he* knew she was not telling the truth but would allow her lie to go unchallenged.

Insufferable man.

"You appeared to be well acquainted with the man you were speaking with a few moments ago."

So, here was the real reason for this dance. But it did not sound like a question, so Freddie did not answer.

"What is the man's name?" he asked, undeterred by her silence.

Her jaw flexed with the urge to tell him to take his probing questions and go to the devil. She compromised by lying again. "I do not know."

"I have seen him several times before, always with Lord Severn."

"How interesting."

"Yes," he agreed, his gaze assessing.

An angry flush spread over her body at his brooding judgment. How was he able to express such disapproval with one quiet syllable? And why did she even care?

Your flush is not borne of anger, and you care a great deal about what this man thinks—especially when it comes to you.

Freddie realized she was scowling and quickly rearranged her features into a bland mask. Already she had attracted more attention than she wanted by dancing with the biggest matrimonial prize of the Season. Marriage-minded mamas would hardly want to engage the services of a woman who threw herself into the path of an eligible bachelor. This single dance with the duke—and Freddie's high color and obvious excitement—would be causing no small amount of gossip.

Just what she needed.

"Regardless of what his name is, Severn's underling is not the sort of person you should be seen associating with, Winifred. At least not if you value your reputation."

"How generous you are to spare such solicitude for me," Freddie retorted heatedly. "Your condescension humbles and overwhelms me, Your Grace."

Amusement flickered across his stern features, the expression so brief and slight she would have missed it if she had not been glaring at him.

Freddie could not blame him for finding her childish behavior entertaining. Just what was it about Plimpton that reduced her to an emotional, argumentative girl of seven-and-ten?

"You are the sister of my oldest friend, Winifred. It is both a duty and an honor to offer you guidance in your brother's absence."

This time Freddie caught her angry retort. The threat in his words was subtle, but it was there nonetheless: if Freddie *misbehaved* or attracted negative attention, the duke would inform Wareham.

"I know nothing about that man," she said, evidently unable to utter anything but lies tonight. "He merely stopped to ask me if I knew where the cardroom was."

Plimpton's eyebrows rose a fraction at her blatant untruth.

The Etiquette of Love

Freddie wanted to howl when her face, yet again, heated under his level gaze.

"He looks familiar to me," Plimpton mused a moment later. When Freddie gave no answer, he pinned her with a sharp look. "Does he not look familiar to you, Winifred?"

Just what was the awful man driving at?

"No, he does not look familiar. Why should he?" she could not help asking.

Plimpton did not answer as he guided her into a turn.

Would this dance never end?

Freddie stared fixedly at his cravat and resolved not to speak to him again.

"I remember the first time I saw you, Winifred."

She instantly looked up. "You do?" she asked, and then was annoyed that she had not managed to quell the question.

"You were at that age when children learn to walk. I had come to stay the Easter holiday with Wareham. Your parents were still alive then."

Freddie hated how much she wanted to hear more—how hungry she was for information about a past and people she could not remember.

Rather than pepper him with the questions churning inside her, she forced herself to cut him a blasé, mocking look. "I did not realize you spent your holidays at Torrance Park in the nursery."

Why did she have such an urge to take digs at him? She *never* behaved this way. And certainly not to a virtual stranger. And *never* with a man of his rank.

If she had been hoping to snub him, she had failed.

Instead, his stern features softened. "You were not in the nursery, Winifred. You had escaped your minder and crawled down the stairs and across half the house, setting all the servants in an uproar searching for you. You were dirty, and crying, and dispirited by the time you discovered Wareham, me, and your brother Piers in the billiards room.

When Wareham went to pick you up, you pushed him away. It was Piers you wanted. And when you saw him, your face transformed, and you promptly struggled to your feet and tottered toward him, as if you had been doing it all your life."

His words created an image that was so vivid that Freddie would have sworn that she remembered it, but she knew that was just her imagination. Nanny had told her she started walking late—so late the old woman had worried that something was amiss—just shy of two years old. Piers and Wareham, separated by only a year, would have been sixteen and fifteen at the time.

"You cried like you were being murdered when your nurse came to collect you, so Piers carried you back up to the nursery himself." Plimpton's lips twisted faintly. "Of course, Wareham and I teased him mercilessly when he returned."

"Adolescent boys are so beastly to each other," Freddie said absently, her thoughts on her long-dead brother.

"Yes, that is an excellent word for them."

"It is hard to believe Piers was only sixteen at the time. He seemed like a god to me."

When the duke did not respond, she looked up to find him staring in the direction of the French doors that led to the terrace, an arrested look on his face.

But when Freddie turned to see what had attracted his interest, there was no one there.

Chapter 2

Freddie stared down at the open ledger that held her monthly household accounts. How in the world would she get by until next year without the small amount that her roommate and dear friend, Lorelei Fontenot, had contributed?

Oh, Lori had not said she was moving away forever when she'd gone to visit her family, but Freddie had a premonition that the younger woman would not be coming back to live with her again, even if she did return to London.

The house Freddie rented was large—five bedchambers along with the carriage house—and she should have sought out more roommates ages ago, after Honoria Keyes and Serena Lombard both left to marry, one after another. But the thought of having strangers in her home had been repugnant, so she had avoided it. But now, that was something she would have to—

"My lady? Lady Sedgewick?"

Freddie jolted and looked up to find her housekeeper hovering on the threshold. "I am sorry, Mrs. Brinkley." She gestured to the ledger. "I was deep in my figures. Did you need something?"

"There is a—a person here to see you." With a pinched look of disapproval, the older woman approached and held out a card.

P. A. Gregg

A voice came back to Freddie. *I will call on you... soon. When I do, we can enjoy a long, private discussion.* The words had hung in her mind, but as the days and then weeks had passed with no visit from him, she had started to believe his threat an empty one.

It was on the tip of her tongue to tell her servant to send him away—why should she admit the man to her house?—but then she recalled Plimpton's interference that night and bridled at the memory. When she opened her mouth, what came out was, "Please show him in, Mrs. Brinkley."

The older woman frowned but nodded and shut the door.

Freddie closed the ledger and set aside her paperwork before standing and checking her appearance in the large mirror over the fireplace. The woman who looked back at her was as neat as wax and just about as exciting. Freddie knew she was considered attractive, but she found her pale face, ash blonde hair, and gray eyes profoundly uninteresting. If she could look like anyone, it would be her friend Lori, whose brilliant green eyes, raven hair, and voluptuous body were a stunning combination.

Unfortunately, she was stuck with colorless and boring.

She heard a step in the corridor and turned from the glass as the door opened.

"Mr. Gregg, my lady," Mrs. Brinkley announced, disapproval radiating from her very pores.

"Thank you, Mrs. Brinkley. That will be all," Freddie added when the other woman appeared predisposed to linger.

The man who had earned Mrs. Brinkley's censure sauntered into the room—and *saunter* was certainly the right word. He moved with unhurried, lazy grace but his sharp dark brown eyes took in every detail of her cozy little sitting room.

Freddie gestured to a chair that was as far as possible from the settee. "Please, have a—" she broke off, stammering, when Gregg kept walking, not stopping until he was mere inches from her.

Freddie refused to step back in her own parlor, so she held her ground, which meant she was forced to crane her neck to meet his gaze.

His almost black eyes were unusual with such light blond hair, which was the sunny gold of ripe wheat. His face was thin—gaunt, almost—and composed of sharp angles. The lines bracketing his mouth and nose and those radiating out from his eyes were the sort that came from spending years beneath a blazing sun. The word *weatherbeaten* came to mind.

Suddenly, he smiled. No, it was a grin, crooked and roguish and charming.

And...familiar.

The Etiquette of Love

A strange sensation—as if she were up high in the sky looking down on herself—caused Freddie to feel nauseated. Her view flickered and then changed to something else entirely, until she was looking at another place. Another *time*.

Another person—one who had died a long, long time ago.

"I—I—you need to state your business and then *go*," she said shrilly, clutching at the back of the nearby chair.

Rather than look offended, his smile broadened. "My business? Why, *you* are my business, Little Bird."

Freddie gasped and heard a distinct *crack*, like the shattering of glass, and then everything went dark.

***

"Wake up, Little Bird," an urgent male voice whispered while a large hand frantically patted her cheek. "Please—wake up." The hand patted harder.

Freddie forced her eyes open and grabbed the arm connected to the annoying hand. "Stop that."

The patting stopped and a voice muttered, "Thank God."

Freddie saw that she was reclining on the rose brocade settee. Kneeling beside her was Mr. Gregg, his tanned face now pale with concern.

"What is your name?" he asked.

"What?"

"Your name—do you know it?"

"Of course, I know my name," she snapped, and then winced and felt her head.

"I just wanted to make sure you didn't damage your head," he explained. "You cracked it hard when you fell. It is not bleeding, but there will be a lump." He held out a glass. "Here, drink some water."

Freddie ignored the glass, her head now pounding as well as spinning. "You said *L-Little Bird*. How do you know that name?"

"How do you think?" Mr. Gregg grinned again. The source of all the unease—the wordless confusion—she had felt the few times that she had been in proximity with this man suddenly became clear. "It's me, Piers. I did not mean to startle you, but I could not think of how else to tell you."

"*Piers?*" she gasped.

Her beloved older brother, whom she'd believed dead, chuckled and said, "It took you long enough to recognize me, Little Bird."

"But—but they told me you died. Wareham told me."

He grimaced. "I'm sorry about that, Little Bird. I had to put an end to anyone searching for me."

"Wait—you mean *you* made up that story?"

"I'm afraid so."

Freddie felt a sharp pang of guilt at Piers's admission because she had immediately assumed that it had been Wareham who had come up with the rumor.

But then she remembered it had been Wareham who had sent Piers away in the first place. "You left because he told you to, didn't you?" she asked, not needing to explain who *he* was.

"Don't be angry with Wareham, Winny; he did what he could to help me. He was the one who gave me the money I needed to get away."

"But he *made* you go instead of helping you," she insisted.

"No, he *helped* me by making me go."

Freddie scoffed. "He could have used his money and influence to clear your name, Piers. He could have—"

"He could not have done that."

"What do you mean? Of course he could have. If an earl had championed your innocence and—"

"He could not help me if I was not innocent, Little Bird."

Freddie's jaw dropped. "Are you saying you killed that man?"

Piers shook his head. "I don't know."

"Good Lord, Piers! How can you not know such a thing?"

His jaw knotted with frustration. "Because I simply cannot remember. I'd had a great deal to drink that night. So much that I have no memory of what happened after a certain point. I recall leaving the Fox and Hounds—the inn where I encountered Wareham and the others, who'd gone there to watch a mill." His dark eyes—the only feature on his face that even remotely reminded Freddie of the fresh-faced boy in her memory—slid to hers and his lips flexed into a self-mocking smile. "Wareham and I got into an argument about the bloody chess pieces again. I insisted on going to Meecham's house even though Wareham strenuously tried to dissuade me and—"

"Wait, Piers. Who is this Meecham and what chess pieces are you talking about?"

Piers's eyes widened. "You haven't heard about the chess set from Stroma?"

Freddie shook her head.

"You don't know who Meecham was?"

"No."

Piers gave a bitter bark of laughter. "Good God. What have you been told about me, Little Bird?"

"Wareham said you'd killed a man in an argument and then fled. And then, several years later, he said you died." She didn't tell Piers that for years Freddie had not believed Wareham. Part of her had always wondered if it was something Sophia had convinced him to say. She felt ashamed now that she had believed Wareham capable of such cruelty.

Piers sighed. "You should know what happened, Winny."

"I should have known a long time ago. Tell me what happened, Piers. All of it. And start at the beginning."

"David Meecham is the man I am accused of murdering. He was the youngest son of Viscount Meecham, but he had been disowned years before I met him and was something of a...well, let's just say he wasn't good *ton*. That summer David became my traveling companion after Wareham banished me from Torrance Park and—"

"Banished? But why?"

"Because I deserved it. Really, Little Bird," he said at her disbelieving look. "I had been playing deeply and got myself in trouble. Wareham had already bailed me out of debt more than a few times." He grimaced and then added, "He had also paid the fathers of two girls I, er…Well, I am sure you know what I mean."

"Oh, Piers."

"I'm sorry, Little Bird. You shouldn't have to hear such things, but the truth is that I was reckless and selfish, and Wareham was hard put to keep me out of gaol even before Meecham was murdered."

"I cannot believe that I have never heard any of this."

"I am sorry, Little Bird. Have I fallen from my pedestal?"

Freddie felt slightly ill. Not so much because she was angry at Piers—although it certainly shocked her to hear her beloved brother had been a rake–but because of the accusations she had flung at Wareham so long ago. Angry words blaming him for driving Piers away from England, accusing Wareham of being glad that Piers had gone.

"Poor Little Bird,' he murmured. His lips pulled into the sardonic smile that she associated with Mr. Gregg—a cynical sneer she had never seen on young Piers's face. The expression was perhaps more of a disguise than his light hair, darkly tanned skin, and lean features had been.

"Before you go on, I need to know about those girls you mentioned. You have two children, Piers?"

"Yes. I sought out both women since my return. Wareham had given the girls enough money that they were able to marry well." He pulled a face. "I am already a grandfather. I earned a great deal of money while I was away, so I've made sure none of them will ever want for material comforts. It does not excuse what I did, but it is all I can do now."

Freddie nodded. "Tell me the rest of your story—what were the chess pieces you mentioned?"

"Meecham and I wandered about the north of Scotland for months. The cold, inhospitable land was an appropriate place for banishment and fit my mood perfectly. Meecham stayed with me not out of friendship, but because he, too, was evading the bitter fruits of bad behavior. In any event, we'd been staying in a village whose name I don't recall when we heard of a shipwreck off the island of Stroma. Many people on the mainland said the islanders on Stroma were wreckers—you have heard of them?"

"People who cause ships to founder and then ransack them."

Piers nodded. "There are even stories that they kill, rather than rescue, any survivors who make it to shore. Whether the islanders were guilty or not, the tide carried a goodly amount of wreckage to the mainland and out of their clutches. Meecham and I were combing the shoreline when we found something." Piers's gaze turned distant. "It was a small chest, and it was obviously very old. It had been badly battered by its rough journey, but fortunately the contents were well-protected from jostling and the elements. It held a chess set of a design that I had never seen." He wore an expression of wonder when he turned to her. "The set was not complete—it was missing five pieces—but we knew that what remained must still be of value. The pieces were mesmerizing, Winifred, they had so much...*personality*, for lack of a better word. Meecham suggested we take them to an acquaintance of his in Edinburgh, a man who belonged to the Society of Antiquaries of Scotland."

Piers stared into the past. "The man was stunned. He immediately said that even incomplete, the set was beyond price. He estimated they originated in the twelfth century and were probably from somewhere in Scandinavia. He offered us money for them—an outrageous sum that Meecham wanted to accept—but I told him we should not be hasty; that we should look for additional verification from some other source. The British Museum, perhaps, or men who were known to collect such things. Meecham took some convincing before he agreed. Together we swore his friend to silence. He agreed only on the condition that when we were ready to sell, he would have first right of refusal. We were badly skint and needed money to travel and so we sold one piece to Meecham's friend. The sale yielded enough money to make us feel as rich as kings, which is exactly how we proceeded to behave." He gave a derisive snort. "We were young fools, Little Bird. By the time we reached Torrance Park we had run through a good deal of our newly acquired wealth. I convinced Meecham that my brother would help us find a buyer for the rest of the pieces. I argued that Wareham would have the sorts of connections in London that neither of us could boast. Meecham knew I was right, and so he agreed to talk to Wareham. But the one thing he remained steadfast about was refusing to allow Wareham to keep the pieces in his vault at Torrance Park. If he had, then none of the rest of what happened would have occurred."

"What happened?"

"To make an already long story a bit shorter, Wareham confided the details of my, er, acquisition, in his closest friend."

"Plimpton?"

"Who else?" Piers asked bitterly. "Plimpton was a close associate of the Duke of Devonshire, who is a renowned collector of such things. Naturally, Plimpton asked Devonshire about the pieces to see what he knew. That was when he discovered the set had been stolen from Devonshire years before."

Freddie winced. "Oh, no."

Piers nodded grimly. "Oh, yes. Wareham, not surprisingly, insisted the pieces needed to be returned—including the one we had sold. He wrote to the man who'd purchased it, explaining it had been stolen, and he paid to recover the piece." Piers's mouth flexed into a scowl. "When I told Meecham, he raged that the set belonged to us by virtue of some arcane finder's law. He said we should sell it immediately before anyone could stop us. I pointed out we could do no such thing even if I had wanted to. Not only did Wareham and Plimpton know the pieces were in our possession, but at least half-a-dozen of their friends who were at that blasted house party had actually seen the set. Its existence could not stay a secret long. And there would be hell to pay if Devonshire learned of it from some other source. We *had* to give it back. Finally, Meecham agreed. Or so I believed," he added darkly. "I'd told him I would arrange with Wareham to use his carriage to take us to Devonshire's estate in the country. It was inconvenient that Wareham was hosting a gathering at the time—one of his bachelor orgies as we used to call them—" he broke off and met Freddie's startled gaze. "Oh, I beg your pardon. Er, they were just parties—nothing out of the ordinary."

"I see."

Piers chuckled. "Look at you—a very disapproving Little Bird, indeed."

Freddie smiled reluctantly, unable to resist his teasing. Some things, it appeared, never changed.

"I gather those parties stopped after Wareham married?"

Freddie nodded.

"I understand from the bits of gossip I've managed to collect that Wareham married a woman who was a bit of a gorgon," Piers said. "How did you get on with her?"

"I do not care to speak ill of the dead."

Piers frowned. "Was she unkind to you, Little Bird?"

"She was not an easy woman to live with."

"Was she the reason you fell out with Wareham?"

"That is not a subject I want to discuss," she said, calmly but firmly.

Piers hesitated, but then nodded. "Very well."

"Tell me the rest of what happened."

"There isn't much more. I went to talk to Meecham and tell him we were leaving. Somewhere between Torrance Park and the house where Meecham was staying I simply lost track of myself. I'd had several drinks while I waited to speak to Wareham—I remember that much—but that is the last thing. I found out afterward that Meecham's house had been ransacked and the chess set was nowhere to be found."

"Did it ever turn up?"

"I wondered about that for years—decades—and the first thing I did when I returned to England last year was—"

"You were here last *year*?"

He gave Freddie a wary, guilty look. "I was."

She was astounded by the pain that stabbed her at his words.

He leaned forward and took her hand, squeezing it lightly when Freddy merely let it sit limply in his grasp. "I am wanted for murder,

Little Bird, and I cannot even say the accusation isn't the truth. I spent my time here last year looking into my past with as much delicacy as I could, hoping to find out what might have really happened. I spoke to Wareham and he and I decided—"

"Wareham knows that you are alive?"

He grimaced. "Yes."

"You told *him*, but not me?"

"I'm sorry, Little Bird."

Freddie's eyes narrowed. "What a fool I am. It was Wareham who told you not to tell me last year, wasn't it?"

Piers opened his mouth, but then shut it without speaking.

So, there was her answer. "What did he say to you? Just tell me, Piers," she demanded when he hesitated.

Piers heaved a put-upon sigh. "He said the chess set was never found. He said that after I left England, he went to Devonshire himself and told him the truth. The duke was kind enough not to bay for my blood. Whether he actually believed that I did not have set, or he simply kept mum out of respect for Wareham—or Plimpton, rather—I do not know. Not that telling the story would have done anything for him at that point. I was long gone, Meecham was dead, and the set had disappeared. Wareham told me last year that the local constabulary had officially closed the murder case when they learned of my death. He said my reappearance would lead to the reopening of the whole mess and there would be nothing he could do to help me." He chuckled. "You are scowling at that, Little Bird. But don't be angry at Wareham."

She ignored his teasing and said, "I know he helped you leave England, but did he ever do anything to find out what really happened, Piers?"

"I believe he tried his best. There just wasn't a great deal to go on, love. Servants heard me arguing with Meecham and the next thing anyone knew, I was found covered in blood in a ditch clutching the murder weapon, the chess set was gone, and Meecham's body—with multiple stab wounds—was discovered in the study where we'd last been seen together." He shrugged. "It is entirely possible I fought him

The Etiquette of Love

in a drunken rage and killed him. In fact, that is probable. What else could have happened?"

"The chess set is *gone*, Piers. That should tell you that somebody else took it."

"Perhaps. Or perhaps Meecham sold it, fearing we would be forced to return it."

"When had you last seen the set?"

Piers chewed his lip. After a moment, he said, "Two—maybe three-days before the murder. We trusted each other no further than we had to. We both agreed to look at the pieces every few days just to keep that trust strong. Maybe I discovered that night that he'd sold it. That would be enough to kill him."

Freddie ignored that last part. "Do you often lose your memory from drink?"

"No. That was the only time. Once was enough," he added grimly.

"You say other people saw the set?"

Piers nodded. "Meecham and I brought it out one night, so most of Wareham's guests would have seen it."

"What if one of them stole the pieces and set you up to be the suspect?"

He frowned. "One of *them* killed Meecham?"

"Why not?"

"Those men were all peers, Little Bird. Every single one of them belonged to the same clubs as men like Wareham, Plimpton, and Devonshire. They were not the sort to steal from each other."

"And you are?"

He blinked at that.

"It seems to me you have accepted your guilt with very little proof, Piers."

"I was covered in his blood and a bloody knife was found beside me."

"Did you recognize the knife?"

"No, but—"

"Are you sure it was his blood?"

"But…how?"

"Perhaps one of them drugged you—that would explain you having no memory of it."

He gave a startled laugh. "Do you really believe somebody hatched a plot to make me look like a murderer?"

"I believe that theory more than I believe you bludgeoned a man to death. Do you really think you are capable of such a thing?"

He slumped back in his chair, looking dazed. "I have believed it for more than half my life."

Freddie could see that he was looking at the event from a different angle for perhaps the first time. How had he allowed himself to believe in his guilt when he had no recollection of it? Was it really so easy for him to believe he was a murderer because of an accident of birth? Because he lacked the same pedigree—or at least the legitimacy—of those other men who had been there. Piers was—or at least he had been back then—a selfish, irresponsible, reckless youth. But a murderer?

Freddie refused to believe it.

"Bloody hell. You really think I might be innocent?"

"In my heart, I know you are," Freddie said without hesitation. "But I know my faith in you is not evidence. It will not be enough to spare you from the noose. We need evidence, although what we can find so long after the fact I cannot imagine. We will have to look at the men who were there when this happened. I suppose maybe one of the servants might have done it, but I truly believe we can rule them out. It has to be one of the other guests who—"

"Who is this *we*, Little Bird?"

"You do not honestly believe that *you* can poke around in these people's lives without drawing attention, do you?"

The Etiquette of Love

"And *you* do?" He barked a laugh. "If what you believe is correct, there is a killer still at large." He shook his head. "No. I forbid you to get involved."

"You *forbid* me?"

"Do not get your hackles up, Winifred. This is my problem to solve," he said sternly. "If I want help; I am a grown man and can ask for it."

She flinched at his cool tone.

"Don't give me that look," he said.

"What look?"

"The one that says I am being cruel and unreasonable by refusing to allow you to risk your neck. Give me your word you will not poke around in this."

"I will give you my word to do nothing…yet."

"*Yet?* What do you mean?"

"I mean I will not do anything until you have time to think the matter over and see the sense in what I have offered."

He looked to be grinding his teeth. "That is not good enough. I want you to *promise* me you will not do anything without telling me first."

Freddie stood, fetched her appointment book off her desk, and flipped to a blank page. "I promise I will not do anything dangerous. But I *can* help you draw up a list of who was there. And I can tell you—"

He gave a dismissive wave. "I already have a list."

"But are you sure it is comprehensive?"

He hesitated.

Freddie seized on that. "I can find out—"

"I said *no*, Little Bird." At her hurt look, he sighed. "I promise that you and I will sit down together—soon—and discuss the matter *ad nauseam*. But not today."

"Why not today?"

"Because I have a few questions for *you*. Why did you marry Sedgewick?"

Freddie reluctantly closed her appointment book. "What do you mean?"

"Don't try that trick on me."

"What trick?"

"Looking all wide-eyed and confused like a—like a harmless kitten."

She could not help smiling. "A kitten? I do not believe I have been called that before."

"Yes, you have; you just don't recall it. Wareham and I used to tease you about those huge eyes of yours in that little face. But do not change the bloody subject."

"*Tsk, tsk*. Language, Piers."

He merely stared.

"What makes you think I did not marry Sedgewick simply because *I* wanted to. He was a very handsome man, after all."

"Damnit! Don't toy with me, Little Bird. Why did you marry him? And why did Wareham allow it? As for Sedgewick's looks, I am well aware he'd been a handsome devil back when I ran with him—"

"You and Sedgewick were friends?"

"I did not say we were *friends*—I didn't care for the scoundrel above half—I said I ran with him. He was a rake and hell on women, and yet he always had more chasing him than you could shake a stick at. But he was twenty years your senior! And given the sort of life he lived I doubt he was much to look at by the time you married him." He swept her person with an assessing gaze. "You are a damned beautiful woman, Little Bird. You can't tell me that you didn't have scads of men after you. So, *why* him? Why Sedgewick? Just tell me the truth, dammit!"

"Why are you so upset about this, Piers? It was a long time ag—

"Was it because of money?"

The Etiquette of Love

Thinking about her awful marriage always left Freddie dispirited and this time was no exception. "I will answer your question if you give me your word this will be the last time we talk about it." A glance into his almost deranged eyes made her add, "And I also want your word you will not confront Wareham about it."

Knots ran up and down his jaw as he glared.

"Promise me, or we are finished with this discussion right now."

He uttered an extremely vulgar word and said, "Fine. I promise."

"You were right when you said Sedgewick drew women in droves. But you were wrong to think he lost his looks." She snorted softly. "If there was any justice in the world he would have looked like a gargoyle, as ugly on the outside as he was on the inside. But I have learned there is no justice. He was twenty-four years my senior, but he was still an extremely attractive man." Freddie chewed her lower lip, not wanting to share this next part, but Piers had just bared a great many ugly parts of his past, hadn't he?

"I wanted to marry him because I was attracted to him. Very much so." At least during their courtship and for the first few months of her marriage.

Piers looked discomfited by her confession. "Oh," was all he could muster.

Attracted was too weak a word; what she had felt for Sedgewick had bordered on fascination. Now that Freddie was older and more experienced, she knew that what had both drawn and repelled her had been Sedgewick's sexuality, which she had sensed even though he had kept a tight leash on that part of himself during their courtship. He had let a little slip once they had been married, not ripping off his handsome mask and exposing her to the full extent of his depravity until she defied him.

After that, Sedgewick had never bothered with his mask again. At least not for Freddie.

As much as she still hated and loathed her dead husband, she had blossomed those first few weeks of marriage, when he had been a generous and attentive lover. She had adored the way Sedgewick had made her feel in the bedchamber. And she had reveled in the naughty pleasures he had shown her.

Later on, when things were at their worst, she had castigated herself for being led by her base desires. For a time, she had hated herself worse than Sedgewick.

But that was ancient history now; it had been years since she had despised the sensual streak in her own nature, no matter that it had led her into a truly miserable marriage.

While she did not hate that part of herself any longer, neither did she encourage it.

At least not until Plimpton.

"Winifred?"

Freddie wrenched her mind away from the too-attractive duke. "Oh, where was I? Yes, my marriage. I was flattered by his attention. Even so, I did not want to marry before tasting the delights of a Season. But Sedgewick did not want to wait six months, and so I decided that accepting him was better than losing him."

"You were seventeen! What could you possibly know about anything? Why didn't Wareham tell him to go to the devil?" Piers demanded. "He never should have considered that snake's suit. It was that goddamned wife of his who put the idea into his head, wasn't it?"

There was no point in lying. The woman was dead and so was Freddie's hatred. "Sophia came to me after I had told Wareham I wanted to wait. She told me how Wareham was deeply in debt to Sedgewick—that the expense of a Season would just be more of a financial burden. She said Sedgewick would forgive Wareham's debt if I agreed to marry him, but that—"

Piers shot to his feet. "That lying *cunt*!"

Freddie gasped. "*Piers!*"

He stared down at her with an almost crazed look. "Have you ever known Wareham to gamble for more than chicken stakes?"

"No," she admitted. "But I assumed that he had learned his lesson after—"

"He had no lesson to learn, Winifred. Those bloody debts were *mine*! And Wareham—goddamn his rigid honor—took them onto his own shoulders and *you* are the one who ended up paying for them."

"I—I don't understand. How could they be yours? You had been gone for years by then."

But Piers had stopped listening. He grabbed a handful of his thick blond hair and groaned. "I cannot believe this," he muttered, more to himself than to her. He paced the room like a caged animal.

"Piers, please—I beg of you. Sit down and calm yourself," she said, when his agitation showed signs of becoming worse.

He spun on his heel. "*I* am the reason you married that monster. And do not try and tell me that he was not a monster! When I heard who you had married, I could not believe Wareham had allowed it. I wondered if perhaps Sedgewick had done the impossible and reformed himself. So, I went to that little village that was scarcely a mile from Sedgewick Hall and bought a few rounds at the local taproom. More than one servant was willing to talk about their dead master and his poor, innocent bride."

Freddie was horrified by what he must have heard. More than that, she was furious at him for doing such a thing. "How dare you pry into my past, Piers?"

"Tell me it isn't true—tell me the man wasn't a beast to you?" His hands flexed at his sides.

"That part of my life is dead and buried. I will not exhume it for you, or anyone else." Freddie stood. "If you are going to indulge in an orgy of guilt about your part in it all—if you had any part at all—then you can do so elsewhere."

For a moment, he goggled. And then, to her astonishment, he laughed. "Good God but you have grown into a magnificent woman, Little Bird. Just like I always knew you would. You are absolutely correct. I have no right to barge into your life and enact dramas in your parlor." He held out his hand. "Do you forgive me?"

Freddie set her hand in his. "Of course, you are forgiven, Piers. Now, why don't you sit down, and I will ring for some tea." She smiled. "If you won't talk to me about that long ago weekend and allow me to help prove your innocence, then at least you can tell me what you have been doing with yourself these past three-and-twenty years."

Chapter 3

Plimpton stared out the window of his carriage as a servant flipped down the steps and opened the door.

He raised his hand in a staying gesture when the footman opened his mouth—obviously to ask if something was amiss—his gaze riveted to the man leaving Winifred's house.

"Damnation," he muttered. It was that bloody pirate who worked for Severn—the one who had somehow managed to get into the Duchess of Chorley's ball; the one who looked familiar, but Plimpton did not know why. What the devil was he doing at Winifred's house?

Plimpton watched through narrowed eyes as the man strolled off down the street, an irksome swagger to his stride.

For a moment, he did not move. What on earth was the woman up to? Was the privateer her lover?

Revulsion curdled in his belly and his entire body grew hot with anger. He had believed she possessed more sense than that.

The woman is a widow on the far side of twenty. What right do you have to be outraged?

Because she is mine, *damn it!*

She is not *yours. And given how much she dislikes you; she might never belong to you.*

He ignored that prognostication. Not only was it highly unlikely, but now was not the time to be thinking about it.

Once Plimpton had tucked away the remnants of his anger, he climbed down from his carriage and strode up the same path the other man had just come down.

His rap on the door was answered speedily by the woman who had just shown the last guest out.

The servant—a housekeeper, judging by her severe black bombazine gown—recognized Plimpton from his one prior visit, when he had come to discuss Winifred sponsoring Becca next year.

"Your Grace!" She dropped a hasty curtsey and then hurried back a step, visibly flustered as she gestured him into the foyer. "Please, do come in."

"I wish to see your mistress," he said, stripping off his gloves. "I will wait here while you see if she is at home to visitors," he added firmly, just in case she had any notion of parking him in a sitting room to wait.

"Oh! Yes, of course, Your Grace," she said, even more flustered at this unconventional turn of events. "Er, you just wait right here, then." She backed away, until her foot hit the bottom step, and then turned and hurried up them.

Plimpton slapped his palm with his gloves and prowled the foyer, studying the artwork that hung there. On two walls were large landscapes, both signed by the former owner of the house, Daniel Keyes, the deceased father of Plimpton's sister-in-law, Honoria. Like his daughter, Keyes had been an acclaimed portraitist, but he had evidently applied his considerable skill to at least a few landscapes in his day. Both were magnificent and Plimpton had just resolved to ask Honoria if she would consider painting a scene around Whitcombe when the housekeeper clattered down the stairs.

"The countess will see you now, Your Grace."

Plimpton removed his hat, dropped his gloves into it, and handed both to the servant. "I will show myself up," he informed her before striding up the stairs.

Winifred rose when he entered the small, cramped parlor, her lovely face as coolly serene as ever. As if she had not just entertained a piratical rogue in her home only minutes before.

She dropped into a low, graceful curtsey that he could not help but admire, regardless of his current irritation. "What a pleasure to see you again, Your Grace."

Plimpton might have laughed at her brazen lie, had he been in the laughing mood.

The Etiquette of Love

"Please, have a seat," she said, lowering herself onto the dainty settee where her needlework basket and standing tambour made it clear she had been working.

Plimpton seated himself across from her.

"How may I serve you, Your Grace?"

Why beat around the bush? "I saw that man Gregg leaving your house when I pulled up outside."

"I beg your pardon?" she asked him frostily.

"Severn's minion," Plimpton said, even though she knew perfectly well whom he meant.

Her delicate nostrils flared slightly—the only outward sign of her displeasure—and she said, "What of it?"

His eyebrows leapt at her curt tone, one he was not accustomed to hearing. At least not directed toward *him*. "We have already discussed this, Winifred. Acknowledging Gregg at a *ton* function is enough to start unpleasant rumors. Entertaining the man in your house will do your reputation irreparable damage."

"Yes, I recall that conversation now. It seems my recollection is a bit different, however."

"Oh?"

"The word *discussion* implies there were at least *two* people involved. What I recall is *you* talking and me listening." She hurried on before he could respond, "Let me just say, yet again, how kind you are to concern yourself with my well-being. But whom I entertain—and where I do it—is not your affair."

"It is if you are launching my daughter." As retorts went, it was less than impressive.

It was her turn to lift her eyebrows. "If you wish to change your mind, please let me know so that I might—"

"I do not wish to change my mind," Plimpton said, hoping to keep their petty exchange of barbs from developing into a roaring row. "What I *do* wish is for you to take more care."

"As I said, it is—"

"As a matter of fact, my lady, your well-being *is* my concern. That is why I am here today."

Her lips parted in amazement. "I beg your pardon?"

"I had a serious conversation with your brother about you recently."

She bristled visibly and opened her mouth.

"Wareham is extremely ill," he said before she could argue—which, judging by the belligerent glint in her pale gaze she had every intention of doing.

"What is wrong with him?" The sudden stiffening of her shoulders told him that she was not untouched by his news.

"He was in a bad carriage accident that killed his valet and—"

"My God! When did this happen?"

"About ten days ago."

"Ten days! Why am I only hearing about this now?"

Plimpton's temper spiked at her question, and he struggled to rein in his anger before saying, "He sent you a letter—which he'd had to dictate rather than write himself, he was so ill. It was returned unopened."

Her throat flexed as she swallowed hard, color flooding her cheeks. After a moment, she nodded. "Yes, that is true. I sent it back. Obviously, if I had known—" her voice broke and naked fear spasmed across her face. "Tell me what happened."

"He was traveling from Bristol—perhaps you read about the severe series of storms they recently suffered?"

She nodded mutely.

"Wareham was caught in one of those storms and the section of road he was on washed away, taking his carriage with it. He broke his arm as well as two ribs."

Her eyes widened, her expression accusatory. "How dare you frighten me like that, Your Grace? A few broken bones are unfortunate, but hardly fatal."

The Etiquette of Love

"They can be if one of those bones punctures a lung."

"His lung? But...can a person survive such a wound?"

"Wareham was fortunate to have a physician who'd spent a great deal of time on the Continent during the war. Thanks to Doctor Madsen's skill with instruments called a cannula and trocar, Wareham's prognosis was excellent."

"You were there?"

"Not during the surgery, of course, but immediately afterward. I was in London when his message reached me, and I went directly to Torrance Park. Wareham was doing better, but still in critical condition. Naturally, he was anxious that there should be somebody he could trust at hand in the event the worst happened." Plimpton pulled a letter from his inner coat pocket. "Wareham sent for *me* because he could not reach *you*."

Once again, mortification seized control of her features. "I did not know he had been hurt or I would have opened it. I thought it merely one of his monthly missives."

"He told me you return all his letters unread and have done so every month for *years*." Plimpton had been flabbergasted by his friend's admission. "What purpose could such childish behavior possibly serve?"

"That is hardly your concern." Her words were cold, but her deepening flush told him she was not as sanguine as she wished to appear.

"I am making it my concern, Winifred."

"Do whatever you please, *Your Grace*; it will have no effect on *me*."

Her dismissive, slighting tone should have been insulting, and yet Plimpton found it... endearing. Yes, that was the word. She was so lovely—so delicate and dainty—that it was like being attacked by a butterfly.

You are going soft in the head.

He was. And he planned to enjoy every step of that journey.

Plimpton thrust aside that happy thought and held the letter out to her. "Take it and read it."

"You are not the master of me, Your Grace."

No, he was not. Yet. But he would be.

Yes, by God, he would be.

Plimpton tossed the letter onto the coffee table in front of her settee. "Your brother made a grave mistake not taking you firmly in hand after Sedgewick's death."

If looks were lethal, Plimpton would be gasping his last breath on the floor. "I am sure you think so, Your Grace."

"I *do* think so." He was amused by the scorching glare she sent him. Plimpton doubted that she knew how lovely she became when she was angry. Or how much the sparks she was throwing his way were encouraging, rather than curbing, his desire for her.

"Wareham has been too light with the reins; he has allowed you to get the bit firmly between your teeth. What you require is a firm hand, Winifred." *And I intend to be the one who provides it.*

She gave a squeak of strangled rage, and it was all Plimpton could do to suppress his laughter. He was behaving badly teasing her—especially given the serious reason for his visit—but he simply could not resist one last, little dig. "Had a sister of mine behaved with such willful, reckless independence I would have put her over—"

"Enough, sir!" She lunged to her feet, quivering with rage.

Plimpton stood, watching with interest as she mastered her temper.

"Your equine analogies are odious and insulting." Her eyes were the steely gray of a winter sky, and her voice was admirably cold for all her high color. Indeed, Plimpton was surprised there weren't snow flurries eddying on the parlor floor between them. "Your comparison of women to horses merely confirms what I have long suspected."

"Oh? What is that?"

"That you are utterly devoid of any sensibility where women are concerned. I am deeply grateful that I am *not* your sister."

The Etiquette of Love

So was Plimpton, albeit for entirely different reasons than hers. He would have liked to keep that color in her cheeks a bit longer, but it was time to finish the matter he had come to address.

"A few hours ago, I received an urgent message from the doctor who had been treating Wareham."

Her frigid glare gave way to confusion. "He is no longer treating him? But I thought you said—"

"Wareham is worse."

"I do not understand. You said his prognosis was excellent."

"It was. Or at least it *had* been. According to Doctor Madsen, Wareham's mother-in-law—the Dowager Lady Telford—arrived at Torrance Park the day after I departed. Her stated purpose was to take charge of your brother's children and bring them back home with her."

She gave him a look of disbelief. "Wareham asked *her* to take the children?"

"I can see you are familiar with the Dowager Lady Telford," he said dryly. "No, he did not want her to have the children. In fact, I delivered them to Wareham's brother-in-law, Lord Telford—who lives only an hour away—when I was there. Rather than return home when the dowager discovered the children were not there, she decided to stay and take charge of your brother's nursing." Plimpton's temper flared and he suppressed it with great difficulty before adding, "And now Wareham is far worse than he was."

"The dowager might be... unpleasant, but she has raised five children in her time and is probably a competent nurse. If Wareham is relapsing, it is likely the severity of his injury."

"That is not Doctor Madsen's opinion. He said the wound only became infected recently—under *her* care. Indeed, that is why he had a falling out with her. The dowager evidently dismissed him for impertinence." He met Winifred's gaze squarely. "I fear Wareham is in grave danger, my lady. You must go to him."

"*Me?* I have no power over the situation. If Lady Telford can dismiss a physician, she will take no heed of anything I say."

"She will heed what *I* say," Plimpton assured her grimly.

"Then you do not need me."

"I need you because I know nothing about nursing. And once I dismiss her, I will require your help."

She stared at him, clearly at a loss for words.

"My carriage stands ready to take you home."

His words, or at least one of them, brought her back to life. "Torrance Park is no home of mine. Wareham and Sophia saw to that years ago."

"Enough of this foolishness," he snapped, losing patience. "Wareham might die—not because he has to, but because that shrew is bungling his care. Is this how you wish to end your relationship with your only brother? If you do not go to him now, you will regret it for the rest of your life. He is my oldest *friend* and I will not have his death on my conscience. You should be ashamed to even hesitate to help him."

Her face, which had been hot with anger, drained of color and she seemed to deflate. "I—I—cannot—" Her jaws snapped shut and she broke off her stammering, dashing a tear from her cheek before nodding and saying, "You are right, Your Grace. Now is not the time for any of…that. Of course I will go to him."

The relief he felt at her words left him lightheaded. "Good—excellent," he amended. "So then, how soon can you be ready to travel?"

"I will take the stage from—"

"You will take my carriage."

Her eyes narrowed. "You are not—"

"This quibbling is wasting valuable time! My carriage will be far faster and more comfortable than anything you can arrange. If you are concerned about being beholden to me, then you should view my assistance not as a favor to you, but to Wareham."

Her eyes glittered dangerously, and she inhaled, swelling in size like an exotic reptile preparing to spit venom.

She looked magnificent in her fury.

The Etiquette of Love

He prepared to quash her next argument, but she said, through gritted teeth, "Thank you, Your Grace. When can—"

"Whenever you are ready."

"I need only an hour to send a few messages and pack my things."

Plimpton stood. "Then I will return for you in an hour. No. Do not get up," he said. "I can show myself out."

But she followed him anyhow.

When they reached the foyer Plimpton paused after he had opened the door, expecting that she had accompanied him to say something. But she stared at a point beyond him, visibly shaken.

Was it preparations for her journey that consumed her thoughts? Or was it concern for the brother whose letters she rejected and whom she had not spoken to for eight years?

Or was she thinking about that bloody scoundrel he had seen sauntering away from her house earlier?

Damnation.

Getting her away from London, Plimpton decided, would serve multiple purposes.

Chapter 4

Freddie was packed, dressed in her best traveling costume, and waiting in the foyer when the duke's coach arrived at her door a few minutes before the appointed hour.

"Good lord," she murmured as she looked out the foyer sidelight at the magnificent black lacquer equipage with its four black horses, liveried postilions, coachman, and four outriders—one of whom appeared to be the duke himself, mounted on a superb black horse.

He dismounted gracefully, tossed his reins to a servant, and then strode toward the door.

Freddie hastily turned away and was pulling on her gloves when he entered the foyer, a servant on his heels.

"Are you ready?" he asked abruptly.

"Yes."

He gave a curt nod and turned to the two valises, one of moderate size and a far smaller one that contained the nursing supplies she had accumulated over the years. "This is all you are bringing?"

Was that judgment she heard in his tone? She met his cool gray gaze, looking for signs of…anything. But the man's thoughts were, as always, a mystery. "Yes, this is all I am bringing," she said more tartly than she would have liked. "I will stay as long as Wareham needs me. But once he is on the road to recovery, I will have to return. I have responsibilities here and cannot be gone indefinitely." Why was she explaining herself to him?

To her relief, he did not argue. Instead, he gestured for the servant to take the bags.

The duke's hand rested lightly on her lower back as he escorted her toward the carriage. She was so distracted by the subtle, commanding touch that she did not immediately notice the woman standing beside the carriage.

"This is Miss Denny," the duke said.

The woman, an attractive middle-aged female garbed in the well-made but modest clothing of a companion, dipped a graceful curtsey. "Good day, my lady."

Freddie gave the duke an exasperated look. "You had time to engage a chaperone?"

"Miss Denny only recently accepted employment with me. She was waiting to accompany me to Whitcombe, but will come to Torrance Park, first."

So, *yes*, in other words; he had engaged a chaperone for her. What an infuriating man.

Freddie hardly required a chaperone—indeed, she *was* a chaperone—but it was not the woman's fault, so she inclined her head politely.

The duke handed Freddie into the carriage. "Unfortunately, there is no moon tonight so we will be forced to break our journey when darkness falls."

Freddie nodded, surprised—but pleased—that he had taken the time to inform her of their schedule, especially since he was the sort of high-handed man who never explained anything to anyone.

To Freddie's further surprise, he helped Miss Denny into the coach himself and then flipped up the steps and shut the door.

Most of the tension that had built within her dissipated the moment she was not directly confronted with the duke.

She put him from her thoughts and took notice of her surroundings. It had been a long, long time since Freddie had ridden in such a luxurious vehicle. Not since her brother Wareham's carriage. Sedgewick had preferred to do his traveling by curricle, which had left Freddie to occupy a decrepit old coach that had been in use since his grandfather's day; a ponderous, sloppily sprung whale of a vehicle that had rattled her bones to dust.

It took only a few minutes in the duke's carriage to appreciate the difference. Not only was the interior—supple black leather seats with thick carpet and elegant wooden window coverings—far nicer than anything she had ridden in before, but the cobble street was like velvet beneath the well-sprung vehicle.

She glanced out the right window to where the duke rode. There was no denying that he showed to advantage on horseback. Not only was his mount—a glossy coal-black horse that matched his team to perfection—magnificent, but he rode as if he'd been born to it. Which of course he had. Freddie decided Plimpton should only ever wear riding clothes, which displayed his fit body to perfection. Especially those muscular thighs of his, which were flexing enticingly beneath his coffee-brown leather breeches. Yes, Freddie mused as she studied him, she much preferred Plimpton's more powerful physique to sleek elegance.

You prefer it? a disbelieving voice mocked.

Just because I find him overbearing and domineering does not mean I cannot admire his form.

Plimpton turned slightly and met Freddie's gaze, his severe resting expression growing slightly sterner, as if he disapproved of her.

As if you were a horse that had the bit between its teeth...

Freddie seethed at the memory of his obnoxious words and narrowed her eyes at him.

If he noticed her anger, he did not show it. She did not want to be the first to look away, but something in his hard gaze caused a flush that started at her face and rapidly spread beneath her clothing. Her chest tightened and it became harder to breathe—

Blast the man! Freddie turned away before she embarrassed herself further.

Thank God he was riding alongside the carriage rather than inside it.

Unwanted, the argument they'd had about Wareham came back to her. Freddie cringed as she recalled her reaction to the news of her brother's injury. Plimpton had behaved with abominable arrogance, but Freddie's petulant, thoughtless behavior had been far worse. How could she have allowed her ancient anger against Wareham to rear its ugly head at such a time? If what the duke said was true, her brother might *die.*

The Etiquette of Love

It pained her to admit it, but she was grateful to the duke for making her see reason.

For the second time in as many minutes Freddie put the man out of her head, opened her needlework bag, and took out her current project. It was the fourth and final cushion cover in a commissioned work and it would pay a great deal—relative to what she usually earned from her efforts—once she could hand it over to the man who bought all her needlework.

She had begun selling her work shortly after she had been widowed. All Freddie's life people had praised the quality of her embroidery. Not until Sedgewick's death had she realized that such a pleasurable pastime could yield money. It was not enough to live on, of course, but it was enough to purchase small conveniences. Or at least it had been when she'd worked at the Stefani Academy. Since that had closed, she'd found herself scrambling to make ends meet. Sponsoring young women did not always yield actual money. No, such an exchange would be far too vulgar. Instead, she was given *gifts*. Sometimes these gifts came in the form of cash, but more often she was given jewelry or other valuable baubles. She had discovered, this past year, that launching the daughters of industrialists was a far more profitable endeavor than sponsoring the daughters of peers. The Conroy twins were an excellent example. Their mother and father had simply named a sum—an eye-popping one—to take charge of their daughters. It had been uncomfortable to engage in such a nakedly commercial exchange, but it had also been a relief. And it had generated enough money to pay several bills that had been about to become an embarrassment.

Thinking of money made her recall Piers's last words to her today. "You needn't worry about money any longer, Little Bird. One of the few wise things I've done in my life is ally myself with Severn these past sixteen years. As his first mate I have earned a great deal of prize money. You never need to work again."

She had been warmed by her brother's well intentioned, but ill conceived, offer. "I cannot stop working, Piers. Nor can I live off your money."

"Why the devil can't you? I am your brother, for pity's sake!"

"What would I tell my friends, Piers? For that matter, what would the rest of the *ton* assume if I were suddenly living as high as a coach horse and stopped working?"

"It's none of their bloody business where your money comes from."

"I can hardly tell people you are my brother, can I? I might as well report you to Bow Street as accept your money."

They had argued briefly before he had accepted her rejection but *only for the time being.* "I will contrive something that will answer," he had promised.

"Concentrate on *contriving* a way to prove your innocence, first."

He had laughed and they had been on good terms as she had seen him to the door.

"I will be gone for some weeks," he had said before kissing her cheek.

"Where are you going?"

"Never you mind, Little Bird."

She smiled to herself at the memory as she finished one edge of her seat cushion and loosened the tambour frame to move the work.

Freddie might not be able to accept financial gifts from Piers, but it felt good to have a brother ready to stand by her side after so many years—even if she could not acknowledge him as such.

Oh, Wareham would offer help, but there would be strings attached.

Miles had always been ready to champion her in any way, but he was a friend and though she loved him, she did not love him like one loved family. Nor did she love him romantically, even though she knew he had been interested in her. Indeed, she had been relieved when he had married Mary Barnett. The prickly little woman was perfect for Miles. Their union had started out as rocky as any she had ever seen, but it had been clear at their wedding ball a year ago that their union had turned into a love match.

The Etiquette of Love

Of all the teachers who'd worked at the Stefani Academy only Freddie and Lori remained uncoupled.

Freddie would never remarry, but she had hopes for Lori, whom she was almost certain had developed tender feelings for Lord Stand Fast Severn. It was a shame there had been such a bizarre misunderstanding involving Severn and the heiress Demelza Pasco. How a marriage announcement came to be made in the newspaper about the pair was quite a mystery to Freddie. But evidently that had all been a terrible mistake and Severn was not the villain Freddie had feared he might be. Lori had fled London after reading the faux wedding announcement, escaping to the country to lick her wounds at her brother and sister-in-law's home.

Freddie needed to write to Lori about the mix-up with Severn and Miss Pasco, but she still had not decided how to relay that news without raising her friend's hopes.

Well, she would have plenty of time to consider the matter on this upcoming trip.

***

Plimpton had made the journey from London to Dorset countless times over the years. He and Wareham had been best friends for three-quarters of his life, after all. But never had he accompanied a woman to the earl's country house.

Cecily had taken an immediate dislike to Wareham's wife the first and only time the countess had visited Whitcombe and had not cared to either visit or entertain the Warehams again.

As a result, it had been only Plimpton and Wareham who'd traveled back and forth over the years.

Not that Cecily had entertained many other guests after those first few years. It had been Plimpton's mother who'd served as his hostess for the better part of the last two decades.

Cecily herself had not left Whitcombe since the death of their last child, Edward. Indeed, she had rarely left her chambers. Once she no longer needed to tolerate Plimpton's monthly visits to her bed, she had requested that she be allowed to move to some other apartment, far away from his. Whitcombe had three-hundred-and-sixty-one rooms, so there had been plenty for her to choose from.

After she had moved chambers weeks, even months, had gone by without catching a glimpse of her. Plimpton had no idea what Cecily had done with all her time. She certainly had not spent any of it with their daughter. For all that Rebecca was their only surviving child, Cecily had always treated the girl as a stranger. Right from the beginning she had wanted nothing to do with the rearing of her, turning everything over to Plimpton and his mother.

Wareham's wife—Sophia—had been the polar opposite of Cecily. She had controlled her children, her houses, and her husband with a proverbial fist of iron. No detail was too insignificant for the countess to manage. She'd been a bloody exhausting woman and he had never understood why Wareham had been so besotted with her. Oh, she had been lovely, that was true. But she'd been hard through and through.

There had not been much to choose from between either of their wives in Plimpton's opinion. And yet until only a year ago Wareham had loved the countess to distraction. His feelings had changed so suddenly it had been shocking.

At that point, just like Cecily, Wareham had moved out of the master's chambers to get away from his spouse.

Plimpton had never asked his friend what had happened. He did not want to know.

While he'd never envied Wareham his wife, for years he had been guilty of a deep envy for the other man's children. Six times the countess had been brought to bed, and all six had survived.

But then Lady Wareham had been a healthy, energetic woman who had scarcely sat still for a moment of the day. If she had not died from a bad hunting accident Plimpton suspected she would have lived to be a very old lady.

Cecily, by contrast, had always been ethereally frail. Not until he'd been married to her for five years did Plimpton discover just how much of her frailty—and her beauty—she owed to the numerous vials and powders that cluttered her dressing table.

He hastily shut the door on those distasteful thoughts.

The Etiquette of Love

Thank God Rebecca had lived through childhood, although her health to this day was still less than robust. He did not like to imagine what his life would have become if his daughter, too, had died.

He would have gone on doing his duty, because that is what he did—and who he was—but life would have been gray and joyless.

He loved his mother and his brother, of course, but there was no love to compare to what a person felt for a child. At least not in his experience.

Plimpton turned to the woman seated in his carriage.

Her head was bent over something—perhaps a book—and her profile was to him. She was a flawless woman; the sort who robbed a man of breath each and every time he looked at her. She was as lovely as Cecily had been and every bit as regal and aloof. Especially around Plimpton.

But although she wore a mask of frigid courtesy in his presence, he had observed the way she interacted with Honoria and their other friends. Unlike Cecily, there was a warm and loving woman beneath her cool, controlled veneer.

But never toward Plimpton. For him, all Winifred had was hostility and mistrust. Did she know about Plimpton's part in banishing her beloved half-brother—a banishment that had eventually led to Piers's death—or was there some other reason she despised him?

***

Even though Plimpton's carriage did not bear his escutcheon, it was clear to anyone with an ounce of sense that whoever the impressive cortege belonged to was somebody wealthy and powerful.

The duke had either been very certain that Freddie would accompany him on his journey and sent his horses ahead, or he routinely kept a change of horses on the road to Dorset because the team that replaced the original four were every bit as magnificent.

Even when there was no change needed, Plimpton stopped to allow the two women to stretch their legs and refresh themselves.

Freddie discovered that Miss Denny was taking a position as companion to the duke's aged mother who had suffered an apoplexy several months earlier and now required constant attention.

If Miss Denny thought this trip to Dorset was strange, she did not indicate it—and not because she was reticent to talk. Indeed, she indulged in an almost constant stream of chatter from the moment they climbed into the coach, only halting the flow when they stopped for refreshment breaks, resuming immediately once the coach started rolling.

Freddie did not mind the woman's chatter. The last thing she wanted to do was sit quietly with her thoughts. Thoughts that were whirling and sloshing like water in a bucket that had been badly jostled.

Between her worry for Wareham and her worry for Piers, Freddie was worn out by the time they stopped for the night and was looking forward to being alone and having a tray in her room.

She should have known better.

"I have engaged a private parlor for us, Winifred," the duke said as he helped her from the carriage when they reached the Knight and Stag, an elegant posting inn that appeared to be quite new.

His words were an order disguised as a request and it prodded her temper like a poker stirring dormant coals to life.

"I am happy to dine in my room." She could not resist adding, "I am sure Miss Denny would be pleased to break bread with you."

He regarded her with a calm, direct look that sent unwanted arrows of arousal throughout her body and made Freddie want to slap herself. Why, oh why, did she have to develop a physical infatuation for this man out of all the hundreds she had encountered over the years?

"Will an hour give you enough time to rest and ready yourself?" he asked, ignoring both her rejection and her comment about the garrulous companion.

Well. What could a person say to that, other than *yes*?

"An hour will be sufficient. Thank you, Your Grace."

He inclined his head and strode away.

The Etiquette of Love

Miss Denny was talking to one of Plimpton's grooms and gesturing toward the second coach, where a haughty looking man who could only be His Grace's valet was directing the unloading of luggage.

Freddie was about to join the other woman and fetch her valise when a tall, handsome young man wearing the duke's silver and navy-blue livery approached her, one of her bags in each hand. "Your chambers are ready, my lady. Right this way, please." He nodded toward the double doors, which the innkeeper and his wife had flung wide open to receive the duke's entourage.

"It seems like His Grace is well-known here," she said as they made their way up the stairs.

"He stays here often, although it is usually one of his stops on the way back from Torrance Park, rather than on the way there."

That made sense as he probably left London far earlier than he had today.

"What is your name?" she asked when they reached the landing.

"William, my lady." He paused outside the second door and opened it.

The room was far larger and nicer than what one saw in most inns. Massive beams held up a freshly plastered ceiling and the wooden floors gleamed. The bed was a huge four poster affair with ivory curtains, fluffy pillows, and gold brocade bedspread.

So, this was the sort of luxury one enjoyed if one was a duke. Or if one traveled with a duke.

"Is there anything I can get for you, my lady?"

She turned from the bed. "No, thank you, William, that will be all."

Before he could shut the door a maid arrived with a steaming ewer. "His Grace said I was to help you dress, my lady."

"Thank you, but I do not require assistance. You can just leave that on the dresser." She reached into the reticule that still hung from her wrist and extracted a coin, handing it to the maid as she turned to leave.

The girl beamed and dropped a curtsey. "Thank you, my lady!"

Freddie locked the door and then stripped off her gloves before opening the larger of the two bags, which held only four gowns. One of the garments was her best dinner dress. It was also her newest gown, which she had bought when Mr. Conroy gave her a bonus. It had been a reckless purchase, but all her dresses had begun to look threadbare. Fortunately, the two modistes that she brought most of her clients to had offered her significant discounts on her own clothing. This dress was the first time she had taken advantage of such an offer.

As she stroked the lovely mint green silk, she chastised herself. Why had she packed such a gown when she might have used the space for something more useful and practical?

You brought it because you wanted the duke to see you in it. You wanted him to observe you in something other than the dowdy and matronly gowns you wear to chaperone your clients.

Freddie ignored the voice and undressed down to her chemise before washing the travel grime from her face and limbs with the deliciously hot water. She unpinned her hair, brushed it until it shone, and then re-dressed it in a sleek chignon.

The gown's buttons were cleverly hidden by a side ruffle, which allowed her to dress without a maid. The pale green color was not a shade she would have believed flattering, but it had been made for a woman who'd never collected it and Madam Therese had urged her to try it on, offering her an even deeper discount than usual.

"It is not a color that will suit many women," the modiste had admitted when she had regarded Freddie in the trifold looking glass. "But with your coloring and slim form"—she had made a gesture with her lips and fingertips that was quintessentially gallic. "You must take this one, my lady. It was meant for you."

As Freddie studied herself now, she had to admit the pale green made her hair look like spun gold and her eyes more silver than gray. Not only did she love the color, but the thin silk caressed her body in a way that felt positively decadent.

"And why are you wearing it tonight, Winifred?" she asked herself mockingly, cutting her reflection a scathing glance as she took out the string of paste pearls that went with every gown ever made and clasped them around her throat. Once, years before, she had possessed a strand of genuine pearls left to her by her mother, a woman she did not remember. The necklace, along with the matching earbobs, she had sold the day she had gone to the asylum to collect Miranda. She had needed the money to bribe the attendant to look the other way.

She had consoled herself with the argument that they were only *things*—that Miranda's freedom and future were more important—but she had felt a twinge of regret at parting with the last connection to her mother.

Freddie screwed the fake pearl earbobs into her ears and then smoothed the fine silk of her skirt, taking pleasure from the feel of the garment as much as the look of it. There was no point in lying to herself; she had brought the gown hoping she would dine with the duke at some point.

Wanting to impress a man—especially one like Plimpton—was… dangerous.

Freddie would need to remain vigilant around him.

Chapter 5

"This is a lovely inn," Winifred said as the servants set out the second course. "I do not recall ever staying here when I traveled between Torrance Park and London in the past."

"It opened for business five or six years ago," Plimpton said, lifting the bottle of wine and refilling both their glasses.

Her full mouth tightened and thinned at Plimpton's gesture. Whether she was displeased because she thought him high-handed or because she disapproved of drinking more than one glass, he did not know.

They spoke of only inconsequential matters while the room buzzed with servants. But he could sense a certain tension beneath her lovely surface and knew she had questions for him. Plimpton had some for her, too.

In the meantime, he relaxed and savored the sight of her. Although she always looked elegant, he had noticed there was a certain shabby quality about her clothing which had surprised him as he'd assumed launching young women into society would be a fairly lucrative endeavor.

The gown she wore tonight was new—or at least he had never seen it before. The dress had obviously been designed by a modiste with considerable skill. The rich silk was such a pale green that it should have reduced her fair hair, skin, and eyes to insipidity, but instead, she looked vibrant and alive, like spring, personified. Indeed, she positively *glowed*, her silvery-gray eyes exhibiting those hints of pale brown that seemed to become more pronounced depending on what color she wore.

She was the most exquisite woman he had seen in years. Possibly ever. And there was a depth to her that transcended mere physical perfection.

Plimpton had his own secrets and plenty of past disappointments and usually had no interest in probing beyond the polite masks of others—either women or men. But the lightning-fast flashes of sorrow that sometimes slipped past Winifred's beautiful veneer fascinated and drew him. What had happened to her during her marriage to Sedgewick? The man had been a rake—no, worse: a debauchee—and Plimpton had been horrified when Wareham had sanctioned the match. Of course, Sedgewick had been Wareham's wife's cousin, so it would have been difficult for him to reject a member of her family.

But he should have.

That sadness he saw in those occasional flashes had come from her time with Sedgewick; Plimpton was sure of it.

And it sickened him to think of what she might have endured.

***

Freddie should never have drunk that third glass of wine. Just because the duke kept pouring it, did not mean she had to keep swallowing it. But she had, her hand seemingly moving of its own accord and her mouth its willing accomplice. And now, somehow, the third glass was empty. She didn't usually have a *second* glass. While her wits were not befuddled, her tongue had loosened as the delicious meal wore on.

For a man who had always seemed reserved to the point of taciturnity, the Duke of Plimpton was an excellent host and dinner companion. He kept the conversation moving smoothly, avoiding subjects that were too uncomfortable or personal while the servants hovered.

Most surprisingly, he spoke warmly about his home, Whitcombe, and it was obvious that he enjoyed ruralizing. And yet she knew he was scrupulous when it came to his parliamentary duties and came to London whenever Lords was in session.

It was also clear—from the way he talked about his daughter, mother, brother, Honoria, and his new nephew—that he cared deeply for his family. He was especially voluble on the subject of Honey's baby, whom Freddie had not yet met.

"Robert is a very healthy baby," he said, the words reminding Freddie that Plimpton had lost several children of his own.

Indeed, the change in the duke at the mention of his brother's child was electric. His features, usually so stern, lightened with something that was almost a smile.

"Have you met him yet?" he asked.

"Not yet," Freddie admitted. She had wanted to be there when the child was born, but she had not been able to leave her client at the time. "Honey says she will bring him to London in the spring."

He frowned at that, clearly not pleased at the thought of the baby traveling. Freddie would like to be a fly on the wall if he ever thought to tell Honey how to raise her son.

"I was pleased that Honoria enjoys the country so much," he said, evidently deciding to leave the matter of the spring trip until some other time. "I know she spent most of her life in London so I thought she would yearn for city life."

"Her love for country living has surprised me, as well," Freddie admitted. "Her letters are bursting with descriptions of Everley's home farm, the new succession house Lord Simon is building, the new stables, and, of course, Robert." Freddie finished the last of her raspberries and cream and the duke gestured for the servant to clear the dishes away.

"Would you care for anything else, my lady?" he asked.

"No, thank you. I have already eaten too much."

The duke nodded his dismissal and the servants noiselessly departed.

Finally, they were alone and could talk freely.

"You said you talked to Wareham about my future."

He nodded slowly, clearly weighing his next words. "Wareham was in a great deal of pain at the time, so his thinking was not quite clear. But one thing was evident, and that was his concern for your future."

"I have not seen my brother in more than eight years. The last time we spoke he told me he would wash his hands of me if I chose to teach school." Her eyes narrowed. "And for the last eight years he has held to that promise. So, why is he worried about my future *now*?"

The duke gave a slight shrug. "That is something you will have to ask Wareham."

"Wareham should be more concerned about his children than me. Especially his daughters. The only woman more manipulative and controlling than Sophia was her mother." Now *that* was something Freddie never would have said without the prompting of three glasses of wine.

"I believe Wareham shares that opinion."

Freddie raised her eyebrows, not bothering to hide her disbelief.

The duke accurately interpreted her look. "Your brother has changed, Winifred. As for the children, Viscount Telford would be their guardian if the worst happened. Naturally, Wareham's oldest boy—who is almost eighteen—would take up his duties as earl if his father were to die. But the rest are still in the schoolroom and would live with Telford."

Freddie shivered, the thought of her brother's death for the first time feeling like a possibility. She had been at odds with Wareham for so many, many years that it was hard to remember the funny, caring brother he had once been.

"Are you cold?" the duke asked, mistaking her shiver. "Shall I have a servant fetch a wrap?"

Freddie shook her head. "I am surprised that Wareham's brother- and sister-in-law are willing to take charge of all five of the younger children."

"The Telfords have none of their own."

"Even so," Freddie said, "that is a great deal of responsibility. Wareham was not close with his brother-in-law back when I lived with him.

"No, I believe he and Telford have only become better acquainted in the last year or so." He cleared his throat. "For a long time, Lady Wareham and Lady Telford were…estranged."

Freddie gave an inelegant snort—something else that never would have happened if she had not drunk so much—and barely managed to bite back some truly ungenerous words about her deceased sister-in-law.

The way the duke eyed her told Freddie that he could guess what she had suppressed. "Do you know the younger Lady Telford?" he asked.

"I only met her a handful of times." She hesitated, and then threw restraint to the wind. "Sophia did not get along with any of her siblings or their spouses. I saw most of them only at my brother's wedding."

The duke nodded, looking unsurprised.

Sophia's manipulative, outspoken tendencies had alienated her siblings and Freddie imagined the entire family had exhaled a sigh of relief when Sophia had married Wareham and moved to Torrance Park.

And then Sophia had become Freddie's problem.

She looked up from her unpleasant memories to find the duke's knowing eyes on her.

"You continued visiting Wareham even after his marriage?" she asked.

"I did."

She was amazed anyone would expose themselves to Sophia's company on purpose. "Of course, Sophia would have adored you. Or at least she would have adored your rank." The moment the words were out of her mouth she regretted them. She could not even fairly blame the nasty comment on the three glasses of wine. Her anger toward her dead sister-in-law had dimmed since the other woman's death, but thinking about Sophia always fanned the glowing coals and brought her hatred roaring back to life. "I apologize, that was—"

"Accurate," he broke in, subtle humor glinting in his eyes. "The Countess of Wareham could be a difficult woman." The words were so ridiculously understated that Freddie felt like rolling on the floor with laughter. Thankfully, she was able to restrain that impulse. Perhaps the *rolling on the floor with laughter* stage only started after one had consumed *four* glasses of wine?

"I don't know if you are aware, but Wareham has long regretted that he did not curb his wife's behavior where you were concerned."

"No, I was not aware of that."

"Perhaps if you had opened any of his letters, you might have been."

His quietly chiding words were like dry tinder on the flames of her anger. She gave an unamused laugh. "I always knew the purview of a duke was extensive, but I never dreamed it included the private affairs of people who are neither related to you nor dependent on your bounty."

The duke's expression did not so much as flicker. "Wareham is especially riddled with guilt when it comes to your marriage to Sedgewick. He fears there were reasons behind your decision to marry the earl that he was not aware of. He blames himself for not noticing at the time."

"He *should* feel guilty. He allowed his wife to rule his household without ever bothering to question her behavior—especially when it came to *me*." Freddie retorted, unwanted memories of life with Wareham's harpy of a wife resurfacing in her memory like bloated corpses floating to the surface of a lake. "Sophia made my life hell from the day she married my brother. No, even before then," she amended.

The cozy parlor pulsed with an uncomfortable silence and Freddie regretted sharing such an intimate detail of her past with this quietly judging stranger.

Oh, what does any of that matter anymore? It happened more than a decade ago. And you did nothing to be ashamed of, in any case.

Emboldened by those thoughts, Freddie forced herself to meet his gaze.

To her astonishment, she did not see censure in his dark gray eyes, but something that looked remarkably like sympathy.

Unhappily, she saw even more in his knowing gaze: The duke did not just suspect that Sedgewick had been cruel, he also knew how depraved her husband had been.

Freddie squirmed at the knowledge in the duke's eyes, ashamed that the world—or at least a man like Plimpton—knew the truth about her dead husband.

She was terrified he was going to ask her something about Sedgewick or her marriage, but she should have known better; he was far too polite and circumspect to delve into that subject.

Instead, he turned the lens on himself. "When a man is as ill as your brother is now, the transgressions of his past weigh heavily." His lips twisted slightly. "I was very sick a few years ago, so I remember well how one's failures can haunt one."

Her friend Honey had told her about the duke's illness, although she had not shared many details, just the fact that he had been close to death. Honey had also mentioned that Lord Simon and Plimpton had been estranged at the time. Freddie supposed that was the *failure* he had just referred to.

Plimpton was not the sort of man to share such a private matter lightly and Freddie appreciated him confiding in her. In his stiff, autocratic way, the duke was trying to be helpful, and it was unfair of her to be constantly ripping up at him. It was also unlike her. If her friends could see the way she had behaved earlier today…

Freddie shuddered. *Do better, Winifred.* She met his inscrutable gaze. "Whitcombe is a great distance from Torrance Park, Your Grace. I know you are putting yourself to considerable inconvenience by bringing me all this way. I—I appreciate it."

Lord. That had been painful.

"I am honored that I can help," he said. "I must tell you that many of Wareham's other friendships have fallen away over the years, Winifred. Your brother is quite isolated, so your presence at Torrance will matter a great deal to him."

Fury rose inside her—the emotion so bitter and powerful she had to clench her jaws to stop it from spewing out of her. She wanted to shout at the duke that Wareham's isolation was his own fault. That her brother had, year after year, chosen his wife over his sister, his family, and his friends.

But the man across from her had done nothing to deserve her rancor. Indeed, his loyalty to Wareham was commendable.

"You have been a good friend to Wareham, Your Grace."

"And he has been a good friend to me."

Freddie believed that.

Too bad Wareham had not been even half as good a brother.

Chapter 6

The duke must have sent word to Torrance to expect them because the front door opened as the carriage rolled up and several footmen and a man who could only be a butler—although he was not dear old Friske, whom Sophia must have driven off—hastened to meet the carriage.

As he had every single time, Plimpton opened the carriage door himself and helped Freddie and Miss Denny out.

"This is Lady Sedgewick, Goodrich, his lordship's sister," the duke said to the dignified looking older man who had approached.

"It is a pleasure to finally meet you, my lady," the butler said, sounding as if he meant it.

"How is his lordship?" the duke asked.

"Doctor Finch was here a few hours ago and he cupped Lord Wareham after observing the deterioration in his condition. He fears the infection has become worse, Your Grace."

The duke frowned. "And the Dowager Viscountess Telford?"

The butler's face tightened almost imperceptibly. "She is still here." He coughed lightly. "Although she has not attended his lordship after he sent her away two days ago."

"I see," Plimpton said after a pregnant silence.

The duke had not raised his voice, but Freddie could feel the force of his anger radiating off his well-tailored person. His jaw muscles flexed, his opaque gaze looking through, rather than at the poor butler, who had developed beads of perspiration on his forehead.

Freddie reflected that the duke would have to shave twice a day given that his beard had begun to poke through the tanned skin, and it was scarcely three o'clock.

She blinked at the strange observation. Why on earth was she thinking about his facial hair?

The duke turned to her. "Would you like to go to your room first and—"

"I would like to see my brother immediately."

For the first time, approval glinted in Plimpton's cold gaze. "I will come with you."

Freddie was more relieved by his words than she wanted to admit. There was a strange, unpleasant atmosphere in the house—a tension of sorts—and after the butler's confession about the dowager, Freddie suspected the older woman was the source.

As the three of them ascended the grand marble staircase the butler turned to her. "I took the liberty of having your old chambers prepared for you, my lady."

Freddie felt a stab of pleasure at his thoughtfulness. "Thank you." How astonishing that her sister-in-law had left any trace of her in the house.

As if she'd spoken the words aloud the butler delicately cleared his throat and said, "Er, the suite was redecorated some years ago."

Ah. She should have guessed.

Torrance Park had been built a hundred and fifty years earlier when the original structure had suffered a devastating fire. While none of the furnishings had been ancient family heirlooms, the house had been, in Freddie's memory, elegantly appointed.

As she looked around her, she could see few things from her childhood remaining. While Freddie wouldn't have called the changes to the furniture, draperies, and art *vulgar*, the modern décor struck her as trying a bit too hard.

Goodrich stopped outside of one of the guestroom doors and knocked lightly.

Freddie frowned. "My brother is not in the earl's chambers?"

"Er, no, my lady. His lordship moved to this suite of rooms some time ago."

The Etiquette of Love

She looked at the duke, but he said nothing. Wareham had occupied the master's chambers at Torrance Park since their parents had died. How odd that he had moved.

When nobody answered the butler's knock he turned the handle. "It is locked," he said, astonished.

Wearing the closest thing Freddie had seen to a scowl the duke rapped sharply on the heavy wooden door.

They waited. And waited.

Plimpton had just raised his hand to pound with the meat of his fist when the door finally opened.

The fetid stench of sickness was the first thing she noticed. Right behind that was the unmistakable odor of gin.

The woman who had opened the door was wizened and ancient looking. A pair of rheumy eyes blinked up at them and a scratchy voice wheezed, "His lordship is sleeping and not to be disturbed."

"This is Lady Sedgewick, his lordship's sister, Mrs. Marley," Goodrich said, his voice frosty with disapproval.

"The Dowager said—"

"Stand aside, woman," the duke barked.

Mrs. Marley's jaw sagged, and her squinty eyes widened as she hastily stumbled out of the way.

Plimpton gestured for Freddie to enter.

Inhaling through her mouth, she almost gagged as she went through the study and into the adjacent bedchamber. Breathing such air would make anyone ill, even a healthy person.

She strode to the window farthest from the bed, yanked back the drapes, and fumbled with the sash before flinging it open and flooding the room with much needed air.

Behind her, the old woman gave a scandalized yelp. "Her ladyship said—"

"You are dismissed," the duke's voice was as lethal as a knife's blade.

"Look here, I don't take orders from *you*. I take my—"

The voices faded into insignificance as Freddie stared in horror at the motionless figure on the bed. Wareham's normally slender, handsome face was so bloated and red that Freddie never would have recognized him as her brother. His breathing was stertorous, and it pained her own lungs just to hear him. She stepped closer and her foot struck something—a bottle, judging by the sound it made as it rolled beneath the bed. A few seconds later the botanical odor of gin—fresh this time, rather than sour and old—assaulted her.

"She is gone, Winifred. What do you need?"

Freddie jolted and turned to the duke. His face had lost all its color, and the nostrils of his aquiline, high-bridged nose were pinched against the smell.

"My valise—the smaller one—if you please." Her gaze flickered over the pillow beneath her brother's greasy head. "Fresh bed linens—indeed, fresh pillows and new blankets; hot water—lots of it—soap, washcloths, and some towels." She glanced around at the dim room. "I'll need more light, and a screen so it won't disturb my brother."

"You will also need help," the duke said.

Freddie nodded and turned to the hovering butler, who was staring aghast at Wareham's prone figure.

"Yes. Send up your two best maids—girls who take initiative and are self-directed. Once they have put his lordship's rooms in order I will instruct them on his care."

"I know just who to—"

"What is the meaning of this?" a strident voice demanded from the doorway, which had been left open by the fleeing Mrs. Marley.

Freddie was about to go and speak to the woman when the duke set a hand on her shoulder. "You stay and take care of Wareham." His lips compressed into a grim smile. "I will see to the dowager." He turned to the butler. "Do as Lady Sedgewick instructed."

The servant nodded and hurried away.

Relieved to have the matter of Lady Telford out of her hands, Freddie turned back to her brother. Steeling herself, she reached for the stained bedding over his chest.

"You have no right—" the dowager began.

"Outside, Lady Telford. Now," the duke added menacingly.

"Do not come the high-handed master with *me*, Plimpton! I will—"

"You will step outside under your own locomotion, or I will pick you up and carry you out, madam."

Freddie's lips quirked into a slight smile at the other woman's scandalized yelp.

Only when the door shut, and blessed silence reigned did she pull back the blanket.

She gasped and caught her lip with her teeth to keep from crying out at the festering wound that met her gaze.

Wareham's nightshirt was almost transparent with sweat. Bloody yellow stains spread out discoloring the formerly white linen.

"Oh, Dicky! What has that witch done to you?" she whispered, calling her brother by his nickname for the first time in almost two decades as a tear rolled down her cheek. "Thank God Plimpton brought me here in time."

***

"You have *no* right to—"

"We will conduct this conversation in his lordship's study rather than the corridor, ma'am," Plimpton said, marching the squirming woman down the corridor.

"Unhand me, you brute!" Her ladyship jerked her upper arm from his grasp. Or at least she tried to, but he held her firmly. Plimpton had to force himself to walk slowly—and not tighten his grip as much as he wanted to—forcibly reminding himself that as loathsome as she was, the dowager was a lady, and an elderly one, at that.

"Will you come peaceably?" he asked coolly.

She scowled up at him. "Yes," she said, forcing the word through clenched jaws.

Plimpton released her and gestured in the direction of Wareham's study. "After you, ma'am."

They made the short journey in blessed silence. The moment he closed the door the dowager turned on him, her expression wrathful. "Edna Marley has worked for my family since I was a child."

"Then perhaps it is time you gave her a pension and allow her to retire, madam. Please, have a seat," he said, gesturing to a chair.

She ignored him, her mouth screwing up like a piece of paper that had been tightly twisted "You have *no* right to command matters here and I will—"

"I have a signed power of attorney from Wareham to see to all facets of his estate, his children, *and* his health."

Her jaw dropped open like a drawbridge whose ropes had been severed. She sputtered, "That is—that is—"

"That is the way his lordship wants it," he finished for her, although not what she would have said if her empurpling face was anything to go by.

"How dare you take charge of my daughter's children and send them to my son and his useless wife?"

"It is what Wareham wanted."

"Those are my grandchildren and should be *in* my care."

Plimpton thought Wareham's children—especially his young daughters—would be better off with a pack of wolves than with their grandmother. But stating that would scarcely be conducive to ending this conversation. "It is my belief that Wareham will soon be well enough that his children do not require either Telford's *or* your care, ma'am. Now, tell me why you dismissed Doctor Madsen?"

She crossed her arms and scowled. "I suppose he is the one who had the temerity to write to you?"

And a damned good thing he had. Plimpton ignored her question and repeated, "Why did you dismiss him?"

"He is a quack! He refused to cup Lord Wareham even though it was obvious that is what he needed."

"Obvious to whom?"

"To Doctor Finch."

"And who is he, pray?"

"Finch is an excellent physician. It was he who treated my daughter after her riding accident."

Plimpton forbore pointing out how well that had ended for Lady Wareham. Instead, he said, "Doctor Madsen is a highly respected physician who has years of experience with the sort of injury his lordship sustained. He believes cupping to be counterproductive to the healing process in this situation and I—*and I*," he repeated in a raised voice to be heard over hers. "Believe him. Not only do I believe him, but Lord Wareham was on the mend before you interfered with his treatment."

She jumped up from her chair. "I will not stay here and be insulted by you!"

Courtesy bred into his bones had him on his feet a scant second later. "Fortunately, there is no reason for you to stay. I will be pleased to offer you the use of my carriage and servants to take you wherever you would like to go." *Preferably to Hell.*

"I do not want anything from you. Your interference in my family's affairs is outrageous. I will contact our family's lawyer about your claims."

"Please do so."

"You will not get away with this!" With that salvo, she turned on her heel and stormed toward the door.

Plimpton lengthened his stride and reached it before her. He set his hand on the doorknob and turned to her, forcing her to meet his gaze. "I think it is an excellent idea to contact your family solicitor. I also want to reiterate, in case you did not hear me, that you are not to interfere with his lordship's treatment again. Nor are you to remove the children from your son's house." Judging by the hatred that flared in her gaze that had been her next step. "Understood?" he asked when she merely seethed.

They locked eyes, the silence unbroken but for her hectic breathing.

Plimpton thought he might be stuck in the room all day with the stubborn old witch when she finally snarled, "I understand. Now get out of my way."

He opened the door, and she fled his presence as speedily as a rat escaping up a drainpipe.

He sighed and rubbed his aching jaw, which he'd been clenching. A soft rasping sound came from his palm, and he grimaced; he needed a shave. And a bath. And a decent night's sleep.

Unfortunately, it would be hours before he could have any of those things.

Chapter 7

"My lady? I've brought fresh ice."

The voice jolted Freddie from her fugue, and she was confused for a moment. The sight of her brother—on clean bedding, wearing a fresh nightshirt, and no longer sweating profusely or a violent shade of reddish purple—reminded her of where she was.

She smiled at the maid. *Betsy*, she reminded herself. One of the clear-eyed and clean young women Goodrich had sent to help care for Wareham.

"I must have dropped off to sleep," she admitted, suppressing a yawn and rising from her chair before taking the basin of ice chips from the girl. "Thank you."

"His Grace said I was to help in any way you needed."

"This is good for now, Betsy."

The girl hesitated.

"Yes?" Freddie urged.

"May I stay and watch? I know only a little of nursing and I would like to learn more.

"Of course you may stay." Freddie poured a tiny amount of the distilled lavender she had brought into the ice.

"Why do you add lavender, my lady?" Betsy asked quietly.

"Some people believe it has a cleansing effect—an astringent. Others believe the smell of it lifts a person's mood." She smiled faintly. "I think a little of both is true. Will you take one of those clean cloths, wet it, squeeze it thoroughly, and then bathe his lordship's forehead, please? I will check his feet to see if they have warmed up."

"Why would his feet be cold if he has a fever, my lady?" Betsy asked, her hands busy while she spoke.

"It can be an indication of a more serious infection called sepsis."

While the maid cooled Wareham's brow, Freddie checked her brother's feet, which were still too cold for a person who was burning up with fever, but at least they were no longer as chilled as the ice in the basin.

As much as she wanted to slip a hot brick into the bed and warm them up, she did not want to hide his symptoms. The wounds on his torso had just begun to succumb to infection, which told her that Lady Telford's recent *care* had been the turning point for her brother; and not a good one.

She was weak with relief that the duke had taken the dowager away. She had only met her once before—at Wareham and Sophia's wedding—and could still recall what an unpleasant woman she was. It was saying something that even Sophia could not tolera—

"Winny?"

Freddie's head whipped around at the sound of her brother's voice. She gestured for the girl to take away the cloth and took Wareham's hand—also cold, although not as bad as it had been. Now that his eyes were open, she saw that they were yellowed and bloodshot, but the pupils seemed to be focusing and he was smiling—albeit dazedly. He was, she suddenly understood, more than a little intoxicated.

Anger and relief mixed in her breast. Anger that the dowager would approve of dosing Wareham with gin, and relief that much of his relapse might be due to alcohol, rather than any worsening of his wound.

"You came." He squeezed her hand so weakly she could barely feel it.

"Of course I came," she said, her vision blurring.

"I am sorry—so sorry. I never should have—"

"*Hush.* I know you are," she said, and squeezed his hand back. "But I will want to have a full, proper apology from you, so you will have to get better to deliver it."

He gave a weak chuckle that turned into a cough and his hand flew to his chest as he wheezed and grimaced. "Hurts," he rasped when he could catch his breath.

The Etiquette of Love

"I will not make you laugh if you agree to eat a little broth."

He nodded.

Before Freddie had to ask, Betsy said, "I will fetch it right away, my lady," and speedily left the room.

Freddie tried to release her brother's hand, but he clung tighter. "Stay."

"I will stay. I am just going to bring my chair closer."

He released her with obvious reluctance.

Once she was seated near the bed, she took his hand between hers. "Is it difficult to breathe?"

He shook his head. "Just…hurts." His eyes slid shakily around the room. "Dowager?"

"She is gone."

The muscles in his face sagged with relief. "Plimpton?"

"He is here." Freddie could not hold back her smile. "It was the duke who routed Lady Telford."

Wareham's lips quivered into a smile. "Wish I…could have watched."

Freddie laughed softly. "Me too."

"Good…friend."

"He is."

Wareham took several breaths and then opened his mouth. Instead of speaking, he coughed.

Freddie squeezed his hand as his body was wracked by paroxysms, tears leaking from his eyes as he gritted his teeth and clutched at his chest.

"Do not try to talk, Dicky. We will have time for that later."

Rather than calm him, her words seemed to agitate him more. "No," he wheezed. "Need…talk." He held up a finger in a *just a moment* gesture and Freddie nodded.

"Take all the time you need. I am not going anywh—"

The door opened and Freddie was marveling that Betsy had returned so quickly when she saw it was the duke.

His normally inexpressive face creased into the closest thing Freddie had seen to a smile yet. "The maid told me you'd awakened and were already shouting orders," he said to his friend, hovering on the threshold. He turned to Freddie. "May I stay for a few minutes?"

"Of course, Your Grace."

He quietly closed the door and approached the bed. "You were doing so well that I obeyed your order to leave and what do I find now that I have returned?" He awkwardly patted her brother's shoulder, but Wareham grabbed his hand. "Thank you., Plimpton."

Freddie was touched by obvious bond of affection between the two men. Touched and also jealous that Dicky had worked to keep his friendship with the duke, but not his relationship with his sister.

"You can repay me by getting better." Plimpton turned to Freddie. "The cook has prepared a late dinner for us."

She glanced at her brother. "I really should not—"

"One of the maids can sit with Wareham for an hour," Plimpton said, looking at the earl and raising an eyebrow.

Wareham nodded. "I will...be fine. Go to dinner."

"Will an hour give you enough time?" the duke asked, taking her acquiescence for granted.

Freddie was too tired to argue. "An hour will be fine, Your Grace."

He bowed and quietly left the room.

A moment later, the door opened again and this time it was Betsy.

"Here you go, my lady. Cook made it just as you instructed."

"Thank you," she said, taking the small tray from the girl. "You may go now, but please return in half an hour."

"Aye, my lady."

The Etiquette of Love

Freddie picked up the bowl of broth and the spoon and turned back to her brother. "Eat five spoonsful and then you can talk for a minute. And then another four or five."

Wareham gave her a tired smirk, looking more like her brother. "Tyrant."

"Yes, and do not forget it." Freddie lifted the spoon to his mouth. It was slow going, but he looked astoundingly better after just a bit of nourishment.

"When have you last had food?"

He shrugged. "Days."

Freddie scowled. What had the dowager been about to starve him and leave him in filth? It was almost as if—she cut off the nasty thought and focused her attention on Wareham.

Once he had swallowed the fifth spoonful she wiped his mouth and sat back in her chair, keeping the bowl in her hands. "Now, you may speak for a minute—no longer."

"Piers is alive, Winny—I was wrong all those years ago. He didn't die. And—and he is back. In England."

It was the last thing she had expected him to say and for a moment, she did not respond. "I know," she finally said.

His eyes widened and he struggled to sit. "How do you know? Did he—"

Freddie held the bowl with one hand and set her free hand on his shoulder. "If you are going to become excited, then we will wait to talk."

He opened his mouth and his eyebrows descended—a sure sign he was angry—but his arms had already begun to tremble under his weight. He made a low growling sound and sagged back against the cushions. "I am as weak as...kitten."

"You are. It is time for more broth."

He gave her an exasperated look but complied.

"I forbade him to drag you into... his dangerous foolishness," Dicky said as soon as he'd swallowed the last mouthful.

Freddie scowled. "He did not ask me for anything, Wareham. Indeed, he wanted to give *me* something."

"Money?" Wareham spat, as if the word were dirty.

"I will not discuss Piers with you. And I will *not* abandon him. And neither of those things is up for discussion. I intended to care for you until you are out of danger, but if you badger me on this point—" She did not want to finish the thought. Instead, she dipped the spoon into the broth and said, "Open."

This time, Freddie didn't stop until the bowl was empty.

"There is danger," Wareham said as she returned the empty bowl to the tray and lifted the glass of water to his lips. She was pleased when he took several swallows without being coaxed.

Once he'd had his fill, she asked, "What danger?"

"Meecham's killer never found…still out there." His voice had become breathy. Freddie knew she should make him wait to discuss the matter, but it was obviously bothering him.

"If you think that, then you never believed Piers did it, did you?"

"Didn't matter what I believed. Evidence was damning. *Still* damning. If he pokes around… could stir trouble."

"Do you truly expect him to stay away from his home forever when he is innocent?"

"Finding the truth too dangerous. For him…and those who help him."

"Who else will pursue the truth?"

"Personal inquiry agent."

Freddie frowned. "Why haven't you engaged one before?"

"I *did*. Turned up nothing."

"So what will change now?"

He shrugged, and then winced. "Don't know."

"If Piers asks for my help, I will give it." She paused and then added, "The same way I would for you."

The Etiquette of Love

He looked sheepish at her words. And then he yawned.

"You are tired," she said, getting up from her chair.

His hand shot out and grasped her forearm. "More to say."

"You can say it in the morning. Right now, you will sleep."

His mouth opened, as if to argue, but another yawn came out. He gave a weak laugh. "Winny wins." His eyelids were already at half-mast. It took less than a minute for him to fall asleep.

Freddie watched him sleep, relieved that his breathing sounded even and unobstructed.

A few moments later the door opened, and Betsy tiptoed into the room.

"He has just fallen asleep," Freddie whispered. "Send for me immediately if he becomes restless or if his fever worsens or—or if there is *any* other change. Otherwise, I will return in two hours."

Betsy nodded.

Freddie's feet led her toward her old chambers without any instruction from her brain. When she opened the door to the room, she snorted softly. No, there wasn't anything left of her old rooms, not even the color. What had once been a lovely Delft blue and was now a nauseating peachy shade. It was too floral and fussy for Freddie's taste, but then she did not plan to be there above a week. Although Dicky was still weak and ill, he had already improved greatly after she had cleaned his wound, fed him, and driven the filthy air from the room. He would be even better tomorrow once the gin he had been dosed with was out of his system and he'd had a few meals of broth and plenty of water.

A maid brought hot water while she was laying out her serviceable lavender evening gown. "Mr. Goodrich said I was to wait on you, my lady."

Freddie hesitated.

"I am very good dressing hair, my lady."

The girl looked so hopeful Freddie smiled. "What is your name?"

"Jane, ma'am."

"Very well, Jane. Just let me wash myself and you can try your hand at taming the mess."

A short time later Freddie admired her new coiffure in the mirror. "It looks very nice. Thank you, Jane."

The girl blushed. "You've lovely hair, my lady. It was a pleasure." She glanced at the pearls Freddie had laid out earlier. "Will you wear these?"

She didn't tell Jane she had nothing else.

After she had dismissed the maid, she examined her appearance, frowning. As always, the addition of pearls made the dress barely acceptable. Like it or not, she would have to buy more clothing soon. She was beginning to look dowdy.

And where will you find the money? Will you stint Miranda so that you might have new gowns?

Freddie paid no attention to the heckling voice. Instead, she sat for a moment, eyes closed, and cleared her head of all thoughts. It was a trick she had learned during her marriage and the only thing that had saved her sanity during those dreadful three-and-a-half years.

The clock was already striking eight when Freddie hurried toward the dining room.

Memories, long forgotten, flooded her as she hurried through corridors that were both familiar and not. It was jarring to see things she remembered as clearly as the back of her hand—a Titian hanging in pride of place on the stretch of wall between the two curving staircases—and a second later noticing the lovely old Aubusson carpet runner had been replaced by one that was a bilious pastel shade.

The duke was already in the dining room when she entered. He was standing in front of the large portrait of Sophia that hung on one end of the room. Wareham's portrait was on the wall opposite.

"I am sorry I am late," Freddie said.

"I just arrived myself a moment ago." He turned to one of the footmen and gestured to the table. "Please move the other setting to this end."

"Yes, Your Grace," one of the men said, hurrying to reset the table.

Once they were finished, Plimpton said, "Tell Goodrich he may serve."

The men left and he turned to Freddie. "The meal is a simple one so I thought we could dispense with servants tonight so that we might speak freely."

Freddie nodded.

"Wareham already looks a great deal better."

"Part of that is simply clean clothing and bedding. But I am pleased to say he ate a bowl of broth and drank two glasses of water. Do you have any way to contact the doctor who had been treating him?"

"I already sent a message to Madsen. He is evidently delivering a child somewhere far afield, but his housekeeper assured my servant that the doctor would present himself at the earliest opportunity."

"Thank you."

"What are your impressions of Wareham's condition?"

"I have listened to his breathing and hear no sign of congestion in his chest. The infection is bad, but it has not settled in, so it must be of recent vintage." She frowned. "The worst of his condition seems to be dehydration. The old woman must have been giving him gin to keep him quiescent."

A brief flash of incandescent rage lit the duke's dark eyes, the expression so vivid and forceful that it left her slightly breathless.

It was gone in less than a second. And when he spoke, he sounded as mild and dispassionate as ever. "One would almost think the dowager was trying to kill her son-in-law."

Freddie was relieved that she had not needed to be the one to give life to the suspicion. "Why would she wish to do such a thing?"

"It defies comprehension," he said, but Freddie knew he had more than a few ideas. "Do you have adequate help? Miss Denny has offered her assistance."

Freddie wondered if the woman would talk as much in a sick room. "The two maids are more than sufficient." She hesitated and then added, "I believe Miss Denny can complete her journey, Your Grace."

Humor glittered in the duke's eyes at her not very subtle suggestion. "She will leave tomorrow."

"For now, I would like a truckle bed set up in Wareham's room. That way I can be close at hand if he needs me."

He frowned. "You will exhaust yourself if you do that. You do not trust either of the maids to stay with him? If not, I can sit with him while you get some sleep."

She was amused at the thought of him serving as a nurse. "I do not think that will be necessary. Although if you can spare your valet, I believe Wareham would appreciate a shave."

"Of course."

He was still frowning, and Freddie knew he was not happy with the idea of her sleeping on a truckle.

She spoke before he could voice his displeasure. "I wanted to thank you for, er, managing Lady Telford." She gave him a rueful look. "I doubt I could have rid Torrance Park of her presence quite so quickly and easily."

Dark humor glinted in his eyes. "One of the benefits of rank, I suppose."

Chapter 8

Freddie did not linger over her dinner. By the time she changed her clothes and returned to Wareham's chambers she found the truckle bed waiting, so the duke must have given the order even though he had not agreed with her decision.

Wareham woke twice during the night, making her glad of her decision to sleep in his room. His fever spiked and Freddie briefly wondered if she had done wrong to send Doctor Finch away when he had made his evening visit to cup Wareham for the second time that day.

"Lady Telford warned me of this," he had snapped when she'd told him he would not be bleeding her brother. He had glared daggers at Winifred as he'd put his cupping implements back in his bag with more force than was necessary. "I wash my hands of this. When his lordship worsens, it will be on your conscience, my lady."

The duke had entered the room for the end of his tirade and had seized the man by the arm. "Apologize."

Finch's eyes had gone comically round at Plimpton's quiet, menacing snarl.

"I—I beg your pardon, my lady. I never should have—"

He continued to apologize as the duke dragged him from the room.

But his threat lingered and left Freddie worried and shaken.

Only the duke's reassurance after he had returned eased some of her concern. "Madsen opposes cupping in your brother's case, Winifred. You did right to stop that butcher."

Both times Wareham woke during the night she encouraged him to drink his fill of water. Once he'd fallen back asleep, she bathed his forehead with cool cloths.

He woke a third time near dawn, needing to visit the necessary. Without his own body servant to help him—the man had died in the accident—Freddie was forced to summon the duke's valet.

Digby came so quickly that she knew the duke must have alerted him yesterday. He was every bit as impassive and taciturn as his master.

"I will help his lordship if you wish to break your fast, my lady."

"But what if the duke—"

"His Grace has no need of me, ma'am. He has gone riding. I am at his lordship's disposal for as long as he needs me."

Likely Wareham would want to shave and bathe. Freddie nodded, "I will return in two hours."

As it transpired, she had just finished indulging in a bath and a breakfast tray in her room when a servant knocked to inform her that Doctor Madsen had arrived.

She hastily dressed and hurried to her brother's chambers, unsurprised to find the duke was there before her.

Both men turned at her entrance and the stranger—a short, stout man—smiled, looking genuinely delighted to see her.

"Madsen, this is Lady Sedgewick, his lordship's sister," the duke said.

The doctor took her hand and bowed over it. "You have worked miracles since I last saw your brother, my lady."

Wareham was propped up against several pillows and was freshly shaved, his hair slightly damp, evidencing if not a bath, then at least a hair washing. He wore a sheepish smile to be the object of such intense inspection.

She smiled at the physician. "I think it is His Grace's valet who effected the miracle."

"No, no. I am told it was *you* who put your foot down and halted the bleeding."

Freddie cut him an apprehensive look. "I hope I did not—"

The Etiquette of Love

"You did exactly the right thing," he assured her. "I managed to bull my way back in here two days ago—before Lady Telford had me forcibly ejected—and I was appalled by the sudden downturn in his lordship's health." A scowl spasmed across his cherubic features, making him look quite fierce. He appeared to master himself with some effort and turned a reassuring smile on his patient. "I am delighted to find you back on the mend. I believe you will continue to get better if you rest, sleep, and submit to your sister's nursing."

Wareham laughed, and then winced. "Don't let her hear that—she is already a tyrant."

"Good." The doctor turned to Freddie. "If you have a moment, I would like to confer with you on his treatment."

"Of course. Let us retire to the drawing room. I am sure you would like some tea."

"That would be most welcome. I have been up these past two nights overseeing a very tricky delivery."

"I'll return shortly," Freddie said to her brother.

Rather than look annoyed that his doctor and sister were leaving to talk about him in private, Wareham nodded, suddenly exhausted, his eyelids sliding closed even as they watched.

"I will stay with him," the duke said, moving a chair closer to the bed.

"I hope your efforts were successful?" Freddie asked the doctor as they made their way to the drawing room.

"I beg your pardon?"

"The baby?"

"Oh, yes, yes. Quite. The child survived and is healthy. And the mother is fine, if exhausted."

He opened the drawing room door and Freddie barely waited until they'd both taken a seat before she asked, "How is my brother, really, Doctor? Please do not mince words."

"He suffered a relapse, there is no denying that." He scowled. "Being bled twice daily was almost as bad as being half-drowned with gin. I am not, as you may have guessed, an exponent of cupping. It is too often used and too little understood."

That opinion probably caused him no end of trouble within the medical community. In fact, she could not recall meeting a doctor who believed there was no benefit to bleeding a patient.

"There is no denying my brother looks a good deal better after just one day without it."

Madsen nodded. "Indeed. I believe he is once more on the path to recovery."

"When you say *recovery*, do you mean he will be the same as he was before the accident?"

"Based on how speedily he was healing before this recent relapse I am willing to say he will eventually function at pre-accident levels."

"What can I do to aid his recovery?"

"Exactly what you have been doing: keep him hydrated and fed."

"Broth?"

"Add some plain scrambled eggs and soups with more substance."

"And when should he be allowed to be up and around?"

"That was what I wanted to talk about, my lady. His lordship should have been walking days ago."

Freddie blinked. "Already?"

"I know it seems soon, but he needs to strengthen his lungs by *using* them. Have him get up at *least* five or six times a day. He should not walk to exhaustion, of course, but enough to get him breathing faster. Increase the time in small increments. It will tire him out, but that is good as he needs lots of sleep and rest. Provide him with distractions, as long as they are not too strenuous. The worst thing for any patient, no matter the injury, is worrying and fidgeting."

"How long should he have around-the-clock observation?"

"If he continues to improve at his current rate, he can do without constant care in—let us say for now—two days. He should be well beyond any danger by then."

The Etiquette of Love

Which meant that Freddie could probably leave far sooner than she had expected.

Strangely, the thought of rushing back to London no longer appealed to her quite as much as it had done.

***

Winifred dined alone with Wareham that evening. But the following day, Plimpton heard his friend insist that she enjoy a proper meal in the dining room. With Plimpton.

Winifred wore the mint-green gown again and Plimpton found it bloody difficult to tear his gaze away. She must have only brought the two evening dresses, no doubt believing that she would not need more as she'd not be staying long. And now, based on what Doctor Madsen had told him, she had been correct about the brief length of her stay.

Which meant that Plimpton had less time with her than he had expected.

"Doctor Madsen is a very capable man," Winifred said, once the footman had set a plate of oysters in front of her.

"He is. He served in the army for almost a decade, which means he has seen more severe injuries in one month than most Harley Street physicians will see in their lifetimes."

"How is it that you are acquainted with him?"

"He cared for my brother when he was injured." And Simon had been far worse off than Wareham. "If not for Madsen I do not believe my brother would be alive," he added, startling himself with the frank admission. And startling her, too, if her expression was anything to go by.

She nodded. Because what else could she do?

There is nobody who can kill a conversation quite like you, Wyndham. The mocking voice sounded like Simon and was exactly the sort of thing he would have said.

After an awkward moment, Winifred delicately cleared her throat. "Now that Doctor Madsen has decreed Wareham out of danger, I have decided to leave four days hence. The two maids who've been assisting me are diligent and intelligent. And one of the footmen—Jacob, is his name—has evinced an interest in filling Wareham's valet vacancy until my brother can make other arrangements." She paused and then added, "I daresay you will be relieved to have your valet back."

Plimpton raised a matter that was more interesting to him than Digby's services. "My coach will have returned to Torrance Park by then. You must allow me to convey you back to London when you are ready to leave, and I will accompany you." And this time Plimpton would sit *inside* the carriage. With no talkative chaperone to get between them.

So much for caring about Winifred's reputation...

"I am sure my brother can see to my transportation needs."

"Actually, he cannot."

She fixed him with a disbelieving look. "I beg your pardon?"

"Lady Telford commandeered Wareham's traveling coach as well as his coachman and postilions. She is evidently in no hurry to send them back."

She was routed, but not defeated. She opened her mouth.

Before she could suggest some other method of transport—stagecoach, mail coach, hot air balloon, oxen—Plimpton said, "Please, Winifred. Allow me to assist you. I, too, will be heading home now that Wareham's circumstances are not desperate."

Her jaw flexed as she regarded him. Plimpton knew she did not care for his informal address. He did not care. She was fortunate he did not call her *Winny*. The only reason he had not adopted the pet name was that he preferred her name unaltered. It was regal and suited her.

"It would be churlish to reject your offer," she said, almost as if she needed to hear the words herself. "Thank you, Your Grace." She pushed to her feet and Plimpton rose along with her. "I should go and check on Wareham."

He inclined his head, and then found himself saying, "Perhaps you might honor me with a game of chess—or a few hands of piquet—once you have settled Wareham for the night."

The Etiquette of Love

She could not have looked more flabbergasted if he had invited her to his bedchamber; the invitation he had genuinely wanted to extend. Perhaps he should do so now?

Instead, he pressed his offensive while she was still rendered speechless. "I recall Wareham saying once that you two played often when you visited him during your school holidays. He said you thrashed him quite mercilessly at chess and he lost thousands of pounds to you at piquet."

Her lips curved into a fond smile. "Perhaps not *thousands* of pounds, but it was certainly a generous supplement to my pin money. It is true that I won more games against him than I lost. But it has been years—more than a decade—and I am terribly out of practice."

"Good. Then perhaps I might have a chance."

She gave a startled laugh, as if surprised that he possessed any wit at all. Well, she wasn't the only one who thought him humorless.

She regarded him thoughtfully with her silvery eyes and Plimpton had no idea what she would say.

After a moment, she nodded. "I would like that."

His heart, which had been dormant for decades, leapt. Plimpton felt as if he'd just accomplished something worth boasting about—like delivering a rousing speech in Lords.

He suppressed the spike of excitement and said, "Shall we say an hour from now—in the library? If Wareham needs you and you find you cannot get away, I will understand."

"An hour," she said firmly.

He strode toward the door to open it for her, and then watched her slender, elegant form until she turned onto the stairs and disappeared from view before making his way to the library, where he could write a few letters while he waited.

How long had it been since he had actually conversed with a woman? Not the empty chatter he'd always engaged in with his mistresses, but genuinely making an effort to become acquainted. Other than his mother, daughter, or sister-in-law, he could not recall the last time, but knew it had been a long, long time ago.

Usually, Plimpton did not have to put himself to any effort at all because women did the work for him. He did not fool himself that they pursed him because he was so handsome, charming, and witty. No, it was his title and status that attracted them, even if the man in question was average looking at best, quiet to the point of taciturnity, and often so terse as to be considered rude. At least he would have been called rude if not for his title.

Yes, being a duke made up for a host of shortcomings, both physical and personal, and rendered Plimpton all but irresistible.

Although his wife had managed to resist him just fine.

Winifred appears to be resisting you quite easily, as well.

He gave a bark of laughter. Yes, she certainly did.

As for Cecily? Well, Plimpton did not want to think about his dead wife—ever—but most certainly not tonight.

He lit several more candles and then sat down at the large cherrywood desk and commenced to write the letters he wanted to go out with the morning mail.

Plimpton was just sanding a rather lengthy list of instructions for his steward at Whitcombe when the door opened and Winifred entered.

He put the letter aside and stood, vaguely surprised that the hour had passed so quickly. "How is he?" he asked.

"He slept through the dinner hour, but I managed to get him to eat a little broth when he woke, even though he said he was not hungry. The moment he finished the last mouthful he fell asleep again."

"Is that normal?"

"The doctor said he would be very tired now that he has begun to walk regularly."

"So, you are free to play, then?"

"Yes."

Plimpton gestured to the game table. "Chess or cards?"

"I think cards. I do not have the proper mind set for chess right now."

The Etiquette of Love

He was relieved to hear it as he *never* had the mind set for the tedious game. "Would you care for something to drink?"

She glanced at the assembled bottles. "If there is any madeira I would have a glass."

There was indeed a fresh bottle. While Plimpton opened it, she fetched a pack of cards and began to absently shuffle them, her slender fingers agile and the movement of the cards fluid.

Plimpton grimaced. "I can already see I am in for a drubbing," he said as he poured two glasses.

She raised her eyebrows at him.

"I can tell by the way you handle the cards that you know what you are about." He set their glasses on the table. "I warn you that my idea of shuffling is to dump the cards in a pile and then mess them about with both hands."

She laughed—a genuinely amused chuckle—and Plimpton could not recall hearing a lovelier sound.

Oh, dear. You are *smitten, aren't you?*

He was; happily so.

Plimpton seated himself and took a drink. "Do you remain in London all summer?"

Her expression, which had been open, shuttered now that the subject had moved from cards to herself. "Yes."

"You do not find it unpleasantly hot and devoid of company?"

"The weather is easy to tolerate as I am at leisure. As for company," she shrugged. "I get quite enough of that during the Season." She set the deck in the middle of the table, and they cut for the draw. Plimpton drew the ten of hearts and she beat him with an ace.

"A portent of what is to come," he murmured, earning another smile. "I understand your housemate, er, Miss Fontenot, is no longer living with you?" he asked as she once again shuffled.

She paused and cocked her head. "How did you—"

"Honoria mentioned it in her last letter."

"Honey writes to you?"

Her obvious surprise amused him. "Yes, she does."

As he watched, a blush swept up her elegant throat to her face, reminding him of a spectacular sunrise. She swallowed and dealt the cards. "I beg your pardon. That probably sounded rude. I just did not realize you were on such, er, easy terms."

"I am fortunate that she is of a forgiving nature and does not hold my behavior from before her marriage against me."

"Your behavior?" she asked, distributing the final card and then setting the *talon* between them before picking up her hand.

Now it was Plimpton who was surprised. Had Honoria not told her friend what he had said to *convince* her to marry Simon?

Guilt, an emotion he rarely allowed to take up any space in his thoughts, prickled him unpleasantly.

"What do you mean?" she persisted.

For a moment, Plimpton was annoyed at his sister-in-law for keeping her own counsel. Honoria's circumspection meant it was up to *him* to inform Winifred of his high-handed—and thoughtlessly cruel—behavior.

Plimpton took a generous swallow from his glass.

***

The duke looked...uncomfortable.

No, Freddie amended a few seconds later; *uncomfortable* was not quite the word for it. Normally, he did not display much of anything. Only on rare occasions did she see any emotion on his face, and then, it was there and gone in an instant. This expression, however, had settled. On any other man's face, she might have called the look *sheepish*.

Surely not.

"I do not know how much Honoria told you about becoming betrothed to my brother?"

"At the time she told me very little," Freddie admitted. "But since their marriage, she confessed how she had been compromised during her stay at Whitcombe. She said you persuaded both her and Lord Simon they must marry. That is all I know." She had no difficulty imagining *that* conversation, and—knowing what she did of the duke—the word she would have used would have been *commanded*.

"She is kind to call it *persuasion*," he said, as if reading her thoughts. "In truth, I threatened her."

"*Threatened?* Surely you are exaggerating."

"No. I am not. I told her that if she did not comply with my demand and marry my brother, I would make it difficult for her to find clients. At least any among the *ton*."

Disappointment—and something close to revulsion—rose up in her at his confession. "That—that was unkind."

"It *was* unkind. Honoria told me to do my worst, that she had enough money from her father's estate to live quite happily. Balked in that regard, I decided to threaten your livelihood, instead."

Freddie could not have heard him correctly. "I beg your pardon?"

"I told Honoria I would make it difficult for you to continue sponsoring young women. I do not think she believed I would do it. So, when she did not capitulate, I encouraged one of your clients to seek a sponsor elsewhere."

"Who?" she said through lips that were numb with shock.

"Lady Mayfield."

Freddie realized she was still gripping the cards, holding them tightly enough to bend them. She carefully placed them on the table. "I remember when Lady Mayfield changed her mind."

"That was my fault," he said, not a flicker of emotion on his face or in his voice. "I did not besmirch your name in any way, but I saw to it that she employed the services of a friend of my mother's, instead. It was at that point that Honoria agreed to marry Simon. I then asked my mother to mention your name to the Countess of Sayle. I believe she became your client."

"Yes," she said faintly. "She did." And Freddie had almost wept with relief as she had counted on Lady Mayfield's employment to pay off long overdue bills.

"I know that doesn't excuse what I—"

"No, it does not."

"I am not proud of what I did."

Freddie laughed hollowly. "Well, that is something, I suppose." She held his gaze. "What would you have done if Honey had not complied?"

He opened his mouth.

"Never mind," she said. "I do not want to hear you say it. Tell me, Your Grace. Knowing what you know now—how I rely on such commissions to feed myself and keep a roof over my head—would you do it again?"

He stared at her for a long moment. "It would be a lie to say *no*."

Again, she gave a humorless laugh. "At least you are honest."

He regarded her with his usual opaque stare, a man who could destroy her with only a few well-placed words.

Freddie shook her head. "We are all just pieces on a board to you, to be used to serve your purposes, regardless of right or wrong. Do you know what I worry about almost every day of my life?"

His jaw flexed, but he did not speak.

"Let me answer that for you: money. That is what I think about, incessantly. In the eight years since Sedgewick's death there has not been a single day that has gone by when I don't worry that I will not have enough money to get by. And then somebody like *you*—a man who has never had to fear losing the roof over his head, or choose between buying food or coal, or wonder what he will sell after he has already pawned away all his valuable possessions—has the arrogant audacity to toy with my future without a second's thought." Her words echoed loudly in the cavernous room, making Freddie realize that she had been shouting.

Yes, shouting. Because she was angry, deservedly so.

She was breathing hard, her hands clenched into fists, and her blood thundering in her ears.

The Etiquette of Love

The duke sat without moving, silently absorbing all her rage. "Everything you said is correct. I did not weigh the damage to other people. In my mind, you were the best tool to achieve my purpose. I am sorry to have caused you anxiety, but I know that is too little, too late."

Freddie looked for some evidence there was an actual man behind his opaque gaze. She saw nothing but a duke, through and through. An aristocrat who would always have his way.

Exhausted by her burst of anger and dispirited at how quickly a night that had promised pleasure had turned sour, she pushed away from the table and stood. "I am tired. I beg you will excuse me."

The duke inclined his head. "Of course." He strode to the door and opened it for her. "Good night, Winifred."

Freddie paused, mortified by her shouting. "I should not have raised my voice and—"

"You do not owe me an apology," he said, as unruffled as ever. "I deserve everything you said and more."

Standing so close to him, she could see that his eyes—which she suddenly noticed were tilted slightly at the outside corners—were not opaque at all, but a cool, translucent gray. She opened her mouth to say…what?

There was nothing to say. The Duke of Plimpton had wanted his brother to marry, and he had done everything in his considerable power to get what he wanted. Regardless of who had been hurt in the process.

Freddie closed her mouth and left without another word.

Chapter 9

Freddie turned on the cot and bit back a groan at the soreness radiating out from her lower back. Even before she opened her eyes she remembered where she was: in Wareham's chambers, sleeping on that blasted truckle bed.

She had been too agitated to sleep, so she had come to check on Wareham. Betsy had been in the chair, nodding off, so she'd dismissed the girl and laid down on the bed. Why not? She could toss and turn just as easily in a truckle as in her bed.

And she had. All. Night. Long.

Freddie yawned. Before she could even blink the sleep out of her eyes a voice above her said, "Good morning, sleepyhead!"

Freddie turned onto her back and immediately encountered a pair of familiar hazel eyes peering over the edge of the bed.

"You are awake," she croaked stupidly.

"I've been awake for ages." Wareham smiled, irksomely bright eyed and brushy tailed. He frowned at the truckle. "I did not think you would sleep here again. You really needn't, you know. I do not require anyone to watch over me while I sleep."

Freddie grunted, not wishing to explain the true reason why she was there. "What time is it?"

"Not quite six."

This time she didn't hold back her groan. "Are you certain you will not go back to sleep?"

Wareham laughed. So, there was her answer.

"Are you hungry? Should I ring for breakfast?" she asked, sitting up and swinging her feet the short distance to the floor.

"No, not yet."

"Do you need me to summon Jacob to—"

"He already came and helped me. You slept right through it."

"Some nurse I am."

"You were exhausted from everything you have been doing. Sleeping on that truckle is not helping."

Freddie did not correct him and tell him she was actually exhausted from all the anger that had coursed through her for hours and hours. Instead, she stood and straightened her dressing gown—which she had fallen asleep in—while fighting back a yawn and failing.

"Winny?"

"Yes?" She glanced in the mirror and recoiled at her reflection. That would teach her for falling asleep without plaiting her hair. She had spun in her cot like a child's top, over and over trying and failing to find sleep after her confrontation with the duke.

Over the long hours of the night the anger that had fueled her had been spent, leaving only smoking embers.

She did not think that what he had done was right, of course, but she knew why the duke had wanted his brother to marry. Honey might have withheld the duke's unethical method of pressuring her to marry, but she had shared many other details about her new brother-in-law, especially the devastation he had suffered over twenty years of marriage and the deaths of three children. When other people might have found solace in their spouse to help them bear such loss, the duke and duchess had withdrawn from each other.

To hear Honey tell it, the duchess had been the one responsible for their profound estrangement. But then Honey was only privy to one side of the story, and that side came from Lord Simon, who would not want to cast Plimpton in a poor light.

"Winny?"

She turned at her brother's voice.

"Would you sit with me for a few minutes?" he asked, his tone no longer teasing.

"Yes, of course."

"I will not keep you long, but there are some things I need to say."

"I am at your disposal."

"First—I wanted to thank you for—"

"Please do not thank me. If you thank anyone, it should be Plimpton. He all but dragged me down here."

"Well, I am grateful you allowed yourself to be dragged. If you hadn't, I daresay we would not be having this conversation right now and my mother-in-law would be planning my funeral."

Freddie could not argue with his assessment.

Wareham held out his hand and, after a brief hesitation, Freddie took it.

He squeezed her fingers. "I have been a terrible brother to you. I have known that for a long time. But it was not until fourteen months ago that I realized just how much damage I have caused."

"What happened fourteen months ago?"

"Piers came back."

Freddie was still irked about Wareham forcing Piers to keep her in the dark, but now was not the time to bring that up. "How did that change your thinking?"

He bit his lip, chewing the chapped skin so hard she saw red splits appear.

She squeezed his hand. "Tell me what happened, Wareham."

"Sophia found out that Piers had returned." He snorted bitterly. "I say *found out*. In truth, she had her ear against my study door. Rather than be ashamed of eavesdropping she had the audacity to confront me about it, chiding me for not reporting him to the authorities." He gave Freddie a look of disbelief. "She thought I should turn in my own brother! We had a bitter argument, and ugly things were said on both sides. I forbade her to speak to *anyone* about Piers." His lips thinned. "Rather than obey me, she immediately—and anonymously—sent word to the local magistrate. Naturally the man paid me a visit, wanting to know if it was true that I was protecting a murderer; the same man I had insisted died years ago." He scowled at the memory. "It was beyond unpleasant."

Freddie waited silently for the rest.

Wareham inhaled deeply, winced, and then carefully exhaled. "Sophia's excuse for betraying me was that she was trying to save me from my reckless, selfish family. She claimed I did not appreciate all that she had done on my behalf. And then she said something I could not believe." Wareham met her gaze. "She admitted—*proudly*—that she'd had to pressure you to marry Sedgwick. When I demanded to know what she meant, she confessed that she had approached you after you'd refused Sedgewick's first offer and she...convinced you. But that was all I could get out of her; she refused to tell me exactly what she said, not that I cannot guess. Will you tell me, Winny?"

The sick feeling in her belly, which had begun the moment Wareham spoke Sedgewick's name, rapidly spread, filling her with nausea. "Why?"

"Please," he said. "I *need* to know."

"She said that you owed Sedgewick a great deal of money."

Wareham slumped back against his pillows, looking as ill as she felt.

"We should not speak of this right now. It is upsetting you."

"Please," he said, pale but firm. "Please tell me the rest. This has been eating at me for more than a year. The only thing that will make it worse is allowing me to go on imagining and not know the truth. *Tell me.*"

"She said that you had very little chance of repaying the debt unless I married Sedgewick. She said a Season would only add more to the burden you already labored und—"

"That *lying* bitch!"

Freddie flinched at the fury—and no small amount of hatred—in his gaze. "*Shhh*, Dicky. I know now that it was Piers's debt, not yours."

"The debt did not matter—regardless of who's it was. I was never so below the hatches that I could not cover Piers's gambling obligations. And while it was true that paying Sedgewick back had required the sale of a small piece of acreage, I was not close to facing ruin, Winny." His face hardened. "And I had already paid him the money he was due before your marriage. Sophia *knew* that. She deliberately lied to force you into marriage."

Freddie did not argue.

Dicky swallowed hard. "When I accused Sophia of selling you to a monster she said that if you had been a more obedient, conformable wife you might have changed Sedgewick for the better." He gave a snort of disbelief. "As if you—or anyone—could have done *anything* to fix such a man." Wareham squeezed her fingers so hard it hurt. His cheeks were flushed, and his skin had become sheened with sweat. "I should have protected you, Winny. Christ! You were only seventeen! Can you ever forgive me?"

"I have already forgiven you, Dicky. I have been at fault, too. I never should have sent your letters back unopened."

He waved a dismissive hand. "I should have gone directly to you and begged your forgiveness last year when I found out the truth, but I was ashamed. I always knew that Sophia often went beyond the bounds of what was acceptable to get her own way, but I never guessed she could be so dishonest and—and so vindictive—toward you for no reason."

It was difficult for Freddie to believe her brother had not noticed how truly manipulative and unpleasant his wife had been, but there was no point in belaboring the issue now.

"She was your wife and you loved her, Dicky. There is no shame in that."

"There is shame in what I allowed her to do, Winny." Again he chewed his ravaged lower lip. "My love for her died after what she did to Piers. And—and when I learned what she had done to you, I actively hated her. The scales had dropped from my eyes and I saw how she had twisted and warped not only my relationship with you, but also my children. And how she was manipulating *them* for her purposes. I know it is an appalling thing to admit, but I cannot mourn her."

Freddie's eyes burned with unshed tears. She did not mourn the passing of the horrid woman he had married, but she mourned her brother's loss of love.

"My dearest Winny—you know I would be honored if you consented to move back to Torrance Park."

"I have my own life to live, Dicky. I do not want to give that up. But I will come and visit often."

"If you won't allow me to give you a home, at least accept your allowance. It is not nearly as much as you should have had from your marriage, but it is *your* money."

A bitter smile curved her lips. "Is it really my money, Dicky? Could I pull it all out of the funds tomorrow if I wished?"

"That would be an exceedingly foolish act," he said, completely missing the point.

"Perhaps, but if it was *your* money and you wished to do so, you could. And without consulting anyone else."

"Yes, that is true. But I am a man and have had charge of such things all my life, my dear. Can you honestly say you would know how to go about managing your own investments? It is my duty and honor to care for the women in my family. And you know I would never hold the purse strings tightly."

How could she explain to him that a purse held by somebody else was *not* hers. "I do not want to revisit this subject, Wareham."

"You are still angry that Sedgewick appointed me your trustee, aren't you?"

"I am not angry." Indeed, she was *enraged* whenever she thought about the terms of her dead husband's will, which had left her Wareham's perpetual pensioner. Any disbursements must meet his approval and he was the one who would set her allowance. It was humiliating.

But she would not argue about that again.

"I gave up any claim to that money eight years ago. And I learned to live without it." Not because she wanted to; because she'd had to.

"I know you could not accept the money then because I required that you lived under my roof and—and I understand how that would have been impossible. But I had hoped now that—" He broke off, but

Freddie did not need him to finish to know that he meant now that Sophia was gone.

The pain that shone from his eyes dulled the edge of her anger "Rest assured that if I need that money, I will ask for it. But I cannot move back, and not because of any estrangement; I have friends who love me, and I have a purpose in my life." She smiled wryly. "I know chaperoning young ladies is not everyone's notion of a dream, but it supports me well enough." That was not the truth, but to share the truth would be the ultimate unkindness. It was not Dicky who stood in the way of that money, but Freddie's own pride.

He sighed and she suspected it was his turn to force a smile. "Plimpton says you have agreed to help him with Rebecca?"

Freddie considered that arrangement from the perspective of what she had learned the night before. But the spark of anger she expected failed to materialize. "Yes, that is true."

"I am pleased to hear it. Have you met her?"

"Not yet."

"She is a delightful girl." He pulled a face. "It is perhaps unfortunate that she resembles Plimpton more than her beautiful mother, but I believe her temperament is sweet and conformable." He laughed. "In other words, utterly unlike either of her parents."

"You knew his wife?" Why had she asked him that? Why was she so eaten up with curiosity about a dead woman?

Distaste flickered across Wareham's face. "To be brutally honest, I do not believe there was much to know beyond her beautiful façade. She was the diamond of that Season, and we were all a little in love with her. But everyone knew she would choose Plimpton. Not because she valued him for who he is, of course, but because her father was ambitious." Wareham shook his head. "I never envied him Cecily. I foolishly believed that although my wife was not as beautiful, at least she cared for me." He gave a dispirited snort. "Amazing one's capacity for self-delusion, isn't it?"

"Sophia loved you, Dicky. And I am sure she loved her children."

"I do not believe that sort of love—cloaked as it was in the need to control—is worth having." He sighed. "But none of that matters now."

There was a knock on the door before it opened and the duke paused on the threshold, his gaze going from Freddie to Wareham to their joined hands, and then back to Wareham. "I apologize for interrupting."

"You are not interrupting," Wareham said, squeezing Freddie's hand. "My sister and I were just talking."

Freddie suddenly recalled what a fright she looked. His Grace, naturally, was as impeccable as ever.

And he was looking at her. "I wondered if you would care to join me for a ride?"

Freddie stared. Had she completely imagined their argument last night?

No, you argued. He just sat there and listened.

"What a capital idea," Dicky said, sounding so excited one would have thought that *he* had been invited. "You should go, Freddie—I was about summon Jacob and your presence will be distinctly *de trop*."

Freddie wrenched her gaze away from the duke and turned to her brother, who was grinning at her with an almost unsettling enthusiasm. "But you said Jacob had already—"

"Yes, yes," he hastily cut in. "But now I need his assistance *again*." He cleared his throat and gave her a speaking look.

"Oh," she said, feeling foolish. "Er, of course. I will leave you to it." She turned to the duke. "I am afraid I did not bring a habit with—"

"Take one of Sophia's," Wareham said.

Freddie eyed her brother. "Her clothing is still here?"

"Yes. I'm afraid I did not know what to do with it," he admitted. "Take a habit. There must be a dozen of them. It will be loose on you, but you are similar enough in height."

Freddie narrowed her gaze. Why was he smiling so dementedly?

Dicky, mistaking her hesitation for an unwillingness to borrow his dead wife's clothing, clucked his tongue and said, "Take a habit, Winny—lord, take any of her clothing you want. It is all just hanging there going to waste. Go on," he urged. "I will keep Plimpton amused while you dress. He can meet you down at the stables in, say, three-quarters of an hour? Is that good for you, Your Grace?" he asked his friend without taking his eyes from Freddie.

"Take as long as you need," the duke said, looking at Dicky with a wry glint in his cold eyes.

He shifted his gaze to Freddie when he felt her attention and their eyes locked. Freddie could not look away and the staring match seemed to last forever, although it could not have been more than a few seconds before her brother spoke, shattering the unsettling bond.

"Hurry along, Winny, the day is wasting."

Freddie opened her mouth to reject the duke's offer, but then realized they would have to discuss what had happened last night eventually. Going for a ride would be an excellent opportunity to speak with the man without being overheard or interrupted. What exactly she would say to the duke, Freddie was not yet sure.

Chapter 10

Plimpton gave his friend a sardonic look once he'd closed the door behind Winifred. "Playing matchmaker, Wareham?"

The earl chuckled. "Perhaps."

"I wish you wouldn't."

"Why not?"

"Because your sister despises me." And Wareham's ham-fisted matchmaking was hardly going to help.

Wareham looked genuinely startled. "You must be mistaken."

"You never were very observant," Plimpton said dryly.

"Why would she hate you? She does not even know you. I did not think the two of you had even spoken to one another since she was a girl."

"I have seen her quite a few times these past few years." Too often for Winifred's liking and not often enough for Plimpton's.

"Ah. Now I recall; she is an acquaintance of your sister-in-law, is she not?"

Plimpton shook his head at Wareham's innocent look. Or at least his *attempt* to look innocent; it was a good thing the other man was not fond of gambling. "You know damned well they are more than just *acquaintances*, Richard."

Again, Wareham grinned, looking so much like his old self—and not the corpse he had been only a few days earlier—that tension Plimpton had not been aware he'd been carrying drained from his shoulders.

"My sister is perfect for you, Plimpton."

He did not argue, because Wareham was right: Winifred *was* the perfect woman for him. Accomplished, assured, and well-bred. As comfortable with the highest sticklers of the *ton* as she was with the humblest servant. She would preside over Plimpton's establishments as if she was born to direct them. Because she was.

Unfortunately, *he* was not perfect for her.

"I do not think your sister is interested in remarrying." Certainly not to Plimpton, and perhaps not with anyone else, either.

"No," Wareham agreed, his expression turning pensive. "I am afraid Winny has developed an abominable streak of independence somewhere along the way."

Plimpton forbore pointing out that she had been forced to take care of herself thanks to Wareham's inability to control his wife's meddling.

"I should have listened to you all those years ago when you warned me about Sedgewick," Wareham said, reading Plimpton's unspoken criticism. "I will be ashamed until my dying breath that I took Sophia's counsel over yours." He looked solemn for a moment, but then perked up. "I can atone for my past mistakes by making Winny see just how well the two of you suit each other and how happy and comfortably settled she could be if she would only listen to reason."

Plimpton bit back a groan; the last thing he needed was Wareham's help.

But the other man warmed to his subject. "Winny is a strong woman and will require deft, but firm, handling, Plimpton. She needs a husband who can master her without breaking her spirit. You are the perfect man to work the odd kick from her gallop and tame the willful restlessness that has afflicted her since Sedgewick's death."

Plimpton could not help being amused. "I would not employ equine analogies in her presence if I were you, Richard."

Wareham gave a dismissive flick of his hand. "Women and horses are much of a muchness and you know it, Plimpton. And men fall into one of three camps where both are concerned. First, there are those like you, who are gentle, dexterous riders and get the best out of a mare without her even being aware she has been mastered."

Plimpton laughed. "Cecily would have begged to differ."

The Etiquette of Love

"Perhaps, but then she was hardly representative of her gender, was she?" Wareham hurried on at whatever he saw on Plimpton's face. "Next there are those well-meaning but cow-handed oafs who cause damage to their mount without meaning to. Finally, and worst of all, there are those brutes who revel in cruelty and will ruin a soft mouth forever with vicious handling. Sedgwick, I am afraid, was a member of that third group."

Thinking about Winifred's soft mouth and Sedgewick's likely vicious handling sent a jagged bolt of fury tearing through Plimpton and he changed the subject. "Rather than cast about for a husband for your sister, you should convince her to accept your assistance."

Wareham shot him an exasperated look. "I have spoken to her about that repeatedly over the years, but she stubbornly refuses to accept my help."

It was on the tip of his tongue to tell his friend to be more persuasive. He was tempted to share what he had recently discovered, which was that Winifred made ends meet by selling her needlework, as if she were some impoverished crone slaving away at piecework in a vile garret.

But he could not bring himself to carry tales, even though he owed Winifred no allegiance. Indeed, if he owed anyone, it would be Wareham, who stood as legal guardian to his sister whether she liked it or not. Just because Wareham had never exercised his authority over Winifred did not mean he could not be roused to do so. There had never been a breath of scandal associated with the Ice Countess, but if word ever reached Wareham's ears that his sister was engaged in trade or—god forbid—associating with scaff and raff like Severn's sailors... Well, the earl had a temper. He also possessed a rigid sense of propriety. It was well within his power to curtail Winifred's freedom—or take it away entirely—if he believed her behavior required checking.

As if Wareham had read Plimpton's thoughts, he said, "I am of half a mind to put my foot down this time, Plimpton. Winny would be angry if I insisted that she live under my roof again, but she would obey me." His jaw worked. "Hell, she'd have no choice in the matter. I daresay she would soon get over her anger once she reaccustomed herself to creature comforts."

Plimpton doubted that.

Now is your chance to drop a word in Wareham's ear about his sister's association with that bastard Gregg. You could have her away from London and that rogue's influence before she could say Jack Robinson.

Yes, he could. And he could earn Winifred's undying hatred in the process.

No, if Plimpton dropped a word of warning in anyone's ear, it should be Winifred's to warn her.

Plimpton snorted unhappily. Why did he think that Winifred would not thank him for such consideration?

***

The duke cast a look of haughty displeasure over Freddie's mount. "That nag is not worthy of you, Winifred."

She patted the old gelding's neck. "Old Velvet will do fine for me. It has been several years since I've ridden." More than eight.

"*Hmm.*" His cold eyes moved over her slowly and with a bold, leisurely thoroughness that implied he had every right to take a complete inventory of her person whenever the urge seized him. Had any woman ever gainsaid his right before? Freddie doubted it; he was a duke, and the rules of etiquette did not apply to him.

As usual, her body responded to his attention like a well-trained animal. Her pulse quickened, her skin flushed and grew damp beneath her clothing, and—worst of all—her intimate muscles clenched and sent distracting, unwanted ripples of pleasure throughout her body.

Freddie gritted her teeth until her jaws ached; the man was *insufferable*.

And you adore it.

"It is a pity you have been deprived of the pleasure of riding," he said, after having utterly shattered her composure. "You are obviously a skilled equestrienne and have an excellent seat. It would be a privilege to have the mounting of you."

While his bold visual inspection had flustered her, his mild compliment and presumptuous offer rendered her tongue-tied.

"I expected you to give me the cut direct after last night," he said when she remained mute. "And I would have deserved it."

His frank admission was unexpected and softened her resentment. "I was furious," she admitted, as if he might not have noticed.

"You had every right to be."

"Yes, I did." After a moment she felt compelled to add, "But I am no longer angry."

His eyebrows, by far his most expressive feature, lifted. "That is generous of you."

"It is generosity directed toward me, rather than you, Your Grace. It would be easy to cling to my sense of outrage and ill-usage, but I would only be hurting myself with such behavior."

Again, he paused before speaking. "Very few people are able to impose logic when strong emotions are involved."

Freddie was amused by his carefully worded observation. "What you really mean is that *women* lack logic when it comes to their emotions."

This time, the humor in his eyes was unmistakable, but he wisely maintained his silence.

She could not resist a bit of goading. "I suppose you are one of those rare people who can impose logic on your feelings."

"I try to keep my heart from ruling my head."

"I would not have thought that would be a difficult struggle."

Although his expression didn't so much as flicker, Freddie sensed she had somehow hurt him. "I did not mean to suggest you have no heart," she lied after a moment.

"If you had meant it, you would not have been the first person. Please, do not apologize for being direct and honest, Winifred. I endorse both. Thank you for coming with me this morning," he said, finished with the subject of his heart or lack thereof. "Not that Wareham was going to give you any choice in the matter."

"No," she agreed, chuckling despite herself. "He is not subtle."

"He only wants you to be happy."

"And *you* would make me happy?" Yet again she regretted her words. Freddie was *never* rude. What was it about Plimpton that made her so combative? Had she really forgiven him for what he'd done? She had believed so. But perhaps she had lied to both of them.

"Would I make you happy?" he asked in a musing tone, his question telling her he was not hurt by her comment as she had feared. Or at least he was not going to show it. After a moment, he shrugged. "I do not know if I would make you happy."

His candor and lack of arrogance surprised her. After all, he was a handsome, wealthy, eligible duke, a combination that was as rare as hen's teeth; he had every right to be arrogant.

"What I do know," he went on. "Is that I admire and esteem you greatly and I am sure that you could make me happy."

"That is kind of you to say, but you do not really know me, do you?" she said, ruthlessly suppressing the thrill she'd felt at his words.

"True, but what I do know, I like very much."

"And what do you know?" she asked, far too curious about what he thought of her to leave the subject alone.

"I know what Honoria has said about you, how you have been a caring and faithful friend to her and all the others who worked at your school. I know how you carry yourself with dignity even though Sedgewick did not leave you in an easy position." His gray eyes seemed to darken a few shades. "And I know that I am attracted to you physically as well as intellectually. No," he amended while Freddie was still reeling at his disclosure. "*Attracted* is incorrect—or at least inaccurate. I desire you, Winifred. More than I have desired a woman in a very long time. Perhaps ever."

Freddie's face had begun to heat after his first sentence. By the end, she was scarlet.

His mouth—normally so severe—curved into a faint but charming smile. "I beg your pardon; I have embarrassed you. That was not my intention."

She *was* embarrassed. But she was also deeply flattered that she had attracted such a man's attention.

But then a less than flattering thought struck her.

"Your interest in me appears rather sudden, Your Grace. Could this have anything to do with the promise you made to my brother?"

"I promised I would take care of you if he could not. Clearly, that vow does not apply now that he is on the mend. You must take my word that my pursuit of you is all my own doing."

"Is that what this is? Pursuit?"

He gave a short bark of laughter and the sound of his mirth—not to mention his openly diverted expression—was so unprecedented that Freddie's jerked the reins, causing poor Velvet to jolt.

"If you have to ask, then I am doing an excessively poor job of it," he said. "Yes, I am pursuing you, Winifred." The humor that lit his eyes faded. "I hope I have not made myself repugnant to you after what I confessed last night?"

There was nothing whatsoever repugnant about the man beside her. Indeed, if she had not already been married once, his stated interest would have come dangerously close to sweeping her off her feet. But she *had* been married. And once was enough to know better.

How had she ever believed him only passably attractive? He was not obviously handsome like his brother, but his dignity and intelligence—not to mention his unstudied, effortless air of command—made him far more appealing than Lord Simon's golden godlike looks in Freddie's eyes.

He was everything she would have wanted in a husband.

Had she been seeking one.

"I will never marry again, Your Grace."

Rather than evince surprise at her claim—or worse, dismissal—he nodded. "Then I will not press you on a matter that is clearly distasteful to you."

Freddie felt oddly deflated by his quick, emotionless acceptance of her rejection. But then why should his lack of passion surprise her? It was common knowledge that his marriage had been loveless. Freddie knew that he had not been faithful to his wife, and neither had he appeared to be especially devoted to either of the two women who had boasted about being his lover. Indeed, any attachment had seemed to be entirely on their side.

Just thinking about the duke making love with those other women caused an unpleasant churning in her stomach.

"—amiss, my lady?"

Freddie thrust away the unwanted mental images and met his gaze. "No. Nothing is wrong."

"Do you recall if it is the right-hand path or the left that leads to the unusual rock formation your brother calls the Three Sisters? It has been so long I cannot remember."

"The left," Freddie said a bit sharply, still nonplussed that he had broached the subject of wanting her for his wife only a few seconds ago and was now content to discuss geology.

Very well, so be it; he was no longer interested in her. Indeed, could he ever have felt much for her to begin with if he surrendered his interest so quickly and easily?

Why did that thought leave her depressed rather than relieved?

***

Plimpton stared at his looking glass as Digby pared his nails. Instead of seeing his reflection, he saw Winifred as she had looked that morning; garbed in a smart riding habit the color of bitter chocolate with a jaunty, matching shako. She had brought to mind a goddess yet again. Not Aphrodite this time, but Artemis. She was a superlative equestrienne, and he never would have guessed that she had not ridden for so long.

Digby relinquished Plimpton's hand and moved to his other side.

Plimpton had committed a strategic blunder by confessing his interest in her so soon. Left to his own devices, he would have planned the moment more carefully. But Wareham—and his awkward meddling—had not given him much of a choice. He frowned; Lord save him from friends who just wanted to *help*.

The Etiquette of Love

Wareham's analogy of his sister as a badly abused filly might have been crude, but he feared it was on point.

Sedgewick had been several years older than Plimpton but the two had crossed path often at their clubs, and also in less savory venues that Plimpton had frequented as a young man.

Although Plimpton had not been monogamous after his second year of marriage, neither had he patronized brothels. Using whores was an irresponsible and repellent habit of young men who did not know better—or at least it should be.

Sedgewick, however, had never stopped haunting houses of prostitution. Not only had the Earl been a man of notoriously lusty habits, but he'd enjoyed establishments that specialized in fulfilling perversions so extreme that most Covent Garden whores refused to satisfy them.

Plimpton's hands curled into fists; just thinking of the debauched cur touching a sensitive woman like Winifred made him see red.

Digby lightly cleared his throat, reminding Plimpton there was a man attached to his fingers. He relaxed his hands, but his imagination refused to be curbed so easily.

Whatever Winifred had endured as Sedgewick's wife, Plimpton did not believe she had been irrevocably damaged. Yes, she was skittish, but she was not uninterested in him. It was not his vanity speaking; Plimpton had seen her disappointment clearly when he had seemingly given up on marriage so quickly and easily.

He had rushed his fences this morning and had no intention of making her shy off again. If it was marriage that caused her to balk, he would make her believe his interest in her was of a less permanent nature.

The *ton* was a hotbed of gossip and while Plimpton had never flaunted his affairs, neither had he made any attempt to hide them. He knew women talked as much as men about such matters, which meant that Winifred would know that it was not unusual for him to take *ton* widows as his lovers. If she was amenable to dalliance, he would open that door. If she did not walk through it then he would find some other way. And another. He would not give up.

Digby finished with his nails and Plimpton inspected both hands before standing and gesturing for his valet to help him into his snug but not ridiculously tight coat.

Once he had adjusted his cravat, he slipped on his heavy gold and onyx signet, chose a quizzing glass from among the three Digby proffered—opting for the simplest of the trio—and then slipped the black ribbon holding the glass over his neck and examined his reflection. Assured that he was presentable, he nodded his dismissal at the valet and walked the short distance to the dining room.

Tonight, he was not the first to arrive. Winifred was looking out the window onto the garden which was still visible at seven o'clock given that the sun did not set until after nine. She was wearing the plainer of her two gowns. Regardless of her simple garb, his breath caught just as it did every single time he saw her face.

"Good evening, Winifred." He waved away the footman and seated her himself. "How did the afternoon go?" he asked after the servant had filled both their glasses. "I understand Wareham's two oldest sons paid him a visit today."

She smiled and the expression was so radiant that Plimpton felt as if she had punched him.

"It was delightful. I had not seen Thomas since he was ten and Robert was just seven. They are young men, now. Their aunt and uncle came with them and promised to bring the four youngest children back for a visit the day after tomorrow. She would have brought them today, but she wanted to make sure Wareham was able to enjoy so much stimulation, first."

Once the servants had set out the first course Plimpton said to Goodrich, "Thank you. We will ring when we need you."

"Very good, Your Grace." The butler and two footmen bowed and left them alone.

If she thought his dismissal of the servants was odd, she did not show it. Normally Plimpton would not have been so forward, but her time at Torrance would soon be over and he did not want to waste any opportunity to get to know her. With servants hovering, they could not speak of anything but pleasantries.

The Etiquette of Love

"I have only seen Wareham's sister-in-law around the children a handful of times, but it seemed she got on well with them," Plimpton said after taking a few mouthfuls of a delicious, chilled lobster consommé.

Winifred nodded. "Yes. They appear to be very comfortable with both their aunt and uncle." She paused, turning her glass around and around and staring at the pattern the foot made on the tablecloth. It was the first time Plimpton had seen her fidget. After a moment, she looked up. "At one point during their visit their mother's name came up and neither of the boys exhibited any sign that they missed her."

Plimpton weighed possible responses and decided on the least jarring one. "It is probable Lady Wareham did not spend a great deal of time with either of her sons, even when they were young."

"Yes, I suppose that is true. Was that how it was with your mother—that you barely saw her when you were a boy?"

Plimpton's initial instinct was to ignore her intimate question, and subtly change the subject. But a wry mental voice stopped him.

This is how people become acquainted and also the reason you dismissed the servants.

He swallowed his distaste at discussing such a private matter and said, "No, that is not how I was raised. I saw my mother often as a boy and we are still...close. The same is true for my brother." He cleared his throat, feeling uncharacteristically awkward. Nobody had ever asked him about his family relations. But she wanted to know, so...

"My father was not an approachable man." That was perhaps the understatement of the century. "He was raised to view open signs of affection or sentiment as weakness." And the duke had done his best to beat weakness out of both his sons, but especially his heir. "To my mother's credit, she defied him on numerous occasions, expressing her love when she believed that we needed such support. Unfortunately, she always paid for her transgressions."

She looked arrested. "Do you mean that he, er..."

"He did not hurt her physically." The duke had reserved corporal punishment for his sons, but there was no point in dredging that up. Still, he could not resist adding, "While he never laid a hand on her in anger, his displeasure was...a powerful weapon." And one that he wielded like a battleaxe of old.

She quietly assessed what he had said. And perhaps what he had left *un*said, as well. "You are fortunate in your relationship with your mother."

"Yes. I am very fortunate." There, that was enough honesty about *that* topic for one evening. He purposely changed the subject. "I was impressed by Wareham's improvement. He said he took six short walks today."

"Doctor Madsen says he will soon be able to go for much longer walks. In fact, Wareham is doing so well that I feel comfortable leaving in three days."

"That is a day earlier than we discussed."

"If that does not fit with your schedule, then I am sure—"

"The day you have chosen is fine," he lied. He had wanted to have more time with her, but he suspected that to argue the matter would only alienate her. He would call on her in London, but it would not be the same as being under the same roof. Here she was more relaxed. To call on her openly—to court her, in effect—would be a trickier proposition.

He did not have much time. He had better make every minute count.

"Will you come to the library and play piquet later?" he asked, putting his plan into action immediately.

She opened her mouth so quickly that he thought she would reject his offer. But then she closed it again, her brow furrowing. A few seconds later, she nodded and said, "Thank you. I would like that. I will meet you in the library in an hour."

Plimpton managed to hide his triumphant smile—fine, more of a *grin*, really—until he shut the door behind her.

Chapter 11

Freddie looked up from the tally sheet and met the duke's gaze.

"I am afraid you lost—again. But it was closer this time, Your Grace."

"I believe you are fibbing to spare my feelings."

His teasing surprised a laugh out of her. "Well, perhaps a little."

"You are a very good player."

"Thank you." She cast him an appraising look. He did not appear concerned that she had thrashed him soundly in all three games.

"What is it?" he asked.

"I do not think you are especially fond of the game."

His lips curled into what Freddie had begun to think of as one of his *almost smiles*, the expression so slight that a person might miss it if they were not watching closely. "Card game are not something I often have time for," he admitted diplomatically. "In fact, the last time I played piquet was with your brother—when we were at university."

"You do not go to gambling clubs?"

"Not often. And when I do, it is not piquet that I play."

"Would you rather play chess?"

"Will you think me a terribly dull fellow if I confess that I am not excessively fond of chess, either?"

Freddie could not help laughing. "I do not think playing chess is generally considered *exciting*, Your Grace. What do you enjoy doing for leisure?"

"I take pleasure in more physical pursuits."

Why did such an innocuous statement make her mouth flood with moisture? And were his eyes a darker, smokier gray then they'd been a moment earlier?

Freddie delicately cleared her throat of the obstruction that had come from nowhere and said, "I take it you mean hunting?"

"I hunt, but I also like riding for enjoyment—like today—or with a practical aim, such as inspecting my estates. What about you, Winifred? Other than thrashing men at piquet, what leisure activities do you enjoy?"

"I read a great deal, and I am fortunate that my house is situated within easy walking distance of Hyde Park. I enjoy games of all sorts, even silly parlor games like Speculation or Charades. I must admit to a special fondness for cards, however."

"And yet you rarely visit card rooms at balls."

"I am all astonishment. I never would have guessed that you took any notice of my actions at *ton* functions, Your Grace."

"Are you?"

"Yes, I am."

"*Tsk, tsk.*" He lowered his voice. "You are fibbing again, Winifred. You *know* that I have watched you this past Season because you have seen me doing so."

Freddie could only hold his gaze for a few seconds before lowering her eyes to the cards still scattered on the table. Pleased to have a purpose, she began to gather them into a neat pile, hoping desperately that he didn't notice the slight trembling in her fingers.

But then his hand, large and warm, laid atop both of hers, his fingers lightly closing and gentling her fumbling.

Had her mouth been flooded only a moment before? Because now her throat felt as if she had just swallowed a lump of chalk.

He was not holding her tightly and Freddie could have pulled her hand away easily. And yet... she did no such thing. Instead, she reveled in the rare pleasure of skin-on-skin contact. She touched other people so infrequently that she suddenly felt starved for it. She embraced her friends, of course, but it had been years and years since she had felt a man's touch. And even longer since she had welcomed it. Not since the first days of her marriage, when she had naively believed her handsome, charming, and worldly-wise husband's promise to cherish, love, and protect her.

"Winifred. Look at me."

She was unwilling to meet his cool gaze when she was in such turmoil. "No."

A soft chuckle drifted toward her and he laced his fingers with those of her right hand and stood. "Come here."

She stood, still unable to look at his face, her eyes mere inches away from his perfectly tied cravat. The pleasant scent of starch, cologne, and a faint hint of port teased her nostrils.

The warm pad of a finger lifted her chin, until she could not avoid meeting his gaze.

Heat and desire blazed in his eyes. Some small part of her brain still capable of rational thought pointed out that *this* was a true sign of what he felt, not the aloof indifference he'd displayed to her that morning when she had rebuffed his interest in marriage.

He lightly skimmed a thumb over her lower lip, his eyes never leaving hers. "I find you irresistible." His voice was lower and not as smooth as usual, a faintly wondering tone threaded through his declaration, as if he could not believe what he was saying. "I know you do nothing to cast out lures and yet your mere existence is a siren call." His gaze dropped to her lips. "I have resisted you for as long as I am able." That was all the warning she had before his mouth lowered over hers.

Her hands, which had hung limply at her sides after she'd stood, wasted no time sliding up the smooth wool of his snug-fitting coat and twining around his neck.

He gave an approving purr at her eager acceptance and stepped closer, one hand cupping her head while the other moved to her lower back and pulled her body flush against his, her breasts pressed flat against his chest, his arousal a long hard ridge against her belly.

It had been so long since she had kissed a man that Freddie was momentarily at sea, exploring him with her hands, but giving up control of their kiss to his expert ministrations. Not content with just her mouth, Plimpton left a trail of butterfly-light kisses across her cheek to her temple where his nose nuzzled gently in her hair. His chest expanded against hers as he inhaled, filling his lungs until they had to be near bursting.

He exhaled a low groan along with air. "You smell and feel every bit as delicious as you look." Heat and hunger infused his words and Freddie would not have believed the voice belonged to the Duke of Plimpton if she didn't currently have his arms around her and his lips on her skin.

When he nibbled her jaw, Freddie tilted her head so he could reach her throat, shivering as he explored the underside of her chin, a spot she would not have believed to be so sensitive until right then.

He caressed down her back, until his hand was firmly cupping one buttock. Freddie shivered when one of his fingers accidently grazed her cleft. But then it settled in place, as if it belonged there, and she knew it had been no accident.

Emboldened by his wicked exploration, she did some investigating of her own. The body beneath the exquisitely tailored garment was warm and hard and divinely muscular. She privately rejoiced at His Grace's love of physical pursuits over piquet.

Freddie used both hands to learn the shape of his broad shoulders and muscular back, following the taut line of his body to his narrow waist. She hesitated only a second before allowing her hands to migrate lower and cup his rock-hard buttocks.

His body shook and her hands froze. When she raised her eyes to his she saw from his amused expression that it was silent laughter she had felt.

"Wicked Winifred," he whispered approvingly, caressing up the curve of her lower back, following the knobs of her spine with one hand while his other hand closed lightly around her throat in a possessive gesture that should have felt threatening but instead made her quiver with desire.

She caught her lower lip, biting back a gasp of delight when he cupped her breast, his thumb lazily circling her nipple while his lips returned to her mouth, his tongue delving deep as his clever hands and fingers flooded her with body with sensation. Pressure built inside her, a hollow aching need to be filled, and Freddie ground her hips against him in wordless demand.

As suddenly as the kisses and caresses had started, they stopped.

Freddie blinked up into eyes that were twin black pools. His lips were no longer a stern slash, but pink and slick and slightly swollen, softening his austere features.

Only when both his hands closed lightly around her waist did Freddie realize that her fingers were still gripping his buttocks, as if to keep him close.

She jerked her hands away as if he had burned her and would have backed away, but his fingers tightened on her waist.

"No." He gave a slight shake of his head. "Do not run away, Winifred."

"It was you who—" She broke off, unwilling to utter the rest of the mortifying and reproachful words.

"I did not stop kissing you because I wanted to. I did it to give you an opportunity to consider what will come next."

His calm words irked her into retorting, "*Me?* What about you? Or do you not require time to consider?"

"No. I already know what I want. I have known for a while." He did not smirk or gloat, he just observed her with the relaxed, confident gaze of a predator eying its next meal, his thumbs lightly, absently, stroking the sensitive flesh of her abdomen over the thin muslin of her gown.

What was wrong with her that she could find him arousing and infuriating at the same time?

"Tell me what you want, Winifred?"

"I meant what I said this morning, Your Grace. I do not wish to marry."

He tucked a loose strand of hair behind her ear and then cupped her jaw as he had done earlier, the gesture making her feel cherished, though she had no idea why. "I know," he said, and then lightly kissed her.

His quiet acceptance confused her. "Then…what does this mean?"

"What would you like it to mean?"

Freddie gave an exasperated huff. "What would *you* like it to mean?"

"I would like it to mean you will come upstairs to my bedchamber and spend the better part of the night indulging our mutual desires," he said without hesitation, kissing her again to punctuate his shocking words.

His shocking and *appealing* words, she amended.

While she gawked up at him in openmouthed stupefaction, he lightly massaged her waist, his eyes flickering over her in an openly hungry way that caused more of the erotic pulsing and swelling that overwhelmed rational thought.

But why did she need to be rational? He knew she did not want marriage, which only left one other possibility. She knew he'd taken *ton* widows as lovers. Why should she be treated any differently? And he was the one who had made the suggestion, so…

He has conveniently forgotten that he is a gentleman right now, *but what will he say after you have consummated your passion? That is when guilt will seep into his thoughts. That is when he will remember that* your brother *is his best friend. That is when he will decide that to save your honor you must marry.*

His hands fell away from her waist and her eyes snapped to his face; his expression was so gentle that she scarcely recognized the haughty, aloof Duke of Plimpton.

"What is it?" she asked, baffled by the sudden change.

He gave a slight shake of his head, brushed the back of his fingers across her jaw, his eyes dark and mysterious. "You are conflicted. You should have all the time you need to make up your mind so that you will not regret anything later. I want you. My mind is made up and will not change. Come to my chambers if yours does." And then he bowed and strode from the room without another word or glance, leaving Freddie standing there, stewing in her own indecision.

Chapter 12

Plimpton was disappointed, but not especially surprised, when Winifred did not knock on his door that night. That kiss in the library had been only his opening salvo. Time was running out, so today he would launch a full offensive.

After he had washed, dressed, and answered some of the never-ending correspondence he received each day Plimpton paid a visit to Wareham's chambers.

Winifred was sitting with her brother, the two of them deep in discussion, but Wareham broke off and called out, "Come in! Come in!" when Plimpton hesitated on the threshold.

"You are late riding this morning," Wareham said when Winifred began bustling around the room, refusing to make eye contact with Plimpton.

"It was raining quite hard when I woke up, so I was forced to look at some of the mail that was forwarded here." He glanced out the window, which he was glad to see Winifred had opened, allowing some fresh air into the room. "It looks as though the clouds have parted—at least for a little while—so I thought I would go now. Would you care to join me, my lady?"

"Yes," Wareham answered for his sister. "She has been in here since the crack of dawn keeping me entertained. She needs exercise and fresh air."

Winifred glanced out the window and then at Plimpton's cravat. At anywhere but his face, in fact. "You think this sunshine will last?"

"Goodrich is certain we will have at least three hours before the heavens re-open."

"Just *go*, Winny."

Winifred gave her brother an exasperated look. "Fine. I will join you, then," she said, still not meeting his gaze. "I will be ready in half-an-hour."

"I will be in the stables," he said, opening the door for her. He had scarcely shut it when Wareham began crowing.

"She likes you, Plimpton—I can tell by how jittery she becomes in your presence. You sly charmer you!"

Plimpton pursed his lips and shook his head at the other man's juvenile behavior. "Careful with that grin, Wareham. If it gets much larger your head might split in half. I'd say all your brains would spill out, but I doubt there is much in there."

Wareham good naturedly ignored his insult. "I think all this hope I am feeling is what is making me better. Now, tell me how you are getting on with my sister? She said you played piquet last night."

Not surprisingly, Plimpton had forgotten all about playing cards, the memory wiped away by the pleasant interlude afterward. "I would not call what happened in the library a *game*. A slaughter is a more apt description."

"She *is* damned good." A sly smile twisted his lips. "Have you played her a game of chess yet?"

"No, but I fear that is coming. I am sure you'll hear the howls of pain in your chambers when we do."

Wareham laughed. "You might be a stupid fellow when it comes to cards and games, but you show to advantage on a horse."

"Thank you," Plimpton said wryly as he stood. "I am going to head down a little early and take a look at what you have that would suit her."

"Who did she ride before?"

"Velvet."

Wareham groaned.

"Any suggestions?" Plimpton asked, pulling on his gloves and picking up his whip.

"Mischief."

"I beg your pardon?" He was momentarily thrown off guard, wondering if the other man somehow knew about the kiss last night.

The Etiquette of Love

"Mischief is the name of the horse," Wareham explained.

"Ah."

"You should ask Goodrich to have a picnic lunch prepared for you," Wareham suggested helpfully as Plimpton opened the door. "Bring Winny down to the lake and make an afternoon of it."

"I will take your suggestion under consideration," he said, drawing the door shut.

"If it rains you can always seek shelter in the gazebo on Frog Island," Wareham shouted.

Plimpton couldn't help laughing. "Evidently matchmaking runs in your family."

"Don't forget you can use the—"

Plimpton shut the door and missed the rest of what his friend said. While Wareham had not come out and begged Plimpton to seduce his sister under his own roof, it was plain that is what he was hoping would happen. The other man firmly clung to the belief that a seduction would lead to marriage.

Plimpton would be extremely satisfied with that outcome, but he did not dismiss Winifred's resistance to remarrying as her brother did.

She was interested in Plimpton sexually, but she was a long way from trusting him.

Plimpton wanted her. Badly. But he was a patient man. The last thing he wanted to do was frighten her off by behaving like a middle-aged Lothario. Although he had not known Sedgewick very well, his dissolute raking, gambling, and evil temper had been legendary. It was understandable that she was wary of men.

He could wait to satisfy his carnal appetite and he would enjoy getting to know her better in the interim. Indeed, he looked forward to savoring a lengthy seduction. Whether it was tonight, or whether it took two months—or even two years—Plimpton was confident that she would come around.

It was not arrogance that made him believe that. It was the fact that he never, ever stopped until he got what he wanted.

And that driven, singlemindedness served you so well with Cecily...

Winifred was not Cecily. Other than their beauty, they had almost nothing in common.

Cecile had looked golden and warm, her hair the color of a freshly minted guinea and her eyes the blue of a robin's egg. But that warmth had been an illusion. Winifred's coloring, on the other hand, looked cool and untouchable but belied a warm, loyal, and caring nature.

It bothered him how often he associated Winifred with Cecily just because both women had been beautiful. They were completely different people and he wanted to divorce the two women in his thoughts. Permanently.

Plimpton was not without his fair share of blame when it came to his disaster of a marriage. He had been a selfish fool when they had married, and it was hardly Cecily's fault that she had never loved him.

Although he *did* blame her for not loving their daughter and would never forgive her for withholding her affection from Rebecca. Over the years he had watched Cecily rebuff Becca's love over and over and over again. He grew to hate her for it, and his hatred had frightened him. Because it would have been all too easy to punish Cecily for what she did to their only child—to use his power as her husband to make her suffer for her unkindness.

Whenever he had felt himself in danger of giving in to those urges, he had fled like a coward to London, trusting only distance to keep him from seeking vengeance.

Plimpton shook off the unwanted thoughts of his dead wife. This was the last time he would allow thoughts of her to contaminate what he was trying to build with Winifred.

***

Winifred wore a different habit today, this one an icy blue with black trim and a sweeping ostrich feather gracing a whimsical twist of a hat.

Her eyes immediately went to the basket the stable lad had attached to Plimpton's saddle. "A picnic?"

"We will miss luncheon so I thought this would stave off our hunger." At least hunger for food.

The Etiquette of Love

She glanced at the sky. "But what if it rains?"

"We will find shelter."

The groom led her horse out of the stable and Winifred's eyes glistened with pleasure. "What a lovely creature." She held out her hand for the animal to inspect.

Plimpton had briefly wondered if the horse was *too* lively when the groom had brought him back to the stall where the gelding had been happily munching hay. As soon as he'd seen the animal he recalled that Wareham had ridden it the last time Plimpton had visited. His friend had had his hands full when the horse was fresh.

He should have known better than to doubt Winifred's abilities. She was a far better rider than her brother, her lithe body moving as one with the spirited horse.

Once the initial friskiness of her mount was no longer consuming her attention the silence between them turned uncomfortable. A fetching pink stain colored the cheek that faced his way, telling him that she felt the awkwardness.

"I should apologize for the liberties I took in the library last night," he said once he had enjoyed her blushes far longer than he should have done.

Her head swiveled toward him, and she fixed him with a narrow-eyed look that was more than a little disgruntled.

Plimpton felt like laughing. Instead, he said, "Although I *should* apologize, it would be dishonest to say that I am sorry, Winifred. I enjoyed kissing you. And I will do it again if the opportunity presents itself."

***

Freddie's heart sped at brief but intense flash of desire that heated his gray gaze.

Calm yourself. You are behaving like a chit with your first infatuation.

The thought was sharp and astringent.

It was also correct.

Had they kissed last night?

Yes.

Had he just threatened to do so again if given the opportunity?

Also, yes.

Was she in danger of giggling like a giddy schoolgirl at such mild flirtation?

Astoundingly, the answer to that was also yes. At least if she did not gain control over her roiling emotions.

Freddie *never* giggled. Not even when she had been a girl. And yet right now a giggle threatened to bubble out of her even though she was a widow of eight years.

A widow who had been too scared and scarred after her disaster of a marriage to take a lover.

That thought killed the urge to giggle.

Thanks to Sedgewick, her life for years had been a passionless wasteland, an existence devoted to finding marital partners for other women. Husbands, but not necessarily *lovers* because women of her class did not yearn for such taboo things within marriage.

Except that Freddie *did* yearn for passion and intimacy and had done for some time. It had taken three- or four-years distance from her traumatic marriage to admit that Sedgewick—who had already destroyed so much in her life—would also rob Freddie of her own sensuality if she allowed it. And so, she had admitted to herself that she had physical needs and there was nothing wrong with her for wanting passion in her life.

She had been strongly tempted on several occasions to indulge those needs, especially when she had first met her friend Miles, the Earl of Avington. Eight years ago Miles had been a younger son with no prospects and every bit as poor and desperate for work as Freddie and all their other friends.

Miles also happened to be the most gorgeous man she had ever seen. Not only was he physically perfect, but he was a lovely person as well.

They had kissed—just once—but rather than stoking her desire, the brief experiment had killed it. Because kissing Miles had felt revoltingly like kissing her brother. She had never told him so, of course, but it had made the decision not to pursue an affair with him very easy.

Now, kissing the duke, on the other hand had set her blood ablaze.

Just imagine what lying with him would do…

Oh, she had. She had. For hours last night she had wondered. Twice, she had risen from her bed, slipped on her dressing gown, and walked toward her bedchamber door.

Twice she had stood staring into the darkness, breathing unevenly, her heart pounding.

And twice she had returned to her bed.

"Shall we take the other path today—the one that leads to the lake?" he asked, his question interrupting her increasingly heated imaginings.

"If you like," she said, grateful he could not hear her thoughts.

The path narrowed not long after the fork and she was spared having to come up with polite conversation. Instead, she could openly admire his broad shoulders, narrow waist, and excellent seat without anyone being the wiser.

You should have gone to him last night.

Yes, she should have.

You should go to him tonight.

Yes, she should do.

But *would* she?

Freddie honestly did not know.

They came out of the trees into the clearing, and the lake—it was too large to be called a pond—stretched out before them, sparkling like a sapphire under the summer sky. Its vivid blue color was not just a reflection of the sky, but a result of the Devonshire limestone that comprised the lakebed. The stone was a distinctive taupe color struck through with non-directional veining, and it not only kept the water clear and cool, but it had also contributed to a lovely section of sandy beach, which was where her great-grandfather had built the boathouse.

The word *boathouse* did not do justice to the airy, elegant structure that perched above the water. It had a small wet dock beneath it that was hewn from the same limestone that had formed the lake, making the house appear as if it had grown up out of the earth.

"Shall we stop here?" The duke glanced at the sky, which still held blue directly overhead, although clouds weren't far away. "If you are hungry, we could see what Cook packed for us."

"I am not hungry yet, but I would not mind having a look around."

The duke gracefully swung from the saddle and came to help Freddie dismount.

She had, shamefully and wantonly, hoped that he would take advantage of an opportunity to hold her a bit closer and longer than was proper, and use his body to ease her way down.

Disappointingly, he behaved like a perfect gentleman.

While the duke loosened the horses' girths and set them free to graze, Freddie examined the boathouse, pleased to see it was weathering time without any visible decay.

The small cottage—for that is what it was—looked like something fairies might have made. Her grandfather had built it as a wedding gift for his wife. Theirs had been one of the grand love stories of their day. Freddie never met either of them as they'd both died long before she was born, her grandfather first and her grandmother of a broken heart a short time later.

"It has been years since I have been here," the duke said as he came to stand beside her. "Wareham used to have parties every summer."

"I recall them quite vividly." They had been magical. At least the earliest ones.

She remembered Plimpton—of course she did, how could anyone forget him?—who had been serious and reserved even then, a sort of *otherness* about him. Freddie did not know at what age he had succeeded to the dukedom, but he must have been trained from the cradle for his position.

Like all the other boys who had come during those long-ago summers, he had treated Wareham's pest of a little sister with casual tolerance. And Freddie *had* been a pest, following Wareham and his friends whenever she could escape the nursery, wanting to be part of whatever they were up to. She had cried more than once when Wareham had marched her back to the nursery.

Some of the boys had teased her, but never Plimpton. Indeed, she did not recall exchanging so much as a word with him.

He looked down and met her gaze. "Your nurse brought you here once—you were tiny, no more than five or six—because she was terrified that you would sneak away and come down on your own and drown. She refused to leave until Wareham agreed to teach you how to swim."

Long buried memories came drifting back to her, like travelers returning from a distant, forgotten land.

Freddie nodded. "Yes, I remember now. Nanny said if I learned, I would be allowed to come to the next party. So Wareham taught me to swim. It was after Piers left," she added, and then shook the sadness away. "You said Wareham *used to* have parties down here; does he not have them any longer?"

"He stopped not long after you got married."

Looking back on it, she was amazed that Sophia had tolerated Wareham's beach parties for as long as she had. Sophia had been an enemy of fun of any sort, and she had especially despised the boathouse and beach, complaining that the bedchambers were too small and damp, and hating that people tracked sand all through the little house. She had never joined in that Freddie recalled and it would have rankled her that Dicky enjoyed an activity that she considered juvenile.

Freddie shrugged away the unwanted specter of her sister-in-law and instead thought back to those long-ago beach parties. A laugh slipped out of her. "Wareham was so competitive about that foolish boat race and used to pout shamefully when he lost."

"Which he was forced to do every time I competed."

Freddie scoffed at the duke's smug words. "You only won because I was not allowed to compete. The *Little Bird* was the fleetest boat on the water." Sophia had made Freddie stop participating when she turned thirteen because she disapproved of Freddie's rowing costume—a prim design of Freddie's great-grandmother's creation.

The duke turned to her, one eyebrow cocked, his gaze speculative. "It seems like I remember hearing that you won one year. A year I did not attend," he pointed out unnecessarily.

The competition had required not just rowing—which Freddie never could have won against the superior strength of the boys—but archery, which she was, or had been, very good at.

"Fancy a race?" the duke asked.

Freddie laughed. "Thank you, no. Not only have I not rowed a dinghy in a decade and a half, but I have not picked up a bow in just as long."

"If you are too cowardly to accept my challenge then perhaps you will allow me to row you around Frog Island for old time's sake?"

Freddie had forgotten the silly name. The *island* he was referring to was dead center in the lake and the descriptor *island* was far too grandiose for the little dab of land. Wareham had come up with the name because of the large community of frogs that lived in a captured pond that had, over time, formed a marshy area.

"I would like to go out to the island," she admitted, even though nostalgia threatened to overpower her. Freddie and Wareham had had such *happy* times here. She even recalled a few sunny afternoons with Piers when she could not have been much more than four.

And one magical morning he brought you here to see swans…

Freddie looked around. "There used to be swans."

The duke frowned. "I believe so."

She did not see any today.

"I wonder if there are any boats left if Wareham no longer uses the place," she said.

"Only one way to find out."

The Etiquette of Love

Freddie followed the duke up the two limestone steps leading to the wet dock. The warped wooden door opened with a screech that said it had not been oiled lately.

"Look! There is the *Little Bird*!" Freddie cried. "Why, it looks as if it has had a fresh coat of paint." Freddie ran her hand along the smooth, pale blue prow.

"What is the significance of name *Little Bird*?" the duke asked, looking from the prettily scrolled name to Freddie.

"You—did you know my brother Piers?"

"Yes, although not well."

Freddie could not see from his expression what he thought about the other man. "Piers is the only one who called me that. There used to be finches in a cage in the sunroom. Evidently my mother liked them and always kept a pair, and it bothered me a great deal to see them living inside the house when it was clear to my three-year-old mind that birds belonged *out*side. In any event, I released the birds one day and was getting a scolding from Nanny when Piers intervened on my behalf." Freddie smiled at the memory, which doubtless had been enlarged and colored by time, the way she liked to imagine it happening; Piers, her brave protector, coming to her rescue. She reluctantly left the memory behind. "The *Little Bird* was made for me, so it is much too small for the two of us."

He gestured to the other two boats. "Take your pick."

"I think the *Island Hopper*."

"Very well. Shall we take the food along, or leave it here in the cool until we come back?"

"Let us leave it here. It will be your reward for hard rowing when we return."

"Ah, I see. I am to be your galley slave."

"That will be a novel, educational experience for you, I am sure."

He merely grunted and left to fetch the basket.

Once he had tucked the basket in a cool spot, the two of them eased the boat off the limestone pier into the water.

The duke handed her in, and Freddie opted for the seat in the bow. She felt a twinge of guilt as he slid the oars into the locks and pushed off from the stone wall. "I do not mind sharing the labor."

"I never go back on my word. You relax and I will row."

Freddie observed his smooth, powerful stroking for a few moments and then said, "You are very good."

"I started rowing at Eton and continued when I was at university. My brother and I have occasionally punted on the Severn, but it has been some years since the last time." He paused, and then added, "I am just now realizing how much I have missed it."

Once they were out on the water, she could see the boathouse more clearly, its many east-facing windows glinting in the sun. Although Wareham kept it well-maintained, Freddie thought the building looked lonely.

"It is shame nobody uses the boats or the cottage anymore," she said.

"I agree. I have always envied your brother his boathouse."

"You don't have one on any of your *seven* properties?" she teased. "You must rectify that oversight."

Humor gleamed in his eyes. "I shall have to correct Honoria—whom I assume is your informant—that I have *eight* properties."

"Eight properties," she repeated., shaking her head in wonder. "Do you visit them every year?" Freddie was fascinated by the thought of owning *eight* houses. Sedgewick had lost all but his family's estate by the time they had married, and Wareham owned three—this one, the London house, and a modest property that had belonged to her mother—but she suspected all eight of Plimpton's were far grander.

"Most years I do, but I never stay long at three of them as they have only a skeleton staff and my presence puts undue strain on them."

"That is very considerate of you."

He lifted an eyebrow at her.

The Etiquette of Love

"I am not mocking you. I mean it." Freddie let one hand hang over the side, dragging a finger in the water. "You must be responsible for a great many people."

"It sometimes feels that way."

"Only sometimes?"

He rowed for a moment before answering. "Like anyone else, I have good days and bad days."

"What is a good day?"

He rowed for a moment, the boat gliding silently, and then said, "A good day is any day when there is no calamity."

"Calamity?"

"No crop-killing frosts, no tenants falling off ladders and breaking their legs, no new leaks discovered in Whitcombe's roof." He shrugged. "Those are good days."

"And what constitutes a bad day—if you do not mind me asking. Aside from those things you just listed, of course."

Again, he pondered her question. He was a precise man who thought before he spoke, and his succinct speech reflected that. Like Freddie, flirtation and badinage did not come easily to him.

"Last year a fire started in an outbuilding at one of my tenant farms. Before we could extinguish it, it destroyed not just his barn, threshing house, and all the other buildings, but his home, as well."

"And his family?"

The duke shook his head. "He, his wife, and their seven children all escaped unscathed—at least in body—but losing one's home and all one's possessions is—" he broke off and shook his head. "Even though I could provide them with new housing and other necessities, I could not replace all they had lost. Nobody could."

She was touched that he would take his tenants' pain so personally. Not all peers cared about their people. Sedgewick's tenant farmers had occupied ramshackle houses, paid steep rents, and barely scratched out a subsistence living on overworked land.

The duke paused and shipped the oars before taking out his handkerchief and wiping the sheen of perspiration from his face. It *was* hot and muggy when the sun burned through the clouds. She was certainly feeling uncomfortably warm in her habit, and she was not the one rowing.

"I will not be offended if you remove your coat, Your Grace."

He glanced up from re-folding his handkerchief. "Thank you, I think I will; it is rather warm."

Freddie could not look away as his long, elegant fingers deftly unfastened the buttons on his coat. Had she felt hot before? Now, she was sweltering.

She watched beneath her lashes as he shrugged his powerful shoulders and peeled off the elegantly tailored garment, which he proceeded to bunched up and was about to shove into a gap in the gunwale beside him.

Freddie held out her hand. "Give it to me. I will hold it for you."

He handed her crumpled coat. "Thank you."

"Look how you have wrinkled it," Freddie scolded as she took it by the shoulders to give it a good shake.

"Be careful there is—damnation!" the duke shouted as something gold and shiny flew out of the garment and into the air.

Freddie lurched to grab whatever it was and was flabbergasted when her hand closed around something round and smooth.

Unfortunately, the duke lunged at the same moment.

It seemed like time slowed as the dinghy flipped—more of a gentle roll, really—tipping both her and the duke into the lake.

Chapter 13

Plimpton knew even as he grabbed for the locket that he would never reach it in time. What he did *not* know was that Winifred would lunge for it as well and their combined weight would not only tip the boat but turn it over completely.

The water was shockingly cold, especially given that the day was so warm, and his wits momentarily froze. Only when he heard splashing and a muffled, "*Help!*" did he regain his senses and tread water, turning in a circle.

He saw…nothing.

"Winifred?" he called. Good Lord! Had she gone under?

Another muffled cry came from the dinghy's hull, which was right beside him.

Plimpton shoved his hand beneath the rim of the boat. "If you can hear me, take my hand," he shouted.

After a moment, slim, cold fingers tightened around his. "Can you swim out?" he asked loudly.

"My skirts are too heavy. I will sink if I let go of the gunnel."

"Release my hand for a moment and I will come under with you and then we can leave together."

There was a slight pause before her fingers slipped away. Plimpton took a deep breath and dove beneath the surface, keeping one hand on the lip of the boat to guide himself.

A few seconds later he popped up into crepuscular light. "Winifred?"

"Right here," she said in a breathy voice.

"Are you hurt?"

"No, I am fine."

"Take my hand and on the count of three stop treading and let me guide you out." He reached out, his fingers encountering something hard and wet—a shoulder, perhaps—and she clasped her hand around his.

"Deep breath—one, two, *three*."

He kicked strongly to get free of the dingy and bright light streamed down through the crystalline water. A moment later his head broke the surface, Winifred's a second later. She sputtered and shook her head, sending diamonds of water flying. Plimpton wiped the water from his eyes, and when his vision was clear, he saw that she was holding one hand fisted above the water.

"Is your arm hurt?"

"No, I have your locket in my hand. At least I think it is a locket."

Plimpton gave a disbelieving snort. "Good Lord. That was an amazing catch. And, yes, it is a locket."

"Considering that I am the clumsy oaf who sent it flying in the first place, it seemed only fair."

Despite their current situation—treading water in his shirtsleeves in the middle of a lake—he was amused by the thought of her being a *clumsy oaf*.

"Can you swim at all?" he asked, already guessing the answer.

"Not with this lead weight around my legs." Even in the cool water her cheeks reddened at the unladylike word *legs*.

"Take the skirt off and I will carry it."

Her eyes and mouth rounded into *O's*.

"If it is too difficult to remove, I can help you to—"

"No, no, it is not that. It unbuttons at the waist, but—"

"But what? Take it off and then we can swim to shore."

"Can we not flip the boat over?"

Plimpton already knew that flipping the boat would not be possible, but he could see she did not wish to remove her habit and was ready to argue, so…

The Etiquette of Love

"I can try," he said, and glanced at her hand, which was resting on his arm. "Are you sure you can stay afloat?"

"For a minute or two," she said in a breathless voice.

Plimpton curled his hands around the edge of the dinghy and lifted. Not surprisingly, he immediately sank.

"No chance," he said, turning to her. "I am afraid we will have to swim."

She cast a yearning glance at the island.

"The island is closer, but there is no boat to take us back. If you do not want to remove your skirt you can clasp your arms around my neck and let me—"

"I will remove my skirt." She began to twist and bob and contort in the water.

Plimpton gave a bark of laughter and her eyes widened. "I beg your pardon, Winifred. I did not laugh at you, but the situation."

"I did not think you were mocking me. I was just stunned that you *can* laugh."

That made him smile.

"*And* you can smile!"

"Very droll. You will be even more thunderstruck when you learn my teeth can chatter."

"Oh, sorry," she muttered, taking his unsubtle hint and struggling one handedly with her garment. "Well, blast. What am I thinking?" She thrust a hand at him. "Here, hold this."

Plimpton took the locket from her hand. He suspected it was now ruined, despite her best efforts.

"What is it?" she asked, her voice breathy and her arms in motion beneath the water.

"A locket."

She rolled her eyes. "I had guessed that much."

"It holds a miniature of my daughter that Honoria painted for me."

"Oh, no! It will be ruined. I am so terribly sorry that I—"

"It was hardly your fault," he said. "And if it is ruined, I suspect I can prevail on Honoria to paint another one for me. It is one of the many benefits of having a painter in the family. Now, give me your skirt."

Her color flared as she lifted the sodden cloth out of the water. Plimpton took it, momentarily thrown off by the weight of it. "Good Lord. You are to be commended for treading water for so long." He draped the skirt around his shoulders. "Are you ready?"

She nodded and they set off.

Unhindered, she was indeed an excellent swimmer. They swam in silence, the exertion slowly burning away the chill wrought by the water and allowing him to appreciate more fully the humor of the situation.

You certainly know how to charm the skirts off a woman, Wyndham, his brother Simon would say if he could see him now.

"Shall we take a break?" he asked after they had swum about halfway.

"Keep…going."

Plimpton smiled to himself at her doggedness. And then he resumed swimming.

***

Freddie was positively mortified. First, she had flung one of his prized possessions from the boat and then she had thrown him into the water.

And now she was half-nude.

At least it is the bottom half.

An utterly inappropriate urge to laugh—more from hysteria than humor—threatened to sneak from her tightly pursed lips. She eyed the rapidly approaching shoreline with trepidation. Her misery was not over yet; she would soon need to struggle back into her skirt in the water and then walk out of the lake with every article of clothing plastered to her body like a second skin.

The Etiquette of Love

Or perhaps she should keep swimming around the lake until darkness fell. That would eliminate the embarrassment of climbing out of the water like a half-drowned rat.

But then she would need to ride home in wet clothing in the dark.

Beside her, the duke began to walk and a moment later she, too, could reach the sandy bottom with her poor, ruined ankle boots. When she thought about the duke's lovely footwear—or formerly lovely, now—she felt the urge to weep.

"Could I have my skirt back?" she asked as her shoulders emerged from the water.

He stopped and turned to her, the water lapping at the bottom edge of his waistcoat. She could not help admiring how nicely the thin material of his shirt clung to his shoulders and biceps.

It was always good to find a silver lining.

"Surely you are not going to wear it?" he asked.

"Of course I will wear it," she retorted. "I hardly wish to ride home in my ch-chemise." It irked her that she stumbled over the word.

"Perhaps there is something in the boathouse we could wear?" He glanced at the sky. "Although perhaps changing into dry clothing—if we can find some—is rather pointless."

Freddie looked at the sky and saw that it had filled with dark clouds as they had been swimming. "There used to be spare clothing for accidents like this one. But I still need my skirt for now."

He handed her the garment without a word and politely turned away while she struggled into it.

"You can turn back now."

He did so and offered her his elbow.

Freddie laced her arm through his as they resumed their walk toward shore. The further they got out of the lake the more she had to lean on him. Only when the water was ankle-deep did she dare release him and wobble the last few steps alone, lifting the hem scandalously high to wring out as much water as possible before ascending the limestone steps that led to the boathouse door.

The sitting room, with its wall of windows, was sweltering from being tightly shut up, the still air rippling with heat. The furniture was draped in holland covers, but there was very little dust so the house must have been cleaned not too long ago.

"It is rather stultifying in here. I will open some of these windows to allow in some fresh air," the duke said.

Freddie nodded. "I will go upstairs and look for some clothing."

The cottage had four rooms, but two were completely empty, even of furniture. The third had a cupboard full of clothing, unfortunately all of it was for young boys.

The last room must have been used by her nieces because it held garments suitable for young girls.

Freddie had just begun to give up hope when she found a banyan shoved into the corner of the armoire, the faded maroon and heavy gold braiding a style from at least fifty years ago.

Freddie smirked to herself as she imagined the duke wearing such a grand, old-fashioned garment.

Unfortunately, that was the only article of adult clothing she could find.

Freddie chewed her lip and her gaze settled on the bed.

***

Plimpton stripped off his waistcoat and hung it over the back of a chair he'd set in front of the window.

He would have liked to remove his shirt, which was sticking to his skin, but if Winifred did not find any clothing, then—

Plimpton heard a step behind him and turned. His eyes bulged out of his head and his mouth quite suddenly went dry.

"I found this for you," she said, holding something out to him.

But Plimpton could not pull his gaze off her person. Intellectually, he knew that what she had done was fashion an astonishingly attractive toga from a bedsheet. But his body responded as if she wore a negligee composed of nothing more than a few scraps of lace and wicked intentions.

The Etiquette of Love

Other than a rapidly spreading blush, her skin was as pale as the soft white sheet, an effect that made her look as if she had just been deposited on earth by way of a beam of sunshine—or a moonbeam would be more like it.

The fact that he was even thinking such drivel shook him out of his daze. He wrenched his hungry gaze from the elegant slope of her bare shoulders to her face, which was flushed a fetching pink.

She looked stunned, almost as if she could read Plimpton's mind, which was currently entertaining visions of stripping her naked and taking her right there in the blazing sunshine.

"Er, Your Grace?"

"I beg your pardon?" His voice sounded as if he had been parched for days.

She lifted her outstretched arm higher, which was when he saw she was holding some godawful scarlet and gold fabric.

He reached for it, out of courtesy more than interest. "Thank you," he said, and then forced himself to look at the garment in his hands, eyeing it dubiously. Her laughter brought his attention back to her beautiful face.

"You should see the expression on your face."

"Abject horror?" he guessed.

Her smile grew into a grin, the joyful expression more devastating than her Grecian apparel.

"If I can wear a bed sheet then you can wear a robe from the reign of George I. If you like, there are even red-heeled shoes with jeweled buckles on them. I could fetch them for you."

"You cannot be serious."

She laughed. "No, I made that up."

"Very droll. And this"—he raised the garish robe—"was all you could find?"

"You don't sound like you believe me."

He snorted at her wide-eyed innocent look. "I will go up and change."

"Oh! I forgot my wet things upstairs."

Before Plimpton could tell her that he would bring them down with him she scampered back up the stairs, giving him delicious glimpses of elegant ankles, shapely, high-arched feet, and a generously rounded rump pressing against the thin sheeting.

Once he reached the second floor she motioned him toward the first room. "You can use this one, my clothing is in the other." She paused and looked him up and down. "Will you be able to remove those boots yourself?"

"Not without a great deal of effort. I will just dry my shirt and waistcoat."

"But you must be dreadfully uncomfortable in all that wet leather."

"It is not pleasant," he admitted. "But it is bearable."

"Were you not the one who mocked me about my skirt, Your Grace?" Before he could say it was hardly the same thing, she gestured to one of the other rooms. "Come. You sit and I will pull them off."

Plimpton knew he should not like the thought of that so much.

He should politely but firmly decline.

She gestured to the room's only chair, giving him an impatient look. "Come. It will be hours before my habit is fit to wear. We can relax and enjoy a picnic lunch while everything dries."

When put that way, it sounded foolish to sit around in wet boots and leathers.

Plimpton sat.

"Give me one foot," she commanded.

He lifted his boot and grimaced. "It's covered with sand."

"Sand washes off." She grabbed his ankle and pulled. Not surprisingly, the soaked leather did not budge. She caught her lower lip with her teeth—an action that did nothing to loosen his footwear but tightened his breeches—and considered the soggy boot before giving another tug, harder this time.

That did not work, either.

She scowled at his boot as if it were personally defying her.

Although Plimpton could have happily sat there and watched her fondle him—any part of him—all day, he had mercy on her. "Well, thank you for trying, Winifred." He began to lift his foot from her grasp, but she held on to it.

"I will use the other way."

"What other way?"

She pursed her lips. "*You* know what way."

Plimpton was beginning to enjoy himself. "Oh, you mean the way a valet sometimes does?"

"Yes, that is the way I mean."

Plimpton did not think he had imagined the slightly dangerous undertone in her voice. "I could not ask you to—"

"You are not asking. I am offering. But you will close your eyes."

"I will?"

"Yes, you will."

"Very well, I will close my eyes." Plimpton fit deed to words and listened to the sound of cloth rustling—the lifting of her toga, he presumed—and then felt warm, firm flesh clamp around his knee.

Plimpton opened his eyes—truly, how could any man resist?—and was faced with the delightful sight of her legs bare to above the knee and her derriere shifting and flexing beneath the shin sheet as she wrestled with the boot until it grudgingly began to move.

All too soon she had it free and dropped it with a *thunk* to the floor.

Plimpton closed his eyes when she began to twist around.

There was a heavy silence, and then she moved to the other leg. He opened his eyes and enjoyed the second half of the too brief show, shutting them again when the second boot hit the floor.

She moved away, taking the warm pleasure of her body with her. "You can open them now." Her voice came from the doorway, where she hesitated on the threshold, cheeks a furious pink.

"Thank you, Winifred." Plimpton only allowed himself to smile after she had darted away, swallowed up by the shadows in the hallway.

Chapter 14

Freddie's face had just begun to cool when she heard the sound of soft footsteps coming down the stairs.

She watched from beneath lowered lashes as he padded on bare feet toward the door leading out to the wide stone balcony that stretched out over the wet dock below. He tossed his boots onto the ground before draping his breeches, stockings, and shirt over the thick railing.

She pointed to the box beside the fireplace when he reentered the room. "There are some old newspapers in there."

He raised his eyebrows.

"For your boots," she explained.

His eyebrows inched higher. "Er, to polish them?"

"To stuff inside them."

"Because...?"

"If you don't, they will shrink as they dry, and you will never get your feet back in them."

"And newspaper will keep them from shrinking, will it?"

"Yes, but you must pack them tightly."

He nodded, looking ridiculously regal in his robe. Once he had fetched his boots back inside, he sat in the chair nearest the fireplace and began pushing full sheets into the neck of one boot.

Freddie sighed and took the next sheet from him, crumpling it into a tight ball. "Like so."

He accepted her instruction with a nod and followed her example with the next sheet. "How do you know these things?"

"Life without a lady's maid."

"Ah." He worked in silence until one boot was full. "Tight enough?"

"A bit more."

Once he had finished, he took them back outside and set them in the sun.

"There is water in the pitcher if you want to wash the newsprint from your hands," she said. "Are you hungry?"

"I am."

As he washed, Freddie set out the contents of the picnic basket. She could not help thinking how domesticated the scene was. Although it would not be a common domestic arrangement for a duke, who would have at least a dozen people to do the sorts of mundane tasks that he was being forced to do today.

He sat down in the chair across from her and she was unexpectedly charmed by how ruffled he looked with his brown hair tousled, his ridiculous robe exposing a very un-ridiculous expanse of muscular throat and chest. A smudge of newsprint on his cheek provided a piquant finishing touch to his dishevelment.

"You are regarding me strangely," he pointed out after she had stared for too long.

"I was just wondering how often you have had to care for your own boots or undress yourself."

Rather than look offended by her question, there was a faint curve to his lips as he reached for the unopened bottle of wine. "Not often," he admitted. "I imagine it was much the same case for you before Sedgewick died."

"Yes, it was eye opening."

He filled both glasses and handed one to her.

"Thank you." She took only a tiny sip. Today she would nurse each glass, rather than quaff down three in rapid succession.

"Tell me about your time teaching at that school. Honoria said it was the Stefani Academy?"

"What do you want to know?"

"How did you find the position? What made you decide to teach? What sort of things did you teach? Anything, really. I will make up two plates of food while you talk." He paused and then added with a twinkle in his eye, "Putting food on a plate is one of my few domestic achievements."

Freddie laughed. "Commendable."

He began to put portions on the plates while Freddie cast her mind back. "My decision to teach was born of exigency. Without going into the gruesome details, Sedgewick somehow got at the money set aside for me in the settlement agreement and spent most of it—or likely just lost it all in various gaming hells. The small amount he did leave behind was in a trust that is administered by Wareham—but I suspect you know all about that."

The duke set a plate in front of her, met her gaze, and said, "Actually, I did not know what had been left or how."

Likely her brother was simply too embarrassed to let that business be known, even to his best friend. Freddie continued, "I knew I would need to find some way to support myself. And yes, before you ask, Wareham offered me a place to live and a generous allowance. What he did not understand that living under the same roof with his wife would have been misery." She met Plimpton's gaze and said frankly, "Sophia was the reason I rushed into marriage in the first place."

"I think your brother knows that... now."

"Yes, he apologized. I blamed him for years for not seeing how difficult Sophia was to live with, but part of me always respected him for showing such devotion to his wife." She shrugged, not wanting to talk about the woman any more than she had to. "Regardless, I knew I could not live under Wareham's roof. And I don't have the temperament to be a companion or a governess, but teaching appealed to me, probably because I enjoyed my time at school so much. I contacted the woman at my school, but she had no position for me. Instead, she pointed me in the direction of the Stefani Academy."

"Honoria mentioned that it was Portia Stefani, rather than Ivo—her famous husband—who was the force behind that operation."

Freddie pulled a face at the memory of the mercurial pianist. "Yes. Other than his grand name, Ivo was more of a detriment. He despised the school and thought himself above it, even though he could no longer play professionally after injuring his hand. The school was doing well without his help, but it could not support his expensive habits. I worked there for four years before matters came to a head."

"Did you enjoy it?"

"I adored it, especially the camaraderie with the other teachers. All of us except Miles—er, Lord Avington—lived at the school. I was the only one of them who did not already have a career." She gave him a wry look. "I, of course, had been raised to view a woman's role as decorative with my primary—my *only*—goal as marriage. You are familiar with Honey's background and know she is a great artist. But the others are just as talented in their way. Portia Stefani could have been a concert pianist but sacrificed her own ambitions when she married. Serena Lockheart—Lombard, back then—was raised by a prestigious sculptor and he'd taught her to follow in his footsteps. Annis Bowman—have you met her?"

"She is the only one of the teachers I have not met. Although I was briefly introduced to her husband, Rotherhithe, a while back."

"Annis would have gone to university and pursued languages if she wasn't a woman. I believe she speaks seven or eight at last count." Freddie couldn't help smiling before saying, "And then there is Miles."

***

Plimpton had been listening with fascination up until that point. But the affectionate, almost loving, expression on her face when she mentioned the Earl of Avington caused a foreign emotion to tighten his chest. He knew it immediately for what it was, but it had been a long, long time since he had last felt such searing jealousy.

"Miles is not an artist on the level of the others, of course, but he is a very talented man."

"Oh?" Plimpton asked, cringing at the hostility in his tone. Fortunately, Winifred was too caught up in her memories to notice.

"He took up carving while he was a prisoner during the war."

Instantly, Plimpton's jealousy dissolved. Having a brother who had endured the horrors of war made it difficult for him to feel anything but sympathy for Avington, no matter how much Winifred might like him.

"He got so good at it that he sold his work."

"Did he?" Now, there was a surprise.

Her warm gaze cooled. "I can hear the disapproval in your voice, Your Grace."

"Then there must be something wrong with your hearing, Winifred because I would never look down my nose at a man for trying to support himself when his family is floundering. I knew Avington's brother quite well, so I was aware of the dire straits the earldom was in. The fact that Miles Ingram worked rather than draw an allowance shows what caliber of man he is."

"I happen to agree." She paused, and then gave him a rather challenging look and said, "I also sell my work. It was Miles who introduced me to the man who buys it."

"You carve wood?" he teased, for some reason unwilling to admit he knew about her needlework.

She chuckled. "No. I ply a needle. The gentleman who buys my work accepts all sorts of items."

"Does Wareham know?" he asked, although he knew the answer.

"No. And I would thank you not to tell him, either."

"I will not tell him what you confide in me."

Red streaks, like twin strokes from a painter's brush, stained her sculped cheekbones. "No, of course you would not. I apologize for impugning your honor."

Plimpton, whose mouth was full of cheese, nodded.

"The last of my colleagues is Lorelei Fontenot. I believe Lori will one day be a great novelist. Unfortunately, she has been forced to earn her living selling stories to newspapers. You might have met her at one of the balls Miles and his wife Mary gave last year."

"I remember Miss Fontenot," Plimpton said. "She sat me down and explained to me why the peerage was—let me see, what was the word she used? Ah, yes, a *leech* on the British people."

Winifred chortled. "Oh, dear. You got *that* lecture, did you?"

"Yes, and at some length. I find interesting that she holds such views and yet lives with a countess, is friends with an earl—" he broke off, squinting as he searched his memory. "In fact, I believe only your friend who married Gareth Lockheart is not a peer."

"That is true." She gave an exaggerated sigh. "Poor Lorelei has had her hands full with the six of us, I fear. She is also vehemently opposed to marriage."

Plimpton had found the talkative, excitable woman tiresome and exhausting. He would much rather discuss the woman across from him. "And then there is you, Winifred."

"Yes, the only one without any particular skill or ability—unless one considers being the widow of an earl a talent. I should not scoff at that, I suppose. It is the one thing Sedgewick left me of any value." She stopped abruptly and blinked. "Goodness, I have done all the talking." She gestured to her plate, which was full, and then his, which was mostly empty. "It is your turn to talk and my turn to eat."

Plimpton had to bite back a groan.

She must have seen his reluctance because she said, "Come now, I have told *you* about my past. It is your turn."

"You told me about your *friends*," he corrected. "But you still did not tell me about teaching school."

"I did not?"

"No."

"Oh. Well, let me see…I taught deportment and conversational arts."

"That sounds interesting. Tell me how one teaches the art of conversation."

She eyed him skeptically.

"What? Why are you looking at me so suspiciously?"

"Because I have a hard time believing you are really interested in such things."

"Believe it, because it is true. So, tell me about teaching conversation."

The Etiquette of Love

"I taught conversation for *females*, so it would hardly be of any interest to you."

"And how would that be different?"

She made one of those subtle, ladylike sounds that could not be called a snort—more of an elegant sniff, he supposed—and said, "When a woman talks to another woman, she actually *communicates*. When a woman talks to a man, she deflects and encourages."

"Is that so?"

"It is so. When a young lady converses with a man, she encourages him to talk about himself and deflects any questions that come her way, turning the conversation back to him."

"Is that what you have been trying to do with me—pander to my pride?"

"Of course not," she said with an admirably straight face.

He chuckled. "*Hmm*, why do I feel as if you are carefully managing me?"

"*Two* laughs in one day? Why, Your Grace, what will the *ton* say about such unbridled dissipation?"

"I believe that was a deflection," Plimpton countered.

"What a quick learner you are, Your Grace."

"Why would you teach young girls such a thing?"

"Because it is what men want—to talk and have their viewpoints affirmed—*not* hear a woman's opinions. When a young woman enters the *Grand Marriage Mart* she needs to understand that, or she will be left sitting by herself and watching others get asked to dance."

"I am not sure I agree with you, but I will leave that debate for another time. For now, I feel compelled to point out that you do not agree with everything *I* say or regard me worshipfully, as if every word that comes out of my mouth is a revelation."

"True, but then I am not a young girl in search of a husband."

"Touché," he murmured.

"Now, Your Grace, it is *my* turn to ask the questions."

***

"What would you like to know?" Plimpton asked.

Freddie could not help noticing the wariness in his gaze.

"First I would like to know about that locket of yours."

"Oh." The duke looked so relieved that Freddie almost laughed. "It is a portrait of my daughter."

"So you said. May I see it?"

He stood and went to the mantlepiece and returned with the oval locket, already open.

Freddie took it and then smiled up at him. "Why, it seems fine!"

"It does. I daresay that is because it is painted in oil. I am leaving it open just in case the canvas is damp."

She nodded and peered at the miniature. The girl in the locket was perhaps sixteen. She was not beautiful; the most anyone could say about her was that she had a lovely smile and pretty eyes like her father. Freddie was unaccountably relieved that Lady Rebecca was not a raving beauty like her mother. Although why that mattered, she did not know.

Freddie looked up and handed the locked back. "She looks delightful."

Plimpton's stern mouth twisted into a doting smile. "She clever and loving and a joy to be around."

Freddie was momentarily stunned by his burst of effusiveness. So, there was something—or somebody, rather—the aloof Duke of Plimpton loved.

He returned the locket to the mantlepiece, still open, and then resumed his seat, his gaze once again guarded as he waited for more questions.

Freddie decided to get her question out of the way before she lost her courage. "Tell me about those naughty parties Wareham used to have—the ones that ended when he married Sophia."

Freddie could see her question surprised him. There was also a hint of relief in his gaze. Had he been concerned she would ask about his marriage.

He shrugged. "They were not so naughty. They were bachelor parties for young, unmarried men. I am sure a woman with your experience can imagine what that entailed."

Freddie could imagine wealthy, indulged young men's obnoxious behavior perfectly well. But that was not what she really wanted. She was hoping to talk about the guests at one party in particular, since Piers's recollection of that fateful night was so fragmented. Her probing needed to be careful, or the duke's sharp mind would wonder what she was up to.

"Were they all school mates at these parties?"

His eyes narrowed slightly, and he said, "For the most part."

"Do you still associate with most of them, or have you drifted apart?"

He relaxed a little at the question. "I see most of them at clubs or in Lords, but I can't say I have retained any of those friendships. Except for your brother, of course. I believe Wareham keeps up with several of the others."

"Does he? That surprises me. Like whom?"

His glass hovered halfway to his mouth and then he set it down without taking a drink. "Why do these questions not sound like casual interest?"

"Because you are of a suspicious nature?" she retorted.

His hard expression softened slightly. "Usually, it is not without reason."

"I am just curious about what life was like back then. I remember some of those parties when I was a few years older, but Nanny always kept me well away from them."

"That was probably wise. We drank a great deal and frequently engaged in dangerous stunts and were hardly appropriate company for young children."

"I notice you said *we*."

"I am sure I was just as stupid and reckless as any other spoiled young peer."

Freddie could not allow that to pass unchallenged. "I recall you—not well, but well enough."

"And what do you recall?" he asked, draining the contents of his glass and lifting the bottle.

God help her, Freddie nodded for more. Clearly, she was a very slow learner.

"I recall you being as quiet and serious as you are now," she said, deciding to try one more lure to see if she could get any bites. "I also recall Lord Trendon and Sir Maxwell Weil, who were very boisterous, but I don't remember them behaving badly.

"No, they were, in general, decent."

"So that is three of you who were not naughty. Who were the wild boys?"

He frowned, but in concentration this time, his gaze going vague as he cast his mind back. "Elliot Jordan, Sutton—"

"Viscount Sutton?"

"Yes."

"He died not long ago, didn't he?"

"Yes, a hunting accident."

Freddie would have sworn that shutters closed over his eyes. She could guess why; it was said Sutton was hurting financially and might have committed suicide to escape his creditors.

"I can well believe Sutton was reckless. Who else?"

"Conrad and Brandon were rusticated at least twice. And…Peregrine Fluke. Well…" he trailed off, looking as if he regretted mentioning that last name. Clearly the duke decided Sir Peregrine's behavior was not fit for female ears.

Freddie knew Lords Sutton, Conrad, and Brandon, but she had never heard of Elliot Jordan. Still, he should not be hard to find if he ran with that crowd. And everyone knew Sir Peregrine, who was not just an extremely flamboyant dresser, but changed his lovers as often as most men changed their stockings.

"Why are you asking about these men—truly?"

"No reason," she lied. A sudden pattering sound on the glass gave her the distraction she was looking for. "Drat! It is raining." She stood, glad to get away from the duke's searching look.

"Sit and finish eating," he said. "I will fetch in the clothing."

Freddie was going to resist his autocratic command, but then decided he had just given her enough information that she could forgive him his high-handed behavior. Besides, she *was* hungry, so she sank back into her chair, her mind churning as to how she could pry more out of the duke without causing his antennae to twitch.

***

They finished the bottle of wine and watched as the rain became heavier.

"This looks to be settling in. It seems we will be stuck here for a while," Plimpton said.

Winifred checked their clothing and shook her head. "Your shirt is almost dry, but everything else is still wet."

He pushed up from his seat. "I will build a fire."

"Do you know how?"

Plimpton was amused despite himself. "You really do think I'm as helpless as a newborn babe, don't you? No, do not answer that," he said, making her laugh. "Yes, I know how to build a fire."

Five minutes later, when he was faced with a sullenly smoking heap of sticks and small logs, he turned to his audience of one and said, "You win. It seems I really am as helpless as a newborn babe, after all. You can do better?"

She rubbed her hands together. "Watch and learn from a master of the art," she said, her lofty look and tone making him smile.

She removed half the sticks and two of the logs and then took one of the newspapers from the stack he had used earlier and crumpled up a sheet before tucking it carefully beneath the rearranged kindling and wood.

"That is not fair," he said. "I did not know we were allowed to use newspaper."

She snickered. "Yes—that is rule number four in the fire-building handbook."

Plimpton deserved her mockery, but he refused to reward her by laughing.

A few strikes of the flint and the paper caught. Soon, there was a respectable blaze. She stood and turned, wearing a smug smile as she dusted off her hands.

She looked bloody adorable gloating, her hair in a bedraggled plait down her back, with enough loose hairs around her face to make her look like she wore a messy silver halo.

Plimpton stepped forward, until his gaudy robe touched her toga. Surprise replaced laughter and she gazed up at him, lips parted. "I lied to you, Winifred."

"You d-did?"

"Yes. I said that I would wait for you to come to me. But I am tired of waiting." He lowered his mouth over hers. There was only a second of stiffness before her body relaxed and she slid her arms around his neck as she had done the night before, once again leaning into the kiss, pressing her uncorsetted body against him.

Her eager, trusting response shot straight to his cock, which had been half-hard since the moment she had descended the stairs wearing her damned toga.

They picked up right where they had left off the night before. Her mouth moved against his with eager abandon, the tip of her tongue meeting his when he slid between her lush lips.

He dipped aggressively deep, and she responded by taking his tongue between her lips and sucking.

Plimpton groaned, his grasp on his self-control fraying like a badly worn rope. He explored her with less than his ordinary finesse, but then, this did not feel ordinary. *She* was not ordinary; nor was his reaction to her. He wanted her with a hunger that sent howling need roaring through his body, the flames of his desire flaring to life like the fire she had just built.

He pulled away slightly—before he lost the ability to think entirely—and met her heavy-lidded gaze. "Let us go upstairs."

As he had feared, the practical words brought her back to the moment. Her face, slack with arousal only a moment before, grew taut. "I need you to promise me something before I go upstairs with you."

Anything. Everything. You do not even need to ask. Whatever you want is yours.

"I will, if it is within my power to do so,' he answered.

"Promise you will not be seized by honorable remorse after we, er… Well, just *after*."

It was bloody hard to bite back his smile. He briefly wondered what she would do if he supplied his own word to describe what he wanted to do to her.

Wisely, he kept his mouth shut.

She continued to babble. "You must promise you will not be tiresome and insist on marrying to save my reputation."

"You want me to promise not to ask you to marry me?"

"Yes."

He considered her words a moment before slowly shaking his head. "As much as I want to go upstairs with you right now, I cannot promise I will not ask you to marry."

Plimpton saw a flicker of feminine satisfaction—pleasure that he had not given up so quickly or easily this time—in her eyes before she suppressed it. "Can you at least promise that you will not ask for a month?"

"Why? What happens in a month?" he asked, intrigued.

She gave a nervous laugh. "Nothing, I just want a—a reprieve."

"A reprieve," he repeated. "That brings to mind executions. I should feel insulted." Instead, he felt amused.

She raised a hand to his cheek, the gesture sweetly intimate. "It is not my intention to insult you. I just… Well, I want to enjoy today—*this*"—she stroked his face in demonstration—"without being made to feel guilty afterward." She inhaled deeply, as if gathering her strength. "I have remained chaste since my husband died. Mostly because I have never really been tempted, but also because I have always, always, always done the *right* thing. The *proper* thing. But I do not want to suppress the desire I feel for you, Plimpton. For once, I want to follow my heart like every other sophisticated *ton* widow. The man I married was chosen for me. *I* want to choose my lover."

Plimpton laid his hand over hers and pressed his cheek into her palm. "You are not like any other widow—*ton* or otherwise. Indeed, you are unlike any woman I have ever met, Winifred" He turned so that he could kiss the tender skin of her palm. "I cannot say how flattered I am that *I* am the man you have chosen. So, I will promise you that I will not ask you to marry me. For at least a month."

Her smile was slow and radiant. "Then…what are you waiting for? Take me upstairs, Your Grace."

Chapter 15

Freddie felt as if another woman had suddenly slipped on her skin and was using her body to carry out her most deeply buried fantasy.

Already she had behaved more openly and freely with the duke than she ever had with any man—or even most of her female friends—but now she was about to move far beyond anything she'd done in the past.

There was something about the duke's air of reserve that made her want to shake it, to cause a crack or fissure in his smooth veneer and then pry it open to see what was inside. He was just so…self-contained it was irresistible.

Never in her life had she felt that way about another person; it was…exciting.

The duke took her hand—as if he feared she might change her mind—and led her up the stairs.

When he would have turned into the room with the sheetless bed, she said, "No, not that one—this one."

He smoothly changed course, released her hand, and ushered her inside before closing the door behind him.

Freddie stood in the middle of the room; her fingers laced to keep them from fidgeting.

Plimpton took her face in both his hands, holding her gently but firmly while he kissed her, not deeply and hungrily as he had done downstairs, but slowly, as if she were an ice from Gunter's, something precious and delicious to be savored.

The kiss was unhurried and not a prelude to something else, but a celebration in its own right, as if they had all the time in the world to explore.

At the start of her marriage Freddie had enjoyed Sedgewick's kisses. But even back then—before everything between them had turned to dross—he had never taken his time like Plimpton was doing. The duke lured and enticed and coaxed her into pure sensuality like a pied piper of kisses.

She fell into an erotic rhythm, accepting when he gave, and giving when he took. Downstairs their tongues had jousted. This was more of a dance where both partners took turns leading. He taught her new steps, nipping at her lower lip and then soothing it with a light caress. He disarmed her with probing, gentle swipes of his tongue, until Fredie surrendered utterly, rational thought submitting to pure sensation.

"Winifred," he murmured, bringing her back to earth, reminding her that the man turning her knees to jelly was the stuffy—no, not stuffy, but *proper*—Duke of Plimpton.

"Yes?" she said in a thick voice that didn't sound like her.

"I want to see your hair free, darling."

A shudder of pleasure rippled through her at the endearment. Who would have guessed that such a stern man could sound so affectionate and tender?

"Please," he added, mistaking her dreaming musing for uncertainty. He stroked the wispy spirals at her temples, those bothersome tendrils that always escaped confinement, no matter how severely she restrained them.

He nuzzled her ear with his cold nose, the unexpected action making her laugh. "Are you mocking me," he murmured, his breath hot on her ear, his voice amused rather than offended.

"Your nose is cold—just like a dog's."

"But not wet and slobbery, I hope?"

Again, she laughed. Could this possibly be the dignified Duke of Plimpton teasing her? Freddie had never before laughed while engaging in erotic endeavors. She never would have believed it would feel so intimate and delightful.

"No. Not wet and slobbery," she assured him, lightly kissing the sharp line of his jaw.

"Take down your hair," he said again, nipping her earlobe sharply enough to draw a soft gasp from her.

Freddie reluctantly released his waist, which she had been massaging like a blissful, languorous cat and drew her thick plait of hair over her shoulder.

His rapt attention was both disconcerting and flattering, his pupils swollen and his lips slack with sensual expectation as if she were Salome in the midst of her infamous dance, rather than a rumpled woman garbed in a bedsheet who smelled of lake water.

Freddie nimbly unraveled the three thick strands and then gave her head a slight shake.

A low, entirely masculine sound of approval rumbled through him, and he carded his fingers into the heavy veil of hair and lifted a thick fistful over her shoulder, his taut expression softening as he combed his fingers through the riot of curls. "I never would have guessed it was so curly. It always looks so sleek…so smooth."

Always? Just how often had he studied her? The fact that he had noticed her hair, not once, but *always* was—

"Yes. I have noticed your hair. I have noticed everything about you, Winifred," he said, making her wonder if she'd spoken her thoughts aloud. "How could I not notice when you attract all the light in any room you occupy?" His hands moved from her hair to her throat and then her bare shoulders, his gaze tracking their journey the entire way. He plucked at where the sheet was bunched at her shoulder. "How do I take this off?"

Still reeling from his romantic words, Freddie reached up with hands that were not quite steady to where the twisted ends of the sheet met beneath her hair.

He set his hands around her wrists. "No, I see it now. I will do it." His lips began to lift up at the edges, not stopping until Freddie caught a flash of white—who would have believed the duke had teeth! "I need to prove to you that I am not utterly worthless when it comes to dressing and undressing."

Freddie laughed. "I am not sure that untying a simple knot will convince me of that."

"A man needs to start somewhere." He slid his hands beneath the heavy fall of her hair, parted the curtain in the middle and then drew the halves over her shoulders, so that the thick curls draped over each breast. Freddie suspected he had done that for her modesty, and she was, yet again, surprised at his consideration.

His fingers moved gently at her neck while he gazed ceilingward, his face assuming a look of extreme concentration. "*Hmmm*, yes...I think I might be able to do this..." The weight of the material loosened, and his eyes lowered to hers as he brought the ends of the sheet between them. "Success." He paused and lifted his eyebrows, as if seeking permission.

Freddie hesitated. Why was he giving her an opportunity to stop him? Was that what he wanted? Sedgewick had never once—

She firmly curtailed that line of thinking; her dead husband had no place here today.

Freddie wanted Plimpton, and that was more than enough reason to meet his gaze and nod her permission.

The sheet dropped soundlessly to the floor, puddling around her feet. The urge to cover her body with her hands was strong, but she *wanted* him to see her, even though tendrils of mortification were threatening to strangle her bold desire.

His eyes lowered slowly and so did hers. She appreciated, for once, her unruly curls which covered far more of her than the straight hair she had always coveted.

The duke hissed sharply at the sight of her nipples, which had hardened to points and thrust eagerly through the curls.

He lifted his hands, his movements as slow and measured as if he were approaching a shy woodland creature. His eyes lifted to hers, and when his palms, smooth and warm, slid around her small breasts, it was her turn to hiss in a breath. Her eyelids fluttered as he stroked the sensitive tips, sending shudder after shudder of pleasure straight to her womb.

Her curls fell away to expose her entirely as he caressed. "Exquisite," he muttered right before his hot, slick lips closed over the aching tip.

Freddie's knees threatened to give out and she clutched at his shoulders to steady herself, her head falling back and a moan slipping from her parted lips as he suckled first one nipple, and then the other, alternating between them until she shook with the effort of containing her cries.

He paused his torture only long enough to mutter something beneath his breath and push aside her hair entirely. Evidently pleased with the result, he resumed his sensual assault, his hands intensifying the already devastating campaign and stroking the sensitive undersides of her breasts while he sucked each nipple to hardness.

Freddie's fingers dug into his upper arms, the thick brocade that covered his hard biceps reminding her that she was naked while he still wore his banyan. It had been a long time since she had seen a male body, and she suspected the duke had a fine one beneath the ridiculous robe.

She tugged at the gaudy gold lapel. "Off," was all she could manage.

He lifted his mouth from the nipple he was tormenting, his lips glistening. "*Hmm?*" He sounded irritated at being pulled from his task.

"Take off your robe."

He gave a low growl, but his hands disappeared from her body and tugged open the sash. He shrugged his shoulders, sending the banyan to join the sheet.

Before Freddie could even sneak a peek at him, he took her hand and led her toward the bed. "Up you go," he ordered gruffly, taking her by the waist and lifting her with no apparent effort.

And then she got her first good look at her lover's body and groaned.

He appeared more muscular without clothing, his hips broader and his powerful thighs heavily thewed. They were the legs of a man who spent a good deal of time astride a horse, the tops of his thighs worn bare of hair from the friction of snug leather breeches.

His arousal jutted straight up from a tangle of light brown curls; the thick shaft wet with his desire. A thin trail of hair led from his groin up his flat, muscled belly to his chest where it grew into a light fleece that spread to encompass his small brown nipples.

His chest and abdomen suddenly shifted and flexed, and Freddie looked up to find that he was watching her. Her face scalded at being caught subjecting him to such intimate scrutiny.

Two warm fingers slid beneath her chin, and he lifted her face—which had dipped in embarrassment—until she was forced to meet his gaze. "You needn't be shy, Winifred; I like having your eyes on me. Lie back on the bed," he added more softly, gathering her hair and holding it out to the side while Freddie wordlessly complied.

His jaw flexed as he stared down at her. No curtain of curls shielded her this time and she squirmed to hide herself but suppressed the urge; he had not hidden from *her* inspection, had he?

His eyes darkened until they were black with a thin gray ring when they finally returned to her face. "I want to pleasure you with my mouth."

Her lips parted in shock as she struggled to accept that a proper man like the duke would engage in such blatantly carnal activity.

"Do you not know what I mean?" he asked, mistaking the reason for her hesitation.

"I know what you mean. I just—I just did not think that you would er, approve of—" she broke off and bit her lip, feeling rather stupid as his gaze changed from concerned to amused.

He joined her on the bed, caging her torso with his hands and knees, and then staring down at her, consuming her with his eyes. "Oh yes, Winifred, I most certainly *do* approve." And then he claimed her parted lips with a hot deep kiss that promised what was to come.

***

Plimpton wondered what it was about him that made Winifred expect such a staid, unimaginative lover. Was it because he was not handsome, but average and boring? Or perhaps his brother's accusation that Plimpton was cold and inhuman—which Simon usually shouted at him in times of anger—was widely shared?

But Winifred was not the only one laboring under misconceptions. Plimpton was more relieved than he could say that she had not shrunk from either his intimate touches or his unconventional suggestion. He had worried that Sedgewick had ruined her for sensual pleasure. But thus far she had exhibited no revulsion, only the mild embarrassment of a woman who had been without a lover for a very long time.

They kissed until the tension that had built in her slender form leaked away. As badly as he ached to taste her and make her writhe with bliss, it was difficult to relinquish her soft lips and eager tongue and begin kissing his way down her body.

Her breasts provided another sweet distraction, their peaks puckered like dark raspberries. He licked and nipped and suckled her until her back flexed and arched and her hands gripped his head to hold him where she wanted.

Smiling to himself, he resumed his erotic trek, enchanted when her fingers tightened, and she attempted to bring him back.

But Plimpton stayed firm in his intentions, only lingering at her navel to kiss the gentle swell of her belly before moving on to the dark blonde curls that concealed his ultimate destination.

He nudged her thighs apart, drinking in the sight of her flushed, trembling body as he spread her legs, easily overcoming her shy resistance and not stopping until she was exposed and vulnerable.

She shifted uncomfortably beneath his gaze.

"You do not like me to look at you?" he asked, stroking a hand up one thigh, firmly caressing the taut muscle and tracing it up to the prominent tendon that pointed the way to her mons.

"It makes me feel immodest and wanton."

"Good."

She gave a startled burst of laughter and then cut a direct look at his hips and said tartly, "I can see you do not suffer from the same reservations."

Plimpton glanced down at his thrusting, leaking cock and laughed. "No, you are right about that."

"You should laugh and smile more; it suits you."

"Does it?" he teased, stroking a finger over the seam of her netherlips, the outline of which was visible beneath her pale private hair.

Over and over, he caressed, pressing a little harder each time, until he breached her puffy lips and slicked the pad of his finger.

She groaned and lifted her hips when he paused his caressing.

"I will smile more if you make that sound more," he promised.

She gave a breathy gurgle of laughter that turned into another, raspier, gasp after his next stroke.

"You are so wet," he marveled, caressing her with two fingers, parting the lips of her pussy to expose the engorged, slick nub. "My God." Plimpton positioned his torso between her thighs with more haste than grace and lowered his mouth over her.

A soft, choked cry broke from her and her hips lifted for more as he licked from her tight entrance to her swollen bud with rhythmic firm strokes. Only when her fingers slid into his hair and she gently but firmly pulled him higher, did he chuckle and suck the tiny bundle of nerves between his lips, giving her what she needed.

***

Freddie's climax built slowly and inexorably like an avalanche as the duke teased and tormented her toward the brink of orgasm, his lips and tongue surely the instruments of the devil.

Even in the midst of her bliss she could not help being amused that it was not the thought of herself splayed, hips bucking, and hands buried in his hair that caused her face to scald. No, shameless hussy that she was, her wanton behavior drew no blushes. Instead, it was the sounds the duke made as he feasted on her with abandoned carnality.

Sedgewick at his best had been enthusiastic but always in a hurry. The duke not only reveled in his possession of her, but he appeared content to spend the entire day where he was, teasing her to the edge of her climax and then—maddeningly—drifting away just at the crucial moment.

The first time he brought her to the brink and then shifted his attention, she thought he had miscalculated and gently brought him back. The third time it happened she knew he was toying with her. And judging by the way his lips curved against her sensitive flesh, he was enjoying himself greatly.

Freddie tightened her fingers in his hair the next time he played his trick and angled his head enough that their eyes met. "Your Grace," she said, forcing the words through gritted teeth.

"*Hmm*?" His shoulders shook slightly and Freddie realized the unrepentant tease was *laughing*.

"You are being…unkind, Plimpton."

This time, he didn't bother to hide his laughter. He fixed her with an innocent look that did not convince her for a moment, and released her with a leisurely lick before saying, "Am I?"

"You know you are."

"I beg your pardon—perhaps *this* was what you wanted?" He lowered his mouth.

Freddie cried out, her head tipping back and her eyes sliding shut. "Yes," she breathed as he gave her *exactly* what she needed. "Yes…*yes, that*!"

This time when she careened toward her climax, instead of abandoning her, he eased two fingers inside her, pumping her with firm, deep strokes as the wave crested and finally broke.

"Yes!" she shouted as she arched off the bed, every muscle in her body locked as she trembled with the force of her orgasm.

***

Winifred was just full of surprises. An Ice Countess? More like a *fire* countess.

Plimpton eased his fingers from her tight sheath and gave her swollen bud a last kiss before rising up on his knees to survey what he had wrought. Not only were her cheeks flushed, but the skin on her chest was passion mottled and a pink stain lightly dusted her belly. She was sleek, delicate perfection, surrounded by a froth of pale blonde curls, her eyes heavy lidded and her expression of slack satiation making her already beautiful face stunning.

Her lips curved slightly as she met his gaze, and he was thrilled beyond words that she appeared to be reveling in her sensuality rather than regretting it.

She raised her hands to him and then—to his delight—she spread her thighs wider, the invitation unmistakable.

Plimpton's balls clenched hard with the force of his need, causing his cock to jerk and drool even more profusely.

Her lazy smile grew into a grin.

"You are enjoying watching me suffer, are you?"

"Yes," she admitted without hesitation.

He barked a laugh, but it quickly turned to a hiss when her hand closed around his shaft and she squeezed him, her deft fingers milking the pre-ejaculate from his slit with a confident dexterity that would have brought him to his knees had he not already been there.

"You are not the only one who knows some tricks, Your Grace."

"So it would seem," he said tightly, having to force the words through clenched jaws as she thumbed a spot beneath his crown that turned him into witless fool. He closed his eyes and pushed his hips closer, not that she needed any direction from him. Her slender hand worked him with firm strokes, her fingers tightening to near painfulness as she pumped him toward climax. He wanted to stop—to pull away—but it felt too damned good.

The orgasm built slowly, her stroking slow enough that he could savor the sensation, but fast enough that this interlude would end far too soon.

He was still trying to salvage the will to stop her, when she stopped herself.

His head felt as if it were full of lead and it took him far longer than it should have to open his eyes and gather his wits.

She was smirking up at him. "What is sauce for the goose…"

Ah. So that was her game.

"I do not think so, darling." He plucked her hand from his shaft and pinned her wrists to the bed beside her head while he lowered his hips.

"You teased me. This is not fair," she pouted.

The Etiquette of Love

"I never said I would fight fair." He prodded the head of his cock against her hot wet flesh, spreading her thighs wider with his knees. She shuddered, her hips canting to take him. The silent, eager gesture of submission sent a blinding wave of lust through him, and he filled her with a hard, deep thrust, not stopping until he was fully hilted.

She whimpered at the sudden stretch, catching her lower lip with her teeth as she slowly stretched to accommodate him. And then her eyes opened the merest slit and she raised her hips to take him even deeper, her inner muscles contracting so tightly his eyes threatened to roll back in their sockets.

Bloody hell. This woman could very well kill him.

And Plimpton might welcome such a death.

***

We fit together like a lock and key.

Freddie was embarrassed by the thought, but only because she had described the perfection of the feeling in such cliched terms. Truthfully, she was too steeped in bliss to think of anything better. And who cared what words she used? It was the *feeling* that mattered. And the feeling was glorious.

He withdrew slowly and then filled her up again with a savage thrust.

"I beg your pardon," he said in a tight voice, misreading her gasp of pleasure for something else. "Are you—"

"Perfect," was all she could manage. Judging by the heat that flared in his gaze, that was exactly the right answer.

Again, he withdrew, but rather than sink back in, he pulsed his hips, his thick crown teasing her entrance as he stared down into her eyes, questions lurking at the edges of his desire.

"What is it?" she asked.

"As this is your first foray into, er, illicit pleasure—"

"I cannot get pregnant."

He eyed her pensively and then asked, "Are you certain?"

"Sedgewick's first wife was pregnant four times; I never conceived."

He hesitated, and then opened his mouth, no doubt to point out the obvious—that perhaps Sedgewick's first wife had been prepared to slip cuckoos into her husband's nest—but Freddie did not want to go over the painful subject of her infertility. Not ever. But certainly not *now*.

She lifted her hips, forcing him deeper, and tightened her inner muscles.

He groaned and his eyelids fluttered, as if he were struggling to resist.

Freddie rolled her hips and Plimpton surrendered with a guttural grunt, sinking deep, until she was almost uncomfortably filled and stretched.

He stayed that way, holding her pinioned with both his brooding gaze and rigid arousal.

"I cannot get deep enough," he said in a strained voice, his shaft flexing inside her.

Something about that subtle movement struck Freddie vividly: there was a man inside her body.

It was silly to be startled by something so obvious, but the erotic thought caused every muscle in her body to tighten.

Plimpton groaned. "Good God," he muttered, his hips beginning to move with agonizing slowness.

"Please…Plimpton," she entreated hoarsely, the need to be taken hard and fast turning her into to a pleading, wanton wreck.

He smirked, clearly pleased and amused by her begging. But his tight jaw and flared nostrils told her she was not the only one barely clinging to control.

"You want more, *hmm*?"

"Yes, please."

The Etiquette of Love

His pupils flared, telling her he liked her prim response, and his hips moved faster, his strokes deeper and harder as he fell into a rhythm that gave her every inch.

Freddie tugged at her wrists, which were still imprisoned in his grasp.

He raised one haughty eyebrow, his hips unfaltering as he filled her smoothly and completely, again and again and again.

"I want to touch you," she whispered, her face flaming at her own boldness.

Holding her gaze, he deliberately released one hand and then the other.

Freddie eagerly raised her fingers to the hard, corded skin of his waist, resting her palms lightly on the fascinating muscles which tightened and lengthened with each graceful thrust.

His eyelids lowered in an expression of animal bliss as she slid her hands around his pumping hips and cupped a taut buttock in each hand. She had felt him the night before, but there had been clothing between them. Who would have guessed they could feel even better—satiny smooth and warm and hard—against her bare palms? She squeezed, digging her fingers into the flexing striations.

"That feels good," he praised, lowering his torso onto one elbow and then sliding a hand between their bodies, the soft pad of his finger unerringly locating her clitoris. Freddie had been too sensitive only moments earlier, but now she welcomed his touch.

"Come with me this time, Winifred," he said in a tight voice, his hips pumping harder and deeper as his slick finger commenced the same magic as before, but without teasing her this time.

Freddie explored from his tantalizing bottom over his tight waist to his flared back, and upper arms. She wrapped her hands—or at least tried to—around his biceps as he worked them both toward bliss.

His hips began to jerk, the rhythm breaking. "Are you close?" he asked in a breathy, strained voice.

Freddie spread her thighs wider, offering herself up to him in answer.

He groaned and his hips began to drum, the fierce thrusts increasingly uncontrolled.

"Yes," she moaned as she exploded, convulsing around his pulsing length as he buried himself to the hilt, the hot rush of his orgasm causing an answering burst of pleasure in her own body. Her contractions seemed to multiply, the orgasm lasting far longer than the first.

A slight tremor shook his arms before he lowered his body over hers. Freddie held him close as his spasms became less violent, the time between each paroxysm increasing until he relaxed with a sigh. He was hot, heavy, and smelled of clean male sweat with the lingering aroma of lake water in his messy hair.

He came back from his small death quickly and she felt awareness invade his body. Rather than leave her, he gently rolled them both onto their sides, keeping their bodies joined.

"There, now you can breathe," he said in a voice already thick with sleep.

Freddie smiled at this very male reaction to ejaculation. She did not want to talk—nothing good could come of it, that was certain—so she snuggled into his arms and laid her head on his biceps. "I need to rest," she lied.

"Very well," he said, the second word made unrecognizable by a huge yawn. "Just for a moment." He had barely finished speaking before his muscles relaxed and his breathing deepened.

Men. How could they possibly fall sleep at a time like this?

That was the last thought Freddie had before warm, velvety blackness claimed her.

***

Plimpton felt so good that he struggled against awakening. This dream was delicious… His cock was hard and pulsing and it was currently lodged somewhere hot, wet, and tight.

Something soft and warm moved beside him and he forced his eyelids open. Curls—beautiful and ash blonde—clouded his vision. He lifted one hand and carefully moved them aside. Winifred was cuddled against him, her soft breasts plastered against his chest, her head on his upper arm—which had fallen asleep—and best of all, one slender leg was draped over his hip, a pose which kept his cock deeply snugged inside her.

The erection which had woken him pulsed happily at the realization that it had not been a dream at all. Plimpton could not resist flexing inside her, but the rest of his body remained unmoving so that he did not wake her.

But she stirred in any case, her head rolling slightly to the side and her drowsy silver eyes meeting his. And then her full, coral lips curved into a smile. "Did we sleep long?"

"I'm not sure; I woke only a few seconds before you." He glanced at the window. Rain still pattered softly on the glass, and it was light outside, although muted. "It could be any time of day out there." He looked down at her, sliding his free hand around her waist and pulling her even closer, until she gave a soft grunt of pleasure, her smile growing when he pulsed his hips. "Are you too sore to take me again?"

She gave a sleepy chuckle. "Strictly speaking, I never *stopped* taking you, Your Grace."

"*Mmm*," he murmured, pulling her closer to claim a kiss. "I am going to take that as permission to indulge."

She did some flexing of her own to demonstrate her approval.

Plimpton cupped her thigh and pulled her tighter to his body, fucking her with shallow, teasing thrusts.

She brought her fingers to his lips, tracing the smile he hadn't known he was wearing.

"Do I really smile so rarely?" he asked, not pausing his gentle stroking.

"I cannot recall you doing so until today."

"It is all your fault," he accused.

"I can accept the blame for that—*ungh*." Her eyelids fluttered when he when altered his thrusting so that he lightly grazed the apex of her sex.

"Do you like it like this? Or do you want it harder?" he asked in a tight voice, amazed that he could be so close to ejaculating again.

She nodded and murmured, "*Mmm.*"

Plimpton smiled at her non-answer. Her hair was a tangled blonde cloud and there was a sleep line on her cheek from the bedding that had become trapped between her face and his arm, but he thought she had never appeared more lovely.

Potent affection surged through him, immediately followed by raw fear and gut-wrenching powerlessness. All three emotions were rare and unfamiliar, but the last one was especially unwelcome. In the past, powerlessness had always followed profoundly unpleasant occasions—like his wedding night or his children's illnesses—those times in his life when nothing good had happened.

It worried him that he was feeling it now with Winifred.

He drew her close enough that she could not see his face and read his thoughts. She was pliant in his arms, her leg tightening around him, as if to bring him more deeply inside her.

And still Plimpton needed *more*. He rolled her onto her back, once again pinning her hands to the bed as he drove into her willing body *hard*, working her with savage thrusts. The harder he fucked her, the more sinuously she writhed beneath him, taking everything he gave her and opening herself for more, inviting him into her body as deeply as he could go.

"Look at me," he ordered in a harsh voice, primitive satisfaction flooding him when her eyes flew open; at least there was one way in which he could command her obedience.

Plimpton stared into her longer and harder than he had ever looked at anyone in his life. Even now, in her passion, there were walls he could not scale or see beyond, barriers she had erected to keep out the likes of him.

Having her today would not purge her from his system, it would only work her deeper, like a sliver that became buried in one's flesh the more one worried at it. Wanting her had settled into his blood like a low-grade fever, and he feared it would only become worse in the days and weeks to come.

The Etiquette of Love

But at least I can make her feel this much, he thought as her orgasm overtook her and her eyes grew wide and unguarded in her passion.

Mercifully, his own climax broke and physical bliss washed away the tangle of unwanted emotions.

Chapter 16

Freddie had barely recovered from the ferocity of Plimpton's lovemaking when he slowly withdrew from her body and rolled away from her, his feet hitting the floor with two soft thuds.

He bent to pick up his robe and slipped into it, tying the sash in a few deft motions, and then strode out of the room.

Her forehead furrowed at his sudden departure. Had she done something wrong? He had looked even more intense than usual as he had driven them both to pleasure. Was he...angry? Disgusted?

Or was this normal behavior after having carnal relations with a lover?

On the good nights, Sedgewick had passed out for a few moments after his orgasm and then bid her goodnight once he'd roused himself and returned to his chambers.

Perhaps this was the equivalent?

She told herself not to feel hurt by what felt like abandonment. After all, she was the one who continued to insist upon—

"Roll onto your back."

She jolted at the sound of his voice. "I did not hear you return," she said stupidly, her body obeying his quiet command.

He knelt on the bed and reached for the sheet she had just pulled up to her breasts.

When she clenched the bedding more tightly, he lifted a cloth for her to see. "I brought this to cleanse you, Winifred."

"Oh." She stared, startled by what was an unprecedented action in her experience. "Er, I can—"

"Let me," he said quietly. Gone was her smiling lover, in his place was the stern, inscrutable aristocrat.

The Etiquette of Love

It embarrassed her to think of him doing something so intimate, but she found herself releasing her vise-like grip on the sheet and opening her legs.

For a man who had been attended by body servants all his life, he was remarkably thorough and gentle. His expression was not lascivious, but...caring.

"There," he said when he had finished, looking up to meet her eyes. "I would draw you a bath, but—incompetent that I am—I have no idea how one goes about heating that much water."

Freddie laughed, relieved that the hard set of his mouth had softened, taking away some of the severity. "It would take too much time and we should probably be on our way."

"Yes, it is barely raining now. I will go downstairs and fetch your clothing. There is more water—cold, unfortunately—in that ewer." He gestured toward the dresser and pushed off the bed.

Freddie waited until he'd padded from the room and then hurriedly tied the sheet around her, although this time it was just hastily draped rather than fashioned into a Grecian garment.

A quick search of the dressing table drawers unearthed a fine ivory comb and brush set. She had no hope of getting all the knots out of her hair, but at least she was able to tame it enough that she could split it into three sections and plait it.

Once she had secured the end with a faded ribbon she'd found beside the brush, she wound the thick rope into a coronet and used a handful of rusty pins to fasten it into place.

She took a step back and grimaced at her reflection; she looked like a woman who'd fallen in a lake, swum for a quarter of an hour, and then engaged in two rounds of vigorous bed sport.

Footsteps on the stairs—booted ones this time—made her turn.

She laughed and then bit her lip.

He gave her a mock chastising look. "Are you making fun of my clothing?"

"Just your shirt," she said, and then chortled again at his bedraggled neckcloth and badly wrinkled sleeves. "And your cravat."

She glanced at his boots, which were now dull and misshapen. "But I cannot laugh at your boots. They were lovely and now they are ruined."

He shrugged.

"Were they easy to get on?"

"Yes, but only because they are still damp."

"Where are my things?"

"I left them in front of the fire as everything is still a little damp." He smiled wryly. "I found a kettle, figured out how to fill it with water, and have miraculously set it to boil. I thought we might have tea. By the time we are done, your things should be close to dry."

"I would love some tea. But first let me repair my toga." She made a shooing gesture. "I will be down in a moment."

Once she'd tidied her *gown* and smoothed down the worst of the corkscrews of hair with a damp comb, she decided that was as good as it would get and descended the stairs.

"You are just in time," he said, gesturing to the teapot and cannister of tea he must have found in the kitchen. "The water is boiling. Tell me, do I put the water or tea in first?"

"Shame on you, Your Grace!" she scolded. "It is always tea and *then* water."

He gave her a meek look she did not believe for a moment. "Consider me suitably chastened."

As the tea steeped, she examined the tray he had loaded and brought from the tiny kitchen. She picked up a cleaver and held it aloft. "What, pray, is this for?"

He gave her a sheepish look. "I thought I would just put some of everything on the tray."

She laughed and shook her head. "Sit and relax and I will perform the time-honored ritual. How do you like it?"

"Black and strong."

Once the tea had steeped enough for her, she poured a cup, added a lump of sugar, and set the pot aside to steep a bit more. An optimistic feeling had been building inside her ever since he had returned to the bedchamber with the cloth. Perhaps it really *was* possible to engage in an affair without a man becoming tiresome? Perhaps she *could* trust Plimpton not to become high-handed and dictatorial.

Perhaps you might actually ask him a few more questions about that fateful weekend...

Freddie glanced up to find him regarding her with a thoughtful, but relaxed, expression.

Maybe now *was* a good time?

"What is it?" he asked. "Do I have something on my face?" He squinted down at his hands, which she saw had smudges from the kettle.

For some reason, it was that normal—rather than ducal—reaction which decided her.

"I want to ask you something."

He immediately looked wary. "Yes?"

"You must give me your word you will not pry into why I am asking."

He crossed his arms, the gesture pulling the badly wrinkled, shrunken vest until the buttons strained. How was he able not only to look *good*, but positively delicious?

"What is this about, Winifred?"

Her gaze jerked up at his clipped question and she saw that his eyebrows, which were a few shades darker than his light brown hair, had drawn down over the bridge of his nose, forming a stern V.

"It is not a personal question about you, Your Grace. I just want your opinion on something."

His eyebrows slowly returned to their normal position, but the tension did not leave his shoulders. "Very well, I will not pry."

She poured a bit of tea, saw that it was dark enough, and filled the cup before handing it to him.

"Thank you."

She nodded absently, wondering how to phrase her question. Direct was probably best. "My question is about that party Wareham had the week my brother Piers disappeared." As Freddie looked into his eyes, she could practically hear doors and shutters slamming shut.

"What about it?" he asked in the most unencouraging tone imaginable.

"Do you recall anything strange about that week? Aside from the murder," she hastily added.

"Why?"

Freddie flung up her hands. "You just *promised* that you would not pry!"

"That was hardly *prying*. I am just...wondering."

"Well, don't wonder."

His jaw flexed as he regarded her, his eyes once again opaque. He inhaled deeply, held it, and then exhaled before saying, "I am afraid that the murder wiped everything else that occurred from my memory."

Fair enough. "And can you recall any people other than the ones you told me about earlier?"

"I do not recall who I named earlier."

"Sutton, Weil, Fluke, Jordan, Conrad, Brandon, Wareham, Piers, you, and Meecham."

His forehead creased at her rapid-fire listing.

"Nobody else?" she prodded.

He stared at her for a long, uncomfortable moment. "Those are the only ones I can remember. If you want a more comprehensive list, ask Wareham."

So, that was it, then. It was crystal clear that Freddie would get nothing more from the duke.

"Thank you." She drained the rest of her tea and began to put the dirty crockery onto the tray.

His hand closed over hers. "You should not be poking around in this, Winifred."

The Etiquette of Love

"I do not know what you mean."

"You are a terrible liar—which is to your credit, by the way—but you needn't have bothered. Wareham told me last night that Piers returned a year ago and has come back again. I also know he is masquerading as your friend Gregg." He smiled, but it was not one of amusement. "I thought there was nothing more irksome than believing Gregg to be your paramour. It seems I was wrong."

She jerked her hand away. "If you knew all that, then why did you ask?"

"I was hoping it was not true."

"You were hoping that my brother had not come to visit me?"

"Yes. You must know that associating with a murderer—"

"An *accused* murderer."

His jaw flexed. "If you are caught associating with a *fugitive* accused of murder you will go to gaol, Winifred. I would have hoped Cantrell would have more regard for your safety and future than to rope you into some hairbrained investi—"

"Hairbrained? Just what do you mean by that? Is he not allowed to prove his innocence?"

He winced at her raised voice, which just made her angrier.

"Oh, you do not care for being shouted at?" she shouted.

"No, I do not."

"Well, I do not care to be chided by somebody with no right to do so, but it seems I have no choice in the matter. For your information, Your Grace, Piers did not *rope* me into anything. In fact, he specifically begged me not to become involved."

"And yet here you are, prying into the matter with as much finesse as a bull in rut. I am at least glad to see that Cantrell's wishes have as little bearing on your behavior as anyone else's."

Her hand closed around the empty cup in front of her.

The duke saw the gesture and shook his head. "If you throw that at me, I will put you over my knee."

Freddie was almost as furious at herself for the idiotic squeak she made as she was at him for threatening her.

She lunged to her feet, drawing herself up to her full height, desperately wishing she was not wearing a bedsheet.

The duke, naturally, stood, robbing her of even the slight advantage of glaring down at him.

"If you expect me to feel guilty for looking into what is obviously a gross miscarriage of justice involving somebody I dearly love, then I am pleased to disappoint you."

"A gross miscarriage of justice? You mean the fact that Piers Cantrell escaped the noose? Because you are certainly right about that."

"You—you—"

"Yes, what am I?"

"I am too polite to say it," she snapped. "You were probably right there with everyone else accusing him, weren't you?"

He leaned forward, his eyes narrowing. "For your information, I was *right there* when it came to helping him escape England and, by extension, justice. And that, Winifred, is something I have regretted ever since."

All the angry, hurtful words she wanted to fling at him got jammed up together inside her head, which felt as if it might actually burst into flames, she was so furious.

"You were not there," he went on, his voice as cool as ever even though sparks lit up his gray eyes. "You do not understand the full extent of the evidence against Cantrell," he said, clearly warming to his subject, his face hard and unforgiving.

"What evidence? You mean Piers waking up in a ditch with a bloody knife? It might have been anyone's knife—and anyone's blood, including that of a farm animal. Piers said he never lost consciousness from drink either before that time, or since. It seems to me, Your Grace, that my brother was drugged and the only evidence of him fighting with Meecham was the word of a servant who—"

"*I* heard the argument, Winifred."

The Etiquette of Love

She blinked. "But—"

"Meecham and your brother had been behaving like a pair of villains in a bad pantomime from the moment they appeared at Torrance Park, alternately celebrating their good fortune and squabbing over how to divvy up their ill-gotten gains. It was a boiling pot just waiting to spill over. And it *did* spill over when Wareham informed Cantrell that the pieces had been stolen from Devonshire's collection. He told your precious Piers not to even *think* about selling so much as one piece because he would be returning them to the duke. Cantrell stormed away in a rage, his parting words some rubbish about the doctrine of treasure trove and how it belonged to him and him alone and that he would neither hand it over to Devonshire nor share the profits with Meecham. Wareham wanted to go after him that night and retrieve the pieces immediately. I have always regretted that I talked him out of it, counseling him to wait until Cantrell's blood had cooled and he sobered up."

Plimpton gazed into the past, his expression of guilt unmistakable. "If I had gone with Wareham that night, we might have thrashed the damned chess set out of the pair of them and they'd have woken up the next day with nothing more than sore heads and a few bruises. As it was, I told Wareham that I would follow Piers home to make sure he came to no harm. I overheard him argue with Meecham, the two of them obviously drunk. I believed they would both pass out sooner rather than later, so I left them after warning the servant to keep an eye on them. You have no idea how often I wish I had stayed there, Winifred. But there is no doubt in my mind that Cantrell fought with Meecham and then killed him, although I suspect it was accidental rather than intentional. Unfortunately, Piers did not remember anything that happened that night, so we will never know."

The fear that Plimpton might be right only added to Freddie's anger.

She shoved away her chair, knocking it over in her haste to get away from both the duke and what very well might be the truth.

"You are *wrong*! I know you are."

"Don't you think that I would *like* to be wrong, Winifred? Don't you think I have not seen how this has weighed on my best friend's

"A lack of imagination?" he retorted coolly, and then ruined a splendid set-down by saying, "I apologize. That was rude, combative and unhelpful."

This was less satisfying than arguing with oneself.

Freddie shoved the tea tray across the table with a loud clatter. "I was going to tidy our mess, but you should continue on your journey of self-discovery and add washing crockery to your list of exciting exploits." She turned on her heel and snatched her clothing off the chair backs where he'd considerately set them to dry. In her haste, she yanked one of the chairs over and it struck her toe.

"Damnation!" she yelped, hopping inelegantly on one foot.

The duke approached her, immediately solicitous. "Here. Let me have a look," he said, dropping into a crouch and reaching for her foot.

Freddie glared down at him. "Do not touch me," she hissed, pleased when he recoiled. She snatched up her boots and stockings and stormed up the stairs.

For good measure, she slammed the bedroom door.

***

Wareham put down his coffee cup, a frown marring his high forehead. "I wish you were not leaving tomorrow, Winny."

Freddie was eating breakfast with her brother, who—with Doctor Madsen's approval—had joined her in the breakfast room for his first meal that was not broth or scrambled eggs.

"I should have left today—or even yesterday—when it was clear you no longer needed constant nursing. Or much nursing at all, really."

"I could have a relapse."

She laughed. "You will not relapse. Doctor Madsen said your recovery is so astonishing he is considering writing a medical article about you."

"That is because of your care, Winny. If you leave—"

"You will be fine. And Jane and Bessy have learned all I have to teach on the subject of nursing. I have already been here longer than I conscience over the years? Eating away at him, a constant source of shame and doubt?"

His tone was weary rather than hostile and that, more than anything, was persuasive.

Good God! What if he was right? After all, Piers had said the sa[me] thing, hadn't he? Perhaps she had judged Wareham unfairly all these years? Maybe he really had saved Piers's life by getting him out of the country.

Thankfully, the duke opened his mouth and stopped Freddie before she could admit her traitorous doubts. "Cantrell should have stayed away, and he deserves whatever happens to him for coming back. Wareham went to considerable expense and effort to stop any investigation into the matter and the man has waltzed back to Englan[d] stirring up trouble. Yet again."

"I suppose you think Sophia did the right thing telling the constable that Piers had returned? Beckam told you that, too, didn't he?"

"Yes, he told me that last night, as well. Of course I do not agre[e] with what Lady Wareham did. Your brother forbade her to speak of [the] matter and that should have been enough to stay her tongue."

She gave a bitter laugh. "Oh. I see. It was not wrong of her because it was morally reprehensible, vindictive, and petty, but beca[use] she disobeyed her lord and master."

He gave her an exasperated look. "If one cannot trust one's spouse, then who *can* one trust?"

The question stopped Freddie like a stone wall. And it only enraged her more because she happened to agree with him. It took [a] great deal of effort to muster a sneer. "What a shame that duty do[es] run in both directions and not just from a husband to his wife."

"Of course, it works both ways."

The man was almost impossible to argue with! "Why do I fi[nd it] so hard to believe?"

should have stayed away. I have a life—I have things that need to be done."

He sighed, reached across the table, and took her hand. "I am only teasing you; I hope you know that. I just don't like to see you leave after we have just patched up our differences." He cocked his head. "We *have* patched them up, haven't we?"

"As far as I am concerned, we have."

"Excellent. Then you will—"

"I will not move under your roof, nor will I accept your money, Dicky. Please," she said when he opened his mouth to argue. "Let us enjoy this last day without arguing."

He compressed his lips and nodded. "Very well. You win—this time. But I will not stop offering."

"And that is your right," she said, spreading marmalade on a piece of bread and eying the chafing dishes, contemplating having a bit more of the coddled eggs.

"Winny?"

"*Hmm?*" she said, savoring the rich flavor of the marmalade, which was made from oranges from Wareham's own succession house.

"Have you and Plimpton had a falling out?"

Her gaze slid back to her brother. "Falling out? How could we, when we never had an, er, falling *in*."

He smiled briefly at her attempt at humor. "You have not gone riding with him since the day you were caught out by the rain. And then you suddenly decided to have dinner with me in my chambers—which I have greatly enjoyed, of course—rather than eating with him in the dining room. As for cards, you have played piquet with me every evening, ignoring poor Plimpton entirely."

"I came here to see *you* Dicky, not the duke."

"True, but I thought—"

"I know what you thought. And that is the main reason I have curtailed my activities with him. When will you understand that I do not want a husband, Dicky? You and I will have a *falling out* if you continue to throw every unmarried man in the vicinity at my head."

"I promise I will not do that. But Plimpton is not *every* man, Winny. Would just anyone have brought you to me? Not only that, but he was steadfast in making sure I had a doctor who wouldn't kill me. Plimpton is a man in a thousand—five thousand, even—honorable and generous and—"

"Wareham, *stop.*"

He lifted his hands in surrender. "I want you to know it pains me deeply to see two people who are perfect for each other and one of them refuses to accept the wisdom of such a match."

"Duly noted," she said. "Now, might we speak of my nephews and nieces? If you are well enough, why don't we see if they can come by this evening?"

But as her brother chatted with her—and eagerly endorsed her plan for an evening of adolescent games and performances on the pianoforte for her nieces—Freddie's willful mind went back to the man she had just told Dicky not to mention.

The days since the boathouse incident had been awkward, to say the least. But she had to commend Plimpton for making his presence scarce when she and Wareham were together. At least that way her brother could not embarrass them by constantly attempting to throw them together.

She doubted Wareham had curtailed his schemes when talking to the duke any more than he had when speaking to her, but at least she didn't have to be with Plimpton while she endured it.

She would have left two days ago if not for the fact that Dicky's coach had *still* not returned and the last thing she wanted was to accept another favor from Plimpton.

That afternoon by the lake had been delightful—at least the first three-quarters—but it had been the last half hour that had sealed their fate. Freddie could never care for a man who would condemn her beloved brother without even considering the possibility that he was innocent.

As much as she had enjoyed her liaison with him, it was all they would ever have.

And if the thought of never spending time with him again caused a heavy ache in her chest she would get over it by soldiering grimly onward. The same way she got through everything painful in her life.

Chapter 17

"Married?" Freddie repeated rather stupidly.

Lori grinned gleefully. "Yes, married." She held out her hand, which sported a plain gold band on her fourth finger. "You see before you Viscountess Severn."

Freddie could only stare.

Lori did not appear to notice her stupefaction and babbled happily. "I am sorry I did not invite you to the wedding, Freddie, but it was a very small one. In fact, it was just Severn, me, and my brother and his family."

Finally, Freddie collected enough of her scattered wits to say, "I am so happy for you, Lori." She took the other woman's hands and gave them a gentle squeeze. "I need not ask if you are happy as you are positively glowing. *And* stylish." She took in Lori's stunning peacock blue carriage ensemble.

Lori grinned. "Thank you. And no, I did not choose it. It is Severn's doing."

"Ah…So, it was the viscount who was your secret admirer and bought you those other lovely gowns."

Lori laughed. "*Secret admirer.* What a quaint term. I like it. And yes, my husband has far better taste in clothing than I will ever have. He purchased a few items for me himself, but he has commanded me to fill my massive dressing room at Severn House without delay."

It was Freddie's turn to laugh. "Why do I find it difficult to imagine you obeying any man's command?"

"I have become wiser already. I have learned that by *seeming* to comply without a struggle one can usually then do what one wants."

Freddie pursed her lips and shook her head. "I predict stormy times ahead for poor Lord Severn."

"It is what he likes best," Lori assured her, making her laugh again. "As for shopping and spending great piles of his money, that is not a difficult command to obey." Her expression turned anxious. "At least not if you will assist me? If you don't help me, you know I will end up with a dismal wardrobe."

"It would be my pleasure," she said, speaking the truth. Freddie had itched to see the other woman wearing flattering clothing for *years*.

"Excellent! When are you free?"

Freddie went to fetch her appointment book. Tomorrow she and Piers were going to the British Museum to talk with one of the curators about the chess pieces. Because it had been Freddie's idea her brother had—grudgingly—agreed to allow her to go along.

"But only to see this museum bloke," Piers had warned. "Do not take it into your head to play sleuth and pursue the killer on your own, Little Bird."

"Freddie?"

She looked up from her calendar at her friend's voice and smiled. "The day after tomorrow I can put myself solely at your disposal."

"Lovely." Lori's joyous expression turned speculative. "I don't mean to pry—" she broke off and frowned at Freddie's disbelieving laugh. "Very well. So I *do* mean to pry. I was worried when you disappeared for more than a week and neither Mrs. Brinkley nor anyone else knew where you'd gone." A notch of concern settled between her glorious green eyes. "Did something happen?"

"How dramatic you are," Freddie chided. "I went to Brighton for a bit of relaxation." She had no earthy idea why she lied about going to see Wareham, the words just came tumbling out. Lying, it seemed, could easily become a habit.

"Oh. What did you—no, I will not pry. I am just pleased to hear you took time for yourself, although perhaps the next time you should tell Mrs. Brinkley as I worried—and I'm sure the others wondered why your letters had stopped so suddenly, too."

"You are correct. I will leave word should I ever do something so impulsive again."

The Etiquette of Love

"It is the first time I can think of—other than the few afternoons every month when you disappear to who knows where for a few hours." She paused, her expression turning hopeful "As you have confided the truth about your impromptu holiday, perhaps you might enlighten me as to what you do on those days." Her forehead furrowed. "Always Wednesdays now that I think of it."

"I cannot confess all my secrets or I will become quite boring."

Lori found that amusing. "What a polite way to tell me to mind my own business."

"What are you and Lord Severn going to do this summer? Surely you will not stay in town?" Freddie asked, changing the subject while she could.

Lori grimaced. "We are going to stay with his grandfather at Granton Castle. Have you ever been there?"

"Actually, I have not. But I have read about it in guidebooks, and it is said to be magnificent. I am sure you will love it."

Lori did not look convinced. "Oh, that brings to mind another question I had for you. When is the best time to have a house party?"

"A house party?"

"Yes. I want to get everyone together as I did not have a large ceremony. You are a far better correspondent than I am—usually," she teased. "Do you have any idea what a good time for everyone might be?"

Here was a subject Freddie could sink her teeth into. It was also considerably safer than her *mysterious* visit to Torrance Park and the Duke of Plimpton's presence there. Lori would be impossible if she ever discovered Freddie had spent time with him. She had once described Plimpton as *stern but delicious.*

Freddie could now confirm that was a devastatingly accurate description.

"Freddie?"

She looked up from her thoughts, annoyed when she felt her face heat.

Lori narrowed her eyes. "Why, Freddie! You are blushing."

"It is hot in here."

Lori glanced at Freddie's light morning gown and then at her own twilled costume, complete with pelisse buttoned up to the neck. "Why are you so distracted today?" she persisted.

"I am not distracted," Freddie lied for the third or perhaps fourth time in the past half-hour. "I was just considering your party. You should definitely avoid August—at least the first few weeks."

Like a kitten confronted with a ball of twine, Lori fell for the distraction. "Why?"

Freddie shook her head in mock disappointment. "My dear, dear Lori! I am beginning to wonder if you should engage my services to bring you up to snuff."

"Why? What did I say?" she asked, bewildered.

"Have you never heard of Glorious August Twelfth?"

"It seems vaguely familiar."

"I should think so. It is the beginning of the shooting season."

Lori wrinkled her nose. "Ugh. What a barbaric sport, although I hesitate to call it a sport—not until pheasants are armed with guns of their own."

Freddie laughed. "I cannot imagine your husband feels the same."

"Actually, Severn despises hunting of any sort."

"Oh. Well, he is in a minority when it comes to the men of his class."

"Yes," Lori said sourly, "I am aware of the aristocratic male fascination with blood sports of all types." She pulled a face. "So, not August, then? How about September?"

"Let me look at my most recent letters. Annis is expecting an interesting event in—"

"Annis is pregnant?"

The Etiquette of Love

Freddie winced at her friend's immoderate phrasing and raised voice. She had not been entirely in jest when she mentioned offering Lori her services. The other woman would have to deal with Severn's grandfather, the Marquess of Granton, a man who was a stickler of the highest order.

"Freddie?" Lori prodded.

"Yes," Freddie said. "Annis is enceinte. Let me confirm with her whether or not she will want to travel all the way from Yorkshire in September."

Lori gave an airy wave of her had. "I shall leave the setting of the date to you if you do not mind?"

"I don't mind at all. Are there any days I should avoid?"

"No. Severn told me to do whatever I wanted." She gave Freddie a smug smile. "He is proving to be a most tractable husband."

Freddie laughed.

Lori glanced at the clock on the mantel and grimaced. "Oh, Lord! Look at the time. I told the coachman to come back for me in an hour." She jumped to her feet and pulled on an elegant pair of dark teal gloves that perfectly matched her outfit. "Why are you smiling like that?" she asked when Freddie joined her at the door.

"Because I am happy for you, Lori." It was the truth, if not all of it. She was also amused to see Lori adjusting so well to having a carriage and servants at her beck and call. It was delightful to see her beauty accentuated by exquisite clothing and the lovely emeralds she wore in her ears.

"Thank you, my friend," Lori said, her huge green eyes suddenly misty. "Are you sure you will be able to continue on here without me contributing my tiny bit to the household?"

"I forbid you to worry about me. I will be fine," Freddie assured her, opening the door and accompanying Lori down the stairs.

"I wish some intelligent, dashing but dignified gentleman—preferably a duke, but not one of those odious, bulging-eyed royal ones—would come along and sweep you off your feet."

Freddie had to laugh. "Listen to you! You have been opposed to marriage the entire time I have known you and now, a bride of less than a month, you are already plotting and scheming how you can lure others into the same snare."

Lori's cheeks darkened. "I should be ashamed of myself, shouldn't I?" She stopped in the foyer and turned to Freddie, impulsively throwing her arms around her and kissing her cheek before setting Freddie at arm's length and saying, "I just want you to be as happy as I am, my dear, dear Freddie." And with that she dashed a tear from her cheek and hurried outside with her mannish stride to where an elegant black barouche waited.

Freddie watched until her friend's carriage disappeared and then quietly shut the door and sagged back against it with a sigh.

Lori could never ever learn about Freddie's ill-advised but memorable afternoon at the boathouse with Plimpton. She would hound Freddie to the ends of the earth if she ever discovered that an intelligent, dashing but dignified duke *had* come along and proposed marriage.

And Freddie had driven him away.

Chapter 18

The Following Wednesday

The Outskirts of London

The brief walk from the staging inn to Mr. and Mrs. Morrison's cottage was normally one Freddie enjoyed. But today she was filled with unease about Miranda and what mood the girl would be in. Although normally a happy child, once Miranda was thrown off-balance, she might stay that way for days or even weeks.

The Morrison's occupied a cheerful red brick house that was large enough to comfortably accommodate both themselves and their three charges. Mrs. Morrison was a loving woman who spent more time on people than she did on housework and her husband had the same attitude toward gardening.

As a result, the yard had gone wild with flowers and numerous windows still sported crooked paper snowflakes from last Christmas.

Freddie heard female voices raised in play before she saw Miranda and her two housemates—Cynthia and Laura—both of whom were many years older than Miranda's own thirteen years.

Freddie paused to watch through a gap in the untidy hedge. They were playing on the slate Scotch Hopper board Mr. Morrison had made several years earlier.

Miranda's childish voice floated on the muggy summer air as she sang the Magpie Rhyme:

"*One for sorrow,*

Two for joy,

Three for a girl,

Four for a boy,

Five for silver,

Six for gold,

Seven for a secret never to be told."

Laughter and a friendly squabble ensued before Laura, a woman in her early thirties, took her turn.

Freddie opened the sagging gate, whose hinges screeched and drew three sets of eyes.

"*Mama!*" Miranda shrieked, running directly toward Freddie and not bothering to go around the slate board, all but running poor Laura down in the process.

Freddie opened her arms to receive the female projectile hurtling toward her, putting her weight on her back foot to keep from being thrown to the ground.

"Where *were* you?" Miranda wailed. "I worried! I was so worried! Mama Morrison said you were busy with something important. But too busy for me, Mama? I'm not important!" Her slim body shook as she collapsed into tears.

Freddie stroked her narrow shoulders with calm, firm caresses. "*Shhh*, Miranda. Nothing is more important than you, my love. But you see, my brother was ill and—"

Miranda's head whipped up, her face tear-stained and her pale blue eyes already red-rimmed. "My brother?" she repeated, the fascinating notion driving away her sorrow for the moment.

"Well, he would be your uncle to you as I am your Mama," Freddie pointed out.

Miranda loosened her vise-like grip just enough to look behind Freddie. "Is my brother here to see me?"

Freddie smiled as she smoothed back the girl's wispy light brown hair. Now that Miranda had heard the word *brother* and had it in her mind, it would take weeks, or even months, before Freddie could get her to remember that Wareham was her *uncle*, and not her brother.

Not that her brother knew of the girl's existence or ever would, of course.

The Etiquette of Love

"—and Gilly gave me the broken biscuits and I saved them in a sock until a little mouse found them and Mama Morrison scolded me for—"

Freddie listened to a frenetic monologue of Miranda's daily life, which tumbled out of her without pause. She saw that Mrs. Morrison had come out to greet her and smiled at the older woman.

"Now, Miranda," Mrs. Morrison chided gently, just loudly enough to be heard over Miranda's increasingly hurried speech. "You must allow Mrs. Torrance to come inside like a proper guest. She has traveled a long way and will want tea."

When that didn't stop Miranda, who was rapidly working herself into an excited lather, talking louder and faster to be heard over the older woman, Freddie lifted the satchel she'd brought with her and said, "Do you not want to see your gifts, Miranda?"

The words worked like a charm.

"Gifts for me?" Miranda asked, bouncing up and down and lightly petting the strap on Freddie's satchel.

Freddie glanced at the other women—it was simply too hard for her to call two women in their thirties *girls*—both of whom had shuffled closer like shy but curious hens. "I have gifts for you and for Laura and Cynthia, too."

Miranda frowned, clearly unsure if she liked the idea of *everyone* getting gifts. But Mrs. Morrison worked fast. "Let us go inside, girls. The sooner you wash up and tidy yourselves the sooner you can have tea and biscuits."

"And gifts?" Cynthia asked hopefully, her childish voice oddly poignant when paired with her lined face.

"And gifts," Mrs. Morrison agreed, shooing her three charges into the house where a maid waited to help keep them on task.

Once they had clattered up the stairs Mrs. Morrison turned to her. "Let me take your coat and hat, ma'am. So excited poor Miranda was to get your message that you'd come today," she said, nattering as nonstop as Miranda, not pausing to take a breath until she had settled Freddie into what was known as the *Guest Chair* in the tiny parlor.

Freddie unpacked her satchel while Mrs. Morrison talked. The visits followed the same pattern each time as regularity was important not only Miranda, but the other two women the Morrison's cared for. Freddie would distribute the gifts and share tea, chat privately with Miranda afterward, and then make her way back to the coaching inn, all within three hours.

"—and she has learned how to tat and is working on a gift for you for this Christmas," the older woman went on, her gaze flickering over the three equally sized wrapped parcels Freddie set on the table. She clucked her tongue. "You are so thoughtful to bring something for everyone," Mrs. Morrison said, as she did every time. "Nobody ever comes for poor Cynthia anymore." Her mouth puckered into a frown. "Indeed, we haven't received her quarterly payment in half a year. Mr. Morrison and I have had her so long she is like our daughter, so we would never send her away. But with no money for her upkeep coming in, poor Cynthia is forced to do without the little niceties."

Freddie had never asked to whom Cynthia belonged, but she knew the woman's relations must be wealthy because her clothing had always been the very best, although she had noticed there had been nothing new for quite some time. Her heart ached at the thought of Cynthia's family abandoning her.

Thinking about Cynthia naturally led her thoughts to Miranda, and what would happen to her if Freddie could no longer support her. Freddie had a will, of course, but she had very little to bequeath. Increasingly, she wondered if she should just swallow her pride and accept Wareham's pension and all the strings that came attached to it. If she did, then Miranda would never have to worry about her creature comforts.

But if Freddie did that, she could never see her again, either.

There was no easy answer. Her dream had once been to bring Miranda to live with her, but she simply could not provide the level of care the Morrison's provided. More importantly, after living with the Morrisons and the other two women for most of her life it would be cruel to take Miranda away.

"—isn't really getting any better, so Mr. Morrison and I wanted to ask if we should continue with the private tuition?"

The Etiquette of Love

Freddie shook herself. "I beg your pardon, Mrs. Morrison, but I am afraid I did not catch the first part of what you said."

"Not, to worry, ma'am. Here I am, rabbiting on when I can see you have heavy matters on your mind. I was just asking if you wanted to keep paying for Miranda's reading lessons?"

Freddie's heart sank. "I take it there has been no improvement?"

"I am afraid not, Mrs. Torrance. Poor Miranda returns home from the lessons so unhappy and frustrated."

Freddie paid the local schoolteacher a small amount to tutor Miranda three times a week, hoping to teach her to read and write. The lessons were a strain on Freddie's limited resources, but she couldn't help thinking of all the joy Miranda would miss out on if she never learned to read—at least to the level where she could enjoy the children's books Freddie had read to her hundreds of times and which Miranda could probably recite from memory.

She hated to give up on the lessons, but... "I suppose three years is long enough to admit that she will never learn."

"You have done your best, ma'am. The tutoring makes Miranda feel as if she is not as clever as the other children. Little boys and girls who started learning years after she did are now reading and—"

"I understand," Freddie said.

Mrs. Morrison brightened. "But her watercolors are another matter entirely, Mrs. Torrance. *Those* are quite something. And getting better with each week that passes." She lowered her voice, even though it was just the two of them. "She painted a special one for you—Mr. Morrison made a frame for it—and she wants to give it to you for your birthday."

Freddie smiled. "That will be my second birthday this year. I am aging quite alarmingly fast."

Mrs. Morrison chuckled.

What sounded like a herd of horses approached the parlor door and Miranda and the two women burst into the room.

They knew which gift belonged to whom without her having to tell them. The pink tissue wrapped package was always for Miranda, the blue for Cynthia, and the green for Laura.

"What do you say, girls?" Mrs. Morrison asked, having to raise her voice to be heard over the sound of tearing paper and excited chatter.

Three pairs of eyes lifted to Freddie. "Thank you, Mrs. Torrance," Cynthia and Laura called out in unison. "Thank you, *Mama*," Miranda said with a slightly smug smile, pleased that Freddie was all hers.

"You are all very welcome," she said, although it was doubtful they heard her as they were each cooing over their spoils.

It always made Freddie weepy at how little it took to please all three. Just a few hair ribbons, small packets of boiled sweets, and a picture book for Cynthia and Miranda, neither of whom could read, and a book with a very simple story for Laura, who read at the age level of a six-or-seven-year-old child.

She had another gift for Miranda in her bag—a trio of new paint brushes and a tin of fresh cakes of paint—but she would give that to her when they were alone.

Tea was a raucous affair, made louder when Mr. Morrison joined them and all three of his charges crowded around him to show off their new gifts.

Once he'd praised the books, admired the ribbons, and kindly rejected offers of sweets, he turned to Miranda and asked, "Where is that surprise you made for Mrs. Torrance?"

Miranda looked blank for a second, but then squeaked, jumped up, and scampered from the room.

"No running inside," Mrs. Morrison called after her to no avail.

"She worked on this painting for almost a week," Mr. Morrison said, looking as proud as if Miranda was his own daughter.

"I don't believe she has stayed with any project for so long before," his wife added.

Freddie knew the woman was right; Miranda had an attention span that usually didn't stretch beyond any given moment. For her to work on something for days, showed growth. She was tempted to change her mind about the tutoring and keep sending the girl, but she simply did not have the heart to make her do something she disliked, even if it might be good for her.

The Etiquette of Love

When Miranda returned clutching a clumsily wrapped parcel Mr. and Mrs. Morrison considerately led Cynthia and Laura off on some pretext or other to give Freddie time alone with Miranda.

The girl plopped onto the settee beside her and pushed the package into her hands. "Happy birthday, Mama."

"Thank you, Miranda. This is very considerate of you and—"

"Open it," Miranda ordered, poking at the brown-paper wrapping with a finger sticky with pink icing.

Freddie couldn't help chuckling at her enthusiasm. But the gasp of amazement she gave when she unwrapped the gift was entirely spontaneous.

"Oh, my goodness," she said in a hushed, reverential voice as she stared down at the magnificent painting.

"It's the sky, Mama," Miranda said when Freddie could only stare. "It's a consta—a consta—" she growled, frustrated by her inability to recall the word.

"They are constellations," Freddie said.

"Papa Morrison said it was cy—n—cygnus," she smiled triumphantly at having produced the word, pointing to the stars that comprised the swan. "And—and a stinging thing." She grimaced and made pinchers with her hands.

"Scorpius," Freddie supplied, astounded by the realism of the painting and the way the tiny daubs of paint looked just like twinkling starlight against a velvet blue-black sky. "Did you see this in a picture, Miranda?"

"No. It's from the sky."

Freddie laughed. "Yes… but, after you saw it, how did you remember where all the stars were?"

Miranda shrugged, already bored with the subject and the painting, her eyes sliding to Freddie's bag.

"I adore it, Miranda," Freddie said, taking the girl's hand and squeezing lightly to draw her attention back from the gifts awaiting her. "Thank you."

Miranda nodded, her pupils moving rapidly, never settling on any one thing for more than a few seconds. The doctor had called it nystagmus and said it would probably worsen as she grew older. He'd recommended spectacles, but Miranda had cried when they had tried to make her wear them, so the dainty glasses had been put in a drawer for the day when they would be needed. Judging by the amazing painting Miranda had just produced, her vision was still acute enough for the spectacles to be unnecessary.

"I am sorry I missed my last visit," she said, releasing Miranda's hand when she began to fidget. Although the little girl embraced Freddie upon arrival, she was not a cuddler unless she was the one initiating it.

"You had im-*por*-dent things."

"I did. Your uncle was ill," she said, hoping to set the girl straight on Wareham's relationship to her.

"My brother was ill," Miranda corrected, making Freddie smile ruefully. Sometimes, it was better to just let her hold on to something.

"Mama Morrison says you do not like your lessons with Miss Franks."

Miranda's face puckered, as if she had just sucked on a lemon. "I don't like it."

"Are you sure you would not like—"

"I don't *like* it," she repeated, but louder this time.

"*Shh*, darling. No shouting. I just wanted to make sure. You won't have to go anymore."

The furrows on Miranda's brow instantly smoothed and her jittery gaze bounced back to the satchel.

Freddie once again took her hand and squeezed. "Would you rather have a painting tutor, Miranda? Somebody who could—"

"No. I don't like it."

"Very well," Freddie said after a moment. Broaching a different sort of tutor right then—so soon after discussing Miss Franks—had likely just confused the girl. "Would you like to see what I have in my bag?"

Miranda bounced up and down on the ancient settee, making the springs creak.

Freddie laughed. "I will take that as a *yes*."

Chapter 19

It was almost eight weeks exactly after her magical day at the lake with Plimpton that Freddie discovered she was pregnant.

As her luck would have it, she was not the only one who learned the truth that day.

She had just commenced a new needlework project when the urge to vomit struck her. She dropped her tambour and hastily scrambled for the small metal basin she kept beside the settee to catch all the threads she generated. There was a rap on the door, and it opened before she could yell *wait*! Not that she could have yelled anything as she hunched over the bowl and voided the contents of her stomach. Fortunately, she had eaten a spartan breakfast as she had felt nauseated upon waking that morning.

Unfortunately, it was not only Mrs. Brinkley at the door, but Piers right on her heels. Both hurried into the room, the babble of voices rushing around her like an incoming tide.

Freddie closed her eyes and tried to clear her mind. But the trick, usually so useful, did not work today.

She retched once more but brought up nothing. Only then did she notice the room had gone deathly quiet. She opened her eyes to find both Piers and her housekeeper bent low, staring down with wide eyes.

Freddie couldn't help a hoarse chuckle. She glanced at the bowl and then Mrs. Brinkley, hesitating. "I am so sorry to ask you—"

Mrs. Brinkley made a scoffing sound and took the bowl. "Don't be silly, of course I will take it away. You just sit and I'll return with something to settle your poor stomach, my lady." She turned her gaze to Piers, her eyes narrowing. "Perhaps I should—"

"It is fine, Mrs. Brinkley. Mr. Gregg may stay."

Still looking skeptical, the housekeeper left the room.

The Etiquette of Love

Piers, who was holding a glass of water in one hand and hovering over her, hastily shoved it at her. "Here. Drink this."

Freddie sipped carefully at first, and then drank more when it was clear she wouldn't immediately cast it up again.

"Thank you," she said, setting down the half-full glass.

"You are ill."

She forced a smile. "I will be fine."

"I should summon a doctor. It is not normal for—"

"Please do not, Piers."

"If you are concerned about the money, I insist upon paying for—"

"I am fine."

He made a helpless gesture with his hands. "You look dreadful—and vomiting is not normal." He strode toward the servant pull. "I'll tell your housekeeper to summon your doctor immediately."

"I do not want a doctor."

He spun toward her. "Goddammit, Winifred! You are willful and independent beyond reason. I am not trying to control you; I am trying to—"

"Pray do not raise your voice and curse at me."

His lips tightened. "I am sorry. I am just concerned for you. Why won't you let me—"

"I am with child."

Piers's dark brown eyes, so different from Freddie's and Wareham's, widened in shock. "But—*how.*"

Freddie laughed.

Piers's face turned scarlet. "You know what I mean, damn it! I know you do not engage in light affairs."

She frowned. "How do you know that? Have you been spying on me?"

"Not lately. I mean—Damnation! I don't want to talk about that. I want the name of the fucking bastard who—"

"*Piers.*"

"I don't care about my language. Who is it, Winifred. Tell me or I *will* start spying. And then I will kill whoever it is." His hands flexed into fists, as if anticipating the event.

"I fail to see how any of this is your concern."

"I am your brother!"

She stood and headed for the door.

"Where are you going?"

"Until you can speak to me in a level, controlled fashion I have no intention of being subjected to your presence."

"I apologize!" he shouted and then shoved his hands into his hair, behaving for all the world like a character in a stage play. "Sorry, I did not mean to yell that, too. Please stay."

Freddie hesitated.

"Please."

Freddie exhaled and sat.

"Thank you." He cleared his throat and lowered himself into the chair across from her. "What are you going to do?"

"I do not know yet. I just found out myself." Although she'd had her suspicions for weeks. It had been ages since she had missed her courses, not since her marriage when she'd been sick with worry and so malnourished that she had become gravely ill.

At first, she had thought perhaps her anxiety over Wareham's illness—and the subsequent fracas with Plimpton—had thrown off her body's rhythm. But she had felt increasingly nauseated these past two weeks. She had hoped that she'd contracted an influenza, but there had been no fever or other symptoms. Although she had been more tired than usual.

But today…Well, today she just *knew*.

Piers opened his mouth.

"No more questions."

"Please, just one."

Freddie glared. "What?"

"Is it Plimpton?"

An unpleasant jolt shot through her at his question. How in the world had he guessed?

"I have told you everything," he said when she did not answer. "Every embarrassing detail of my past."

"Hardly *every* detail."

"Well, maybe not *all*, but certainly the most relevant and the worst. By doing so, I have demonstrated that I—"

"Yes," she said, too weary to argue. She also felt as if she might throw up again.

He frowned, visibly confused. "I beg your pardon?"

"I said *yes*, the child is Plimpton's."

Before he could speak the door opened and Mrs. Brinkley entered with the tea tray. As she fussed around, Freddie could not help being relieved by the interruption. Already she regretted telling her brother the truth. She should have never opened her mouth. Men—even brothers—could not be trusted.

***

The next eight days were some of the worst of her life. Thankfully, Piers had commenced his investigations into the men who had been at that fateful house party and was too busy to haunt her house and give her speaking looks every time she made a dash for the nearest basin or rubbish bin.

Mrs. Brinkley, on the other hand…

Freddie had not been so fortunate as to escape the sharp eyes of her housekeeper. Or her cook, Una. For the first time since Freddie had known the two feuding women, they were united in their efforts.

Those efforts included alternately coddling her to the point of madness to regarding her with disbelieving, disappointed looks when they thought she would not notice.

Their clucking and fussing were enough to fray every last nerve. She could only be thankful that none of her friends were in London to add to her persecution. Indeed, everyone who was anyone had fled town weeks before. Lori and her new husband had been among the last to leave, Lori begging and pleading Freddie to join her.

"I cannot believe you would rather be here in August—*alone*—than with me at Granton, Freddie. It will be cool and quiet and a relief after this sweltering, hellish nightmare."

Indeed, it was exceptionally hot for early August—the hottest anyone could recall—but the last thing Freddie wanted was to spend more time beneath Lori's hawklike gaze.

To be honest, she was enjoying her time alone.

She had no clients to demand her attention and no housemates to provide distractions. For the first time in years, Freddie had the entire house to herself. The only time she left her cozy nest was to see Miranda or visit her circulating library. Otherwise, she spent the best part of most days curled up in bed, alternately reading and dozing.

Freddie's days and nights took on a sort of warm dream-like languor. She re-read books she had enjoyed in her youth, gentle, happy stories that took little conscious thought to ingest. Unsurprisingly, a big part of her thoughts was on the being growing inside her. A child. *Her* child. Someone to love of her very own.

She loved Miranda dearly, but she had never been allowed to raise her and care for her properly. What would it be like if she were free to publicly claim her daughter or son? She would be forever cast out of society, but if she accepted Wareham's offer, then…

Plans and dreams swirled inside her during those sultry dreamy days, problems all pushed away until…later.

She did not care if the child was female or male. Having a little boy to cherish would, however, be a different experience. Would he look like his father?

The Etiquette of Love

Freddie shied away from thoughts of the duke, which increasingly brought shame in their wake. If she went to Wareham for help, she would need to lie about the child's father. Because Freddie knew what would happen if Plimpton ever discovered she carried his child. Already he possessed a keen desire to make her his wife. Not only because of his connection with Wareham, but because he saw Freddie as epitomizing everything he expected from his duchess.

If he heard of her pregnancy, he would not step aside as he had done all those weeks ago at Torrance Park. If he knew about the baby, he would *force* her to marry him.

And then she would once again find herself the possession of a man who did not love her for *her* but wanted her for *what* she was. Freddie knew Plimpton would not be cruel or dangerous like Sedgewick. She would not need to hide in her room for weeks to conceal the bruises and black eyes and even broken bones on two occasions.

Plimpton would never harm her. At least not physically. But neither would he ever love her.

Sometimes Freddie had to laugh at herself. How could she continue to believe in love after what she knew of men?

Or at least how could she believe in love for *her*. Because she knew it existed for some people. After all, her friends from the Stefani Academy had found love, although only Serena and Lori had married for love while the others had been thrown together by circumstance and were fortunate to grow to love each other.

But Plimpton, as passionate as he had been in the bedchamber, was not the sort of man who fell in love—at least not for long. He wanted a wife and a duchess. With the dukedom secured by the birth of his brother's child he had accepted that Freddie could not have children. But if he learned that she not only *could* get pregnant but was even now carrying his child? Then he would take her to the country and wrap her in cotton wool. Yes, if he knew she was capable of breeding, he would regard her far differently than he had before. She did not believe he had a mania for a son of his own body as Sedgewick had, but he would certainly want more children from her if he knew she were capable.

That thought in itself did not worry her—after all, Freddie would love a nursery full of children—but she did not want to share a family with a man who did not love her. The fact that he'd carried his daughter's miniature in his pocket told her the duke was capable of deep affection for his child, but she suspected such love extended only to those of his own flesh and blood.

Freddie sighed uncomfortably at the jostling of the coach and forced her thoughts away from the duke, instead turning to stare out the stagecoach window. She felt awful and desperately wished that her regular, bi-monthly journey was shorter today.

The movement outside the window elicited a now-familiar nausea in her belly and Freddie immediately looked away, closing her eyes and willing her stomach to settle.

She should have stayed home. It would be mortifying to be sick in the confines of the coach, not to mention how appalling it would be for the other five people crowded in with her.

Freddie had considered canceling her visit to Melinda, but she had already missed a Wednesday when she had gone to Torrance Park so she could *not* miss another one so soon after.

She felt a light touch on her tightly laced fingers and opened her eyes to find the woman across from her, a kindly looking grandmotherly type, giving her a knowing smile. "Peppermint."

Freddie blinked. "I beg your pardon?"

The woman lifted her hand and Freddie saw there was a white lozenge in her gloved palm.

"Take it," the woman urged, and then leaned closer and said in a loud whisper that surely all the other occupants could hear. "It will settle your stomach."

Face flaming, Freddie took the peppermint and forced a smile. "Thank you."

She nodded to indicate Freddie should put it in her mouth. "Go on and chew it."

Freddie did so, her tastebuds and nostrils immediately assaulted by the strong flavor of mint.

The Etiquette of Love

"Thank you," she said again, her filling the close quarters of the carriage with peppermint.

"Buy yourself a packet and keep them on you for the first few months." She gave Freddie a conspiratorial smile that made her eyes narrow to amused slits. "I ate them up by the handful for all seven of mine, sometimes for as long as three months."

Freddie's eyes slid to the prim-looking woman seated beside her benefactress, who had flushed to the roots of her hair to overhear such a conversation.

Only when Freddie swallowed the last of the pulverized lozenge did she notice her nausea had indeed abated a little.

A quick glance around the stagecoach at the other occupants told her that now Piers, Mrs. Brinkley, and Una were not the only ones who knew about Freddie's *interesting* condition.

***

By the time Freddie's visit was over three hours later she had needed to run to the necessary twice and vowed to purchase peppermints before she climbed into the coach for the ride home.

The day was exhausting not just for her, but also for Miranda, who had been more restless than usual, becoming sleepy-eyed and lethargic after opening her gift.

Miranda tolerated Freddie's kiss, mumbled *thank you* for the new sketchbook and pastels at Mrs. Morrison's urging, and tiredly trudged her way up the stairs.

Freddie watched her until she disappeared and then, blinking away the tears that built in her eyes every single time she had to say *goodbye*, turned to Mrs. Morrison. "Thank you for allowing me to visit. I know my appearance here upsets your schedule."

"It is always a pleasure to see you, Mrs. Torrance And all three girls look forward to your visits," Mrs. Morrison assured her with a genial smile.

Freddie handed the older woman a slender packet. "There is a little extra included for this quarter."

Mrs. Morrison blushed as she took the money. "Thank you so much, Mrs. Torrance. I hope you know we'd take Miranda without pay if we—"

"*Shh*, of course I know that."

"Are you sure you won't accept a ride today? This storm won't hold off much longer," Mrs. Morrison said, eyeing the darkening sky.

After politely declining a ride in the Morrison's gig—three times—Freddie was allowed to set off on foot, her heart aching as it always did when she left Miranda behind. The money she had given Mrs. Morrison was scarcely more than a pittance, but it was still enough to make inroads into her careful budget. There would be no sugar for tea and the tea itself would need to be rationed more carefully.

Rain began to fall, interrupting her unpleasant thoughts, and a sudden gust of wind caught at her bonnet.

Freddie scowled, more at herself than the weather, and opened her ancient umbrella.

The raindrops grew fatter, and the breeze tugged at the fragile umbrella, almost tugging it from her grasp several times.

"Oh, bother!" she exclaimed as a gust pulled it hard enough to bend the delicate infrastructure.

Freddie was wrestling with the device when the rain suddenly stopped.

"Good afternoon, my lady."

She gave a startled yelp, her head whipping around at the Duke of Plimpton's voice.

He had somehow come up alongside her, without her even noticing, and was holding a large black umbrella over her head.

"Wha—what are you doing here?" she demanded, her eyes rapidly moving over his person—exquisitely garbed in riding gear—and then darting up to his face.

"Waiting for you. Come, your umbrella is not salvageable," he took it from her unresisting fingers. "We cannot stand here without getting

The Etiquette of Love

soaked and drawing unwanted notice." He offered her his elbow and she linked her arm with his without thinking.

Angry at herself for obeying him without hesitation, Freddie tried to jerk away only to find that he held her lightly, but firmly.

"Do not be foolish, Winifred." His voice was frosty and sharp.

Rather than make a scene, Freddie quit struggling and walked beside him, nodding a greeting as she walked past Mrs. Corbin, the owner of the town mercantile. The woman didn't just run the store, she was also the town crier when it came to gossip. No doubt everyone within a fifty-mile radius would soon know that *Mrs. Torrance* had been walking arm and arm with a strange man.

"How did you find me?" she asked in a tight voice,

"I followed you." Rather than sound remorseful, his tone was even haughtier than usual.

"Why would you do such a thing?"

"To see where you were going."

She sucked in a breath at his audacity. "What gives you the right to invade my privacy in such a way?" she blustered, not stopping to wait for his response. "Following me is obnoxious and offensive enough. But your unapologetic—nay, proud—admission is—well...it is unspeakable!"

"Clearly it is *not* unspeakable, as you have just spoken at some length on the subject," he coolly retorted. The muscles of his face subtly shifted beneath his skin, and the erstwhile warm, sultry summer rain seemed to carry a new chill.

As much as she longed to lash out at him, she gritted her teeth until they ached and forced her next words out through rigidly smiling lips. "How *dare* you spy on me?" she hissed, nodding politely to the left and right as more and more people suddenly decided to step out onto their front stoops to watch the rain.

"I am not sure I would speak of *daring*, if I were you, my lady."

How could the words *my* and *lady* be made to sound so...accusing? Freddie decided that she would not have minded him using her Christian name at that point.

"I do not know what you mean by all this," she lied—poorly, she suspected.

He regarded her with a cool, snubbing look that was the conversational equivalent of hurling lamp oil onto her banked temper. Freddie opened her mouth to say something lacerating, but he was not finished.

"My carriage had just pulled up in front of your house when I saw you climb into a hackney. I wished to speak to you, so I followed you. When your carriage dropped you off at the Green Man, I became curious."

Freddie sorted through various responses, but possessed enough sense to hold back words she would doubtless later regret. What eventually came out was, "How would you like it if I followed *you* and spied on *you*?"

"I am not hiding anything, so I would not mind."

A rude, scoffing sound of a sort she'd never before made, tore out of her mouth. "Is that so? I can just imagine how delighted you would be if I followed you to one of your mistress's houses."

His eyebrows lifted fractionally, and he looked down at her with a lofty, vaguely amused expression that made Freddie want to hit him. "I would be stunned if you did so."

"Why? Because ladies do not do such things?"

"No, because I do not *have* any mistresses to visit."

Disappointment, sharp and searing, stabbed at her. She had believed the duke many things, but never a liar. "I am sure Mrs. Palfrey will be disappointed to hear that."

What had come over her to say such a thing? Honestly, this impulse to blurt out every thought that came into her head was so unlike her that she no longer recognized herself!

But the duke did not even blink at her words. "I doubt that. She and I went our separate ways months ago." He paused, and then added, "And I parted with my other lovers immediately upon returning to London from Torrance Park."

The Etiquette of Love

Lovers? Freddie knew her expression—that of a stunned carp—was not attractive, but she couldn't help her open-mouthed outrage, or her disappointment. Just what was it about men that one woman was never enough for them? Why did so many of them require *multiple* lovers to satisfy their needs? It seemed that in this one regard, Plimpton was not so unlike Sedgewick, after all.

The duke put one leather-clad finger beneath her jaw and lightly pressed it closed. "I am not sure what that look was for, Winifred. How could I possibly want any other woman after having had you?"

Freddie swallowed the lump in her throat—this one the result of pleasure rather than ire—and said, "You ended those liaisons because of *me?*"

"Only partly. I also ended them because they held no appeal for me." He walked her around an especially mucky spot in the road, angling the umbrella so that it would shield her better. "You are the only woman I want, Winifred."

A fog seemed to be building inside her head and Freddie hastily shook it away. *Do not let him charm you,* the voice of self-preservation advised.

And just where were you back in the boathouse at Torrance Park, Freddie demanded.

But the voice had already fled.

"It does not signify why you ended those, er, liaisons," she said in a prim voice she despised. "I have no intention of resuming any—any—" she broke off and glared at him when he merely regarded her with mild interest rather than help her find an acceptable word. "You know what I mean."

"I do know."

Freddie narrowed her eyes at him. Had that been a smile tugging at his lips?

He returned her gaze, no sign of anything—humorous or otherwise—in his cold gray eyes.

"That episode at Torrance—er, in the boathouse—was the first and only time," she said, wanting to kick herself: As if there could be any doubt as to what *episode* she referred to.

"So, you have said. Several times and at length."

Yes, he was definitely smiling.

Looking at his severe pink lips reminded her of how much they could change. Of how they had become slick and red and swollen that afternoon.

Freddie swallowed, a sudden, vivid memory of what he had *done* with his stern mouth—

"Winifred." The quiet word was edged with exasperated amusement.

Her eyes darted up to his. "What?" she demanded rudely.

"If you look at me like that, I cannot promise to control myself on the journey back to London."

Her mind seemed to split into two pieces. One went romping after the tantalizing fantasy of the duke losing his control. The other part, far more tiresome, became snagged on the far less fun aspect of his threat. "You cannot go on the stage with me!"

"You are coming back with me in my carriage."

"Your carriage? But you are dressed for riding." As if that made any difference *at all*.

"I will explain why that is when we are on our way back to London."

"What makes you think I will accompany you?"

"You can either ride with me, or I will purchase a seat on the stage, and we can have our discussion in front of a no-doubt fascinated audience."

"You would not dare."

His gaze was level and bland. "I always do what I say I will do, Winifred."

The Etiquette of Love

Freddie's breathing became labored as his pupils shrank to pinpricks, making his gray eyes appear lighter—and far steelier—than usual. "Wh-what discussion?"

"I think you know exactly what I want to discuss."

***

Plimpton could see she was angry. That was fine; he was angry, too. Actually, he was *furious*. His temper had cooled slightly on the ride from his home on Grosvenor Square to Winifred's house. But it had spiked again when he had followed her hackney cab to the bloody Green Man.

He had fumed all the way from the busy inn to the Spotted Sow in the little village of Spenham. He had become even more displeased upon discovering that Winifred was well-known—as was her errand—by everyone in the little village, while he had been utterly in the dark. *Mrs. Torrance* had been coming to visit her daughter at the Morrison's house, on the first and third Wednesday of each month, for almost nine years.

For nine years she had somehow managed to keep her child a secret from Wareham as well as the rest of the world.

Plimpton could not decide what disappointed him more. The fact that she had a nine-year-old daughter she had tucked away for almost a decade, or that she had lied to him about her inability to bear children.

Those thoughts led directly to a third thought, one that did not just disappoint him, but enraged him: the Countess of Sedgewick was carrying *his* child. A child she had fully intended to conceal from him.

Plimpton had not been this angry in—hell, he could not recall ever being so furious. Or so bloody *hurt*.

Even his brother Simon, one of the most obstinate, argumentative men alive had not provoked him like this, although not for a lack of trying.

As if the secret she was keeping was not bad enough, the messenger had made it even worse. Plimpton was now indebted to Piers bloody Cantrell, a man for whom he held nothing but the deepest suspicion. So, yet another complaint he could lay at this woman's door.

As furious, and—yes, pained—as he was, he refused to give in to his base emotions and rant at her. And so it was with his usual cool courtesy that he ignored her scowls and assisted her into his coach before handing both his umbrella and hers to one of his servants. The man, Albert, looked at the bedraggled umbrella. "Er, what should I—"

"Get rid of it," Plimpton said, and then climbed in and took the back-facing seat.

Once Albert had closed the door he tapped on the roof and the carriage rolled smoothly forward.

Winifred glared, her arms crossed over her chest and her chin jutting combatively. "Perhaps now you can explain what was so important that you spied on me, followed me, and intruded on—"

"Were you ever going to tell me about *our* child?" Try as he might, Plimpton could not keep every trace of anger and pain from his voice.

As it had done earlier, her jaw dropped open like a trapdoor with a defective hinge. This time, her stunned expression did not amuse him in the least. Quite the contrary; it stirred the coals of his wrath.

Plimpton abruptly leaned forward, his elbows resting on his knees as he closed the distance between them. "Has the cat got your tongue, Winifred?"

Her jaw shifted from side to side, a pugnacious expression settling onto her delicate features. "Who told you?"

He flung up his hands. "*That* is what you have to say?"

"I want to know who betrayed my secret."

"Just how many people know about this?"

Was it wrong that he took pleasure in the way she flinched at the naked menace in his tone?

"I—there are only three," she admitted.

"And who are those three, pray?"

"My two servants are aware of my condition, but not who the—" she broke off and caught her lower lip with her teeth.

The Etiquette of Love

"Is *father* the word you are seeking? Come, I know you can say it if you try. Or perhaps I should *define* it for you?"

Her full lips thinned at his sarcasm. "I apologize for my stupid question. It was Piers, of course. He is the only one who knows the complete truth." Disbelief, fury, and betrayal flitted across her face and Plimpton felt a sharp pang of guilt at being the one to cause her distress. He was seized by a powerful urge to take her in his arms and comfort her, to smooth away the furrows in her brow and kiss away the frown on her lips.

But then he recalled she had just come back from visiting her hidden daughter and was evidently preparing to do the same with *his* child.

"Tell me, my lady, were you planning to tuck my son or daughter away like you have with the girl? Was it your intent to visit him or her twice a month while going blithely about your life? Is your daughter the reason you refuse to accept Wareham's help? Because you know what he would do if he found out?"

Plimpton had not known exactly what to expect from her at that accusation, but it certainly had not been mocking amusement. "Why are you bothering to ask me any questions when you think you already know the truth?"

Her careful wording penetrated the fog of anger around him. "What do I not know?"

She turned and looked out the window, her profile set in such obstinate lines that he marveled; who would have believed this elegant, sophisticated woman was even capable of such a sullen, childish expression?

"What do I not know, Winifred?" he repeated in a voice carefully stripped of all emotion.

She merely lifted one shoulder.

The infuriating woman.

"Were you ever going to tell me about the baby?"

"I do not know," she admitted after a long pause, still refusing to make eye contact with him.

Plimpton was grateful for her honesty, even though her response almost gutted him. Did she really find the notion of a child with him—a future together—so repellent that she would keep his own flesh and blood from him?

The thought made any sadness or regret he was feeling evaporate. In its place was iron resolve. "We will be married within the week."

She turned to him, her eyes like pools of molten silver. "Your arrogance—your belief that your word is to be obeyed without question—is precisely why I never told you about my baby!"

"If by *arrogance* you mean a father's desire to make sure his child is born within wedlock, then I am happy to accept your accusation."

"Oh, I understand perfectly your *desire* to assure your child's legitimacy. But you do not stop at merely *desiring*. You *demand*, and I am allowed no say in any of it as you have already decided for both of us how the future will be."

Plimpton sat back, astonished. "Please—enlighten me as to what other possible future you envision? Would you raise this one yourself and bring him or her up in genteel poverty? How would you earn your crust? Do you think the *ton* would tolerate your presence, not to mention give their daughters into your keeping, if you had an illegitimate child? How would you feed, clothe, and house our child if you were a pariah?" His eyes narrowed and he allowed a cruel, cutting edge to sharpen his next words. "Or I suppose you would act in keeping with your current behavior and hand our child off to an elderly couple residing in rural squalor to—"

"I would *never* do that with my baby!" Her eyes blazed in self-righteous fury.

Plimpton shook his head, confused. "Why would this child be any different to you than—"

"Miranda is not my daughter, Your Grace!"

"If she is not yours, then who—"

"I am not going to tell you whose child she is. Suffice it to say that I took her out of an asylum where she was starving and chained to a wall, made to sit in her own bodily waste while people paid a few pence to gawk at her. She has no mother and no father. *I* am what she has."

The Etiquette of Love

Her silvery eyes were lighter than ever as she fixed him with a fierce glare.

Plimpton was utterly baffled. What the devil did she mean? Had she just plucked a child at random out of some horrid institution? But what had made her—

He reined in his pointless musing. The identity of the child—as long as it was not hers—was of negligible interest to him. For now, all that mattered was that she had not planned to condemn her own flesh and blood to being raised by strangers. It was not much, but it was better than what he had believed half-an-hour ago.

He turned his attention to the more important matter. "You know we must marry."

She closed her eyes, a shudder racking her body, an expression of profound misery taking possession of her delicate features.

So, I will marry yet another wife who hates me to the core of her being.

The chilling thought struck him like a kick to the chest.

Plimpton thrust the pain aside, something he was so skilled at doing that it had become as natural as breathing.

She opened her eyes and squarely met his gaze. "Yes, I know."

***

Freddie was so tired. Not just from the day's journey and the emotional strain of encountering the duke, but from years and years of hiding so much of her life from *everyone.*

She stared into the eyes of the man whom she had suspected for weeks—perhaps even longer; perhaps from the moment she had reluctantly, almost unwillingly, waltzed with him at Miles's wedding ball more than a year ago—would become her husband.

The fury that had caused his pupils to shrink to punishing black dots had disappeared and he was once again the cool, untouchable aristocrat. "We still have a month or so before we need marry. If your current condition leaves you too tired, my secretary can draw up a guest list, send out invitation, and manage all the—"

"I want no grand ceremony." She felt her face twist into a sneer and the words spilled from her mouth like venom, "*If it were done when 'tis done, then 'twere well It were done quickly.*"

A dull red stain spread across his austere features, as if she had struck him.

Remorse at her cruel words flooded her. "I—I apologize. That was—"

"Dramatic?" he suggested, his expression of frigid hauteur sitting oddly on his flushed face.

"I was going to say cruel and unnecessary."

"But it was honest," he replied in an inflectionless tone. "We should at least know what we have in one another, should we not?"

Her face heated in well-deserved shame, both at her viciousness as well as the painful acknowledgement that keeping his child from him had been monstrous in the extreme. Had it been possible for their positions to be reversed—and for him to do the same to her—Freddie was not sure she could find it in herself to ever forgive him.

"I can respect brutal honesty," he said. "And I can give it in return." His gray eyes were as flat and flinty as slate. "Although I fear my grasp of Shakespeare is not so impressive as yours, so I am relegated to using my own words." An emotion she could not read flickered across his face, and he said, "If you have any intention of slipping away from me and running from this marriage, I want you to know that there is no place on earth you can hide where I will not find you."

Chilled to her very marrow, Freddie nodded stiffly. "I give you my word I will not leave or try to keep your child from you." *Again.*

His jaws flexed as he stared at her—as if seeking to confirm the truth of her words. Whatever he saw must have satisfied him because he abruptly turned away from her and stared out the window.

They did not exchange another word until they were standing in front of her door what felt like an eternity later.

He paused, his hand resting on the door handle. "I will call on you tomorrow so that we can discuss—"

The Etiquette of Love

"I do not need to discuss anything, Your Grace. I will leave the planning to you. I would prefer that the ceremony be as small as possible. And I would ask that you delay making any public announcement until I have had a chance to speak to Wareham and my friends."

"I, too, would like to speak to my family before sending word of our marriage to the newspaper. However, know that I cannot keep the matter private for long." He must have seen the skepticism in her eyes, because he said, "I will have to procure a special license, which means the archbishop will be aware of my plans and he will pass along that information to whomever he believes needs to hear it. One of those people will be the Regent."

Freddie knew what he said was the truth. A duke marrying by special license was highly irregular. And the Regent was not known for keeping secrets. That meant she had a few days at the most to write her letters.

His lips turned down at the corners. "Normally, the prince would be in Brighton right now and I might have an excuse to not seek his blessing. But he has returned this past week given the unrest that is building in the North. He can be prickly if he believes the proper homage has not been given, so I will have to tell him."

"I understand, Your Grace."

His jaw flexed—a subtle action Freddie was beginning to realize was the equivalent to another, less reserved, man's grimace—as he stared down at her. After an uncomfortable silence, he said, "I will return seven days hence if that will be enough time for you to prepare?"

Seven days? A hundred years would not be long enough to reconcile herself to marrying again. But she had already spewed enough bile at the man who would soon own her body and soul for as long as they both lived. And so she inclined her head and politely said, "Thank you. Seven days will be sufficient."

He opened the door, waited until she had entered the foyer, and then shut it without another word.

Freddie collapsed against the cool wood of the door and closed her eyes. Seven days. She would be married *again* in seven days. She would be another man's chattel—*again*—in seven days. A possession to be sent away at her husband's whim. A pawn to be moved about in any manner her master saw fit, to be commanded and ordered. And if she disobeyed, to be beaten and locked away—

Plimpton is nothing like Sedgewick and you know it.

Freddie wanted to scream and rail against the cool voice of reason that usually guided her thoughts, no matter how right it might—

"Little Bird?"

Her eyes flew open at Piers's tentative voice. He was standing on the stairs, looking down at her, an expression of concern creasing his deeply tanned face.

"You!" Freddie lifted her arm to hurl her satchel at him. Only at the last moment did she recall that Miranda's framed painting was inside it and lowered the bag. "You—you—"

"Bastard?" he suggested with an unhappy smile.

"Why, Piers? Just...*why*?"

"Why do you think, Winifred? Because I could not let you do this—not to yourself, and especially not to your child."

"What gives you the right to make that decision for me?" she shouted, too furious to care that she was behaving like a fishwife. "You who have been gone for most of my life? How can you—"

"My lady? Is aught amiss?"

Freddie's head whipped around, and she met the horrified gaze of her housekeeper. She forced a reassuring smile. "Nothing is wrong, Mrs. Brinkley. I will ring if I require your assistance." It was the closest Freddie had ever come to throwing the woman out of a room.

"Of course, my lady." The housekeeper said stiffly, and then fled.

Freddie regretted having to dismiss her in such a way and knew she would need to make amends to the kindly woman later.

For now, however...

She turned to Piers and her anger returned with a vengeance.

She yanked on the ribbons of her bonnet and flung it onto the nearby table with punishing force before marching up the stairs and poking her brother in the chest. "It was not your secret to share, Piers. Nor was it your problem to solve. How would you like it if I decided to make those sorts of decisions for *your* life? You asked me to keep my nose out of your business—not to meddle—and I adhered to your wishes." She felt a twinge of guilt at the memory of her gentle *prying* into the matter with the duke that day in the boathouse, but brutally dismissed it. "Why do I not deserve the same treatment?"

"It is not the same thing, Lit—"

"Do not *dare* use my pet name to manipulate me right now! How is it not the same? Because I am a mere woman, and you are a man who naturally knows what is best for me? You took away my choices, Piers—all of them, not just about the child, but about who I would marry. About the very fact that I now *have* to marry. You took away my *future*."

His dark eyes suddenly flared to life, and he shoved his face close to hers, startling her so badly she took a step back and would have fallen if he hadn't grabbed her upper arms.

"*Your* choices?" His face contorted with anger. "What about your child's choice, Winifred?"

"That is something I would have decided after I had given the matter—"

"You are a smart woman and yet you ask me *why*? Why the hell do you think? What was there for you to consider? The time to consider was before you spread your—"

Freddie wrenched her arm away. "How *dare* you? Who are you to judge me? You who have probably wenched your way around the globe and back again!"

Dark amusement glittered in his black eyes. "You have a point there, sister. Please forgive me; my accusation was not only crude, but it was also hypocritical. And it was also beside the point—which is the future of your child. I am sure I do not need to explain to you the slim chance of an illegitimate daughter making a decent marriage. But perhaps you are enjoying scrimping and saving so much that you have no qualms about condemning a female child to a similar existence?" he asked sarcastically. "But have you given any thought as to what would happen if you refuse to marry and then give birth to a son? How will he feel when he is old enough to understand that some younger—but *legitimate*—son of Plimpton's has inherited what should have been *his*?"

Frightened by his anger, Freddie tried to retreat, but he held her immobile. "How will he feel being forced to fight for scraps of respect and love from everyone around him—all those who know him for a bastard—while some other *younger* son becomes a goddamned *duke*? Tell me what you will think then, Winifred?" he shouted, shaking her until her teeth rattled.

"Piers!" she gasped as she stared into the face of a stranger.

He froze, his hands still clamped painfully tight, his nostrils flaring with the ferocity of his breathing. "You are right about one thing, Winifred. I *did* take away your choice. And I would do it again in a heartbeat. It might be unfair, but I have a damned sight more knowledge about what it is like to be a bastard than you ever will. I can live with what I did. You may never forgive my betrayal, but one day your son or daughter will thank me for my meddling." He firmly set her aside before descending the stairs two at a time. He snatched his hat and gloves off the table, not bothering to put either on before flinging open the door and shutting it behind him with a sharp *bang*.

Leaving Freddie stunned and alone with her unwanted thoughts.

Chapter 20

Freddie studied her reflection in the looking glass, wondering what Plimpton would think when he came to collect her in less than an hour.

A glowing bride, she was not.

Freddie sighed and opened the bottom drawer of her dressing table and extracted a small bag of cosmetics she had only ever used in emergencies.

"This *is* an emergency," she told her reflection.

A light dusting of rice powder beneath her eyes concealed the worst of the dark rings.

Before she could think better of it, she put a dab of rouge high on each cheekbone and rubbed until only a faint, healthy shadow remained.

There. That was all she would do.

Worry about the future was only part of what had put dark smudges beneath her eyes. Yesterday had been the first day she had been able to keep down her breakfast of plain toast, tea, and half an apple.

"If you have one good day, you'll have more," Mrs. Brinkley had assured her. "Those who are sick all the way through don't usually have a reprieve, my lady."

Freddie had eagerly grasped at the older woman's prediction, praying it was true. Being ill every day for the next six months did not sound pleasant under the best circumstances. Vomiting every day while trying to adjust to marriage and a new husband who now hated her would be a nightmare.

As haggard as she looked, at least her clothing was smart and fashionable. It had pained her to use so much of her tiny nest egg on a gown when she would much rather give it to the Morrison's for Mirand, but she had rebelled against the idea of going to Plimpton dressed like a beggar.

Besides, her small savings hardly signified now that she was to be married. Wareham—who was, thankfully—recovered but not so much that he had insisted on making the journey to attend what was likely to be a grim wedding ceremony, had written to congratulate her on her nuptials. His joy in the marriage of his only sister to his best friend had fairly leapt off the page.

Freddie had written to him, but Plimpton had reached him even before her letter. Evidently the duke had set off the same day he'd collected her in Spenham. He had gone to negotiate the details of the wedding contract. Judging by her brother's ebullient letter, the duke had not shared the reason for the speedy nuptials. Freddie had been relieved Plimpton had not told anyone else she was enceinte. She should have known he would not broadcast such a private piece of information.

She still had not decided whether or not to tell her closest friends about her condition. A good part of her reticence was pride. Freddie had always been the calm, practical, and sensible one in her group of seven. She had already relinquished all claim to those characteristics around Plimpton, but that did not mean she was in a hurry to admit that to her nearest and dearest.

Right now, every ounce of her strength was devoted to facing the man who would be her lord and master.

She looked away from her reflection, glancing at her two trunks and two valises. Astoundingly, this was all Freddie had to show for the last eight years of life: some clothing, a few books, personal treasures that were valuable to nobody but Freddie—paintings Miranda had given her, letters from her friends, a carving of a swan Miles had made for her last birthday—and other sentimental bits and bats.

The house and all its furniture belonged to her friend Honey, who had first been her roommate and then her generous, absentee landlady.

Honey had been the first person she had written about her impending wedding. It had been a difficult letter as she'd needed to announce not only her intention of vacating the house, but also her betrothal to Honey's own brother-in-law.

The Etiquette of Love

Honey's response had come by courier and had rivaled that of Wareham when it came to excitement and enthusiasm.

She assured Freddie that the house would continue the way it was, the four servants—Mrs. Brinkley, Una, Sarah, and John Bowman—would remain in Honey's employ after Freddie paid their wages the last time. Even though she would never again occupy the charming but humble house, Honey would not sell it.

"It is all I have left of my father," she had explained in her letter. *"I will keep it for friends to occupy when they visit London. I might even use my father's old studio when Simon and I begin to spend Seasons in the City. Do not worry about anything house-related, my dearest friend, I am sure you have plenty on your mind to occupy you.*

As for your choice of Plimpton? What can I say? You are perfect for each other. Simon is so thrilled you would think it is OUR marriage he is celebrating. I wish you were having a grand wedding ceremony for us all to attend, but I am delighted that you and Plimpton are so eager for marriage you do not wish to wait."

Freddie had laughed out loud at that part.

She had been touched that the replies from her other friends—Portia, Serena, Annis, Miles, and Lori—had also reached her before today, the last one, from Annis, arriving yesterday. Their letters had brimmed with congratulations and pleasure that Freddie, the last of their number, would not be alone. And if there was an undercurrent of confusion and many questions unasked in each letter, Freddie knew her friends were far too polite, not to mention too accustomed to her intense privacy, to plague her on her unexpected marriage.

Well, all except Lori, whose letter—an ironically brief scrawl from a woman who happened to be a novelist—promised, or threatened rather, to pry all the juicy details out of Freddie when they met at her house party. *"Now it is a party to celebrate not just my own marriage, but yours as well, dearest Freddie."*

Freddie had groaned at the thought of contending with all of her friends at once, but finally decided that baptism by fire was probably the best approach. Besides, she could hardly cry off the party when she had been the one to advise Lori on the date.

Writing letters and packing was not all she had done over the last week. She had also made an unscheduled visit to Miranda.

The Morrisons had been embarrassingly grateful for the money she brought with her.

"But you already paid for this next quarter, Mrs. Torrance," Mrs. Morrison had said.

"This is something extra—for all three, er, girls."

Mr. Morrison had taken the packet, his eyes widening at the thickness of it. And then widening even more when he had opened it and looked inside. "This is too generous, Mrs. Torrance. Far too generous," he'd protested.

"No, it is not," she had assured him. "Nor is it going to be the last of the money. From now on, there will be enough to command not just the bare minimum, but enough to afford all of you more comfort."

"But—and please forgive me if I am encroaching—how is all this possible?"

She had hated to do it, but it would be impossible to keep her identity secret in the future. Perhaps if Plimpton had not known…but he *did* know.

"A *countess*!" The color had drained from Mrs. Morrison's face after Freddie had confessed her identity.

"Perhaps you should sit down for this next part," Freddie said, terrified the woman would go into a swoon.

"There's *more*?" she'd shrieked, leaning heavily on her husband who led her to a chair.

Both the Morrison's had been well beyond awed and deeply alarmed at her next news."

"A *duchess*?" Mrs. Morrison had whispered, as if the word was somehow holy.

Freddie supposed that it was to common folk. There were dukes and then there was the king. It was like the firmament and the stars, and all were equally out of reach to most people.

"I am not sure how often I will be able to visit," she had confessed.

"No, of course you cannot come here," Mrs. Morrison had agreed.

The Etiquette of Love

"You misunderstand, Mrs. Morrison. I will not stop coming completely." At least she hoped Plimpton would not forbid the visits. She had been stupid not to insist on it when he had asked to discuss their marriage, but it was too late for that now. "However, I do not know when and how often."

"But...a *duchess*, visiting here? Is—surely your husband, er, the *duke*, will not permit it?" Mr. Morrison had asked.

Freddie had bristled at the old man's question but could not deny it. "Right now, I cannot make any firm promises. And I *know* that will upset Miranda." Just coming on a day that wasn't Wednesday had already alarmed the girl, who was up in her bed resting after the confusing surprise.

"No, she will not care for such a change," Mrs. Morrison agreed, dubious. "Perhaps—" she broke off, biting her lip.

Freddie had felt a heaviness at the other woman's expression. "Go ahead, Mrs. Morrison—speak plainly, please."

Mrs. Morrison glanced at her husband. He had nodded, the two communicating without words the way some long-married couples seemed to do. "What my wife was going to suggest is that it might be better if you do not, er, come visit."

Freddie had been angry—no, furious—and it must have shown.

"Only for a while," he hastily added.

"It is just a suggestion," Mrs. Morrison hurried to assure her, now pale *and* terrified.

A few deep breaths and a moment of reflection had convinced her they were right. "What will you say to her?"

"Nothing right away. We will not tell her until Wednesday. You know how it is difficult to talk to her about matters that are not directly before her."

Freddie had nodded because Mrs. Morrison was correct. For Miranda there was the first Wednesday and the third Wednesday. And there were other days—laundry day was every Monday and market day Thursday—and changing those days in her mind would be a Herculean undertaking.

But there was no helping it. Not only would the duke not wish to live in London during the summer but she doubted that he would want her to come to town next Season now that she was increasing.

No, she could not make plans for first and third Wednesdays. Not anymore.

A hot streak down one side of her face pulled Freddie from her unhappy thoughts. A glance in the mirror confirmed that she was well on the way to red-rimmed eyes and a swollen nose.

"Drat," she muttered, quickly extracting the small bag again and repairing the damage as best as she could.

Freddie was inspecting the results when there was a light knock on the door. She hastily shoved the rice powder back into the bag as if it were the vilest of contraband before saying, "Come in."

Mrs. Brinkley opened the door a crack and then a bit wider when she saw Freddie was dressed and waiting. "You look lovely, my lady," she said, the flattering expression on her face bearing out her compliment.

Ah, the wonder of cosmetics.

"Thank you, Mrs. Brinkley."

"A carriage and footman have arrived to collect your things, my lady. His Grace will be along in a quarter of an hour."

Freddie nodded, her heartbeat speeding at the thought of seeing him again. She was *such* a besotted fool. She could only hope he never guessed that."

"This is from the four of us, my lady." The housekeeper gave Freddie an uncharacteristically shy smile as she held out a prettily wrapped package.

Freddie felt the telltale burning in her eyes that always heralded tears. Why was she such a watering pot? "Oh, Mrs. Brinkley, you shouldn't have."

"Nonsense. You have been a lovely mistress, and we will miss you dearly. I hope you will visit us."

The Etiquette of Love

"Of course I will." She glanced at the package. "Should I open it now?"

"Yes, it is for today."

Freddie unwrapped the box and smiled when she looked inside. "These are lovely," she said, picking up the fine linen and lightly rubbing a finger over the blue horseshoe embroidered in one corner.

"It isn't nearly as nice as the work you do, but I am accounted no mean hand."

"The are beautiful," she assured the other woman, touched.

"Look beneath," Mrs. Brinkley ordered, dashing a tear from her cheek.

Freddie's eyes widened when she saw the filigree cross on the bed of cotton wool. "This is much too nice! I could never—"

Mrs. Brinkley chuckled. "Never you worry, Una is only *loaning* it to you."

"Er—"

"*Something Old, Something New, Something Borrowed, Something Blue, A Sixpence in your Shoe.*"

Freddie laughed. "Ah yes, of course. Please tell Una I will return it in good order."

"Of course, my lady. But there is something more—sandwiched between the two pieces of wool to protect it."

Freddie gasped when she saw the tiny blue egg. "Why, that is the smallest egg I have ever seen."

"It is a dunnock egg, my lady. Sarah made it."

"She made it?"

"Aye, you see the colorful floss? Pick it up."

Freddie gingerly picked up the bright red embroidery floss and saw it went through the egg, which had been cleverly hollowed out. She felt sad for the bird that had given its life for the bauble, but it was pretty."

"It's beautiful."

"Sarah said to tell you the eggs were left to rot in the nest, my lady. She said, *I know my lady loves all creatures—be sure to tell her naught were harmed, Mrs. Brinkley.*"

"Well, thank her for that. It *does* make me happier."

"You cannot *wear* it, of course, but you have the handkerchief to satisfy the blue."

Freddie laughed. "Ah."

"There's one more thing under *that* piece of wool."

Beneath the last piece, resting on the bottom of the little box, was a shiny new sixpence.

Freddie chuckled.

Mrs. Brinkley rolled her eyes. "That is from John Bowman. Lazy bugger. Er, begging your pardon my lady."

"You tell them thank you for me."

"They would have given it themselves if you hadn't been so kind as to allow them the day off."

"I gave it to you, too, Mrs. Brinkley."

"Tisn't right for you to be readying yourself alone on your wedding day, my lady."

Before Freddie could answer, there was a tap on the door.

Mrs. Brinkley opened it and one of His Grace's footmen—Freddie recalled his name was William—bowed and said, "Begging your pardon, my lady, but His Grace is below."

Freddie opened her mouth, but the older woman spoke first. "You take your new mistress's bags below. The countess will be down when she is good and ready."

Humor glinted in the young man's eyes, but he inclined his head respectfully to the older woman and said, "Of course, madam. Are these all?" he asked, easily picking up the four bags in two hands, making her life's possessions seem even more paltry.

"Aye," Mrs. Brinkley said. "Get on with you."

Once the servant had gone, she turned to Freddie, her expression expectant.

"Er, yes?"

The housekeeper gestured to the box. "I'll help you with the necklace and sixpence, my lady."

Freddie laughed at the other woman's adherence to superstition but handed her the box and sat.

"It never harms a man to be kept waiting," Mrs. Brinkley muttered, clasping the pretty cross around Freddie's neck. "Even if that man be a duke."

***

On the morning of his second wedding Plimpton found himself wishing for his brother Simon's counsel. Plimpton rarely engaged in confidences, preferring to rely on his own judgment when it came to making important decisions. Only now, faced with something that would change his life by several magnitudes, did he admit how much he would have liked to confide in another man—one he trusted.

Plimpton had always valued his brother's opinions where women were concerned. Once upon a time, when Simon had been young, single, and carefree, Plimpton had greatly envied him. And then Simon had returned from the War a husk of his former self and he had been reminded why it was never wise to envy another man.

He did not envy Simon now; he was glad that his brother had found happiness. In the process, however, their relationship had become less important to Simon. Plimpton saw him less and less now that he had a wife and child. It had been a long time since he had spent time with only his brother, just the two of them together.

There was Wareham, of course, but Plimpton could hardly tell Winifred's brother how he had debauched his sister under his roof, impregnated her, and then threatened her into accepting his offer of marriage.

Plimpton grimaced. Hell, it hadn't been an offer, it had been a demand of marriage. An order. A *command*.

"Damnation," he muttered. He ought to have done better. He *ought* to have controlled his temper.

Digby paused, the razor slightly above Plimpton's chin. "Your Grace?"

"It is nothing," he said, feeling like a fool for muttering like a madman.

His valet bit back a yawn as he deftly finished shaving him and placed a steaming towel around Plimpton's race.

The poor man was exhausted and so was Plimpton. And yet the day had scarcely begun.

The two of them had spent the last six and a half days on the road, traveling *very briefly* to Whitcombe to inform his mother and daughter of his news, and then to Torrance Park, arriving back in London late last night.

He'd only had time to see his mother and daughter at Whitcombe—both had been pleased, albeit startled, by his announcement—leaving them to share the news with Simon and Honoria.

Wareham had been delighted by his surprise visit, his delight reaching near unbearable levels when Plimpton confessed the reason behind it.

"Marrying Winny?" Wareham had bellowed, his healthy but still too-thin face wreathed in smiles. "By God, I knew you could charm her, Plimpton. If any man could talk my stubborn sister around, it would be you."

Plimpton had been darkly amused by his friend's optimistic assessment. He knew that he and Winifred could not hide the truth behind their sudden marriage forever, but by the time the child came, nobody would comment that the baby was two months early.

At least they would not dare comment to Plimpton or his wife.

He had worried that Wareham might cavil at the haste with which the marriage was taking place. He should have known better.

"Good God, Plimpton! Don't wait for me—or anyone else—drag my obstinate sister to the alter with all possible haste," Wareham had commanded when Plimpton had apologized that they were not waiting until the earl was ready to travel. "It is a second marriage for both of you, I can understand why you would not wish to engage in all the frippery and foolishness."

The gentle clearing of a throat pulled Plimpton back to the present.

"What is it, Digby?" Plimpton asked, buttoning his waistcoat.

"I believe Your Grace had decided to wear the cerulean and silver waistcoat to match her ladyship's gown."

Plimpton blinked at his valet. "What are you babbling about?"

Digby held up a blue and gray waistcoat. "I think Your Grace will prefer this waistcoat."

"Will I?" he asked dangerously.

Digby held his ground. "Yes, Your Grace."

Plimpton snorted and began *un*buttoning his waistcoat. He did not care if Digby radiated smugness at his easy capitulation. Arguing with his valet was like arguing with the tide.

"I presume you have arranged for Lady Sedgewick's maid?" he asked, narrowing his eyes at his servant when the other man looked like he was going to adjust Plimpton's cravat. He might give in on the subject of waistcoat choice, but he'd be damned if he'd allow his servant to tie his cravat as if he were still in leading strings.

"I have, Your Grace. I interviewed ten prospects from the agency but, in the end, decided Mary Compton was the best choice."

Plimpton frowned as Digby helped him into his coat. "Compton? Frank Compton's daughter?"

"Yes, Your Grace. She is the youngest of his eight daughters."

A grunt of amazement slipped from Plimpton. He'd known the tenant farmer had a large number of daughters, but not *that* many. "The youngest, you say. Is she not a bit young?"

"She is eight-and-ten, Your Grace, but she has ably filled the position of parlor maid for two years now. I am impressed with her maturity and dedication."

"Well, if she impresses you, I am sure she is an excellent choice."

"I am gratified by your faith in me, Your Grace."

Plimpton snorted and selected a pearl cravat pin from those Digby held out on a tray.

His valet cleared his throat.

"Oh, for pity's sake. What is wrong with this?" he asked before he could stop himself.

"Her ladyship is wearing silver, Your Grace."

Plimpton grunted, displeased that Winifred had nothing but paste pearls and silver jewelry. He returned the pearl pin to the tray. "Well?" he said when Digby merely stood silent and unmoving like a totem. "Which is it to be?"

"I believe the sapphire pin would be best, Your Grace."

Plimpton tucked the sapphire pin into the folds of his cravat and slipped on his signet ring before turning to inspect his appearance in the glass. He saw the same average-looking, bland-featured man he had seen his entire life. The only differences between his reflection at twenty and almost three-and-forty were the deeper lines around his dull, slate-colored eyes and the amount of gray in his boring brown hair.

He met Digby's gaze in the looking glass. "I trust you have made arrangements at the Bird in Hand for this evening?" he asked, naming the inn where he would spend his first night with his new wife.

"I reserved their best chambers as well as adjacent rooms for Compton and myself."

Plimpton nodded and reached for the gloves and hat Digby was holding. "I will see you there."

"Very good, Your Grace."

Ten minutes later Plimpton hopped out of his travelling coach—the one that had the escutcheon emblazoned on the doors rather than the unmarked carriage that he normally used—in front of Winifred's house. His baggage coach was already there and waiting. In fact, the front door of the house was opened by one of his very own footmen, William.

"Where are the servants?" he asked the younger man.

"The housekeeper said her ladyship gave them the day off, Your Grace."

"Where is the housekeeper?"

"Upstairs with her ladyship."

"Please notify them I have arrived."

"At once, Your Grace."

Plimpton examined the small foyer as he waited, recalling well the last time he had been in this house.

As he paced, he wondered, not for the first time, if he should have spoken to Winifred before today and consulted her opinion on matters, even though she had asked him to make those decisions himself. If not the place and time of the ceremony, then perhaps the bridal journey.

He shrugged off the thought; it was too late to change things now. If she did not like Sweet Clover Manor, they could rest a few days and go someplace she *would* like.

Do you think there is such a place if you will be there with her?

Plimpton snorted; probably not.

He turned at the sound of footsteps to see William descending the stairs with two bags beneath his arms and another two in his hands.

"Her ladyship will be down directly, Your Grace."

Plimpton jerked a nod. "Perhaps you should bring help on your next trip," he suggested wryly as the man fumbled with the bags.

"Er, this is the only trip, sir."

"That is *all* the countess's luggage?"

"Yes, Your Grace."

He nodded his dismissal and waited, once again alone with his thoughts. His mind wandered to the letters he had received from his family upon returning to Plimpton House yesterday.

His brief visit to Whitcombe had taken his mother and daughter by surprise so that neither of them had asked many questions. But they'd had five days to collect their wits and their letters had, with varying degrees of subtlety, expressed their curiosity.

He'd received one from Honoria—with a postscript from Simon declaring Plimpton a *sly dog*—a much longer letter from his mother, and a brief missive from Rebecca.

His lips twitched as he thought about his daughter's letter, which had begun with the cheeky question: *"Are you marrying Lady Sedgewick to avoid the expense of paying her to sponsor me, Papa?"* But his smile drained away when he thought of her regret at not being involved in the wedding.

His mother's letter had said much the same thing—not the jest about the expense, of course—but that she regretted the hurried nature of the marriage. Although she did not put it in such direct words. He knew what she was thinking—that he was marrying in haste and would repent at leisure. She would be worrying he had chosen another wife based solely on her appearance. What might have begun that way, had altered greatly along the way. While it was true Winifred would make a perfect duchess, it was no longer those qualities he appreciated most in her.

But he did not tell his mother that. She would discover when she met Winifred that he had not fallen into the same trap twice. Plimpton felt certain that both his mother and daughter would like his new wife exceedingly.

He turned at the sound of footsteps and could not help smiling at the sight that met his gaze. No wonder Digby had been so bloody insistent on his waistcoat. Winifred's blue gown was an exact match to the subtle stripes in his own garment. What color had Digby called it? Celestial? No, that wasn't it. Cerulean.

Plimpton thought celestial was a better word for his betrothed, who with her delicate blonde beauty looked exactly like the sort of being one would expect to find reclining on a cloud plucking a harp. Yes, she looked like an angel, at least Plimpton's idea of what one should look like.

"You look lovely, Winifred," he said as she came to halt in front of him.

The Etiquette of Love

Her cheeks, already bearing an attractive rosy blush, darkened even more and she gave him a deep, graceful curtsey. "Thank you, Your Grace."

Plimpton stared down into her magnificent but veiled eyes. "Are you ready?"

She swallowed, took a deep breath, and nodded. "Yes, I am ready."

Chapter 21

Freddie had believed the duke's first carriage had been the peak of luxury, but she had been mistaken. Not only was *this* one larger and far more opulent inside, but the exterior bore the ducal escutcheon of her new husband. *Her* crest now.

Perhaps the biggest difference between the last carriage and this one was the fact that the duke was inside it rather than the garrulous Miss Denny.

Freddie glanced up through her lashes at her husband of roughly one hour. He occupied the back-facing seat with an elegant sprawl that was entirely masculine. His profile was toward her while he stared out the window at the perfect late summer day.

Objectively, she knew that he was not handsome. But flashes of him the way he had been that day at the boathouse kept flickering through her mind's eye. She now knew there was a deeply sensual man lurking beneath all his quiet dignity. He might not be capable of love, but he had shown himself to be a master of sexual pleasure—both giving and receiving. Freddie knew that she was fortunate in that regard. Many men of their class would never share with their wives even a fraction of the sensuality that they would with their mistresses.

Based on Plimpton's history with his first wife Freddie knew he would eventually tire of her and take mistresses. The fact that he had dismissed his *lovers*—plural—after their tryst at the boathouse did not mean his attraction for her would last forever, or even for long.

Sedgewick had returned to his mistresses long before he and Freddie had fallen out with each other. He had not been secretive about his affairs and had brazenly told her about his *women* just a few months after their wedding night.

Freddie recalled the night well. He had been lying beside her at the time, naked and flushed after what she had believed to be a satisfying bout of sexual congress. Seemingly out of the blue he had told her that although she had pleased him that night, he generally preferred two or even three women at once.

Freddie had felt as though he had thrown a bucket of ice water at her.

He had laughed at Freddie's revulsion. "What a little prude you are turning out to be, Winifred. How can you dismiss something without even trying it first?"

But she *had* dismissed it, that night, and every time he had suggested it afterward.

He had not laughed for long, but had turned ugly, especially toward the end of their marriage.

Was that what Plimpton had meant about *lovers*? Would he, too, expect such a thing of her?

The thought of it made Freddie unspeakably weary.

"Have you spent much time in Sussex?" the duke asked, thankfully bringing that unpleasant train of thought to a halt.

"Only to pass through it. Where are we going?" she felt compelled to add, when her first comment sounded too abrupt.

"To my smallest estate. I thought we might enjoy a bit of privacy." He paused and then added, "The name of the house is Sweet Clover. The property came to my family through a great aunt on my distaff side. Great Aunt Horatia was a bit of an eccentric and had a mania for bees. You will find evidence of that passion throughout the house as well as the property. The area around the manor is one of the biggest honey producing areas in Sussex. Another reason I thought we might enjoy Sweet Clover is the annual Honey Fair, when people from all around come to sell wares, a good many of which have something to do with either bees or honey."

"That sounds delightful," Freddie said, wishing she did not sound so stiff. The truth was that it would be good to get away from London and the heat and the noise and the crowds. She loved the country but had felt uncomfortable at Torrance Park because of the weight of her past. It would be nice to be somewhere completely…fresh.

Without warning, the duke suddenly shifted across the narrow gap that separated them and lowered himself onto the seat beside her. She subtly inched toward the carriage door, but they were still touching from thighs to shoulders.

He turned to her, his knees brushing her legs, and held out his hand, which he must have stripped of his glove at some point since their mercifully brief ceremony.

Freddie hesitated a few seconds before setting her hand in his. She still wore the pale blue kid gloves she'd purchased to match her wedding outfit, but she could immediately feel the warmth of him through the thin leather barrier.

"I would not have this awkwardness between us, Winifred. I know this marriage is not what you desire, and I hardly helped matters when I lost my temper with you the last time we spoke. I regret I did not exercise more tact and kindness and I apologize for my anger and the hurtful words I spoke that day.

Freddie was startled and embarrassed by his gracious apology. But she was more embarrassed by her own intransigence. Because not too deep down, she knew that she was the one who had been in the wrong. What they had done at the boathouse had been mutual and yet she had treated the outcome—their baby—as if it belonged to her alone.

She made herself look up from their joined hands. While his gaze was shrouded with reserve, she saw a glimmer of the man he had been that day at the boathouse.

He is trying to make the best of an unhappy, but inevitable, situation, Winifred.

Yes, he was.

Freddie sighed and said, "Piers was waiting for me when I came home from Spenham."

The duke nodded.

"Given his circumstances, he was especially eloquent on the selfishness of my behavior. And he argued on behalf of my—our," she corrected with a slight smile, "unborn child. He was most persuasive. What I am trying to say, not very articulately, is that I look back on my thoughts of a mere week ago and am appalled that I could contemplate depriving you of your child. I would never forgive you if the situation had been reversed. I am humbled by your forgiveness and deeply regret keeping the knowledge from you. I like to believe that I would have seen the error of my ways sooner rather than later, but that is no excuse."

Some of the tension left his face. "I believe you would have told me in your own time." He gently rubbed the top of her hand with his thumb, the absent gesture strangely affecting, as if even when he was not conscious of it, his nature was to comfort, protect, and soothe. "I think we neither of us displayed to advantage on that ride back from Spenham." He lifted her hand and held it between his palms, the gesture beseeching and hopeful. "We are husband and wife now, Winifred, and I want this to be a *good* marriage." His serious mouth flexed into that charming, boyish smile she had seen only on that magical day. "Even if the wedding *was* less than auspicious."

Freddie smiled. "It *was* rather grim, wasn't it?"

"It would have been a somber event with only the two of us, but the vicar did not help matters with his infernal sniffling."

He sounded so offended that Freddie laughed. "We will both be lucky if we do not catch sick from him."

He gave a bark of laughter. "The ultimate gift for newlyweds."

They both chortled together for a moment. When they stopped, the duke looked at least five years younger. "A wedding is just a brief ceremony, Winifred. A marriage, on the other hand... Well, in between his sniffs there was one line in the vows that stood out to me: the one about our union lasting for as long as we both shall live. I hope that is many, many years. And I do not wish to live those years estranged from my wife and lover." He paused, and then startled her by adding, "Not this time. Half a life spent with a woman who could not abide me is half a life too much."

***

Plimpton had not intended to add that last part, but there seemed no point in lying about his past.

Winifred's fingers shifted in his grasp until they were laced with the hand that had been palm-to-palm with hers. She squeezed firmly, her eyes glassy with emotion. "Thank you for taking the first step, Your Grace. I agree with what you have said. My marriage—as the entire *ton* must know—did not end happily. But this is a second chance." She chuckled and then explained at Plimpton's questioning look. "I am laughing because I recalled a saying one of my friends told me years ago. You have not met Annis yet—she is Lady Rotherhithe now—but she has a saying, in one language or another, for almost every occasion. This one, I think, is Chinese: *The best time to plant a tree is twenty years ago. The second-best time is today.*" Her expression turned wry. "In other words; we are neither of us young and should not waste one more day."

Plimpton lifted her hand to his lips and kissed the back of it. "Gardening is yet another activity—along with laundering clothing, washing dishes, and many other practical matters—that I have no experience at. But I am willing to learn, Winifred."

"I am an excellent gardener," she assured him. "I have not grown anything useful like a tree, but I can be a boon to your rose gardens."

"But my turnips will languish," he teased, earning one of her charming gurgles of laughter. Plimpton did not want to ruin the light mood, but there were questions that needed answering. And the sooner it happened, the sooner they could move forward with their lives.

"You are looking serious," she said, her smile fading.

"I want to ask you some questions, but I do not want you to feel...persecuted."

"You want to know about Miranda."

He nodded. "That is the name of the child you visit?"

Her lips twisted into a smile, but it was an unhappy one. "Yes. That is her name: Miranda de Montfort."

Plimpton frowned. "De Montfort? But...that is the Earl of Sedgewick's family name."

"Yes."

He shook his head, confused. "You told me that she was not—"

"She is *not* mine. She was Sedgewick's child by his first wife." She held his gaze, her chin trembling slightly. "You said once that trusting one's spouse to keep a secret worked both ways—for husbands as well as wives—what I have just told you is the most precious, potentially devastating secret I possess. I am asking you now, please do not tell anyone whose child she is."

"Are you telling me that you *stole* Sedgewick's daughter?"

"No! At least... I did not steal her from Sedgewick." Her voice had risen, and Plimpton could tell she was struggling to remain calm. "He never wanted Miranda, and he ordered me to pretend as if she had died."

"*What?*"

She nodded, a tear sliding down one pale cheek. "When we married Miranda was barely nine months old. That is part of the reason Sedgewick wanted to remarry so quickly—even before his mourning period was over—to have a mother for his child." She swallowed twice; her voice unsteady. "I loved Miranda on first sight. It was one of the main reasons I accepted his proposal."

"The other being to avoid living beneath Wareham's roof. With Wareham's wife."

"That was the main reason," she admitted. "But I have to admit I would have married him just for Miranda." She smiled, her thoughts obviously in the past. "Not because she was a pretty baby. Indeed, she was scrawny and hairless and cried incessantly. None of the servants in the nursery could soothe her when she fell into a rage." Her smile grew. "But I could. At first, Sedgewick was delighted that she had taken to me. He commended me when she put on weight and grew healthier." Her smile faded. "But he did not like how much time I spent in the nursery." Her eyes slid to Plimpton's. "I will tell you now, Your Grace, that I refuse to be rationed when it comes to spending time with my child. And as for sending her out to a wet nurse for the first year as my mother did with me, I absolutely—"

Plimpton squeezed her hand. "*Shhh,* darling. You are becoming upset for no reason."

She tried to yank her hand from his, but he would not allow it. "Are you saying I do not have the right to spend as much time as I want with my own child?"

He smiled at her ferocity. "That is not what I am saying at all. I have seen Honoria with Robert—and Simon, too—and they are not ashamed to spend time with their child. My mother was hounded just as you were because my father believed it was degrading for his duchess to nurse her children. He forbade it and both Simon and I were sent away to a wetnurse for not just the first year, but three." He still could not believe the cruelty of the man. "He was adamant that any sort of affection on her part would make his heir and spare—yes, that is how he referred to us—weak and soft. On the surface my mother appears to be of a yielding disposition, but her core is pure steel, and she sneaked away to visit both of us in turn. Some would say she was wrong to disobey my father, but I believe Simon and I would have rebelled violently against our father's strangulating control if not for her. What he saw as a feminizing, weakening influence actually made us stronger." Plimpton met her gaze squarely. "I am *not* my father's son in that regard, Winifred. I do not believe that the most defenseless among us must be neglected in order to be made strong. I honor you for loving Sedgewick's daughter—a child not even of your own blood—and acting as her champion when she could not champion herself. Now," he said, taking his handkerchief from his inside pocket and lightly blotting her tears. "Tell me how she came to live with that couple."

***

Mrs. Brinkley had assured Freddie that the emotions roiling inside her would one day begin to settle.

Unfortunately, that day was not today.

She did not know whether she wanted to sob on the duke's shoulder and beg him to hold and comfort her, or crawl into his lap and kiss him until he took control and brought them both the pleasure they had experienced the day their child was conceived.

"Winifred?" His eyebrows had lowered, a deep notch of concern between them. "Do you not wish to tell me?"

"No, it is not that. It is just—I am so relieved that you do not think spending time with an infant is a ridiculous waste of a mother's time."

"Simon would correct you and say it is not a waste of a father's time, either."

The Etiquette of Love

"Yes, Honey says he spoils Robert with his love."

"Is it possible to give a child too much love?"

The question took her breath away. Could this really be the distant, implacable Duke of Plimpton? The same man who had threatened to destroy Freddie's livelihood to force Honey to bow to his will?

"Why are you looking at me that way, Winifred?"

"No reason," she lied, and then lightly cleared her throat. "To answer your question, Sedgewick was…" She chewed her lip, searching for the right words.

"Childishly selfish?" Plimpton offered wryly.

"Yes. That describes him perfectly." Freddie considered her dead husband's various perversions and amended, "At least it describes his attitude toward getting what he wanted. We were neither of us in love, but the early days of our marriage—before I defied him regarding Miranda—were at least enjoyable." Freddie chewed her lip, pensive. Sharing this next part would be uncomfortable, but it needed to be said.

"I know a great many people are aware of Sedgewick's, er, proclivities, so let me address that matter. At first, we had a…satisfactory physical relationship and he was considerate and gentle." She cleared her throat, her face heating. "At least I thought it was. It was not until later that I learned about his more, er, uncommon tastes. I believe he tried to be a good husband, at least to begin with, but he ceased making any attempts once I held firm about Miranda. The more I dug in my heels about her, the more he punished me."

"By punish, do you mean—"

"Yes, he became violent, but not until the very end. At first, he found more devious ways to bend me to his will. He took away small things."

"Such as?" he asked, once again expressionless.

Freddie found talking about this part of her relationship with Sedgewick embarrassing rather than upsetting. Speaking the words aloud made her realize just how petty and small her first husband had been.

"He forbade me to ride. And then he had the servants deny my friends when they came to visit. He hid my correspondence and did not allow me to visit my brother."

"In other words," he said grimly. "He was building a cage around you."

She was relieved he understood. "He became angry when none of that served to change my mind where Miranda was concerned." She swallowed. "Finally, he—he brought in a doctor, a man who relied on him for his living and needed to curry favor—and the man told me that Miranda was deathly ill. That she was contagious and I would risk my life to tend her. I did not care—I begged Sedgewick to let me nurse her. That was the worst thing I could have done. It was what he had wanted all along: to get a reaction from me. To see evidence of my suffering. If only I had been less—less—"

"You cannot blame yourself for not playing games with a deranged man, Winifred."

"I know, but—" A sob interrupted the last word and Freddie paused, taking a moment to calm her rioting emotions. "Long before matters reached that point, I had not wanted him to come near me. I—I hated him by then and I fought him with every ounce of my strength. But—but my resistance only excited him more."

Plimpton briefly closed his eyes. "No wonder you did not want to marry again."

Freddie licked her suddenly dry lips. "Sedgewick also, er, installed two of his women in the east wing." Ancient rage bubbled up inside her. "In my own *house*. It was humiliating, but I was glad of it if it kept him away from me. But again, I erred. He *wanted* me to notice what he was doing—how he was humiliating me—and when I did not, he came to my bed and—and brought them with him."

"Dear God." The duke shook his head, his expression one of disgust. "What Sedgewick did to you was *not* normal, Winifred."

"Then you—you would not expect such a thing?"

Plimpton's jaw dropped. *"What?"*

"I just meant—well, you mentioned your *lovers* before, so—"

The Etiquette of Love

"God, no!" He shoved a hand through his hair, his expression rigid. "I apologize for that, Winifred. I just said it to—"

"Get a rise out of me?" she guessed, too relieved to be angry.

"Yes. I am sorry. And I hope you believe that I would *never*—"

"I believe you." And she did.

He hesitated, as if to pursue the matter, but then nodded and said, "What happened with the child?"

Freddie was grateful to him for steering the story away from her disgusting marriage. "Understand that this went on over several years—it was like a pot that boiled slowly. Only during the last year did it become unbearable. Partly that was due to my resistance, but there was another reason: Miranda herself."

"You mean because she is simple?"

"They told you about her at the Spotted Sow, I presume?"

"Yes. They said this elderly couple had three girls, none of them right in their heads."

Freddie frowned. "I despise that way of describing them, but there is no denying that Miranda, Cynthia, and Laura are not like other people. They could never live on their own as they are children in many respects. Miranda is only a child, but the other two are in their mid-thirties."

"I presume Miranda's condition was not evident until she was older?"

"Yes. Sedgewick was devastated when the doctor told him she would never be like other children. He was not distraught on Miranda's behalf, but his own. He was consumed with the fear that somebody would find out that he had sired an idiot—his word for his own daughter, not mine. And so he decided that Miranda had to die—oh, not really, but for me and everyone who knew about her. With the help of his pet doctor, Sedgewick was able to persuade me she was dead. I—I don't want to go in to—"

"You do not have to," the duke assured her.

She swallowed and nodded. "Sedgewick assumed I would go back to being his wife and countess as I no longer had her presence to distract me. Instead, I sank into a deep depression. I was inconsolable and—and to be honest, I would have welcomed death. Sedgewick washed his hands of me. I think he, too, wished that I would die and leave him free to marry again—to somebody who could give him an heir. We had been man and wife for more than three years and had— had engaged in regular conjugal relations even for the last part of our marriage—and still I had not conceived."

"Have you ever considered the possibility that Miranda is not really Sedgewick's child?"

"That did not occur to me until I learned I was enceinte." She gave him a wry look. "I suppose that makes me a fool."

"It makes you a trusting person, and there is no crime in that."

"No crime, maybe, but had I known the truth, I never would have—" Freddie broke off and laid a hand on her midriff, which felt no different than usual yet. "I was about to say I would go back and change what happened that day in the boathouse, but that is not true. I cannot regret this child. For years I believed I would never have one. If we had not been together, I might never have known. So, no, I do not regret what we did."

"Good. Neither do I. You had not finished your story."

"There is not a great deal more. Sedgewick behaved increasingly recklessly not only when it came to drinking and women, but also at the card tables. He was, in crude language, *all done up*."

"You believe his hunting accident was no accident?" the duke guessed.

She nodded.

"So… you were free."

"I was free," she agreed. "But I was broken hearted—not for Sedgewick, but for Miranda."

"How did you find out she was alive?"

"Sedgewick had pensioned off her nurse and given the woman a tiny cottage—more of a hut, really—on the estate. She was old and dying and consumed with guilt. It was she who told me that Sedgewick had given Miranda to a hospital for the mentally insane." Freddie felt sick when she thought of that place. Not just Miranda's condition, but the dozens of others she could not save. "It was dreadful, Plimpton. Absolutely horrifying. Even pigs are kept in better conditions."

"And so, you stole her away."

"And so I stole her away," Freddie said, giving him a mulish look.

But instead of chiding her for stealing a child that was not her own, the duke said, "I applaud what you did, Winifred."

"You do?"

"Yes. Any decent person would. What I do not understand is why you have kept everything a secret."

"Have you met the new Earl of Sedgewick, my husband's cousin?"

An expression of distaste flickered across the duke's face. "Yes, unfortunately."

"He is exactly the sort of selfish, insecure man who would put Miranda right back in that place for no reason other than he would not want anyone thinking he did not look after his kin. And his notion of *looking after* means condemning Miranda to a short, ugly, brutish life."

The duke nodded, but he looked distracted.

Unease simmered in Freddie's belly at his pensive expression. "What are you thinking?"

"That she is Lady Miranda de Montfort."

"What of it?"

"You do not think she deserves more than to be tucked away like a dirty secret?"

"But Sedgewick won't give her *more*. He will lock her away somewhere horrible."

"He will not do anything of the sort if I stand as her protector."

Freddie stared. "You—you would *do* that? Oppose him?"

"I doubt I would have to do much—the man not only resembles a weasel physically, he has the characteristics of one. He would not want to make an enemy of me; he will readily agree to hand wardship of her over to me."

"I—that is a lot to consider," Freddie admitted once she had gotten past her shock at his offer. "I do not mean to sound ungrateful, but I am not sure that bringing Miranda to live with us is the best thing for her. You see, she has lived most of her life—at least what she can recall—with the Morrisons and the two women who live there. You would have to meet Miranda to understand just how important routine and ritual are to her. To most orphaned girls of thirteen living in a castle as the ward of a duke would be a fairytale come to life."

"But not Miranda?"

"No, not Miranda."

"What do you wish to do, then?"

She sighed. "I do not know. I have been thinking about it constantly, but—"

"But you worried what I would do or say?"

"Yes," she admitted. "But now that I know you will champion Miranda, I can decide based on what is best for her, rather than out of fear. Thank you, Your Grace, I am…extremely grateful."

"It is my pleasure," he said, lifting their still-joined hands and kissing her bare wrist. His lips curled up slightly at the corner. "By the way, I believe it is time for you to call me Wyndham."

For some reason, the invitation to use his Christian name felt almost as intimate as what they had done that rainy afternoon in the boathouse.

Freddie smiled shyly. "Thank you for what you have offered to do for Miranda…Wyndham."

Chapter 22

The distance to Sweet Clover Manor was not nearly as far as that to Torrance Park, but Plimpton had decided to make the journey in two easy stages rather than all in one day as he normally did.

He was relieved he had decided to split the journey. Because even though they stopped well before nightfall, the dark smudges beneath Winifred's eyes, which had been only hinted at earlier that day, had grown considerably more pronounced.

She had mentioned earlier—after much gentle prying—that she had been ill most mornings until just a few days ago. That would explain her weight loss, which he had noticed immediately today.

Plimpton had experienced a familiar and unwanted gnawing in his belly when he'd asked about Winifred's pregnancy. Because whenever he had inquired into Cecily's health, she had seen it as a sign of his concern for the baby, rather than any real interest in her.

By Cecily's third pregnancy Plimpton had learned not to ask her anything, relying only on whatever the doctor told him.

Winifred had seemed embarrassed by his questions, but not angry. But then she was a completely different sort of woman than his dead wife. That was clear by the way she cared so much about her stepdaughter Miranda that she had gone into decline when she had believed the girl to be dead.

Cecily—

Plimpton caught the thought before it could fully form. Cecily was his past; Winifred was his future. He had been given a new opportunity and he needed to put his dead wife behind him.

But just because he forgot about Cecily did not mean he could forget how fragile some women became during pregnancy. This was no normal wedding night; his bride was already carrying his child so there was no need to rush a consummation.

That is what he told himself.

He also told himself he was going to leave Winifred to rest tonight, no matter how badly he wanted her.

Plimpton had not believed he would have the strength of will to stick to his resolution until Winifred had almost fallen asleep over her custard during dessert.

"Come," he said when she had yawned for the third time in as many minutes. "I will escort you to your room. You should have an early night as we will be leaving at first light tomorrow."

She blinked up at him, clearly nonplussed that he wasn't going to insist on his conjugal rights. Plimpton was nonplussed, himself. And disappointed that he was exercising such restraint. What sort of man did not take his new wife to bed on their wedding night, regardless of whether she was breeding or not?

But as he led her up the stairs, he could see her feet were so heavy she could scarcely lift them. No, he could not, in good conscience, importune her tonight.

"Oh, by the by," she said, the second *by* split by yet another yawn. "I wanted to thank you for Compton. I believe we shall deal very well together."

"I cannot claim the credit for your new maid; that is all Digby's doing."

"Please thank him for me."

"Of course." Just what his already smug, arrogant valet needed: praise from Plimpton's new wife. "I arranged for a bath to be prepared while you were at dinner. A good soak will relieve some of the aches caused by travel."

"How kind of you! Thank you." Her eyelids lifted and the smile she gave him was radiant and went a long way toward erasing signs of her weariness.

It also went a goodly way toward erasing his self-restraint.

"You are welcome," he said hastily, pressing a chaste kiss on her forehead once they had stopped outside the room Digby had reserved for her—the best the inn had to offer. "This is a well-run establishment—and safe—but you must still lock the door once you are inside. I doubt your maid will know that as she is as green as new grass." He hesitated and added, "Lock the door between your room and hers once she has retired, just to be safe."

She gazed up at him with a teasing, sleepy smile that made him instantly hard. Or, harder, rather. "What about the door between my chamber and yours?"

"That should be the *first* door you lock. I will wait here until I hear the tumbler turn."

She laughed. "Good night, Your Grace."

"Sleep well, Winifred."

Plimpton really did wait until he heard the sound of the tumbler turning in the lock before making his way down to the taproom. It was going to be a long, long night. There was no reason to face it entirely sober.

***

By the time Plimpton tottered up to his room three hours later he was both a trifle disguised and still just as aroused as he had been earlier from thinking about his wife sleeping above his head. Mingled with his desire was a feeling of virtuousness at his own self-sacrifice.

As morally rewarding as that feeling was, he could not help wishing he had not behaved *quite* so virtuously. Indeed, a far smaller amount of virtue—taking her only once tonight rather than the three or four times he had envisioned—would have sufficed. But then he had never done anything by halves, had he?

Plimpton fumbled with the key, jabbing it futilely at the lock several times before sliding it home. The symbolism of his clumsy thrusting did not escape him. It was probably just as well he had not made love to Winifred tonight.

Chuckling to himself, he opened the door. And then froze like a bird dog detecting game. Winifred lay atop the bedding on her side curled into a tight C shape with her arms holding a pillow to her midriff.

He carefully closed the door, wincing at the squeak of the hinges. But she did not stir.

Plimpton silently thanked his foresight in dismissing Digby earlier that night. Thinking of his officious valet made his gaze slide to the door that led to the adjoining rooms—not Winifred's, but Digby's. He scowled when he saw she had not thrown the latch, and a possessive, primitive displeasure spread in his belly at the thought of any other man, even his loyal servant, observing his wife as she slept. He took a step to remedy the oversight, freezing yet again as a floorboard groaned beneath his boot.

Blast and damn.

But when he looked at the bed, it was clear Winifred had not moved. It seemed his new wife was a sound sleeper.

By the time he had locked the door and removed his boots and coats, he had amended *sound sleeper* to *sleeps like the dead*. She had not so much as twitched at all the bumps, knocks, and squeaks he had created, even though he had moved with more care than a man trapped in a cave with a sleeping tiger.

Risking a few more noises, he poured himself a glass of the brandy Digby always provided for him when they traveled—complete with cut crystal decanter and glasses—and then lifted one of the wingchairs and carried it closer to the bed.

Glass in hand, he gingerly lowered himself into his seat with a quiet sigh and sipped his drink as he regarded his sleeping wife.

She wore the sort of high-necked, prim white nightgown that he had not seen in years. Cecily had worn something similar for his rare visits to her bedchamber. He only knew that because he had made the unfortunate mistake of lighting the candles in her room on their wedding night, eager to see his beautiful bride, a woman he had not-so-secretly coveted for close to a year before she had accepted his offer.

That night had been the first and last he had wanted any light in the bedchamber.

That had been the last night for a great many things.

Plimpton's father and hers had been friends since the cradle and had all but arranged the union between themselves. It had been Cecily's mother who had insisted on a Season for her daughter before she married.

The Etiquette of Love

Plimpton, by in large obedient to his father's whims, had initially balked at marrying a woman of the duke's choosing.

Until he saw Cecily.

Love at first sight was a common concept. During that Season and right up until his wedding night he had believed that is what afflicted him.

Only after he had accepted that there was a person behind Cecily's beautiful face and desirable body, had he discovered the truth: he had been infatuated. And not even with *her*, but with her appearance. What he had believed to be love, had been shallow and fleeting, a product of his testes rather than his mind or heart. In retrospect, Plimpton could not blame Cecily for despising him; he had been no better than a hound in rut.

Cecily's story, he discovered that first night, had been an all too common one. She had been in love with another man, a squire's son who had neither the rank nor fortune to tempt her father to change his mind. Instead, Cecily's father had sold his daughter, not caring that she had never wanted to marry Plimpton.

Because Cecily could not vent her fury on her father Plimpton became—until her dying day—a convenient target for all her wrath and hatred.

He studied the second woman he had forced into marriage. Her lips were slightly parted, and her chest rose and fell in a gentle, regular rhythm. The conversation they'd had in the coach that day had left him almost giddy with relief. Because it could have so easily gone the other way, cementing their enmity instead of easing it.

She had not only been gracious in her acceptance of his apology but had gratified him with one of her own. He had not needed her to acknowledge the error of her actions, but it had soothed some of the pain he'd been feeling.

Today, for the first time in years—decades, even—he felt hopeful of the future. Yes, part of that hope was because of the child in her belly. But the greater part by far was because of *Winifred*. Not only because of her beautiful face and desirable body. And not even because she epitomized what he wanted in his duchess. No, he was filled with excitement and optimism because she was everything and more when it came to what he had always wanted in a wife, companion, and lover.

Plimpton took a sip of his brandy and savored the pleasant burn that warmed his throat. Winifred's words from earlier—those from her friend Lady Rotherhithe—came back to him. Today he and his new wife had planted a tree—the first of many, he hoped. And perhaps—just *perhaps*—that tree would take root and flourish.

***

Some awareness in her sleeping brain caused Freddie to open her eyes.

The first sight that met her bleary gaze was that of a man, coatless and cravat-less, sprawled in an armchair beside the bed.

Not just any man; her husband.

Plimpton smiled. "The sleeper has awakened," he said, his quiet voice tinged with amusement.

Freddie rubbed her eyes and pushed up into a sitting position. What had seemed like a good idea earlier—coming to her husband's room—now seemed…awkward. "Have you been here long?"

"Not very long."

Freddie's gaze moved down his bare throat, across his broad chest, out to the glass—empty—that he held in a negligent grasp. Her eyes darted back to his face.

"I am not cup shot, if that is what you are wondering."

It had been. And she was relieved to hear he was not. Sedgewick had been nasty at the best of times, but drink had exacerbated his propensity for cruelty.

She saw that her hem of her nightgown had ridden up and carefully pulled it back down, trying to hide the action.

Based on the way his eyes crinkled at the corners, she failed to hide her bid for modesty.

She tossed aside the pillow she'd been clutching and wrapped her arms around her legs and rested her chin on her knees. "What were you doing?"

The Etiquette of Love

"Watching you sleep." His eyes, usually so piercing and aware, were heavily lidded, their expression relaxed and almost lazy.

Freddie should have contrived a plan of action rather than simply coming to his room and waiting for him. But then, she had not expected to fall asleep and—

He unfolded his length from the chair with fluid grace and set his empty glass on the nightstand. "Why are you here, Winifred?"

It was not the question she'd anticipated—indeed, she'd expected no questions—and she cleared her throat. "Er, you said—at Torrance—that I should come to your chambers when I was ready." Freddie felt her blush spread over her entire body, not just her face.

He stared at her broodingly.

"I am sorry," she said, scrambling for the edge of the bed.

"Stay," he said quietly.

She stopped, feeling like a fool.

He reached out to touch her face and she startled.

"*Shh*," he murmured, tracing the line of her jaw with one finger. "Look at me."

She inhaled deeply and looked up, not even trying to conceal her confusion and embarrassment.

"I was attempting to be a considerate husband by leaving you alone tonight."

She nodded, pinioned by his gaze as she so often was. "I know."

"I had removed myself from temptation." His finger slid over her chin and rested on her lower lip. "But temptation has come to me."

"Do you want—should I leave?"

He cocked his head. "Do you know, Winifred, that I do not believe you *could* leave at this point. One self-sacrificing gesture per day is my limit."

A nervous laugh slipped out of her. "That is a good thing for a wife to know."

He held out his hands. "Come here," he urged when she hesitated.

Once he'd brought her to her feet, he stroked the thick rope of hair that lay over her right breast. "I want to see it loose. Does that bother you?"

"No, not at all." It took a great deal of time to brush it out, but Freddie suspected he would make it worth the effort.

"I will do it," he said when she reached for the plait.

He untied the ribbon Compton had used to secure the end, his eyes tracking the motions of his fingers, as if his task was worthy of his complete attention. The softness he had displayed on rare occasions once again tempered his stark features as the plait came apart and the curls sprang free like prisoners liberated from their shackles.

The same rapt look she had seen the last time they'd been together slowly spread over his face. Once he'd freed her hair he finger-combed it until it was a thick, heavy curtain that hung to her waist. "It is still damp."

"Yes. It takes hours to dry, and I was too impatient to sit by the fire."

"I am impatient, myself." His fingers moved to the row of buttons that ran down the front of her best nightgown.

Freddie's breathing quickened; he was going to strip her naked, as he had the last time. She both yearned for and dreaded being bared to him, her skin tingling with excitement when his fingers brushed against the fine muslin.

Once he'd reached the bottom button he looked up. "Over your head or down your hips?"

"It will only fit over my head," she confessed, blushing furiously at the admission that her hips were too broad.

"Is that so? What a lucky man I am," he murmured, slowly bunching the fabric with his fingers but not taking his eyes from hers.

Freddie was very aware of her breathing—the speed of it and the harshness—and was pleased to note that his chest was rising and falling faster than before.

She closed her eyes when he raised the nightgown over her head, keeping them closed when it was gone.

"Are you shy, Your Grace?"

Her eyes flew open, and she found him regarding her with lazy amusement. She also found him fully clothed.

Stifling her cowardice, she reached for his shirt. "It is my turn, now."

He looked pleased by her eagerness, watching her intently as she tugged the long hem of his shirt from his pantaloons. He raised his arms without being asked and Freddie leaned close, standing on her toes to lift the garment over his head.

The scent of him caught at her. Not lake water this time, but clean starch, cologne, and the nutty, faintly sweet aroma of brandy.

She stepped away with reluctance and tossed his shirt over the chair he had just vacated. When she looked at him, she saw his eyes were on her body, his face hard with desire. She indulged herself with an inspection of her own, pleased that her memory had not exaggerated his muscularity or his… proportions.

She swallowed down the moisture that pooled in her mouth as her gaze hovered over the thick ridge distorting his tight pantaloons. Freddie loved fine clothing and the fabrics that comprised it—seeing it, feeling it, and even reading about how it was made.

Pantaloons, for example, were cut on the bias, a procedure which created the stretching effect that made for such a flattering fit. Or at least it was flattering when stretched over a fine body.

And the duke had exceptionally magnificent thighs and calves.

She leaned closer so that she could reach behind him to unlace the gusset that gave the pantaloons an even snugger fit.

He hissed when her erect nipples grazed the thin skin of his torso and his arms closed around her. "Are you trying to unman me?" he asked in a low voice, nuzzling her temple and ear with his nose.

"I am trying to *un*dress you," she corrected, her voice every bit as strained as his.

Her fingers finally located the ends of the laces and tugged. The fabric sagged slightly and Freddie slid her fingers between warm linen and hot satiny skin and eased the garment down over his narrow hips.

The duke moaned and his teeth nibbled her ear, startling a giggle out of her.

She bit her lower lip, mortified at the sound.

"A giggle? Why Your Grace, I never would have believed you capable of making such a sound." His hand slid up her spine and cupped her head, turning her slightly so that he could claim her lips. The kiss was slow, deep, and so drugging that Freddie forgot all about his pantaloons.

He pulled away after a long moment. "I am thrilled that you came to me, Winifred."

She swallowed and nodded.

He gestured to his pantaloons, which had slid down just enough that the slick crown of his erection was peeking over the top, like a helmed soldier peering over a wall.

"Oh," she said, enrapt by the erotic image.

The duke's hands came to rest just above his waistband, the gesture causing muscles all up and down his abdomen and chest to flex. He cleared his throat and Freddie's head whipped up.

"They go down over my hips, rather than up over my head," he pointed out helpfully.

Freddie couldn't help laughing. "And here I thought you could not dress or undress yourself."

He raised his eyebrows, his regal, haughty stare, utterly at odds with the twinkle in his gray eyes and his jutting arousal.

She had barely shoved his pantaloons to his thighs when he caught her up in his arms again, trapping the hot brand of his erection against her belly.

"Get on the bed," he said, his voice raspy, no laughter in his hot eyes now.

The Etiquette of Love

Freddie scrambled backward with more haste than grace, wanting a good vantage point to watch the duke's doings. She arranged her arms and legs so that she was as modestly covered as possible. But the duke was not paying her any mind at the moment. He had shoved down his pantaloons and drawers in a rush and was now cursing beneath his breath when he could not pull the narrow bottoms over his feet.

Freddie could not resist making a *tsk*ing sound. "I see I was premature with my praise. You need to unbutton the ankles, Your Grace." She cocked an eyebrow. "You probably were not even aware there *were* buttons, were you?"

"Hush, wife," he retorted imperiously. "Of course I knew they had buttons." A slight flush stained his cheeks and a rueful smile pulled at his lips. "I have seen Digby buttoning and unbuttoning them times beyond counting."

Freddie laughed and, acting on impulse, shed her modest pose and pulled him onto the bed. "You sit," she ordered, and then—before she could lose her courage—she slipped from the mattress and lowered herself to her knees.

Not until she looked up and saw Plimpton's expression of shock as he gazed down at her did she realize the audacity of her action and how exposed it had left her.

But it was too late to change her mind, so she lowered her bottom onto her heels and bowed her head as she took the hem of the pantleg closest to her. Rather than the more common cloth-covered buttons, the duke's were nacre; a lovely dark gray shade that matched the color of his pantaloons—and his eyes—perfectly. The unexpected elegance of the buttons surprised her. The duke's clothing was always of the finest cut and fabric, but his style was one of almost Puritanical simplicity. These buttons were unlike him.

"What are you doing down there?" he asked peevishly.

"Examining these lovely nacre buttons."

"Nacre?" he repeated, visibly betwattled.

"Nacre is a type of—"

"I know what nacre is," he retorted.

Yes, he was *definitely* peeved.

"Are these special pantaloons, Your Grace?"

"What are you driving at, Duchess?"

"Did Digby purchase them just for today?"

His eyes narrowed when he realized she was roasting him. "You think I lack the style necessary to choose nacre buttons."

She bit her lip. "Not at all."

His gaze dropped from her face to her chest, which she had forgotten was bare.

She gasped and lifted an arm to cover herself.

"You will hardly be able to unbutton those *nacre* buttons with only one hand," he taunted.

She took great pleasure in proving him wrong, unfastening four in rapid succession and then tugging on the hem hard enough to yank the fabric over his foot. "You were saying?"

"*Hmm*," was all he replied as she switched arms over her chest and unbuttoned the other side just as deftly. "Impressive."

"I feel certain a man of your abilities could learn to do it given enough time and practice."

He gave a bark of laughter. "Impudent minx." He shoved off his pantaloons and kicked the tangled garments off his feet. Moving swiftly, he took her hands and lifted her from her knees. "Straddle me," he said, his eyes locking with hers.

"But—"

"No *but*s." He nudged her thighs with one of his knees. "Do it, Winifred. I promise I will make it worth your while."

His gaze was so searingly commanding that her clenched legs spread without further urging. He nodded, his eyes still on hers. "Good. Now, put your knees beside my hips. Go ahead," he said when she once again balked.

As if in a trance, she complied with his scandalous order and he immediately slid his hands up her outer thighs and around to her bottom, gently but firmly pulling her closer and spreading her even wider in the process.

He lowered his gaze and his jaw muscles flexed beneath the taut skin of his jaw. "Look at us, Winifred."

**

His wife's body trembled beneath his hands. Plimpton knew part of that was from embarrassment at the vulnerability of her position. But part of it, he could tell by the hammering pulse at the base of her throat, was from pure excitement.

Her forehead brushed against his face as she gazed down to where they touched. Her almost inaudible grunt of arousal was more erotic than the sound of her screaming his name.

Although Plimpton would have that from her as well, before the night was finished.

He reached down to where his cock jutted up from her dark blond curls and the lips of her sex were parted by his shaft. Carefully, he exposed her slick, swollen peak, dipping his finger into her slippery heat and using the copious moisture her body was producing to caress the thrusting little nub of flesh.

A shudder racked her body and one of her hands lifted to his shoulder, her touch as light and tentative as butterfly landing on a flower.

Her other hand closed around his cock.

"God, yes," he whispered as her slim, cool fingers tightened around his hot length and she pumped him firmly from root to tip.

He hated to admit it, but Sedgewick had taught her well. Just like the last time she'd handled him; she knew how much pressure to exert and exactly where to employ it, stroking beneath his crown with each caress.

Plimpton slid his finger through the swollen petals of her sex until he reached her tight opening and buried himself to the third knuckle, working her until he was slick with her arousal and then adding a second finger.

At first the only noises in the room were ragged breaths and occasional grunts or moans. Soon, the sound of wet flesh joined the erotic symphony.

Rarely, if ever, had he been brought to the point of climax so speedily and he shook with the effort of containing his orgasm. Between her skilled hand and her tight, wet body his control frayed just as quickly as his virtuous intentions had done.

Before he could shame himself, the pumping of her fist began to falter so he intensified his own efforts and was rewarded when her body suddenly went stiff and froze.

"*Wyndham*," she gasped, a shudder rolling through her slender frame as her cunt squeezed his fingers, one convulsive wave after another, each less powerful than the last.

Not until the last one had faded away did Plimpton withdraw from her and close his hand around the one of hers that was now only resting lightly on his cock. He used her fist to stroke himself, cupping her hand tightly. It took barely a half dozen pumps of their joined hands before he exploded, emptying his long-suffering ballocks against the soft curve of her breasts, painting her with his seed.

Plimpton collapsed against her, sapped of energy, his hand falling away as Winifred milked him until there was nothing left.

He leaned back just enough that he could admire his work, sliding his fingers into the cooling ejaculate and spreading it over her breasts and belly until she was liberally coated.

Rather than be repulsed, she arched her back to give him better access. Plimpton had rarely seen a sight as arousing as that of his hand stroking her small, perfect breast, its tip erect and dark pink, the pale globe glistening wetly.

But then he lifted his eyes and encountered an even more satisfying sight: Winifred heavy-eyed with satiation, her lips curved into a tiny, smug smile.

A man, Plimpton decided, could become very accustomed to seeing that expression. Indeed, he could quickly become addicted to it.

Chapter 23

As the coach began to climb a gentle rise Plimpton gathered his papers, slipped off his spectacles, and put both into his lap desk before setting it aside and crossing over to sit beside Winifred.

She glanced up from her book as his body slid in beside her.

"Look," he said, timing his command perfectly to when the carriage crested the slight hill.

He watched her, rather than the sight before them and was not disappointed.

Her lips parted and her eyes went wide with wonder as she got her first look at Sweet Clover Manor. "It is *adorable,* Plimpton! You did not say it was Tudor. Wattle and daub is my favorite—and that jettied upper floor and those mullioned windows and dormers and—oh, I just love all of it. When was it built?"

"I am told it is a classic example of the mid-Elizabethan Period. Rather than E-shaped, Sweet Clover is laid out like an H, with a central hall connecting the two wings. It has many features that are typical of the era, such as flagstone floors rather than wood, and oak paneled walls and ceilings. There is also a coffin drop and—my favorite part—an inglenook fireplace in the library."

"A coffin drop?" She frowned. "I have not heard of that."

"It is a section of flooring on the second level that is removable so large items can be raised and lowered. The staircase, you will see, is too tightly spiraled to allow for moving anything too big."

"What an interesting driveway. Is there a reason for the design?"

Even though the terrain was level and not heavily wooded, the narrow, crushed rock drive weaved back and forth in uneven zigs and zags.

"An ancestor, I cannot recall the name at present, believed such irregularity would deter evil spirits from reaching the manor."

She laughed. "Because spirits only travel on well graveled paths."

"Just so," he agreed. As they neared the house, he saw that the Bensons, the married couple who took care of the house, had lined up the servants, who numbered no more than twenty, both indoor and out.

Plimpton had deliberately chosen Sweet Clover because it was the smallest of Plimpton's houses by an order of magnitude. He had no interest in awing her with grandeur; he wanted to help her settle comfortably into her new life. To do that, they needed intimacy. Judging by the cozy feel of her London house, he thought Sweet Clover might feel more like home to her.

He had never visited the property long enough to encourage social calls, so they would not be bothered by neighbors. It would be the perfect place to become acquainted with each other.

Plimpton stole a gaze at her rapt profile as she gazed at the approaching building. He hoped she would not feel trapped or bored with only him for company.

If that proved to be the case…Well, it was better to find out sooner rather than later.

***

Freddie fell in love with Sweet Clover Manor on sight, and her affection for the charming old house only deepened in the days that followed.

It was cozy enough for the two of them, while still affording them enough space for their individual needs. There were very few servants to manage, and Mr. and Mrs. Benson did an admirable job of seeing to Freddie and Plimpton's comfort without overwhelming them with attention.

Plimpton had chosen well; it was the perfect place for a bridal holiday.

The Bensons were an elderly couple who had managed the property since Plimpton's father's time and it was clear they were both overjoyed that the duke had remarried, and also that His Grace had chosen to bring his new wife to Sweet Clover before any of his other properties—even before taking her to Whitcombe.

The Etiquette of Love

Mrs. Benson, who showed Freddie to her room, was all but bursting with excitement. "Benson and I were thrilled the duke chose Sweet Clover for your bridal journey, Your Grace."

"So am I, Mrs. Benson. I am already enchanted with the house."

The older woman glowed at Freddie's praise, as if Sweet Clover belonged to her. Freddie suspected it felt that way when one only saw the owner once a year for a week or two.

The housekeeper led her to an intricately carved door near the end of the corridor. "This is the mistress's chambers."

Freddie entered the red and gold room and smiled at the old-fashioned, but era-appropriate furniture and heavy velvet hangings. "It is lovely. And it suits the character of the house."

Mrs. Benson looked gratified by her praise. "I have freshened it over the years. His Grace's mother—the last to occupy the chambers, and that a good thirty years ago—requested I keep it as it was when she visited as a young bride."

"I could not agree more," Freddie said.

The housekeeper looked relieved. She gestured to a door in the east wall. "This door was added much later than the original construction to form connecting chambers. This is His Grace's apartment." The room was almost identical in size and layout as her bedchamber. Mrs. Benson closed the door and crossed the room to the last door, on the opposite wall. "There were no dressing rooms in the original design, so an entire bedchamber was converted to make a commodious boudoir."

"Lovely," Freddie murmured.

"I have put your maid in the attic. There are just five rooms, so she is sharing chambers with Bessie, one of the parlor maids." She gave Freddie a slightly apprehensive look, no doubt concerned not to offend the new mistress by slighting her personal servant.

"I am sure it will be fine. Compton was a parlor maid in His Grace's London house and has not yet developed the expectations of a more seasoned dresser."

Mrs. Benson laughed when she saw that Freddie was smiling.

"If there is anything you need, Your Grace, please let me know immediately."

"Thank you, Mrs. Benson. Everything is lovely."

Once the servant had left, Freddie wandered to the windows, which looked out over a charming back garden which buzzed—literally—with late summer life. The bee hives Plimpton had mentioned dotted the fields as far as the eye could see. It was clear the area was devoted to agriculture. Rather than woods, there were abundant orchards. And instead of decorative water features and man-made lakes, there was a river, or stream, rather, that helpfully snaked its way through fields and orchards alike, providing decorative, but practical, irrigation.

As she turned and surveyed her chamber for the next month—the period the duke had suggested they spend in the countryside before journeying to Whitcombe to begin their married life in earnest—she could not help feeling that the environment her new husband had chosen was delightfully…intimate. Sweet Clover, as beguiling as it was, must certainly be among his smaller holdings, and probably the by a long chalk.

His message in choosing such a location for the first weeks of their married life was clear: they would have the time and opportunity—if they wished to take it—to get better acquainted with one another.

A wave of heat spread through her body as she glanced at the ancient four-poster bed, the sight of it reminding her of last night at the inn.

She raised her hands to her hot cheeks at the recollection of her boldness.

Her new husband, so aloof in general, had proven for a second time that in the bedchamber, he willingly and eagerly cast off his restraint.

Freddie felt a giddy, hopeful smile stretch her lips. While she still had reasons to regret the need for her hasty marriage, she was quickly learning there was also much to recommend it.

***

They ate dinner in a small room which Plimpton had converted into a breakfast room years before.

The Etiquette of Love

"You probably did not notice it on your quick journey through the great hall—which also historically served as a dining room—but there is no source of heat there."

She paused in the act of lifting a bite of trout—fresh from the stream on his land—to her mouth. "None at all?"

"None," he confirmed. "It is not so terrible in the summertime, but in the winter the wind howls through the myriad cracks and crevices and rattles the windows all the way to the attic." He pulled a face. "An unheated two-story atrium is visually stunning, but hardly conducive to comfortable dining. Now the hall is only used for dinner parties, so we will eat all our meals in here."

"And do you have many of those—dinner parties, I mean?"

"There has not been a party at Sweet Clover since Simon and I were lads. My mother and father brought us here only once. I do not recall the occasion for the rare family trip, but I do remember the massive oak table in the entry hall was full at least twice."

"And that was the only time your family traveled together?"

"The only time," he confirmed. He did not tell her that the unpleasant occasion was burnt into his memory. His father, not easy to be around even at the best of times, had suffered a gout flare up during the journey. Traveling with him in the carriage must have been as pleasant as traveling with a nest of angry hornets for his mother.

Plimpton and Simon had been in the second carriage. He must have been eleven—too young to ride alongside the coach, unfortunately—which meant Simon would have been five or six. His brother had been a dreadful passenger and their nurse had spent the long journey both ways cleaning up vomit.

He looked up from his unhappy memory to find Winifred watching him. It occurred to him that she would have never traveled with her mother and father as they had died in a carriage accident when she was four or five.

"Your first wife never visited Sweet Clover?"

He blinked at the unexpected question. "No." The single syllable sounded too abrupt, so he added, "At the beginning of our marriage Cecily did not care for travel. And then later on, her health prohibited all but the shortest journeys." A more honest answer would be to say she had not wanted to go anywhere with *him*—or be anywhere Plimpton was—but he did not feel compelled to be *that* honest with his new wife.

He changed the subject to the walks and sights in the vicinity and dinner passed without further inquiry into his unhappy first marriage.

***

"Thank you, Compton. That will be all for the night," Freddie said. Her new maid was very enthusiastic about her job and would have fussed for an hour with Freddie's hair if she had allowed it. "Try and get some sleep tonight," she added in a teasing voice. Last night the poor girl had stayed awake half the night mending Freddie's dismal wardrobe. "His Grace tells me there is an excellent modiste in the village so we can replenish my wardrobe over the next few weeks."

"Very good, Your Grace," the girl said, looking as excited as if *she* were the one who would be getting new clothing.

Once her maid had shut the door behind her Freddie turned to the mirror and commenced giving her hair the requisite fifty strokes, a habit she had employed since girlhood.

Not surprisingly, her thoughts turned to Plimpton.

Last night at the inn was something of a fever dream. The duke might not have been drunk, but he had certainly been…loose. Never before had he smiled, laughed, or teased so much.

He had fallen asleep soon after gently cleaning her—an act that had been more surprising than spending on her breasts, which was something she had endured often in the past as Sedgewick had found it terribly exciting. Freddie had never understood the appeal or the eroticism of the act until last night. Something about watching her stern husband revel in marking her in such a primitive fashion had made her own climax more intense.

Freddie had slipped back to her room after Plimpton fell asleep and had laid awake until an hour before dawn, her brain churning.

Two hours later she had been red-eyed and woolly-headed as she had eaten breakfast across from her husband—who had been as reserved, courteous, and clear eyed as ever despite his night of drinking—and Freddie had wondered if she had imagined the entire episode the night before. Who *was* this man who could be two so completely different people?

All day long in the carriage they had read, relaxed, and spoken desultorily of casual matters. It was as if the day before—both the intensely personal conversation they'd had after the wedding as well as their torrid night of passion—had left them both exhausted.

Tonight at dinner Plimpton had continued his civil but impersonal conversation throughout the meal—as if he entertaining a guest—and then he had joined her in the library after enjoying his after dinner port and cigar.

For two hours she had worked on her new needlework design while he had sorted through the mail he had brought with him from London.

It had all shrieked of domesticity.

And then suddenly, half an hour ago, he had put away his letters, removed his spectacles, and politely—but firmly—informed her that it was time for bed. Yes. He had *informed* her, not asked.

Upon leaving her outside the door to her chambers he had said that he would come to her in half-an-hour.

Again, it had been an *informing*.

He bore *no* resemblance to the hot and fierce lover of the night before. She saw not even a glimmer of the man who had painted her belly, breasts, and even her chin with ejaculate and then sleeked it over her skin, admiring his work before tenderly bathing her clean again.

Freddie felt like there were two Plimptons, and neither of them knew anything about the other one, both living entirely independent lives.

She glared at her reflection as a confusion of emotions roiled within her. There was no denying that she desired him with an intensity which made clear thinking difficult.

He was not the handsomest man she had ever met, and he was certainly not the most equable or charming. Indeed, he was often taciturn, cold, and so remote as to be antisocial. But he was also physically superb, utterly masculine, clever and witty, and his quiet aura of power—even his untouchability and exclusivity—all combined to make him irresistible.

Indeed, if Freddie could have created a man herself, it would be Plimpton.

But *that* Plimpton only came out in the bedchamber. Only when their clothing came off did he allow her to see that he wanted her. But that was the *only* time he made his desire apparent.

Was that because sexual desire was *all* he felt for her? Is that how it had been in his first marriage? Would that be the blueprint for how their own marriage would progress? Well, with the notable exception that she might very well give the duke what he had always wanted: a son.

Regardless of whether she did so or not, he would live as he chose; Freddie knew that meant he would resume taking lovers. If she provided him with the requisite heir and spare, would she be allowed to take lovers, as well?

Why did such a future fill her with despair?

The sound of a door opening made her set down her hairbrush and turn.

The duke, garbed in a robe of dark gray silk, paused on the threshold his gaze lingering on her hair before his eyes slid to her face. "It is beautiful. It pleases me to see it down."

Freddie appreciated the way he couched his commands as compliments. It was another behavior Sedgewick had never learned. Or at least he had never employed it with her.

The duke closed the distance between them, not stopping until he was only inches away from her. He carded his fingers into her hair, his gaze on the pale locks as he sifted the strands through his fingers, his eyes growing dark with desire.

"You feel tense," he observed.

Freddie *was* tense.

"Should I leave you and return three hours from now as I did last night?"

The Etiquette of Love

The Duke of Plimpton sober *and* teasing? No, that was not possible.

His eyes moved back to hers when she did not answer, and his lips curved into a smile that grew and grew.

A dimple she never would have guessed existed showed itself on his right cheek. The striations that were always visible at the corners of his eyes deepened as did the parenthesis that bracketed his lips. His eyelashes—the only soft part of him—were thick but blond-tipped and their lushness was not apparent until a person was close.

"A genuine grin," she could not resist saying.

"You sound so surprised," he murmured, his delightful smile sliding away as he eased his fingers into the fine hairs of her temple and gently combed through the loose curls. "I seem to recall smiling that day at the boathouse."

"That was a smile; this is a grin."

"Ah. Well, I hope to do more smiling in the future. And I hope you will, too. I want to make you happy, Winifred."

It was an evening for shocks.

"I promise I will do all that is in my power to make you never regret our union," he saud, stroking her hair until she all but vibrated with pleasure. It had been forever since anyone had touched her so…lovingly. Even that day by the lake Plimpton had not been so tender. True, he had taken his time with her, but it had been desire that guided him. Now she saw desire, but also affection.

Something in his steady gaze made her eyes itch and fill with tears so quickly that one slid down her cheek.

Horror, lightning fast, flickered across his face. "Winifred! My God…what is wrong?"

"It is nothing."

"It is something."

"Lately, I am emotional often. I have been told it is because I am—the, er, my condition." She felt like a ninny for her inability to say the word *pregnant*.

"Ah." He kissed her cheek, and when he pulled back, she saw his lips were wet. He slid his fingers through her hair again, but less carefully this time, and rather than comb through the curls, he caught a thick fistful and lifted it to his face, the ash-blonde cloud obscuring everything but his eyes; eyes that burned with raw desire as he inhaled. "Why do you smell so good?"

"I, er—"

He dropped the silken mass without waiting for an answer, lowering his mouth over hers, his blazing eyes keeping her pinioned in place as he devoured her.

Heat rolled through her body as his lids drooped and he cupped the back of her head, positioning her so that he could ravage her with a deep, searching kiss that left her breathless when he finally pulled away.

"As magical as last night was," he began, his eyes glimmering with humor when her face flooded with heat. "Ah, you recall that, do you? I thought maybe you had forgotten."

"I thought *you* had forgotten," she accused in a choked voice. "You—you came down to breakfast this morning and looked at me as if we had never met!"

"Did I?" He kissed the tip of her likely bright red nose. "As magical as last night was," he repeated, "I had planned on something a bit less selfish for our wedding night."

"That was selfish? For you? Or for me?"

"You are sweet," he murmured, kissing her again before studying her dressing gown, one of the new garments she had purchased for her tiny wedding trousseau. It was a pretty pale pink moire taffeta with blonde lace and buttons all the way up to the neck. "May I?" he asked.

She jerked a nod, her nervousness earning a curious look from him.

But then he reached the fifth or sixth button and caught a glimpse of what was beneath the taffeta and Freddie saw *his* throat bob.

He stopped unbuttoning and slowly parted the edges of the gown. "Uh." His throat flexed again, and he lightly traced a finger down the narrow gap, his skin hot over the gauzy material.

The Etiquette of Love

His eyes lifted to hers and one of his eyebrows arched high. "I feel as though I must have been very, very good to deserve this."

She gave a startled laugh.

He stroked the lace again, harder. "This *is* for me, is it not?"

Freddie did not think she imagined the slightly dangerous tone underlaying the question. "Of course it is. I would hardly buy such a thing for myself."

His eyebrow cocked again.

Freddie felt like an idiot. "Oh. You did not mean *me*. I bought it this week." Why was she babbling? Probably because she had never, ever owned such a garment in her life. She would not own it *now* if not for the fact that Madam Therese, a woman Freddie had brought a great deal of business to over the years, had not commanded her to purchase it—and then made it impossible for her not to do so by lowering the price of the garment to almost nothing. Well, since it was composed of almost nothing that seemed appropriate.

"You bought it for me?" he said.

Freddie almost asked whom else she would have bought it for, but then saw way the corners of his mouth had curled, his tiny smile so pleased and smug that she did not have the heart to crush it.

"Yes, I bought it for you. Wyndham."

He inhaled deeply and then lowered his gaze and continued with the buttons.

***

Plimpton feared that his fingers might stop working before he reached her waist. If they failed him *after* that, he was certain he could get the dressing gown off her body one way or another. But if they stopped before…He would have to tear the blasted thing off her and buy her another one.

Thankfully, it never came to that because the buttons suddenly stopped beneath the cloth belted around her narrow waist.

He parted the garment, made a noise unlike anything he had made in his life, and rasped, "Good God."

She glanced down at herself, as if she had somehow forgotten the devastating garment she had obviously purchased from Satan's own clothier. "Do you not like it? Madam Therese said—"

"I like it." Plimpton's fingers shook as he pushed the dressing gown from her shoulders, like a man unveiling a priceless masterpiece.

The taffeta slid to the floor in a whisper of fabric.

Plimpton swallowed. And then did so again, his throat strangely parched while his mouth was flooded.

The gown was like gossamer, the color a shade too dark to be called cream, perhaps closer to very milky tea. Such a description did not do the color justice. Whatever one called it, it somehow managed to make her look more naked than naked.

Her breasts were clearly visible beneath the filmy fabric, which was gathered at each shoulder and then plunged to the waist, where it was tied with a ribbon of the same shade and then billowed out like fog swirling around her legs and feet.

Her hard nipples thrust against the gathered gauze, looking sharp enough to puncture the fine fabric.

Plimpton reached out and lightly caressed one of the tiny pebbles with the palm of his hand.

She drew a shuddering breath, the action causing her breasts to shiver in a way that made him feel as if he had been clubbed over the head.

He wanted to rip the gown off her body.

He wanted to ravage her while she wore it.

He could not decide what he wanted to do…

"Plimpton are you—"

"*Shhh*," he murmured, gently turning her around until she was facing the dressing table mirror. He stood behind her, drinking in her reflection. "You are the most beautiful thing I have ever seen Winifred."

At his words, a slow tide of pink spread from her chest up her throat.

"No," he amended. "*Now* you are the most beautiful thing I have ever seen."

She twisted around, until she was facing him, and then burrowed into his chest. "You are embarrassing me."

All he could manage was a less than articulate, "*Ugh.*" Because now the mirror showed what he had somehow not noticed: the back of her body.

The gown was almost laughably simple in construction, but the way the voluminous gauze both hid and exposed at the same time meant a complicated design would have been superfluous.

Her elegant shoulders tapered to a waist he could almost span with his hands before her hips swelled, the luscious globes of her buttocks pressing against gossamer. There was a thin shadow where her legs were pressed together, leading from the cleft of her delectable arse down to the floor.

She squirmed closer and he groaned when his rock-hard erection pressed against her soft belly.

"On the bed," he growled, finding her hand and pulling her toward the four-poster monster that took up fully half the bedchamber.

She hesitated, gesturing to her gown. "Should I take this—"

"God no. Leave it on."

She seized handfuls of diaphanous material, lifted it to her shapely calves, and ascended the steps to the mattress.

"Lie down on your back, darling. I'm afraid this first time will be fast."

"First time?" she asked, a teasing glint that he liked very much lighting her eyes.

Plimpton pulled the sash on his robe and shrugged it to the floor before climbing onto the bed.

He flung up her skirt and spread her thighs wide with indecent haste, sliding his finger through her slick folds just enough to assure himself that he would not hurt her. And then he lined himself up and buried his cock all the way with a single thrust.

Her arms and went around him when he stilled and she lifted her knees to take him deeper.

"My God, Winifred," he breathed, his heart almost pounding its way out of his chest as he struggled for control.

And then she wrapped her legs around him and tightened her inner muscles and he was lost.

Chapter 24

Freddie woke with a rope around her neck. For a moment, she felt blind panic and clawed at the noose. A twisted panel of gossamer came loose with scarcely a tug.

She stared at the silvery taupe material in her hands and gave a breathless laugh. It was her nightgown; she had fallen asleep in it.

She rolled her head to the side and squinted at the clock on the bedside table, blinking with surprise when she saw it was already nine o'clock. She was not surprised to find the bed empty as she remembered Plimpton kissing her goodnight sometime after their third round of lovemaking.

She smiled at the word: *lovemaking*.

Her smile grew as she remembered his reaction to Madam Therese's nightgown. The woman certainly knew her business. Plimpton had appeared deranged from the moment he had disrobed her until he had spent inside her that first time.

His sheepish look afterward had been another emotion she'd not seen on his face before. He had further delighted her by insisting she keep the gown on.

"But it is becoming badly creased and wrinkled," she had protested.

"I will buy you another. Ten more."

"In all different colors?" she had teased.

"Yes. No. Only this color." He had rubbed the thin material between his fingers, looking perplexed. "What *is* this color?"

"Taupe? Fawn?"

"Taupe?" He pulled a face. "I don't like how that sounds. But fawn," he repeated. "Yes. I like that. It is the same shade that is in your eyes; fawn, mixed with silver. I have never seen a color like it. Unusual and beautiful."

His thoughtful scrutiny had embarrassed but pleased her. She was no stranger to male admiration and compliments but coming from a man like Plimpton—who did not waste words—the compliment moved her.

The door opened and Freddie glanced up, expecting to see her maid. Instead, it was Plimpton.

"Ah, you are finally awake." He strode into the room, his eyes roaming her person with obvious interest.

She pulled the sheet a bit higher and treated herself to an examination of *his* person. "You have been riding," she said, hearing the disappointment in her voice.

"No. I am *dressed* for riding. I am waiting for you."

"You delayed your morning ride for me?"

"I did. Would you like to go?"

"Very much." She bit her lower lip. "Can you give me a quarter of an hour."

"Take half-an-hour. I have something yet to do before I am ready."

"Thank you."

"I will send in Compton."

The second the door closed behind him she shoved back the bedding, struggled out of the miles of her nightgown, and snatched up her dressing gown.

Freddie knew he preferred to ride first thing and was touched that he had waited for her.

He might look cool and aloof when they were not in the bedchamber, but the countless thoughtful gestures he made were beginning to convince her the man who had ravished her three times last night was closer to the *real* Plimpton than the one who surveyed the world with an opaque, emotionless gaze.

Freddie believed the process of peeling back the layers and getting to know that private man might just be her new favorite pastime.

The Etiquette of Love

***

Freddie's days quickly fell into a pleasant pattern.

After the first morning, she instructed Compton to wake her as soon as Digby had woken the duke.

They went riding, rain or shine, and Plimpton took her to a different part of the estate each morning. It was a small holding, only a little over two thousand acres, but nearly all of it was under cultivation and productive.

A quarter of his tenant farmers made their money from orchards and the other three quarters from mixed crops. All of them followed the Sweet Clover tradition of raising bees, a side industry that supplemented their income.

"Nobody relies solely on one crop—like corn," Plimpton told her one morning. "Although the harsh weather a few years ago devastated many English farmers, ours here did better than most as they have always been encouraged to keep large parcels for experimental crops."

Freddie was fascinated by how devoted and knowledgeable Plimpton was about all facets of agricultural life.

When she mentioned it on their third or fourth ride, he merely shrugged. "It is my livelihood and those of thousands of my people. I could hardly show my face on my estates if I did not know how they supported themselves."

She did not mention Sedgewick's approach to *his* livelihood—which had been to squeeze his workers and farms like they were wet rags to be rung dry—but she could not help mentioning Wareham's attitude, which was laissez faire at best and benign neglect at worst.

"Yes," the duke had agreed, "Wareham is what I would call a casual steward of his land. Thankfully he does not compound that inattention with gambling or profligate spending, so his estate can prosper. Your brother and I have had dozens—probably hundreds—of discussions over the years regarding the need for agricultural improvements. The great landed estates of England are struggling—as are all farmers—since the War." He momentarily looked grim. "The time when landlords could rely on their farms to support them are quickly coming to an end. Only innovation will save English farmers, and, by extension, the aristocracy that draws its wealth from them." He had glanced at her, his mouth flexing into a rueful moue. "But there, you see? You have started me on my hobby horse. If you are not careful, I can bore on at you for hours."

"I find it interesting."

Rather than take up the invitation in her words he merely nodded and changed the subject. "Today I will show you around Chessley. It is a small village, but I believe you will be pleased with the selection of shops. Digby mentioned your maid had inquired about the modiste."

Freddie had quickly discovered that the duke's valet was all knowing and all seeing. "Compton is very eager to replenish my wardrobe," she admitted.

"I will show you what there is today, and you can return at your leisure."

Chessley was a charming little Tudor era village only four miles from Sweet Clover. It was obvious to Freddie that the townsfolk knew the duke was in residence. And it was equally apparent that they adored him.

Plimpton paused often to speak with various people—always by name—and ask after their family members.

"I am very impressed you know so many people personally even though you are here so rarely," Freddie murmured after he'd just finished listening to a rambling description of yet another elderly, ill relative.

"It is my duty to know," he said as he led her away from the village inn, where they had left their mounts.

"Do you enjoy it?"

"Yes, I do." He nodded a greeting to a passing couple garbed in the humble clothing of farmers. "It is what I was born for. I am fortunate it suits me. I am *very* fortunate." Before Freddie could answer, he gestured to an adorable wattle and daub building with the distinctive diamond pane windows of the era. "Shall we go in and say hello to Mrs. Yarrow?"

Dresses and hats and gloves were displayed to charming advantage in the bow window.

"You do not mind?"

"Not at all."

The moment they entered the small shop Mrs. Yarrow hurried over and the other two women inspecting various wares turned and curtsied.

"You honor me, Your Grace," the modiste gushed, her eyes sliding to Freddie, no doubt taking in the details of her habit—one of the two that had belonged to Sophia—and marveling that a duchess would wear such an outmoded, ill-fitting garment.

"It is a pleasure to see you again, Mrs. Yarrow." Plimpton nodded at Freddie. "Her Grace will return later in the week with her dresser to shop in more depth. Today, however, she is in need of a new umbrella—do you have some we might look at?"

His promise of future commerce made the shopkeeper deliriously happy. "Oh, what an honor! But of course, I have some umbrellas. Some just came in last week. If Your Graces will have a seat, I can bring them to you."

"An umbrella?" Freddie murmured once they'd sat on the elegant settee that had probably never been used to sell an umbrella before.

"My servant disposed of your last one," he reminded her.

"Ah."

The shopkeeper returned with her assistant, both women carrying an armload of umbrellas.

Freddie was hard pressed not to laugh when they began unfurling them and the duke scrutinized each one as if the purchase was of great moment.

"This one most closely resembles the one that was destroyed, does it not?" he asked her when the shop assistant modeled a plain black one.

"Yes, that is exactly—"

"What about that one?" Plimpton asked, pointing to an umbrella that had not yet been opened.

"This is one of our newest," Mrs. Yarrow said, eagerly unfurling a truly gorgeous red umbrella.

"What do you think of that one?" Plimpton asked, reaching for it.

"Oh. It is very…red."

He held it slightly behind her, his eyes darkening as they slid up her person—nowhere near the umbrella Freddie could not help noticing—lingering on the bust of her habit, which was tight as Freddie was slightly larger in that area than Sophia had been. Finally, his gaze lifted to her face, no doubt as red as the umbrella now.

"I have changed my mind about only gowns in fawn. You should have one in this color," he said in a low voice.

Memories from the night before assaulted her and Freddie gave a laugh crossed with a laugh. "Plimpton," she murmured.

And then he did something truly shocking; he winked at her.

"We *do* have a lovely silk that is similar in color," Mrs. Yarrow said, naturally mistaking the duke's meaning altogether.

Plimpton looked amused. "You must remember to look at that material when you come back, Winifred."

She nodded dumbly.

"We will take both the black and red umbrellas, Mrs. Yarrow. Please have them sent to Sweet Clover," he told the modiste, finally looking away from Freddie, who felt as if she had just been ravaged by a fever.

"Oh, but the black one will be sufficient," she said in a stupidly breathy voice.

"You will look stunning with the red," Plimpton said, nodding at the shopkeeper and repeating, "We will take both."

Once they'd managed to escape the woman's effusive farewells, the duke offered Freddie his arm and they meandered down the bustling street.

The Etiquette of Love

"It did not occur to me until just now that you rarely wear vivid colors. Do you not care for them?" Plimpton asked. "Because you really did look lovely against that red backdrop."

"I do like colors," she said after a moment. "But you are correct in that I rarely wear any." When had she stopped wearing bright colors? Indeed, she'd not worn any colors at all, other than lavender, for years. The first thing she had purchased that wasn't gray, cream, brown, or lavender had been the pale mint green dinner gown.

A memory slowly surfaced. "I used to wear red. In fact, I had a wool coat that was bright red." And she had dearly loved that coat.

"What happened to change that?"

Like so many things, it had been Sophia who had put an end to both the coat and her love of colors. Her sister-in-law had supervised the purchase of Freddie's first trousseau. One of the things about being a married lady that Freddie had looked forward to was wearing whatever color she wanted, rather than white or the pale pastels that unmarried young women were permitted to wear.

They had been shopping and Freddie had fallen in love with a peacock blue habit.

"A woman with your coloring—or *lack* of coloring—can never wear such a vivid shade," Sophia had said as Freddie stood draped in the lovely fabric. "You must avoid bright colors altogether. Beiges and grays are much better for you." She had hesitated and then added the killing blow. "Wearing such a gaudy color would embarrass your husband."

And so that is what Freddie had worn ever since: beige and gray and lavender.

"I don't know why I stopped wearing colors," she said when she saw Plimpton was waiting for an answer. "But perhaps this umbrella will mark a new beginning for me."

***

Most afternoons Plimpton took care of estate business. This was not just their bridal holiday, it was also his annual visit to the estate, so there was much for him to do..

"Perhaps you might like to accompany me on some of these visits? If you have time, that is," he had asked her the third morning at Sweet Clover.

Freddie could tell by his almost tentative question that he expected rejection. It was a small thing, but it was a clue as to what his marriage had been like.

"I always helped at Torrance Park and one of my favorite parts of living at Sedgewick was becoming acquainted with the tenants."

Plimpton's expression at her words had been the nearest she had seen to those he wore in the bedchamber, which told her he was greatly pleased.

Once Freddie had been introduced to the people on the estate, she felt comfortable paying visits by herself. She especially enjoyed visiting the elderly who lived on the estate. The wives of the tenant farmers were doubtless honored when she called but she knew that all their work had to stop when the duchess visited. But the older people—or cottagers as they were called—lived alone and, for the most part, enjoyed company. They were also able to tell her a great deal about her new home and even a little about her husband, although not much.

Only when she began to be drawn into the lives of the people on the estate did she realize how much she missed country living. At Torrance Park she had been discouraged from visiting after Sophia Became mistress.

At Sedgewick, she had adored visiting both the infirm and the healthy people on the estate. It had pained her to see the condition of the farms, but she had quickly learned her lesson not to mention any of the repairs that were wanted to Sedgewick.

"Your business is to provide an heir. Why don't you see to that before taking on my job?" Sedgewick had retorted the first time she had mentioned the condition of somebody's thatched roof. And that had been one of his kinder comments.

While their afternoons at Sweet Clover were often spent apart, their nights were always spent together.

After dinner Freddie retired to the library and Plimpton joined her after his port and cigar. At first, he had offered to play card or chess.

The Etiquette of Love

But it was quickly apparent that the only pleasure he got from either pastime was making her happy. When she told him that she would rather read or work on her needlework, she had seen the relief in his eyes.

At ten sharp every evening he would close his ledger, put away his correspondence, and say, "It is time for bed, Your Grace."

And then they would spend the hours between ten-thirty and two in the morning exploring each other's bodies.

They talked as well, but the confidences Freddie had hoped would come—such as what Plimpton's first marriage had been like—never materialized.

Every night, between one-thirty and two he would retire to his own chambers.

The one time she mentioned that he might stay, he had politely, but firmly, declined her invitation, stating that she needed her rest.

He was the perfect companion, lover, and protector.

Which made Freddie wonder why she felt such unease simmering just below the surface of those happy days.

Chapter 25

Their second week at Sweet Clover the days were unusually warm. Even the nights were hot, the air not really cooling until early morning for an hour or two, and then it would gradually heat up again.

"Is it always this warm?" Freddie had asked one afternoon, when the heat had driven her in from the garden and she had actually taken a nap.

"No, this is hotter than any summer that I can recall."

Plimpton had taken to opening the window in her room when coming to her bed. The breeze not only cooled her heated skin but perfumed the air with the faint scent of honey and the not unpleasant smoke the men used to calm the bees as they harvested their crop.

It had occurred to her, belatedly on the second evening they made love with the windows open that everyone in the vicinity had likely heard her cries of passion. When she had mentioned that fact to Plimpton, he had given one of his rare chuckles and said, "Good."

"Good?" she had exclaimed. "I will not be able to show my face."

"You should be proud, not ashamed. These are country folk, Winifred. Fornicating is the chief form of entertainment when one goes to bed with the sunset and rises with the cock crow. They approve of a lusty wench who can satisfy her lord and master."

"Lusty wench?"

He had laughed when she had gawked at him in disbelief.

And then he had proceeded to make her scream his name more loudly than ever.

That had been four nights ago, and he'd continued to do so every night since.

Tonight, her lord and master had just finished satisfying *her* twice—he had been prepared to go a third time, but she had pled for mercy—and was now drowsing with her head on his chest, boneless

The Etiquette of Love

with pleasure as she toyed with the light fleece that grew thickest between his small brown nipples. "I think you like hearing me beg," she accused in a sulky tone that fooled neither of them.

"I think you are correct," he replied without hesitation.

"Beast," Freddie muttered with a smile, amused when his chest shook with silent laughter that turned into a yawn.

She carded her fingers through the damp springy hair, sighing with contentment as his palm stroked languidly from her shoulder, down her spine, to her buttock.

This is a perfect moment.

Freddie's hand paused and she turned the thought around in her head, viewing it from several angles.

It *was* perfect. How often did that happen in life? Not more than a handful of times that she could remember. She opened her mouth to share the thought, but hesitated, wondering how to express herself in words. What if he did not feel the same way?

Assaulted by indecision, the moment passed.

There would be more perfect moments and the next time she might know how to share it.

She resumed her caressing, fascinated by the combination of rough hair, hot satin skin, and hard muscles.

"Are you grooming me?" he asked in an amused, sleepy voice.

"I found a gray hair," she informed him.

He hesitated only a fraction of a second before saying, "I am sure you have mistaken one of my *blond* hairs for gray."

She bit the inside of her cheek to keep from laughing. "Blond like the ones at your temples?"

A low growl vibrated his chest.

Freddie grinned. "No, this hair is definitely gray." She tugged gently on the pale intruder. "Should I pull it out? It would hardly take any—"

The hand not stroking her back settled over her hand. "I think not."

Freddie laughed. "Coward."

He guided her hand away from the offending hair toward his nipple. "If you want to pull on something, pull on this."

She lifted her head and met his slitted gaze. "You—you would like that?"

"*Mmm-hmm.*"

Freddie lightly tweaked the petite brown bud, her curiosity piqued when his body stiffened.

"Harder," he murmured. He gave a sharp groan of pleasure when she complied. "More."

"It does not hurt?"

"Just enough to feel good," he assured her. His eyelids lifted when she hesitated and he frowned at whatever he saw on her face, his hand again covering hers. "Winifred? What is it? You have a—a, well, I don't know what to call it, but an odd look. Is something the matter?"

She chewed her lower lip as she searched for words that would not be clumsy or insulting.

"You do not have to do this if you do not like it," he said, guessing the general trend of her thoughts but misattributing the reason. His long fingers curved beneath her chin and lifted her face, until she could not avoid his troubled gaze. "I do not want to let matters fester between us. Particularly when it comes to what we do in the bedchamber. Tell me what you are thinking."

"It is difficult to say."

"Take your time," he said, caressing her cheek and stroking a curl off her temple, tucking it behind her ear.

"Sedgewick liked to be birched," she blurted.

So much for taking your time.

His hand stilled, but Freddie could not read his expression. Why was he so inscrutable to her when she was an open book to him? Could she really be so unobservant?

"Are you asking me if that is something I enjoy?"

She nodded.

"No. I do not like to be whipped." After a pause, he added, "Nor do I like to *do* any whipping. At least not unless my lover wished for that."

She gave a sigh of relief, and a pleasurable tingling penetrated her embarrassment at the sound of the word *lover* on his stern lips.

Plimpton's hand resumed its caressing. "Is that what happened, Winifred? Did Sedgewick force you to birch him?"

She shook her head.

He hesitated, his expression finally one she could read: grim. "Did he birch *you*?"

She held her breath, and then nodded.

"Did you give him permission?"

She hesitated and then said, "I did not want to deny him—and—and I *was* curious," Freddie's voice trembled with shame at her admission. "He promised me that if he did it, it would only be lightly." She swallowed hard. "Not the way he liked it…which was so hard that he was often scarred for weeks, and sometimes there was b-blood."

"And?" he said, his gaze intense.

"He drew blood."

His face hardened—not in disgust, but in anger—and he briefly closed his eyes, as if he needed a moment to control his reaction—before opening them and sliding a hand behind her head. "Come up here."

She glanced at his nipple, which was no longer erect thanks to her introduction of a distasteful subject. "But—"

"We will make time for that later," he assured her. "Come here," he repeated, exerting gentle pressure to help bring her up the length of his body, until they were face to face. He rolled onto his side and propped his head on one hand, caressing her with the other. "If Sedgewick were alive, I would beat him to a bloody pulp. And then I would wait until he regained consciousness and beat him again."

Freddie could not help the smile that took over her face. "Is it wrong for me to enjoy the thought of that?"

"No." He caressed her cheek, his eyes flickering over her face, as if he were searching for something. After a few seconds, his fingers lightly glossed down her sensitive throat, over the thin skin stretched of her breastbone, and then stopped on the slight swell of her belly. He cupped her with one hand and they both looked down.

His skin appeared dark compared to the fish belly whiteness of her midriff and he gently stroked the slight curve of her stomach, his touch worshipful. "I appreciate you telling me something that was difficult and embarrassing to confide." He dipped his little finger into the dimple of her navel, his gaze jumping up to hers when she stifled a laugh. "Ticklish?"

"A little."

"How about here?"

Her breathing quickened as he cupped her mound.

"No. That is not ticklish... yet. Perhaps if you try a little harder."

He looked amused, the warm pads of his fingers easing into her slick, swollen folds and caressing and exploring, until a familiar tension began to build in her sex.

But then his hand stilled and he cupped her again, his touch soothing rather than arousing. "I want to tell you something."

She wrenched her eyes from the mesmerizing sight of his fingers toying with her curls and met his gaze. "You do not need to tell me something difficult or embarrassing just to make me feel better."

"I know. This is neither of those things. Although I assure you that I possess my fair share of embarrassing and difficult memories." He paused, reflected, and then added, "This is something that probably *should* embarrass me, but it does not."

The Etiquette of Love

"Now I am intrigued." Freddie lifted her hand to the nipple she'd been teasing earlier and pinched it.

He shuddered and gave her an approving look. "Wicked girl." He teased the seam of her lower lips in a way that made her tremble for more.

When his hand again stilled, Freddie knew he was teasing her not by accident, but on purpose.

She lifted her hips slightly in a gentle reminder. But he merely gazed down at her, mildly haughty. Now *this* was a look she could read; it said he would do what he wanted, when he wanted, and not a moment before. Freddie adored it.

"Are you Wareham's age?" she asked, returning to her stroking, but not giving his nipple the hard pinches he sought. Two could play at this game, after all.

Her frowned. "Why do you ask?"

"You know *my* age."

He grunted. "I will be three-and-forty on my next birthday."

"When is that?"

"February twenty-second," he said. "And yours is April the twenty-first."

"How did you know?"

"I know many things about you."

Freddie rolled her eyes. "Tell me your secret—the one that *should* embarrass you but does not."

He massaged her belly in light circles. "Sometimes when I am doing other things—tedious things such as going over accounts with Kaplan or reading crop reports—my mind wanders."

Freddie gave an exasperated huff. "*That* is what you wanted to confess?"

"Do not be pert." He gave her mound a sharp tap.

It was not very hard, but Freddie shivered at the strange blend of pleasure and pain.

His eyelids lowered. "Ah."

She squirmed under his brooding gaze. "What does that mean—*ah*?"

"Just...*ah*."

"Fine. If you refuse to explain *ah,* then tell me why you mentioned your mind wandering." He raised his eyebrows, giving her that haughty look again. "*Please* tell me, Your Grace," she amended.

"Since you ask so nicely, I will tell you. My mind wanders because I cannot stop imagining what you will look like in three, four, or five months hence."

"That is no great mystery," she said with an embarrassed laugh. "I will be as big as a heifer and will probably waddle. You will be grateful to hide me away in the country."

"When did I say I was going to hide you away in the country? Or anywhere else, for that matter."

Freddie's eyebrows shot up. "Wh-what do you mean?"

"I mean that I will enjoy taking you to town and parading you before the *ton.*"

"*What?*" she demanded with a scandalized laugh.

His hand resumed its soothing caresses. "I will want it to be known far and wide that I am responsible for your swelling belly. That *I* am the one who put a child inside you."

Every drop of moisture drained from her mouth. "Er... that sounds—"

"Primitive? Yes, it is. I get the most primitive satisfaction from my imaginings." His lips spread into a slow smile that caused her sex to tighten. "And it makes me hard. Every. Time." He punctuated the last two words with two more sharp taps on her mound.

Freddie groaned.

"Ah." He leaned closer, his middle finger curling and parting her swollen lips, the damp pad finding the perfect place and then applying the *perfect* amount of pressure. "When I have those thoughts, I get the strongest urge to find you—no matter where you are or who you are with—and take you." His finger moved lower, until she felt a prodding at the opening to her body. "I imagine bending you over whatever is convenient, lifting your skirt, and filling you." He thrust two fingers inside her, the stretch so sudden and intense her body tightened as if to keep out an intruder.

"Yes," he murmured, holding her full to the top knuckle, his fingers curling in a beckoning motion inside her. "I would give you every inch—hard and long and deep."

"Plimpton," she gasped.

"*Hmm?*" His fingers caressed in a firm, gentle rhythm that was just enough to make her thrum with pleasure, but not enough to move her from pleasure to bliss.

"Please." She raised her hips.

"Please?" He eased his fingers out of her body and then lightly, maddeningly, stroked her throbbing peak. "Is this what you want? To be touched here?"

"Yes... that. And..." she bit her lip.

"And—what?"

"Just that."

"You should not lie to your husband." He gave her engorged bud a hard squeeze.

Freddie blurted, "I didn't mean to!"

"What else do you want?" he asked, easing the pressure, but keeping the bundle of nerves imprisoned.

"I want... more."

"More?"

She growled. "I want you inside, as well."

He thrust back into her, once again filling her. "You want more of this?"

"*Yes.*"

"Then you will have it," he said in a voice that pulsed with erotic menace. He rolled her onto her back and spread her legs wide before kneeling between them, watching intently as he worked her vigorously enough to shake her breasts with each thrust.

Freddie reached up to steady them.

"No," he said, his hand ceasing its stroking. "If you want to grab something, grab your knees."

"What?"

"Yes, like this." He positioned her hands the way he wanted. "Now pull them toward your chest.

She gawked at him. "But, Plimpton, I will look like—"

"You will look delicious. Do as I say and I promise to make you writhe with pleasure."

Face scalding, she did what he said. Never in her life had she felt so exposed and vulnerable. Or so wicked and desirable.

"Look at you," he murmured softly, his eyes blazing and his lips parted hungrily, starved expression causing her inner muscles to clench. "You are perfect," he said, lowering himself onto his stomach, his hand resuming its pumping, his breath hot on her exposed sex. "It arouses you to be looked at and worshipped, doesn't it, Winifred?"

It *did* arouse her. But that did not mean she wasn't squirming at what he must see in such proximity.

He gave a low chuckled. "Your blush extends even down here." He parted her netherlips, spreading her open only inches from his face.

"Plimpton!" Freddie gasped, but she forgot all about her mortification when he lowered his mouth over her.

Her eyes rolled back in her head, and she pulled on her knees even harder.

A smug, low laugh vibrated from her mound to her belly, but Freddie could not bring herself to care about her wanton position or her greedy behavior.

The Etiquette of Love

As he had done before, he pleasured her so noisily, and with so much abandon, that it was hard to reconcile the haughty aristocrat with this almost diabolically carnal creature.

The contrast between the man the world saw and the one currently feasting between her thighs made his actions even more arousing. Powerful contractions seized her body, the rhythmic spasms scarcely dying away before his lips once again closed around her throbbing bundle of nerves, his fingers working her with mortifyingly wet sounds.

"Please…" she gasped. "Plimpton—just—just a moment to—*oh my!*" Freddie arched her back and moaned as he did something with his tongue that turned her inside out and drove every single thought from her head.

***

Plimpton worked four orgasms from his wife's delectable body before yielding to her pleas to stop.

Even then, it was difficult to make himself release her. Once he had committed himself to a course of action, he liked to see it through. When he admitted as much to Winifred, she groaned.

"If you see it any more *through*, I will lose what few wits that remain to me."

"A witless wife?" he mused. "Not entirely a bad thing, I think." He made as if to lower his mouth again and she yelped and tried to close her legs. "No! Please, please, please. Just—a quarter of an hour to recover."

"*Hmmm.*"

"Please… Wyndham."

She knew it softened his resolve when she used his Christian name. She was a wise woman and employed her weapon judiciously.

He gave an exaggerated, self-sacrificing sigh. "Very well, a quarter of an hour."

She nodded, her eyelids already sliding shut.

It took less than a minute before her breathing turned regular and deep.

He snorted softly, amazed at how quickly she fell asleep. But then many things about her amazed him.

For a woman who appeared as ethereal and delicate as an angel, Winifred was remarkably practical and sturdy. Her dainty façade hid a constitution of iron and near boundless energy.

He hated to compare her to Cecily, but it was inevitable given how much they resembled one another on the surface. But whereas both women appeared cool and serene, a warm and passionate nature was just below the surface of Winifred's façade. Beneath Cecily's surface perfection had been…more of the same. She was like glass, with only more glass behind the glass.

What a literary masterpiece of comparative thought.

Plimpton snorted softly. It certainly was.

Plimpton sighed and wrenched his hungry gaze from Winifred's face. A quick look at the clock showed it was just shy of three. Already he had stayed unconscionably late in her bed. As badly as he wanted to curl around her warm, soft body and drift into sleep beside her, he knew that sort of overly affectionate behavior would be met by annoyed resignation if not outright rejection on her part.

As for his part?

He was already taking more of his new wife's time than she had likely anticipated.

Besides, she was breeding and needed her rest. If he stayed with her, the last thing she would get is rest.

He left the bed, careful not to disturb her, took one last greedy look at her passion mottled body, lingering on the gentle swell of her belly, and then covered her with the sheet and blanket before shrugging into his robe and opening the connecting door to his chambers.

It felt as if scarcely five minutes had passed between the time he'd crawled into his bed and closed his eyes and when Digby opened the drapes, flooding his chambers with pale early-morning sunlight.

Biting back a groan, Plimpton pushed back the covers and swung his feet to the floor.

The Etiquette of Love

Digby, who needed even less sleep that Plimpton, instantly emerged from the dressing room with a banyan draped over one arm and a pair of slippers in his hand.

It was Plimpton's preference that their morning routine be conducted without unnecessary chatter, so Digby wordlessly held out the robe and Plimpton slipped into it, yawning as he tied the sash. His valet dropped to his haunches and matter-of-factly put a slipper on each foot, much the same way a nurse would dress a toddler. Plimpton was amused that these sorts of observations had only begun to occur to him since becoming acquainted with his outspoken wife.

He stared down at his servant. "I know how to put on my own slippers, Digby," he said, sounding peevish to his own ears.

Anyone else might have blinked at the non sequitur. Digby, as featureless as a wall of ice, rose to his feet and said, "I have never doubted it, Your Grace." And then, without pausing, added, "Shall I set out your riding gear?"

Plimpton frowned, certain that he had somehow been put in his place. "No. I will wait until the duchess wakes."

"Very good, Your Grace."

"Have a tray sent up; I am going to work in my study for a few hours. I want only coffee and a bit of bread and butter." He gave the other man a stern look. "That is *all* I want, Digby. Do not load up a tray and try to stuff me. You know I don't care to eat a full breakfast before I ride." He was irked by the vaguely querulous tone in his voice—when had he begun to sound like his great aunt?—and then he was irked that he cared.

"Of course, Your Grace," Digby agreed in a blandly soothing tone that told Plimpton he would soon be facing at least a rasher of bacon, several boiled eggs, and a rack of buttered toast.

He jerked the sash of his robe with unnecessary force before going to the desk in his study. Why was he so irritable this morning?

Because you should have never left your wife's bed last night.

Yes, that was true. But already he had the restraint of a dog in rut, going to her every night, staying for hours, having her multiple times and in multiple ways. In short, he was treating her like a back-alley whore instead of his duchess and the mother of his child. He needed to take himself in hand and moderate his hunger for her.

Why don't you allow her to tell you when she has had enough?

He was struck by the thought. But immediately dismissed it. She would see accepting him into her bed, as well as her body, as her duty.

The thought that she might be complying with his demands merely to please him—the way she had obviously done with Sedgewick—made Plimpton shudder. She had already been married to one pig of a husband; she did not need another.

If she despises your touch so much, then why did she *come to you on your wedding night?*

Plimpton's hand froze in the act of lighting one of the candles in a branch. The annoyance that had been building within him began to dissipate, like steam from a kettle that had been removed from an open flame.

She *had* come to him. And after he had purposely made it clear that he had no expectations.

He smiled to himself as he lit the rest of the candles, his mind inevitably reliving how erotic she had looked kneeling at his feet. His morning erection, which had just begun to subside, roared back to life.

He glanced down at the vulgar bulge in his robe. "You are of no use to me right now," he accused. And then felt more than a little foolish for addressing his cock.

He shifted his gaze to something sure to kill his ardor: the pile of correspondence that lurked on the corner of his desk like a coiled adder.

"Damnation," he muttered. He had spent three hours whittling down the pile yesterday, until only one letter remained, that from Jeffers, his steward at Whitcombe. He did not need to read Jeffers's letter to know what it contained. The man would have written to nag him about replacing the seventeen windows in the north wing. Plimpton did not require his servant's nagging. He *knew* the windows needed repairing, but it was on his mother's side of the house, and he disliked the thought of displacing her from her rooms while repairs were made. She had been ill last winter, and her health had not been robust since. Moving her from her chambers would agitate her. It

The Etiquette of Love

would have to happen, of course, but not right now. Perhaps when Winifred was at Whitcombe she would have some idea of how to make the repairs with the least amount of stress.

The thought of Winifred in his home—which he loved dearly, despite the fact that it was a constant drain on his purse as well as his time—caused a pleasing sense of anticipation. This marriage had had a rocky beginning but seemed to get better and better every day. And every night.

He savored the thought for a moment and then reluctantly put it aside, slipped on his spectacles, and commenced to work his way through *today's* pile.

Chapter 26

"I think Sweet Clover is the most restful place I have ever been," Freddie said at dinner several nights later, spooning up the last of her trifle with a sigh of contentment.

"I have often felt as if it were not just off the beaten path, but somehow outside time," Plimpton replied.

"Speaking of being outside of time, did you know the beekeeper who worked here during your great aunt's time is still alive?"

He paused in the act of lifting his glass to his mouth, his forehead furrowing. "Samuel Timkin?"

"Yes, Mr. Timkin."

Plimpton's eyebrows rose slightly, and he lifted his glass the rest of the way and took a drink of wine before setting it down. "He must be close to one hundred."

"Ninety-seven."

"You have spoken to him?" the duke asked, shaking his head when the footman would have refilled his glass.

"I encountered him when I was out walking by the maze. He was sitting on the stone bench just outside it."

"Did you enter the maze?"

"Not after Mr. Timkin told me that your brother was once lost in there for five hours."

Plimpton looked amused. "Simon was only six at the time. I am sure you could do better. At least no more than three hours."

She laughed. "You flatter me."

"Why don't we go there tomorrow?" He paused and added, "I will have the kitchen pack us a picnic lunch."

Freddie knew her face was heating at the memory of their *last* picnic lunch. How silly of her! She was expecting a child and had laid

The Etiquette of Love

with her husband every night since their marriage. Why was she still shy?

She looked up to find him regarding her in the direct, assessing way that always made her long to know what he was thinking. But they did not know each other well enough for her to ask him that question. Freddy wondered if they ever would.

She daubed her lips with the napkin and set it aside before saying, "I will leave you to your port."

The duke stood and walked her to the door, opening it for her even though there were two servants present to carry out the task. "Will you be working in the library?" he asked, just as he did every evening.

"Yes."

He inclined his head. "I will join you shortly."

***

Plimpton took a drink of port and puffed on his cigar. Neither activity, usually so pleasurable, afforded him any enjoyment tonight. Nor had it done so the night before. Or the night before that.

He did not want to be sitting alone and drinking port and blowing a cloud. He wanted to be in the library with his wife. He would read the tenant reports he'd received that day and Winifred would work on the secret project she refused to show him.

His lips twitched as he thought *said project*. It had been their second night at Sweet Clover and he had wandered over to see what she had on her tambour. She had immediately hidden her work from him.

"You do not like anyone seeing it until you are finished?"

"I don't mind that." She had hesitated and then said in a rush, "This is a wedding present for you."

A curious warmth bloomed in his belly at her unexpected disclosure. No one, so far as he knew, had ever made anything for him with their own hands. His family had given him gifts in the past, of course, but none made by their own hands. Both his mother and daughter disliked needlework. As for Cecily? The only thing she would have made him would have had arsenic in it.

Winifred must have mistaken his silence for something other than pleasurable wonder. "It is nothing so valuable as the lovely pearls you gave to me," she said, her tone more than a little defensive.

"If you make it with your own hands then it will be *more* valuable, Winifred."

She had blushed, but it was clear to him that she did not believe he was sincere. It was difficult to explain to people like Winifred—who had worked hard for her money, often going without—that when a person could afford to buy anything he wanted the only items of real value were those few things that could *not* be purchased. Or replaced.

Plimpton returned from his recollection to find that his right hand rested on his chest over the slight bulge caused by the oval locket. Although Digby had never said, Plimpton knew it caused his meticulous valet no small amount of heartache that his master insisted on disfiguring every coat he possessed by keeping the painting in his breast pocket.

Plimpton smiled. So, he did not lose *every* battle to Digby.

He lifted the cigar and stared at the glowing tip, his amusement fading.

Why are you sitting here alone? he asked himself. *Is maintaining a hollow ritual more important than pleasing yourself?*

He stubbed out his partially smoked cigar and shoved back his chair so abruptly that both footmen startled.

"Your Grace?" William said, looking confused.

"I need nothing further tonight," he said, and then strode from the room, feeling their startled looks.

To hell with what they wondered. He was a newlywed. And he wanted to sit with his new wife.

***

A few mornings later, Freddie received four letters.

"How fortunate you are," the duke said as he handed them to her, his tone a shade grudging.

The Etiquette of Love

Freddie looked pointedly from her slender pile of correspondence to the three-inch stack beside his breakfast plate.

"Ah," he said, observing her glance. "But these are bills and reports and other business-related missives while yours are from people who do not want money in return."

"Poor Plimpton. Do you never get any personal letters?"

"Wareham writes, but I am not sure you would call them *letters* so much as illegibly scrawled billets that are rarely longer than three or four sentences."

Freddie could not help smiling. "So, you get those, too?"

"Yes, and not often. But a little goes a long way; it once took me a month to decipher one of his three-line letters."

She laughed. "There are some I have *never* translated."

He buttered a slice of bread and continued, unusually talkative for the breakfast table. "My mother writes regular, thorough accounts of household and village matters and Rebecca's letters, while rare, are engaging. But Simon's scribbling is even worse than Wareham's. Honoria, I am pleased to say, has proven an excellent, entertaining correspondent, but her letters are infrequent now that Robert has learned to crawl."

"They will be rarer still when he learns to run."

The duke chuckled.

Freddie was riveted by his easy humor and the small lines that radiated out from his eyes. Eyes that did not resemble ice-covered steel these past days, but instead were frequently warm, relaxed, and—yes—even affectionate. Although rarely outside the bedchamber

As if feeling her gaze, Plimpton lifted his eyes from the offending stack of bills, his eyebrows pushing together. "What is it, Winifred?"

"Nothing," she lied, not knowing how to express what she was feeling, and not wishing to make him feel self-conscious even if she did.

The duke gestured for the servants to leave and when the door shut, he said, "Does talking about Robert make you think of Miranda?" His question demonstrated a level of empathy she never would have expected. Behind his thick wall of reserve was an attentive, perceptive, and considerate man.

"I think of Miranda all the time." Although lately her thoughts gave her more anxiety than joy. She still had not resolved the issue of what to do about the girl. Regular two-week visits were obviously impossible. What did that leave?

"You miss her."

"Yes."

"We briefly discussed the issue of her care once before. Have you given it more consideration?"

"I have." How could she tell him that much of her indecision was created by the fact that her life was no longer her own without sounding ungrateful? "I have ruled out taking her from the Morrisons and bringing her to live with us. As generous as your offer is, such a decision would be more about pleasing me than Miranda."

He nodded. "Twice monthly visits are not practical in the late summer and fall, when we will be at Whitcombe. But during the rest of the year my duties bring me to London for long stretches." His lips compressed briefly as if something unpleasant crossed his mind. "My presence will be even more necessary given the current situation."

"You mean because of the worker unrest in the North?"

"Yes."

Freddie would have liked to know his position on the growing dissatisfaction, but his expression was not one that encouraged questions. Also, there was a part of her that was afraid she might learn things about his political position she would not like if she began asking questions. She knew he was a Tory, but not all the men in that party shared the same principles. Given the compassion he had displayed when it came to his tenants and servants, she wondered how he reconciled his personal and political beliefs.

He swallowed his mouthful of buttered bread, took a sip of coffee, and said, "Two weeks would be difficult, but visits every three weeks would be possible."

The Etiquette of Love

She studied his face, looking for some sign of whether such recent trips from Whitcombe, his country seat—where she assumed they would spend most of their time away from London—would put an added strain on their marriage.

Again, he read her thoughts, "If it proves too hectic a schedule then we can revisit the subject."

"You do not mind me leaving every three weeks?"

"You will not travel alone."

"Oh." The fact that he would have to go, too, had not occurred to her. "You would not need to suffer the inconvenience of accompanying me.".

"You will not travel alone," he repeated gently.

Freddie understood. She also understood that his quiet decree applied to more than just travel. As softspoken and benevolent as he appeared, there would be only one master in the Duke of Plimpton's house. And it would not be her. While he might handle Freddie with velvet gloves, she should never forget the iron they sheathed.

She saw he was waiting for a response. "I understand, Your Grace."

He nodded and turned back to his breakfast.

She experienced a pang of regret but knew it would do her no good to chafe at her loss of her independence. Not when she had signed it away in the small church on Hart Street more than two weeks ago.

And he was not behaving autocratically; he was attempting to find some solution that would both please her and still be feasible. She owed him at least as much cooperation in return.

"I think once a month would be more practical. I can balance the reduction in the number of visits by saying overnight at the village inn. That way I will see her for a few hours on two days." She could not help smiling. "The owner of the Spotted Sow will be beside himself with ecstasy to count a duke among his patrons."

"You are sure?" he asked, and she knew he wasn't asking about staying at the inn, but the length of time between the visits.

"I am sure."

"If we leave next Monday, we could begin your new schedule on a third Wednesday. At least the day of the week would remain the same for Miranda."

"That is generous of you," she said. More than generous; it was thoughtful of him to recall the day. "But it was your intention to remain here until the two new cottages were completed. Leaving on Monday will be too soon for that."

"I can see them the next time we come to stay. Miranda is more important." His words were as soft spoken as ever, and yet they hit her like a mallet, knocking the air from her lungs.

"What is it?" he asked, concern furrowing his brow. "You have gone pale. Has the, er, breeding affliction you suffered before returned?"

Despite the fact that her throat was suddenly so tight it was hard to breathe Freddie was amused by his carefully worded euphemism for *daily vomiting*. "No, no, I am not bilious."

It was an entirely new affliction; one that affected her heart, rather than her stomach. Somehow, Freddie had contracted a severe case of love for her husband after less than three weeks of exposure to him. If it was already this acute, what would it be like in three months? Or three years?

"Have you contracted a cold? Digby said one of the footmen was laid low in his bed today. Should I summon the doctor?"

She met his calm, level, gaze, looking for signs of something deeper reflected in his eyes.

But all she saw was concern for her health. And that of the baby, of course.

Freddie forced a smile. "I am fine. It was just a momentary indisposition," she lied. "You need not fear that it is contagious."

Chapter 27

Now that a date had been set for leaving Sweet Clover, Freddie felt frantic to do all the things she had planned before they departed.

"I will miss the Honey Festival," she said, sitting with her appointment book on her lap, rather than her needlework. They were in the library after dinner, discussing what needed to be done in the time remaining.

It had been more difficult to work on Plimpton's wedding present since he had begun foregoing his after-dinner ritual of port and cigars. Her husband had become a bit sneakier in the evenings, drifting behind Freddie's chair for no apparent reason, as if he were trying to catch a glimpse of her work. She never would have expected him to be driven by such curiosity.

The pleasure of his company had more than made up for the minor inconvenience of having to hide her work. Besides, she had plenty of time during the afternoons to work on it and was almost finished.

"We will come back again next year," Plimpton reminded her, looking up from his never-ending pile of papers.

"I know we will, but it might be a different season and there will be new things that I will want to do."

"We will come back any time you wish," he assured her.

"I hope the weather cools so that we can have our picnic at the maze before we leave," she fretted. Plimpton had decreed it was far too hot for her to be out of doors in the afternoon and Freddie had to agree. That meant they'd had to cancel it several times now.

"Perhaps we should have an evening picnic?" he mused.

She perked up. "I like that idea."

"I do, too." His eyelids lowered.

As usual, her body tightened at the subtle heat in his gaze and the air seemed to crackle.

"I will see what I can arrange, Winifred."

When he turned his attention back to his work, she felt like she could breathe again. How did he *do* that to her so quickly and effortlessly?

Shaking her head, Freddie flipped through the pages of the appointment book, pausing when she saw a notation she had made weeks ago regarding Lady Rebecca.

She looked up, suddenly struck. Her plans for launching her new stepdaughter next Season would need to be altered now that she was with child. "Plimpton?"

"*Hmm?*" He was glancing from one document to a thick ledger that was open beside it, as if checking something. He wore spectacles and Freddie thought they made him look scholarly. She did not share that observation as she doubted that he would find it flattering given the few comments he had made about his less than enjoyable stint at university. Not that he had said much.

It occurred to her, not for the first time, that her husband did a great deal more listening than talking. Especially when it came to personal subjects.

Meanwhile, he knew all the sordid details of her marriage, not just the part about Sedgewick's treatment of Miranda. And he had known of her falling out with Wareham and Sophia. He knew—well, to put it bluntly—he knew the worst of her past.

Freddie, on the other hand, knew next to nothing about him. Certainly, she knew nothing about his marriage, which had lasted for two-thirds as long as she had been alive.

He was a sensual, generous lover and a considerate and intuitive husband. His concern for her relationship with Miranda was an example of how he was always thinking about what would make her happy.

But he was still a complete enigma.

The Etiquette of Love

It was obvious he cared about her, and not just because she was carrying his child, although she could sense his interest sharpen when it came to that subject even though he kept his curiosity firmly in check.

That careful, circumspect behavior alone told her more than he himself ever had. It told her that his wife had discouraged his concern or interest in her pregnancy. Perhaps that had only happened after she had lost three children. Or perhaps she had discouraged him from the beginning because aristocratic women considered subject like childbirth and children solely a woman's purview, and a working-class woman, at that.

She burned to ask him about his marriage, but she did not want to bring that chilly look into his eyes, the one that said she was not allowed into that part of his mind—his heart—and never would be.

It was odd being the reserved one in a relationship. For years, she had been the self-contained strong one, the one all her friends had come to with their concerns, fears, and questions while she had held her own counsel. Not because she hadn't *wanted* to confide in somebody, but because they had all struggled with serious problems of their own. None of them had a wealthy brother willing to pay their debts if they could not make ends meet. That knowledge had embarrassed her and kept her quiet. After all, somebody like Miles had shouldered the burden of caring for dozens of family members and a crumbling estate. There was nobody waiting to rescue him with a large allowance and comfortable house if he decided to give up playing at working.

Recently, she had without realizing it shifted her troubles onto Plimpton's broad shoulders without hesitation.

And he had accepted them with the same quiet grace he did everything.

Love, almost suffocating, flooded her as she regarded him. His normally perfectly groomed hair was mussed and in tufts. As she watched, he thrust the fingers of his left hand through the already disheveled locks, disturbing them even more, still bent in concentration over his desk. He might not be capable of romantic love—and he would eventually lose interest in her physically and take other lovers—but he would always put her needs before his own, of that she was certain. He would do the same thing for their child. And, unlike

Sedgewick, he would never, ever banish his son or daughter if they were less than perfect.

Most aristocrats barely even noticed their female children. They barely noticed the male ones other than their heir. But Plimpton carried a locket with his daughter's miniature next to his heart.

How could Freddie *not* love him?

But she wished that she didn't. If she could merely *like* and respect him, her life would be so much easier. But love? No, love meant the future would likely be a special sort of hell. When Sedgewick had taken other lovers, Freddie had been both relieved and hopeful that he would leave her alone. When Plimpton tired of her and took a mistress, it would kill her. Oh, not *literally*, but she would be dead inside.

All her life she had hoped for love; now she wished it had passed her by.

Plimpton looked up from his ledger, his eyes distracted behind his spectacles as if he were consumed by some thought. But they sharpened when he saw she was looking at him. "I beg your pardon, Winifred." He removed his glasses and regarded her with a rueful look. "You said something to me a moment ago and I am afraid I was wrestling with this column of figures and did not hear what you said."

Winifred shook her head, so emotional she could not even recall what she had wanted to say.

"It was nothing," she managed. "I was just thinking out loud."

***

Freddie reread Piers's brief letter, frowning to herself.

I called at Plimpton House only to learn you and your new husband were on a bridal journey to one of the duke's smaller holdings.

By now, after several weeks of marriage, you have either forgiven me for my interference or you will hate me forever.

Freddie stopped when she came to that part, her heart squeezing painfully. She should have written to him already; she should have apologized for the angry words she had flung at him that day.

She sighed and turned back to the letter.

The Etiquette of Love

Hoping for the former, I will confide the results of my recent search to you.

I have worked my way through the names on the list and have discovered… nothing. At least nothing that will acquit me of the charge of murder. I believe the men whose steps I have retraced after that fateful party and whose lives I have—well, let me use the word 'scrutinized' as this is being immortalized on parchment—are innocent of both the crimes of theft and murder.

By *scrutinize* he meant utilizing unethical or illegal activities like bribery, breaking and entering, stalking, spying, and misrepresenting his identity and lying his way into the households of these men in any way he could. She did not agree with his methods, but to catch a killer it was probably not possible to post an advertisement in *The Times*.

She continued reading.

While it is possible that my investigations may have failed to turn over some vital piece of evidence, it has not been for a lack of digging. If any of these men are concealing the truth, it will likely die with them.

In any event, I have searched my own soul in the process and have decided this will be the end of my investigation.

Severn has requested that I attend his wedding party before I leave England, so I am staying at Granton Castle until then. After that, I must go, Little Bird, and this time it will be for good.

The words blurred on the page, but Freddie forced herself to finish.

I have accepted Severn's invitation not because I wish to attend his house party but because I would like to spend my last days in England in your company and staying at Granton Castle together seems the easiest way. If you would rather I take my leave now, I will be guided by your feelings on the matter.

With all my affection,

Piers

She brushed aside the tear that had escaped her tight control and frowned at the postscript.

P. S. please thank your husband for his information but tell him that it came to nothing as the man in question died years ago and his son was unable to offer me any information. Even so, I am grateful to Plimpton for making the effort.

Freddie slowly folded the letter, while inside she felt as if she were collapsing. This was just as painful as losing Piers the first time. Worse, maybe, because she could do nothing to help him.

She set aside the letter and glanced up to find Plimpton's eyes on her. He made a subtle gesture, without taking his attention off her, and the two footmen quietly left the room.

Only then did his eyes slide to the letter. "I hope it is not bad news."

"It is from my brother. Piers," she said, and then felt foolish as Plimpton had been the one to hand her the letter.

He nodded.

"He—he says he will be leaving England after Lord Severn's house party." She had to several to clear her throat several times before she could finish. "He will not come back again."

Freddie was grateful Plimpton did not rush to offer either condemnation or sympathy. Instead, he reached across the table and set his hand over hers. The fact that they rarely touched outside of her bedchamber made his gesture all the more affecting.

"He said to thank you for something you told him," Freddie said. "What did he mean?"

Unease flickered across the duke's face, and he withdrew his hand. "It was not much. I recalled something about that house party."

"What did you recall?"

Plimpton hesitated.

"He mentioned a man who died. Piers said he was able to talk to his son. Which man?" she pressed. "Please, tell me."

"Why do you wish to know?"

"Why do you hesitate to tell me?" she countered.

His lips tightened almost imperceptibly. "Because I do not want you involved in this matter."

"Yes, you have said as much before, as has Piers. And I have given my word to him," she retorted, her temper flaring. "But it is over now—I have just told you as much. Soon, he will be gone from my life forever. Surely you can at least tell me how you helped him?"

Rather than soften at her words, his face hardened. "You have not given your word to *me*, Winifred."

"Fine," she said, having to shove the word through clenched teeth to keep from shouting. "I give you my word that I will not involve myself. That I will not help my brother clear his name of murder."

He eyed her levelly for a long, uncomfortable moment before saying, "I remembered a man who was at the house party. I had forgotten about him because he was not one of Wareham's regular friends. Indeed, he was one of mine."

Freddie's jaw dropped. "You forgot your own friend?"

His jaw flexed at her disbelieving, scoffing tone. "His name slipped my mind because he is dead, Winifred. And he has been for a very long time. Also, I forgot about him because he was not there by the time Meecham was dead. He'd been called away on some emergency before all that happened."

"And you say he was a friend of yours?"

The duke shrugged. "A neighbor and we were of age, so…I invited him."

"Why did you tell Piers about him?"

"Because I thought it might help."

"I thought you did not like Piers. I thought you were of the opinion he never should have returned?"

"I am of that opinion, Winifred. But you love your brother and I do not like to see you hurt. So, I offered what help I could."

Freddie was momentarily distracted by his words.

Plimpton glanced down at his plate, but not before Freddie noticed the slight addition of color to his cheeks. "As your brother said, my information was useless. I suspected as much since Luton's son could not have been more than ten or eleven at the time."

"Luton?"

He looked up and Freddie saw a gleam of wariness enter his gaze. "Yes."

"Baron Luton is the neighbor you meant?"

"Yes."

She *definitely* saw wariness. "Ah."

"Ah?" he repeated.

"Yes…*ah*." Plimpton used the word often enough to end conversations he did not care to continue. Why shouldn't she?

He nodded slightly at something, as if she had spoken.

Freddie thought he might pursue the subject—perhaps even make her to swear not to visit the Luton estate, especially since it was a scant four or five miles away and one of Sweet Clover's nearest neighbors—but his next words were on a different subject entirely.

"It occurred to me that between the visit to Miranda and the party at Granton Castle there is not much time to go to Whitcombe."

"What are you saying? That we should stay in London?"

"Perhaps. Or we might go to Granton earlier."

"But what about visiting the Dowager and Rebecca?"

"My mother has repeatedly counseled me to enjoy my bridal holiday before I am pulled back into estate duties. As for Rebecca, she has been invited to Granton and can meet us there."

For once, Freddie saw though him as easily as a pane of glass. He was suggesting the change to their schedule so that she could spend more time with Piers before he had to leave. He was thinking of what *she* wanted and what would make *her* happy.

"Thank you," she said. "That is very thoughtful of you."

If anything, his expression became even more haughty. "You are welcome."

The rush of love Freddie felt for the emotionally repressed, achingly proper aristocrat across from her almost choked her.

But the guilt she felt at what she was about to do was even worse.

The Etiquette of Love

***

Freddie could not help comparing the dilapidated, moth-eaten appearance of Luton Priory with the well-tended, burnished glow of Sweet Clover.

The woman currently pouring tea across from Freddie was perhaps the shabbiest feature of the room they were currently occupying.

Baroness Luton looked up with an apologetic glance when the teapot she had just lifted rattled noisily against the cup she was attempting to fill with a hand that was badly afflicted with palsy.

"May I help, my lady?" Freddie asked.

The other woman's already stooped shoulders sagged with relief. "Thank you, Your Grace. I'm afraid even the smallest tasks are beyond me these days."

Freddie took charge of the tea tray. Scarcely any steam rose from the spout and the silver pot was badly tarnished. The maid who had brought the scantly laden tray had set it down with a jarring clatter, eyeing her mistress with scathing derision before asking if she needed anything else.

As Freddie prepared the weak, tepid cups of tea she wished desperately that she had not made the journey. And not just because of the depressing state of affairs at Luton Priory, a house that was hardly in the condition one would expect if the owners had a fortune in antiquities in their possession.

No, she was regretting her decision because of the nagging shame that she had not only defied Plimpton, but she had brazenly broken her word. Indeed, she had given it with the foreknowledge that she would break it.

Not only had coming to Luton Priory been *wrong*, but it was increasingly clear to her, once her initial optimism had fled, that finding anything out about a party the dead baron had attended twenty-three years before was not going to be an easy task.

If Freddie could manage to end this uncomfortable meeting within the next quarter of an hour she might be able to return home before Plimpton noticed she was gone.

But would concealing her visit really be any better?

Shame swirled in her belly as she stood and brought the baroness's cup and saucer to her.

Lady Luton was understandably flabbergasted that the new Duchess of Plimpton had called on her. Especially since the woman had not moved in society for more than a decade, the palsy that caused her hands to shake so badly also confining her to a Bath chair.

"Thank you," the older woman murmured, the chipped crockery clattering in her hands. "How kind of you to call," she said for the fourth time. "I rarely get any visitors these days."

Freddie sipped her awful tea, bit back a grimace, and set the cup and saucer on the tray. "Have you suffered long from your affliction?"

"More than two decades, although it has become worse these past few years."

"And there is no help for it? Perhaps taking the cure at one of the watering holes? Or would such a trip be too difficult?"

"My physician does not believe such a cure would help."

Freddie scrambled for some way to get to the point. "You have been a widow for some years?" she asked, wincing internally at the clumsy foray, but Lady Luton did not appear to find her indelicate prying offensive.

"Almost twenty."

"You have a son, I believe?"

The cup and saucer clattered badly as the other woman tried to set it on the table.

"Allow me." Freddie sprang up and took the dishes from her; perhaps not all the chips in the China were the fault of the slatternly maid.

"Thank you, Your Grace."

Freddie sat. "You were telling me of your children?"

Lady Luton's pale eyes lowered to her lap, where her hands lay tightly clenched together.

What was the matter with the woman?

As if she had heard her, the baroness looked up. "Luton is my only son."

"He must be a comfort to you."

The other woman gave her a look of incomprehension.

"Because you are housebound and cannot travel," Freddie explained.

"Oh. Yes, he is."

It was like trying to hold a conversation with an oyster, except the little bits she was managing to extract were hardly pearls.

"I was recently visiting my brother Wareham and he mentioned your husband," Freddie lied, deciding to go to the heart of the matter.

The other woman reacted as if Freddie had hurled a lightning bolt at her chest. Her wheeled chair jolted violently enough to knock into the table beside her and send the long-suffering cup and saucer to the floor. Even the sound they made was pathetic—not a crash so much as a dull *clunk* before they broke into a few large pieces.

"Oh, dear," Freddie said. "Let me clean that up."

The baroness looked even more horrified. "No! Your Grace, you should not! Please, ring for a servant to—"

But Freddie was already picking up the pieces. The last thing she wanted was an interruption, not when she was getting such bizarre reactions from the woman at the mere mention of Wareham.

"Wareham said your husband once spent a week at Torrance Park," she hurried on, purposely prolonging the clean up by dropping a few pieces and then mucking up the spilled liquid with one of the frayed table napkins.

Lady Luton stared down at Freddie as if she were an evil apparition that had risen up through the gaps in the floorboards. "I—I do not, that is—"

"Wareham said your husband was suddenly called away—an emergency of some sort." Freddie paused for a fraction of a second and then took a wild leap. "Before he left, however, he seemed especially fascinated by a chess—"

"Good heavens, what has happened here?" A cool male voice came from behind Freddie.

She pushed to her feet and turned to find a tall, gaunt man of indeterminate age hovering on the threshold, his pale eyes—like his mother's—flickering between Freddy and the baroness.

"This is Her Grace of Plimpton," the baroness wheezed shrilly. "Duchess, this is my son, Luton."

The baron entered the room and shut the door behind him as Freddie deposited the crockery shards on the tray and turned to face him.

He bowed low. When he stood, Freddie saw the expression in his pale eyes.

And that was when she knew she had made a very grave mistake.

Chapter 28

Plimpton looked up from the latest progress reports from the builder. "I think the delay will be longer than the two weeks the thatcher is projecting," he said to Edward Cocker, his bailiff.

Cocker nodded. "Aye, Your Grace. So do I."

"Keep a close eye on him when I have gone and let me know immediately if he asks for another extension. The rains will be coming soon, and this delay could prove disastrous."

Cocker nodded and made a notation and then turned to another sheaf of papers. "About the fence dispute, Your Grace."

A deliciously cool breeze tickled the hair at his nape and Plimpton glanced at the partially open window. Fluffy clouds were scudding across the blue sky, bringing down the temperature until it was quite pleasant.

He made a sudden decision. "The fence dispute will have to wait until tomorrow, Cocker. I promised Her Grace that we would have a picnic at the maze days ago, but the weather has been too stifling. I think today would be perfect." It would also give him an opportunity to make amends for his abrupt behavior at breakfast that morning. Winifred was justifiably concerned about her brother, and Plimpton had allowed his worry for her safety to overset his equilibrium. In short, he had been rude, and she deserved an apology.

Cocker smiled in a way that said, *ah, newlyweds*. "Of course, Your Grace." He began shoving papers into his battered leather satchel, but then paused. "I doubt Her Grace has returned from her ride, but perhaps you can—"

"Her ride?" Plimpton repeated. "What ride?" She had ridden with him that morning.

Cocker recoiled at Plimpton's sharp tone. "Er, when I arrived half an hour ago young Jeb was giving her directions and helping her into the saddle."

Plimpton lunged to his feet, the cold, hard knot in his belly grew to the size of a fist. No. She would not dare.

Oh, yes she would.

"Directions to where?" he barked at his gaping servant.

"I believe she wanted to go to Luto—"

"Damnation!" Plimpton strode toward the door as fury and something else—fear?—flooded him.

"What is it, Your Grace?" Cocker asked, his eyes wide.

"Gather two of the brawniest servants you can find and meet me at Luton's estate as quickly as possible."

"Go to Luton's with servants? But—"

"Just do it, man!" Plimpton shouted, the sick dread inside him threatened to choke him as he strode from the library.

If he was wrong and dragged Cocker and his employees over to Landford's for no reason, then he would look like a fool.

But he would rather look like a fool than be mistaken.

Plimpton cursed himself for his willful blindness. He had seen the glitter of resentment in Winifred's eyes this morning when they'd discussed Baron Luton. Damn it! Why hadn't he paid attention?

By the time Plimpton reached the bottom of the stairs, he was running.

***

Freddie swallowed down the sudden lump of fear in her throat and forced a smile. "It is a pleasure to meet you, Lord Luton."

"The pleasure is all mine," the baron corrected in a low, pleased purr, taking her hand and holding it in both of his, no gloves to separate her fingers from his cool, moist flesh.

Revulsion traveled up her arm and she tugged, gently at first, and then harder, until he released her.

"To what do we owe the honor of your visit?" He moved closer to his mother and set his corpse-white hand on her shoulder.

The Etiquette of Love

The baroness flinched and blurted, "Her Grace's brother was a friend of your father's."

Luton's eyes widened, but he looked anything but startled. He looked...*furious*. "Is that so, Your Grace?"

Freddie eased back a step and forced a light chuckle. "My brother Wareham mentioned it in passing and I recalled the name when I found myself in the vicinity. I decided to pay my respects. But I fear I have overstayed." She turned to the baroness. But the other woman looked right through her, as if Freddie was not even there. "I will come back tomorrow, my lady. Or—or perhaps the day after, if you are amenable," she said in an unnaturally high voice.

"Must you leave so soon?" the baron asked, his gentle tone ill-matching the dark glitter in his eyes.

"I am afraid so. You needn't show me out," she assured him hastily when he released his grip on his mother—whose body sagged with relief—and strode toward Freddie.

"Nonsense, I will walk with you." He took her arm in a grip that felt light, but the tension in his almost emaciated form told her it would be unbreakable.

"You are so kind," she murmured, her mind racing as he nattered on about the upcoming Honey Festival, the weather, and other pleasantries.

Freddie must be imagining the menace—another symptom of her condition. Why would he want to hurt her? After all, what did she know? And it would not have been *this* Baron Luton who had killed Meecham as he would have been far too young.

Her thoughts snapped to the present when she saw he was not leading her toward the dusty, gloomy foyer, but in a different direction. "This is not—er, where are you taking me?"

"To the stables."

"But—"

"This is a shortcut," he assured her.

"You need not walk me all the way." She began to pull away, but his hand tightened like the vise she had expected. "You are holding my arm rather tightly, my lord. Would you please—"

"I want to show you something," he said, his hand like a manacle around her arm when he stopped and fished a ring of keys from his pocket with his free hand.

"I would love to see whatever it is some other day, but I'm afraid—*help me!*" She shrieked when he opened the door and pulled her inside.

He jerked her around to face him and Freddie hunched her body, expecting a slap or even a punch. Be Luton just chuckled. "You can scream all you like. I dismissed the servants—such as they are—when I discovered who had come poking around."

"I do not understand what you mean." She jerked on her arm. "You are hurting me, my lord. Let me—"

"Quit trying to get away and it will not hurt," he responded reasonably. "As for not understanding, you know precisely what I mean. I want to show you the chess pieces. Isn't that why you came?" He strode to the window, easily dragging her with him, and reached for one of the badly faded drapes. For a moment she thought he was going to draw them back. If so, she could smash the glass. Surely somebody would notice if she broke one?

Instead of the drape, he grabbed the faded gold cord and gave it a vicious yank, filling the air with dust motes that made her cough.

"Terrible, isn't it?" he asked in a conversational tone while his hands moved deftly to tie her wrists. "One gets accustomed to it after a while," he assured her. "Quit squirming, Your Grace, or I will be forced to make you stop." The words were uttered in the same gentle tone, but the expression in his eyes was a petrifying combination of grim determination and maniacal obsession as he stared down at her.

"There now, that is much better," he said when fear froze her in place.

"What are you going to do to me?"

"I told you; I am going to show you the chess pieces."

"I don't think you understand what your father did to get them, my lord."

He laughed. "Of course I do."

A chill settled in her bones. "My brother was wrongly accused of the murder and has run all his adult life. You could help clear his name with very little effort."

"Why would I do that?" he asked, looking genuinely confused.

Freddie gaped at him.

"My father told me all about Cantrell; he said the man was a bastard and a gamester. Why shouldn't he take the blame? He and Meecham were going to split up the set, they did not value it at all. My father had to rescue them."

"Rescue them?"

"Yes, *rescue*." The expression in his eyes was that of a religious zealot ready to face death for his cause. "They cannot be separated; it is a crime." His lips tightened. "I thought my father understood, but he didn't."

"Wh-what do you mean?"

"I mean he began to sell them." Luton scowled. "I had to stop him before he did irreparable damage."

"Stopped him how?"

He pursed his lips and gave her an exasperated look. "How do you think, Your Grace?"

Freddie recoiled in horror. "You killed your own father?"

He did not appear to hear her. "He sold three of them." The flames in his eyes leapt higher. "It has taken me years to locate them and bring them home."

"You purchased them?"

He cut her a haughty look. "I certainly did not *steal* them."

Hysterical laughter bubbled up in her at his insane moral parsing. "But—but your house is falling down around your ears. Why would you spend money on game pieces?"

He sneered. "That stupid question just proves how unworthy you are to even look at them, not to mention take them away from me."

"I was not going to take them—I just—"

"I am not a fool."

She swallowed at the menace in the quiet words and changed tack. "My husband will expect me soon. We were to meet after I had paid a quick call. If I do not—"

"There is no point in lying. I am sure you came alone to do your spying. Plimpton is not the sort of man to allow his new wife to wander around prying into theft and murder, is he?"

"He knows I am here."

Luton shrugged. "I will tell him—and my mother will confirm—that you never arrived."

"The stable lad who took my horse—and the maid—"

"Finding a good position is not easy for a servant these days. And it is getting harder all the time," he said, shoving her down in a chair. "Please stay put, or I will have to tie your ankles as well." He waited until Freddie nodded, and then turned.

She glanced around the study, which was as faded and neglected as the drawing room.

The baron went to the nicest piece of furniture she had seen in the house, a desk that looked ancient, and unlocked one of the drawers.

There were windows on one wall and just the one door. Freddie could not jump out the window without risking damage to her baby. But she might be able to reach the door.

The baron rummaged in the drawer and Freddie slowly pushed to her feet, grimacing when the chair creaked.

His head whipped up. "*Ah, ah, ah*! You promised, Your Grace."

She sank back into the chair. "You will not get away with this. My husband will—"

"He will search and search and search and never find you." Luton grimaced with effort, as if he were pulling something in the desk, and

The Etiquette of Love

the room suddenly echoed with the sound of a bolt being thrown. He glanced up at Freddie while dropping to his haunches and flinging back a threadbare carpet, causing another cloud of dust. "There are some benefits to poor housekeeping." He sneezed and then shoved against the desk. "I suspect I should oil it more often, but the last thing I want is somebody sliding it open by accident." The huge desk began to slide in an arc.

"What on earth are you doing?"

He smiled at her. "Clever, is it not? Luton Priory is actually older than Sweet Clover, but it is in such poor repair it never gets the attention in the guidebooks that your husband's house does." He stopped pushing and dropped into a crouch again, feeling for something on the floor. A moment later, he stood, lifting a thick wooden slab with him. "But there are some benefits to not being lauded in guidebooks and one of them is that Luton has retained her secrets. You see, my ancestor leveled the priory walls but left what was beneath them." He laid the heavy panel on the floor with a grunt and then stood and paused to massage his lower back. "I now understand why my father was so lazy as to leave the hatch wide open when he went down to gloat. If he hadn't...well, I might never have found the treasure." He strode toward her. "Who discovered it was my father who killed Meecham? You or your brother?"

"My brother?" she repeated pressing back against the flat stuffing of the chair as if she could get away.

He took her elbow and easily lifted her to her feet. "You are a truly beautiful woman, Your Grace, but you are a terrible liar. I know it was Piers Cantrell who came to see me in London, even though he claimed to be a Runner." Luton grinned. "He is not the only man who can spy and bribe people. He should have covered his tracks better, but I suspect he truly believed what I told him." Luton's pupils shrank as he stared down at her. "You should have left well enough alone." He began to pull her toward the black hole in the floor.

"No!" Freddie cried, digging her heels in, but skittering hopelessly.

"If you do not quit that right now and—" he stopped and cocked his head, like a bird listening.

Freddie heard it, too. The sound of baying.

Langdon scowled at the insistent wailing, which was getting louder and louder. "What in the world—"

"*Winifred!*"

It wasn't baying; it was Plimpton!

"Good God!" Luton snarled, pulling harder.

"*Plimpt—*"

Luton wrapped an elbow around her throat, cutting off the word and her breath along with it.

"Oh no you don't," he grunted, and then began dragging her toward the hole again.

Freddie's head grew hot, but she fought like she was fighting for her life. Her hands were useless, but she flung her head back, earning a gratifying *crunch* and howl of pain.

"You *bitch*!" Luton punched the side of her head with a closed fist and stars exploded behind her eyelids.

Pain vibrated through her skull and precious second slid past before she realized he'd loosened his hold on her neck to strike her.

"*Wyndham!*" she screamed. Or at least she tried to, but the word was weak and reedy.

"I don't think so," Luton muttered.

A hand landed on her back and shoved.

Freddie tried to dig her heels in, but he was too strong and she skittered dangerously close to the hole before having the sense to drop to the floor like a sack of rocks, earning a painful knock on her tailbone for her efforts, but stopping her progress.

"*Goddamnit!* Move!" Luton drew back his foot.

Freddie curled into a ball, protecting her stomach and gritting her teeth against impact.

But instead of a kick, an enraged *Winifred!* came from somewhere very close by.

The Etiquette of Love

Freddie risked peeking and was just in time to see the door explode. The room filled with the sound of splintering wood and the maddened roar of an animal.

No. Not an animal, but Plimpton. Her husband moved like a blur, charging toward Luton, who was slack jawed and still poised mid-kick.

The duke picked up the other man up as if he were a toy and then flung him into the dark hole in the floor.

"*Nooooooo*!" Luton's bloodcurdling scream was accompanied by a series of muffled *thuds*.

And then silence.

Freddie only realized she had squeezed her eyes shut when hands like grappling hooks closed around her upper arms and lifted her to her feet.

"Winifred?"

She stared up into eyes that were even more demented than Luton's. Gray eyes—not cold or distant—but bulging with fury, terror, and…fear.

"Are you hurt?" Plimpton asked hoarsely. "Winifred!" he repeated, his fingers biting into her flesh when she merely gawked up at him.

"No, no, I am not hurt." It was a lie; his hands were crushing her. But it didn't seem like the time to point that out as he still looked at least three-quarters mad. "I am fine, Wyndham, I promise."

The sound of his name seemed to jolt him.

"Truly, I am fine," she insisted. "You came just in time. He—he was going to kick me and—"

"I saw," he growled. And then he yanked her against his chest and wrapped his arms around her so tightly that she saw stars for the second time in less than five minutes. His palm spanned the back of her head and held her against his heart, which was pounding so violently that Freddie could not believe he had not passed out. "Winifred." Tremors racked his body as if he had a fever.

"I am fine, Wyndham. He did not hurt me—or the baby. You saved us both."

But his arms would not loosen, and his shaking did not subside.

Only when his bailiff, Cocker, hurried into the room with two footmen and a groom, did Wyndham finally release her, although he still kept her close.

The room, which was suddenly crowded with bodies, was eerily quiet. All eyes were on the duke, who was unrecognizable.

"Your Grace?" Cocker said.

But the duke did not seem to hear him.

Freddie took her husband's face in her hands and stroked his cheeks until he stopped shaking. "I am unhurt, Wyndham." She kissed him gently on the mouth, not caring how many people were watching.

Slowly, like ice melting, the blank look leaked from his eyes. He swallowed and set his hands over hers, lightly squeezing them before lowering them, lacing the fingers of one hand with hers and turning to Cocker.

"Luton is down there," he said gruffly, pointing to the hole without looking. "He is either stunned or unconscious." He paused and then added, "Or dead."

Cocker nodded carefully. "I will see to it, Your Grace," he said, and then turned and murmured quiet instructions to the servants while Wyndham led her from the room.

When Freddie gasped he immediately stopped and accused, "You *are* hurt!"

"Just my ankle. It is not broken, it is just—"

He lifted her in his arms, cradling her, his grip almost uncomfortably tight and his eyes still wild as they stared down at her. "I am taking you home." He spoke challengingly, as if she might argue.

Freddie smiled up at him. "Yes, Wyndham. Take me home, please."

Chapter 29

Freddie tried to speak to her husband several times on the half-hour ride back to Sweet Clover, but the duke seemed to have retreated to someplace deep within himself and did not respond to her questions.

The only time he said anything was when she tried to walk from the stables to the carriage.

"I will carry you."

He spoke in a tone that brooked no argument.

Mr. and Mrs. Benson already had the door to the foyer open and were hovering, confused but aware something awful must have happened.

"Have a bath prepared in Her Grace's chambers immediately and summon her maid to attend her," Plimpton ordered sharply, marching past them and up the spiral staircase without pausing.

Compton was already waiting in her room, which had meant there was no opportunity to speak to Plimpton in private. He deposited her on the bed, turned to Compton and said, "Do not let her walk. Help her to the bath when it is ready. Do not allow her out of your sight," he added. And then he turned and strode from the room without a word to Freddie.

Freddie and her maid locked eyes, the younger woman's brimming with questions—and something that looked like shock.

"I sprained my ankle." Freddie attempted to smile reassuringly but did not do too well judging by the maid's expression.

Only when Freddie glanced in the mirror a moment later did she understand the Compton's distress; her neck was a raw, angry red and her temple and cheek were swollen and mottled. In short, she looked as if she had engaged in a mill and lost.

By the time she had finished soaking, and Compton had dried her and carefully applied a botanical smelling unguent to her scrapes and bruises, almost three hours had passed. And still Plimpton had not returned to her.

There was a soft knock on the door, and she looked up eagerly. But it was only a housemaid with a bowl of gruel. "His Grace said you were to eat this," the maid said, looking discomfited at giving her mistress orders, even if they were not her own.

"Thank you," Freddie said, and quickly ate the food even though she was not hungry.

"Is the duke in the house?" she asked Compton after she'd given her the empty bowl.

"Yes, Your Grace."

"Is he alone?"

"I believe the constable just left, but I think Mr. Cocker is still with him."

If the constable had been and gone, Plimpton would have answers.

"You may go, Compton."

"But His Grace said—"

"I know what he said," Freddie said, not unkindly. "And I know you will have to go and tell him I have disobeyed him. When he asks, tell him that I sent you away. Go on," she urged.

The maid gave her a last, reluctant glance before leaving.

Freddie stared at the clock on the bedside table. Not even a minute elapsed before she heard the staccato drumming of bootheels coming down the hallway.

Her door flew open and her husband glared at her, eyes blazing. "I gave a direct, explicit order and you countermanded it."

"I did."

He was momentarily nonplussed, but his face quickly hardened. "If I have to tie you to the bed, I—"

"You will not have to do that if you get in bed with me."

He blinked, his surprise so complete that Freddie chuckled.

The Etiquette of Love

It was a terrible idea.

He stalked toward the bed. "Do you think it is amusing to defy me and almost end up dead?" he thundered.

She immediately stopped smiling. "No, Your Grace. I do not."

Again, he was stopped short.

Freddie lifted a hand toward him.

He stared at it as if he had never seen it before.

"Please," she murmured.

His jaw hardened, but he reached out and took her hand. Despite the abruptness of his movements, his touch was gentle—the way a man might pick up a piece of spun glass. Well, Freddie could not have that.

She squeezed his fingers and pulled him closer.

He resisted. "You are hurt. I should not—"

"It is not my ankle you will be touching."

For the first time in their acquaintance, *his* lips parted in surprise.

Freddie struck while he was wrong footed. "Please, Wyndham. Get into bed with me." She patted the mattress beside her. "I need to be held." Remarkably, it was the right thing to say.

He sat, leaned against the pile of pillows, and slid his arm around her, holding her close."

Freddie smiled into his shoulder. He was still fully garbed for riding, butter soft buckskins stretched over his ridiculously muscular thighs. His feet were sheathed in fine leather riding boots with wide white tops, which she found stimulating in a way that should have embarrassed her.

"I was hoping you might get undressed and get beneath the covers," she said, her voice muffled against the wool of his coat.

Rather than chuckle or comply, he carefully held her away from him and stared down at her. Hard.

Freddie sighed. "You want to scold me, and I deserve it."

"You gave me your word."

"I did."

"You broke it."

"Yes."

"In fact, you gave it to me knowing you would break it."

"Yes."

"I cannot trust you."

"You can."

"How?" He crossed his arms.

She opened her mouth, but then closed it and shook her head. "I cannot say anything that will make you trust me, Wyndham. You will just have to do it anyway."

He looked profoundly confused by her answer.

Well, he was a gentleman, and a gentleman's word was as important to him as his life. More so, given that many of them were willing to duel to the death to protect it. He simply could not comprehend ever breaking it.

"You will need to trust me; I promise I will never lie to you again."

His brow furrowed and a struggle raged in his normally shuttered eyes. "You might have *died*," he accused.

Any humor she had been feeling about the situation dissipated at the raw terror on his face. How had she ever believed he was incapable of deep emotion? His behavior in that nightmare room today had told her everything that he had not said with words. He cared for her. And the thought of losing her had turned him into a maddened, baying beast.

A goodly part of his fear was undoubtedly for the child she carried, but Freddie knew some was for her, too.

She had scared him—badly—and a man like Plimpton probably did not have much experience with that emotion.

Freddie set her hand on his thigh and squeezed. "I am *truly* sorry I did not ask you to go with me." She paused. "Would you have?"

"Yes," he said without hesitating.

"Even though you believed that Piers was guilty?"

"Yes. I would have done whatever you asked not because of your brother's guilt or innocence. But because *you* asked it of me."

Freddie was humbled. "I beg you to accept my apology."

"I already have. But I am not sure I can trust you again—at least not when it comes to your safety."

"I know. You can keep me close. Will that help?"

He stared broodingly at the wall, as if he could not bear to look at her. "I do not know. I have not felt this—this—"

"Love?" she blurted before she could lose courage.

His gaze sharpened and focused on Freddie, but he did not speak, going so still and motionless he might have been a statute if not for the streaks of red on his cheeks.

His reaction struck Freddie like a proverbial lightning bolt: Plimpton was not purposely withholding his love from her to seize the upper hand in their marriage; he simply did not *know* how to manage the emotions shaking his well-ordered world from its foundations.

He might not even know that love was what he was feeling.

But Freddie knew. And there was no excuse for keeping her feelings to herself anymore—if there ever had been. "Because that is what I feel for you: *love*. I love you, Wyndham—with all my heart."

***

Plimpton had only been this emotionally wrought three other times in his life. And all three of those other days had been when one of his children had died.

In those situations, there had been no words. Not then nor any day since. What could a person possibly say?

But today was different. Perhaps as different as it could possibly be.

Plimpton had almost reached the age of three-and-forty and had never heard the words Winifred had just spoken. At least not directed at him.

Not until his brother's marriage had he heard the words spoken aloud between a man and a woman. Indeed, Simon and Honoria said them often and with seeming ease.

Why couldn't Plimpton?

Could it be that he believed what his father drummed into him? That love was a woman's emotion and a sign of weakness that no real man would succumb to.

Every day, year in and year out, his father had pounded that same message into him, like a human mallet with one stubborn peg that refused to be driven into its hole. The old duke's notion of what made a man was warped and twisted and—Plimpton had eventually decided— just plain *wrong*.

His brother Simon—who had faced bullets and artillery and torture without flinching—was more of a man than anyone Plimpton had ever met, and he loved his wife and son with an openheartedness that made Plimpton's knees weak. *That* was strength.

He looked down into Winifred's patiently waiting face. This woman—this clever, strong, resilient woman—*loved* him.

The choice at that moment was crystal clear. He could either remain in a cage of his father's construction, or he could push open the cell door and let himself out.

"What is it, Wyndham?"

"You have the most mesmerizing eyes I have ever seen," he said, his voice strangely raw, almost as if he had been shouting.

It wasn't what he'd expected to say, but her soft, full lips turned up at the ends. "Thank you."

"I do not mean the color—although that is stunning—I mean the expression in them. The kindness and warmth and compassion." His jaws flexed, as if to halt the fatuous words from pouring out. But they would not be stopped. "I have never told a woman I loved her. Until these past weeks, I did not believe I was capable of the emotion. With my first wife, I mistook infatuation for love. How I thought it could be anything else when I did not know her"—he shook his head. "Well, I was young and stupid. It took years to discover my error and when I did, I took comfort in the fact it had never been love. Because the alternative would have been…devastating."

Plimpton picked up her hand and smoothed the palm with his thumb while he sought the words he needed. "Cecily hated me from the day we married until the day she died." He gave an unamused laugh. "That is not accurate; she hated me well before we married, but I only learned the truth on our wedding night. You see, she was in love with somebody else."

"Oh, Wyndham," she murmured, caressing his cheek with her free hand.

He pressed his face into her palm, seeking the comfort of her touch and not caring that the reaction was one his father would have sneered at.

"I daresay an older, more self-aware, man would have noticed something amiss in his bride-to-be even with the small amount of time we spent together. Or perhaps *because* of how carefully we were kept apart." He shrugged. "But I wanted her too much to care about anything but my own desire." He was ashamed by his admission, but he also experienced a sense of liberation. He had never told anyone about his disastrous marriage, although many people would have guessed the truth. His mother certainly had. And probably Simon. He hoped to God that Becca was too young to understand how loveless her parents' marriage had been, although that was probably wishful thinking.

"Cecily told me she would do her duty, but otherwise begged me never to come near her." He laughed bitterly. "She needn't have wasted her breath; the last thing I wanted to do was force myself on a woman who loathed me. Unfortunately, I had a duty, as well. And that meant I went to her bed for a handful of miserable nights until she was breeding. Then we did not have to see each other again until after the child was born. She lived her life—one of self-imposed isolation—and I lived mine." He met her open, loving gaze. "What I am trying to say—very, er, *wordily*—is that our marriage is already utterly different than my last one. So different, in fact, that it has taken me until today to admit something very important. And that is that I love you, Winifred. I love you with a ferocity that terrifies me."

Her lips parted, her expression one of wonderment.

"Why do you look so stunned? Surely you must have guessed?"

"I *hoped*, but I did not know. You hide your emotions well."

"I do not want to hide them from you, Winifred. Today, when I thought I might be too late to save you, I realized that such love has a steep cost." He squeezed her hand until she winced. But he did not apologize. "I never want to feel that fear again."

"I am so sorry, I—"

"I know you are." Plimpton released her hand and gently lifted her by the waist until she was sitting on his lap. He wanted her close for this last part, so he wrapped his arms around her. "There is more I need to tell you. And it is…ugly."

She nodded.

"After the death of our second child the doctor came to me. He said part of the reason our babies had been so weak and ill was Cecily's use of arsenic."

Winifred winced. "For her complexion?"

Plimpton nodded, his eyes sliding over her beautiful skin.

"I have never used it," she said. "On occasion I have used powdered rice, but never anything else, Plimpton."

He nodded, relieved she had not made him ask.

"Did—did she stop using it?"

"No."

Winifred squeezed her eyes shut, but a tear escaped. "I am so sorry."

He kissed her lightly and continued. "Unlike her first two pregnancies, I did not go my own way for the third one. I stayed at Whitcombe the entire time she was breeding, and I paid attention. I saw the effect the arsenic had—it was not difficult to notice if one actually *looked* at one's wife every day. I forbade her to use it, but she defied me.

The Etiquette of Love

I had her chambers searched and seized the substance. But she kept getting more."

"Her maid?"

Plimpton nodded. "I threatened the woman, but she continued to obey her mistress. So, I dismissed her. The maid had been with her since Cecily was only a girl and she was distraught. Matters became even more… unpleasant when Cecily stopped eating. The doctor said she was already so thin the baby would be starving. He said she must be made to eat, or she would lose the child. He recommended several methods." He saw her shocked look. "No. I could not do what he suggested, which was to restrain her and force feed her. Instead, I told her I would bring her maid back if she would give her word not to use the arsenic."

"And did she?"

"She promised, but I was too cowardly to have her rooms checked."

"That is not cowardly. What else could you have possibly done?"

"I could have done what the doctor said. If I had valued my child's life above my wife's freedom and sanity, I could have had her locked up, forced food down her throat, and kept her away from anything harmful."

"That would have been barbaric."

"That is what I told myself. And when Becca was born and survived—although she was never strong—I thought perhaps the doctor had overreacted. Or that Cecily had kept her word and stopped."

Plimpton's mind unwillingly traveled back to the day his daughter was born. "Cecily was furious when she found out Becca was *only* a girl—those are her words—and she raged at me, becoming so violent that even her maid said she should be restrained before she hurt herself." He briefly closed his eyes. "The last time, we waited two years before—" he swallowed down the words and said, "After our son Edward was born—he would be our last child—Cecily took pleasure in telling me that she had used arsenic during her entire pregnancy. Edward was so much healthier than any of the others, even Becca, that I thought maybe the doctor had been wrong, after all. But the birth had

354

been difficult and the doctor said she was too fragile for more children. We were both relieved. Edward was doing so well—" he broke off and shook away the memory of the soul-destroying day the nurse had come to him, weeping and holding his son's lifeless body.

"I cannot imagine what you must have felt," Winifred said, stroking his arm.

"I hope you never have to experience that feeling, Winfred. I hope neither of us do. It would have been unbearable under any circumstances, but perhaps—had we been able to draw comfort from each other—it would not have been quite as devastating. But Cecily did not grieve. Or at least she claimed she was glad. And she never once held Becca or showed any interest in her." He met Winifred's gaze. "How could a mother hate her own child so much?"

"I cannot believe that she did, Wyndham. She must have been suffering greatly and simply did not have enough strength to spare for anyone else."

"I want to believe that," he said. "I truly do." But he didn't. Not that it mattered any longer.

After a moment she said, "Compton said the constable was here?"

Plimpton felt a rush of gratitude that she had changed the subject. "Yes. He told me they had to restrain Luton to get him out of there."

"I am surprised the fall did not kill him."

"He did suffer a broken leg."

"And the chess pieces?"

"They were down there. Evidently Luton kept them in a shrine that dated back to the days when the building had been an actual priory." He snorted. "It gives new meaning to false idols."

"He looked like a religious zealot when he talked about the set—as if the pieces were alive and needed his care. He killed his father over them."

Plimpton stared at her. "Good Lord! He told you that?"

"He said he did so to stop him from selling the pieces." She shook her head. "His obsession drove him mad and turned him into a murderer just like his father. And all for pieces of stone." She gave him a curious look. "You saw the set?"

"I saw them all those years ago and the constable brought them with him today. They are currently down in my vault."

"What do you think of them?"

Plimpton shrugged. "They are chess pieces, that is all. I certainly did not think they were worth killing for."

"Nothing is."

He took her chin between his fingers. "You are, Winifred," he said, and then he kissed her. He had intended it to be a gentle, light kiss, but she wove her arms around his neck and shifted closer until her nightgown rode up to her thighs.

Plimpton slid his hands around her bare legs and leaned back to see her. "Your poor face, darling… And your neck and ankle. I do not want to hurt—"

"You will hurt me more if you stop touching me," she promised, rubbing her unbound breasts against his torso in a way that immediately got his attention. "I—I need you, Plimpton. Something about almost dying has—" she broke off and shrugged, blushing.

"Are you sure, sweetheart?"

"Yes." She lowered her hands to his fall.

He chuckled. "Wait, I need to remove my boots before—"

"No. I want you to take me with your boots on."

Plimpton groaned, almost ejaculating in his breeches. "My naughty wife has hidden depths," he muttered, unfastening the first few buttons on her nightgown. "I want this off you first. Arms up," he ordered, carefully easing the bunched fabric around her bruised temple and then tossing it to the side.

He sucked in a breath when he saw her throat. Without any material in the way he could actually see the indents left from Luton's fingernails. "That must hurt like—"

"I hardly notice," she said, and then grabbed the flap of his fall, which she had been fumbling with, and yanked.

He gave a startled laugh at the sound of tearing seams.

"I am sorry," she said, not sounding it. She grabbed handfuls of buckskin and yanked his breeches down, snagging his erection in the process.

Plimpton hissed and lifted the fabric away from his prick. "Mind the jewels, darling."

She paused just long enough to laugh and say, "The jewels?" And then she grabbed his stiff shaft and pumped him hard, making him forget about everything else. "I want you, Wyndham."

He forced himself to still her magical fist. "Then you had better stop that right now." He glanced doubtfully down at his breeches, which imprisoned him at the thighs. "If I could remove—"

"No," she barked, and then she did something utterly, erotically shocking and turned away from him, positioning herself on her hands and knees.

Plimpton stared in awed stupefaction.

Winifred twisted around and scowled at him. "What are you waiting for?" And then she leaned lower, until her shoulders and head were on the bed, presenting herself to him.

"My God." He slid a hand between her spread thighs and thrust a finger deep inside her.

She hissed and pushed her bottom against his hand in counterpoint to his thrusting. "I want you inside me," she said, her voice muffled by the bedding.

"What a tyrant you are turning out to be." Plimpton reluctantly released her so that he could ungracefully struggle to his knees. "Are you sure I need to keep all this on? You cannot even see—"

"Wyndham!"

He bit back a grin. "As you command, darling." He positioned his crown at her entrance and filled her with a thrust powerful enough to drive her body up the bed. "Is that what you wanted?" he asked harshly, keeping her tight sheath full and flexing inside her.

She wiggled her hips. "Move."

He laughed and slid one arm around her waist, circling and stroking her slick nub while he fucked her with deep, steady strokes.

She groaned and then gasped, "Yes, please, just like that."

Plimpton did not work her long before her body stiffened and convulsed around him. He ceased his thrusting to relish her contractions, buried deep inside her as the waves of her orgasm crested and then ebbed.

Once passion released its grip on her, he withdrew with a reluctant grimace, and flipped her onto her back.

She blinked up at him, her breasts rosy from chafing against the bedding, her hair a tangled, glorious mess.

Her brow furrowed when she saw his still hard prick. "Why are you stopping? You didn't—"

"No, I didn't. But I thought you had a reason for keeping me clothed?"

She stared, adorably dazed.

"My boots?" he reminded her.

"Oh. Yes, please."

"So polite," he teased, awkwardly getting down off the mattress before taking her hand. "Get on your knees, darling." She hesitated for only a second before hurrying to obey. "Take hold of my shoulders," he ordered, sliding his hands beneath her lush buttocks once she had complied. He lifted her with a soft grunt, holding her up high while he lined his aching cock up with her entrance.

"My God," he muttered as he lowered her slowly, not stopping until she took every inch.

"Why are you standing?" she asked, squirming in a way that was sure to hasten his pleasure.

"Look to your right," he said, his breathlessness reminding him that he was sorely missing his weekly sessions at Angelo's and Jackson's.

Her jaw dropped. "Oh, Wyndham," she cooed, staring at the image in the mirror while his eyes were riveted on her face.

Plimpton rolled his hips, spreading his feet wider to keep his balance, but not too wide since his bloody breeches hobbled him.

And then he proceeded to fuck her while standing, something that was not as easy as he had hoped, although Winifred's rapt expression made it more than worth the effort.

"I like this," she said, her breathing almost as labored as his own.

He barked a laugh. "Enjoy it while it lasts," he said tightly. "Which won't be long."

A smile of wicked delight spread across her face. "Let me help," she said, and bounced against him in counterpoint.

Well, that was the end of that.

***

Plimpton laid her out on the bed with a groan.

"That was lovely," Freddie said.

"Lovely, but far too brief," he agreed wryly.

Freddie could not help admiring the way his chest swelled his coat with each labored breath.

Plimpton began to undress, his hands shaking from either the effort of their recent coupling or as a result of his orgasm.

"Could you put your boots back on after you remove your breeches?" she asked when he dropped into the nearest chair and began struggling with his footwear.

He raised his head slowly and gave her a look of stunned disbelief. "You cannot be serious."

Freddie laughed. "But I *am*."

He groaned. "Let us leave that for another day, shall we, darling?"

It was not a direct *no*, so she did not press him.

An amusing four or five minutes ensued as he struggled out of the last of his clothes. Finally, he joined her on the bed.

"On top of me," Freddie said.

The Etiquette of Love

He frowned.

"Please, Wyndham."

Freddie smiled to herself as he grumbled but did as she bade him, gingerly lowering his naked body over hers. She reached around him and pulled him close, until they were touching from ankles to shoulders.

"I must be crushing you," he said into her hair, and began to roll off her.

She tightened her arms. "No. Stay."

"A compromise," he said, and then raised up onto his elbows.

Freddie smiled up at him. "Your hair is a mess."

"Not as messy as yours."

"No, probably not," she conceded.

He frowned as he looked at her neck. "Does it hurt?"

"No," she lied.

"Yes it does."

"Just a little."

"How the devil did it happen? Was he—was he choking you?"

Freddie did not care for the dark look that crept into his eyes. "I do not want to talk about it." She caressed up and down his upper arms; the muscles were attractively taut from holding his weight.

"Of course, darling. What a brute I am to make you relive it."

"Oh, it does not upset me to remember it."

"Then why—"

"Because I can see what it does to *you*."

He opened his mouth, but then closed it and nodded.

Freddie was glad he decided not to deny it.

"You should have seen yourself when you came through that door."

"What door?"

"Into Luton's study."

He looked blank.

"You don't recall his study?"

He shook his head, a subtle flush spreading over the chiseled angles of his face, softening them. "I remember saddling up Thunder myself and riding full out. The next thing I recall is setting you in the gig Cocker brought to bring you home." He frowned pensively. "How odd that I cannot remember anything else."

"You were not yourself."

"What do you mean?"

"You were baying."

His eyebrows shot up. "Baying?"

"Yes. It was most unnerving. In fact, it was enough to frighten Luton into dropping his guard, which is when I was able to hit him with my head."

"Baying?"

"Baying. And when you burst into the room you broke the hinges off the door."

He gave her a skeptical look.

"You did," she insisted. "And you picked up Luton as if he weighed no more than a feather and threw him down the hole. That is the truth, Plimpton."

He stared unseeingly at her. "I recall nothing."

"I think you must have gone berserker."

He laughed.

"I am serious," Freddie said. "I could see in your eyes that it was not you. And you have no recollection of it, so—"

"Berserker," he repeated.

She reached up and smoothed her palms over the rounded caps of his shoulders. "I am sorry I caused you to be so afraid."

"It wasn't fear that I felt," he corrected. "It was terror."

"I will never forgive myself for putting our baby in such danger."

"It was not fear of losing the baby that drove me to the brink of madness, Winifred. It was fear of losing *you*."

Her pulse sped at the raw look in his eyes.

"I know we married because of our child, but I wanted you when I believed you were barren. I wanted *you*. I am delighted you can have children, but it is *you* I want. For the first half of my life, I had one goal—one driving reason to get up each morning and go on living, even when I was so empty of everything except duty that it was a burden to open my eyes." He held his weight on one arm and reached out to trace her eyebrow with one finger, the love in his eyes stealing her breath. "I'd been attracted to you since Avington's ball—the first one—but I knew I had to have you that night at the Chorley ball—it struck me like a cudgel to the head."

She laughed. "That sounds pleasant."

"It was bloody terrifying. I had lived for so long not wanting anything for myself that I felt as if I were leaping off a cliff into the great unknown." His lips twisted. "When I saw Piers approach you that night, I wanted to strangle him for even daring to look at you. I wanted you all for myself, but every time I got near you, I managed to put your back up about something or other."

Freddie caught his hand and kissed his palm. "I have a confession to make; I put my own back up because I was far too attracted to you for my own comfort. I had been living my life as the Ice Countess"— she nodded at his look of surprise. "Yes, I know about that name. I cultivated it for years. Those first months with Sedgewick made me realize that intimate relations could be fulfilling and enjoyable. But he did an almost thorough job of destroying that opinion over the three and a half years that followed. I knew it was not the act of physical love that was bad, it was Sedgewick. Even so, I did not meet any man worth taking a risk over until you. Whenever I was around you, I felt…things I had not felt in years. I wanted *no* part of those feelings, even though I knew you were nothing like Sedgewick." She smiled. "I think I fell half in love with you when you took charge of the mess we found at Torrance Park, throwing out Wareham's awful mother-in-law and the grim nurse without blinking an eye. I fell a little bit *more* in love when I discovered you kept a miniature of Rebecca close to your heart. But the more I liked you, the more frightened I became. And so I behaved like a fool and hid our child from you." She kissed his hand again. "For years I thought the only person I could rely on was myself—even my friends were all struggling too hard to help save me if I truly stumbled into trouble. But today—when you roared into that house and rescued me you make me feel loved and cherished and protected. You are the sort of man who will always sacrifice your own needs and think of me first—even when I do not deserve it."

Plimpton kissed her. "It is no sacrifice, my darling wife. It is a labor of love. And one I will gladly shoulder every day of my life, if it means I get to live it with you."

Epilogue

Freddie grinned across the carriage at Piers, who was staring in disbelief at the small foldout table littered with playing cards. "Piqued, re-piqued, and capoted, my dear brother."

Piers shook his head and gave her a look of disgust before glaring out the window at Plimpton, who was riding alongside the coach. "No wonder he wanted me to *relax* inside the coach with you. Relax? Ha! He just didn't want to get his arse kicked—" he broke off when Freddie cleared her throat. "I beg your pardon, Duchess, I meant to say that your husband did not want to get his bottom spanked—that is what you aristos like to do, is it not?"

"Piers!" she squawked. "You are a respectable citizen now—not a wanted felon. You need to learn to behave properly in public."

He snorted. "Have you heard Severn and that black-haired wench of his go at it hammer and tongs? I tell you, Little Bird, I learned a few new words from that shrew."

Freddie hid her smile only because she knew it would encourage her brother's bad behavior. But he was right; Lori had a far more vulgar mouth than many a dock worker and sailor.

As Piers shuffled the cards—evidently eager to have his *arse* kicked a bit more—Freddie glanced at her husband.

As always, Plimpton looked mouthwatering on horseback. Her gaze dropped to his boots—a glossy black pair today, the white tops pristine—and her heart fluttered when she recalled him wearing them the night before, with nothing else, while *swiving* her. That was a wicked word Plimpton had taught her. She wondered if Lori knew *that* one.

In the weeks since her brush with death, Freddie had learned more and more about the man who hid behind her husband's mask. Plimpton would always be the same aloof, haughty aristocrat in public—she knew that now—but behind closed doors he became a man that only Freddie got to see.

Her skin tingled and she knew before she wrenched her gaze from his thighs that Plimpton would be looking at her.

He was. And he was wearing his stern-faced look, one of her favorites now that she knew what lurked beneath it.

He raised one eyebrow slowly and Freddie felt it all the way in her womb.

"Talk about behavior that is inappropriate outside the bedchamber," Piers groused.

Her head whipped around. "I do not know what you are talking about."

"Your wildly blushing face suggests otherwise, Little Bird."

"You are imagining things."

He grinned. "There is an excellent duchess glare if I ever saw one."

Freddie couldn't help laughing. "Thank you for riding with me, Piers. Plimpton doesn't care for coaches."

"I can understand why if you thrash him at cards."

"Would you rather play chess?" she asked sweetly.

"*No.*"

She saw that he had put away the cards rather than dealing them out again. So, they were done with that, then. "How long until we get there?"

"About an hour."

"You told me the same thing an hour ago."

He cocked his head.

Yes, she *did* sound a bit plaintive.

Freddie knew she was behaving badly, but something about being in the company of her siblings seem to bring it out in her. She had spent all last week with Piers *and* Wareham and Plimpton had said it was like living with a trio of twelve-year-olds the way they bickered.

Perhaps, but Freddie felt as if they were all making up for lost time.

The Etiquette of Love

All jesting aside, it warmed her heart to see how well her older brothers appeared to be getting along. Wareham and Plimpton had both used their influence to clear Piers's name of any wrong-doing, which meant that her brother was able to walk the streets of England as a free man for the first time in over a decade.

Which reminded her…

"Do you really have to leave next week?" she asked, not for the first time.

"I don't *have* to do anything—now. But I miss it, Little Bird."

"You are a contrarian. When you were not supposed to be here, you were here. And now, when I want you to stay, you are leaving."

"Only for a few months."

"It is a dangerous occupation."

"Not really. All the fun has gone out of being a privateer now that the war is over."

"I think your notion of *fun* might be just a little warped, my dear brother."

Piers laughed and carefully folded up their game table.

Freddie had loved spending this extra time with Piers before Lori's party. Naturally, the idea had been Plimpton's. He had suggested that Piers should come and stay at Plimpton House and then the three of them could make the journey to Granton Castle together.

Piers had accepted the invitation with flattering alacrity, joining Freddie and Plimpton in London shortly after they had returned from their first trip to Spenham to see Miranda.

Freddie had worried that her first visit as the Duchess of Plimpton would be awkward, but she had been relieved by how quickly everyone had adjusted to her change in status.

Predictably, Miranda had been disconcerted by the shift in the visitation schedule and also anxious to meet Plimpton for the first time, but he had charmed all three of the Morrisons' charges—not to mention surprising Freddie—by performing some impressive sleight of hand tricks for everyone's entertainment.

"And here I thought you only performed tricks in the bedchamber," Freddie had whispered into his ear after Plimpton had produced a gleaming sovereign seemingly from thin air, making his small audience shriek and clap with delight.

Plimpton had barked a laugh. "I have some special tricks to show you this evening, my naughty Winifred," he had promised, giving her a smoldering look and making good on his promise later that night at the Spotted Sow. Indeed, his *tricks* had been so impressive that Freddie feared those people below in the taproom might have heard about them.

"Look, Little Bird," Piers said, pulling her from her erotic reminiscing.

Freddie looked to where he was pointing and gasped. "It is just like something from a storybook." They were on a hill slightly above the castle, which looked as if it were rising from the middle of a lake.

"Impressive, isn't it?" Piers asked.

"Indeed." Granton Castle had a massive, crenellated drum tower at each of the four corners with a high curtain wall and parapets. "I cannot imagine Lori being mistress of *that*."

"You will find that she has taken to it like a duck to water."

A drop of rain smacked the window. "Oh! Poor Plimpton. He will get wet," Freddie said, glancing about for her husband. "I do hope he does not catch a chill."

"Lord, but it's nice to see you so smitten, Little Bird."

Freddie pointedly ignored her brother's laughter.

A short time later they crossed the drawbridge and entered beneath the massive barbican where two carriages were already being unloaded.

A much more modern structure had been built along the base of three of the interior curtain walls. Judging by the style of the construction it dated to the early 1600s, so a good three hundred years after the original structure.

"Oh, there is Lori now!" Freddie reached for the door.

"Just a moment, Little Bird. We wouldn't want *you* to take ill, would we?" Piers took her umbrella, opened the door, and hopped out, unfurling the vivid red canopy and holding it over her head.

Lori—dressed in the height of fashion, but just as headlong as ever—came streaking across the courtyard.

"Freddie!" Lori cried, flinging her arms around her.

Piers winced. "Take this," he murmured, pressing the handle of the umbrella into Freddie's palm and sidling away.

Lori released Freddie and snickered at Piers's receding back. "I think I frighten your brother."

Freddie thought Lori probably frightened most people, men and women, but kept that opinion to herself.

"I would have thought Piers would be accustomed to you by now," Freddie said.

"No, he hides from me. And the castle is big, so it is hard for me to find him." She paused thoughtfully. "Sometimes I think Severn has shared secret hiding places with him."

Freddie laughed.

With Piers's permission, she had divulged his story in a series of letters to all her friends. Most of them would respect his privacy. Lori, she knew—and so did Piers—had boundless curiosity and was not afraid to satisfy it.

Well, that was for Piers to deal with.

"I adore your umbrella, Freddie—I don't think I have ever seen you so close to a bright color before," Lori teased. "Unless you are standing next to somebody else, of course."

"It is a gift from Plimpton," Freddie said, irked when she felt her traitorous face heat.

"*Hmmm.* Where is the delicious duke, anyhow?"

"*Lori!*"

"Sorry. But I recall telling you to snap him up ages ago."

Freddie shook her head and deliberately changed the subject. "The castle is magnificent."

Lori pulled a face. "It *is* magnificent to look at but living in it"—she shuddered. "Severn said we don't have to spend more than a few weeks here a couple times a year, but I know he worries about the marquess, so I daresay we'll be here a great deal."

Lori meant the Marquess of Granton, whose title her husband, Lord Stand Fast Severn, would one day inherit. Lord Granton was one of the great sticklers of society so it would be interesting to see how he and Lori engaged with one another.

"Freddie!"

She turned at the sound of Miles's familiar and beloved voice just in time to be caught up in a tight embrace and whirled around until she was dizzy and a bit wet from some errant rain drops.

"Married!" he whispered in her ear. "Congratulations, my dearest Fred." He gave her a smacking kiss on the cheek, released her, and stepped back smiling. But Freddie, who knew him best of all her friends, saw the questions in his celestial blue eyes. Eyes that suddenly slid to Freddie's right, his smile stiffening. Freddie knew who it was before he opened his mouth.

"Plimpton. It is good to see you again," Miles said in an overly hearty voice.

The duke inclined his head slightly. "Avington."

Freddie frowned at the faint chill in his voice. Before she could examine it more closely, a ravishing black-haired woman and a man who resembled a male Galatea came trotting after two toddlers, their coloring so like their respective parents that Freddie was momentarily distracted.

"Come here, you," Eustace Harrington, the Earl of Broughton growled as he snatched up a child as devoid of pigment as he was. The little boy squealed with delight and turned his face toward the sky, sticking out his tongue to catch raindrops.

"Freddie!" Portia threw her arms around Freddie, squeezing the breath out of her.

Portia then held her at arm's length and examined her with a gimlet eye. "You are happy," she declared, only a touch of Italian showing in her English accent.

"I am happy," Freddie agreed. She felt something tug on her skirt of her periwinkle blue traveling costume and looked down to find a girl who resembled her mother so much that Freddie laughed. "Hello, Isabelle!"

The little girl soundlessly held out her arms to be picked up.

Freddie was flattered. "You remember me?"

Isabelle nodded.

Freddie handed the little girl the umbrella. "You will need to hold this up to keep us dry."

Isabelle nodded again and Freddie swept the toddler up, groaning when she settled her on her hip. "You are so big!"

Isabelle merely smiled.

Freddie met Portia's gaze and the other woman shrugged. "Not yet."

Portia meant that Isabelle still wasn't speaking. Her brother, Ian, on the other hand, had not stopped talking since his father picked him up.

"This one is like his mother," Portia said, smirking proudly as her husband handed her their son.

"Papa!"

Freddie turned in time to see Plimpton catch a young woman in a hug. He was facing her and had closed his eyes, his expression one of pure happiness as he embraced his tall, slender daughter.

He opened his eyes, immediately saw Freddie, and his face flexed into what she thought of us his *public smile*, which was an almost indiscernible curving of his lips. "There is somebody I want you to meet Becca." He turned his daughter toward Freddie. "This is my wife, Winifred."

Freddie had seen Becca's miniature, but the girl was older that she had been in the portrait. She looked so much like Plimpton that Freddie instantly felt drawn to her.

"Hello, Becca—may I call you that?"

"Of course, er—Your Grace."

Freddie smiled. "Why don't you call me Winifred—or Freddie, if you like."

Becca's eyebrows lifted, the expression so much like Plimpton's that Freddie laughed for no reason other than she was happy. "I am so glad to meet you finally. I feel like I know you, I've heard so much about you."

The girl blushed. "I have heard about you, too."

"You have?" Freddie turned to look at Plimpton.

Becca laughed. "No, not from Papa. He never tells me anything. It is Honey who talks about you all the time. Ah, here she comes."

"Robert wants his cousin," Honey said, handing her remarkably fat, healthy baby over to Rebecca, who actually looked small holding the child. Honey shook out her arms. "He seems to gain a pound a day. How are you, darling Freddie?" she asked before Freddie could comment on her child's astonishing size.

"I am well." She returned her friend's gentle embrace.

"We are real sisters now," Honey murmured, and then kissed Freddie's cheek. "I cannot wait until you are living at Whitcombe. We can see each other every day."

"That is not fair!" Portia protested. "Stacy," she said to her husband, not caring that he was in the middle of a conversation with the Earl of Rotherhithe, Annis's husband. "I want a house beside Honey and Freddie."

"Of course, my dear," Lord Brougham said, and then turned back to Rotherhithe and continued his conversation.

"I don't think he really heard me," Portia told Honey.

The Etiquette of Love

"You can come live with us if he proves stubborn," Honey assured her. She lightly pinched Ian's cheek. "And you can bring this little monkey with you."

The little boy thought that was hilarious.

"Where is Annis?" Freddie asked, gently bouncing Isabelle on her hip and turning in a circle.

"Over here, with Oliver." A slight figure waddled forward and Freddie could not help staring.

Portia leaned close and whispered, "She looks like she may have the child any minute. But she is only five months, if you can believe it."

Annis squeezed Freddie's shoulder and smiled, her huge blue eyes always making Freddie feel as if the other woman could see right inside her. "It has been such a long time, Freddie," she said softly, her gaze sliding to Plimpton, who was chatting with Becca, Piers, and Simon. She lowered her voice even more and whispered gleefully, "A duke, Freddie!"

Freddie laughed.

"She only married him to outrank us," Lori chimed in, holding out her arms. "It is my turn with Isabelle." The girl eagerly switched to the other woman and Freddie relieved her of the umbrella and subtly flexed her arms.

"It is like losing two stone in an instant, is it not?"

Freddie turned at the sound of a French voice.

"Serena! How lovely to see you." She embraced the beautiful, always slightly disheveled woman.

"I have missed you, Freddie," Serena said, her hard belly jutting against Freddie's and reminding her that Serena was, just like Annis, expecting an interesting event in four months.

"It is good to see you again, Mr. Lockheart," Freddie said to Serena's gorgeous, albeit odd, husband.

"Duchess," Gareth Lockheart murmured, bowing in Freddie's general direction before turning to Lori and demanding, "Where is Declan McElroy?"

Lori looked amused by his abrupt question. "He is not here yet."

Mr. Lockheart frowned. "He told me he would be arriving yesterday."

"Yes, that is what he said when he accepted the invitation."

Lockheart kept staring at Lori, as if she might produce the missing man if he looked hard enough.

"Gareth, darling, don't worry so much," Serena soothed, looping her arm through her husband's and pulling him closer. "Declan is a big boy; he can make his way to a country house party."

Gareth did not look convinced by her words.

Serena met Freddie's questioning gaze and rolled her eyes.

Freddie knew Mr. McElroy was a very close friend of the reclusive Lockheart, but Serena was not exactly fond of the man, who evidently drank a great deal and was a confirmed skirt-chaser into the bargain.

The rain began to fall harder.

Lori handed Isabelle back to her father and then clapped her hands. "Come inside, everyone! We will ply you all with tea and then show you to your chambers."

***

Plimpton leaned against the wide doorframe between the double drawing rooms, nursing his drink and covertly observing his wife chatting with her friends while a small, sharp-eyed man whose name he had already forgotten stood in front of him and babbled about a hunt party he'd joined the month before. If there was anything more tedious than listening to somebody share a minute-by-minute description of a fox hunt, Plimpton could not recall it at that moment.

"Here you are Gervaise."

Plimpton turned at the sound of his brother's voice.

"Ah, Lord Simon," the man—Gervaise, apparently, said. "I was just telling His Grace about—"

"Miss Middleton is looking for you, Gervaise."

"She is?"

The Etiquette of Love

Based on how stunned he looked and sounded Plimpton surmised that people were more in the habit of running *from* Gervaise than toward him.

"Yes, she seemed most eager to talk to you. You should go to her," Simon urged.

Gervaise glanced into the mirror that hung over the fireplace, slicked back his eyebrows with his thumb and forefinger, and then drained the contents of his glass. "Where is she?" he asked, handing the empty glass to Simon.

Simon pointed. "Go that way and take a right past the statue of Venus and you can't miss her."

The other man went hurrying away.

"Is Miss Middleton really looking for him?" Plimpton asked, sipping his drink.

Simon snorted. "The man is a crashing bore; what do you think?"

Plimpton regarded his brother briefly before turning back to Winifred.

"I just thought I'd bring you a spoon, old boy." Simon lifted a dessert spoon from the small pocket in his tailcoat. "Here you go."

Plimpton stared. "Are you foxed?"

Simon laughed. "Not even close."

"What the devil would I need a spoon for."

Simon gestured to where Freddie was sitting. "You have been eating her with your eyes; I thought a spoon might help."

Plimpton gave a bark of laughter. "Very droll." He paused and then said, "Am I so obvious?"

Simon grinned. "Only to somebody who has spent a lifetime Wyndham watching."

"*Hmm.*"

"I can see married life is treating you much better this time," Simon said after a moment, because he was the sort of person who was not comfortable unless he was talking.

"Is there a question in that collection of words?" Plimpton asked.

His brother laughed and slapped him on the shoulder. "Good old Wynd. You haven't changed a bit."

Simon, he realized, was not a very observant man.

***

The following evening...

"Where did Gareth go in such a hurry after dinner?" Lori asked Serena.

"He has gone to talk to one of our footmen about going to the London house to see when Declan left. Or *if* he left."

"Why do you want to know where Gareth went?" Honey asked Lori. "Did you want to torment him some more?"

Freddie, Serena, and Miles all laughed.

"It is not called torture, *Honoria*. It is called conversation," Lori retorted icily.

Honey smirked. "Simon said talking to you was like shoving a live ferret down his breeches."

Miles, who had just taken a drink, doubled over and fell into a coughing fit.

"You deserve that," Lori said, slapping him on the back with more force than necessary. She turned to Honey, "And *you* should be less concerned about my interview technique and more worried about the fact that your husband knows anything at all about shoving rodents in his breeches."

Honey laughed. "I said exactly the same thing to him when he told me."

"Ferrets aren't rodents; they are weasels," Annis corrected softly.

Lori gave the other woman a look of amazement. "Why on earth would you know something like that?"

"All knowledge is valuable," Annis said mildly.

The Etiquette of Love

Lord Severn drifted up behind his wife. "Are you being rude to our guests, my dear?"

"Of course not," Lori retorted. "I am being the perfect hostess," she added, sending Miles off on another coughing bender.

Freddie had missed her friends—had missed the hundreds of evenings they had spent together at the school, teasing and bickering and slowly building friendships that just got better every year. Often in the time since the school had closed, she had yearned to go back to that time again and appreciate it more fully, rather than taking it for granted.

And yet right now…

Her gaze drifted across the room and locked with Plimpton's. He was standing talking to Lord Simon and Lord Broughton. Actually, Lord Simon was talking, and Plimpton was staring at Freddie, giving her one of those blandly assessing glances that used to irk her and now made her feel as if he could see right through her clothing.

Miles said something that made the others laugh, but Freddie didn't catch it. Instead, she glanced at the clock. How soon could she politely excuse herself and go up to bed without becoming the target of the next round of teasing?

***

An hour and a half later…

Plimpton had Winifred stretched out facedown beneath him and nibbling on her neck and holding her wrists pinned to the mattress while he stroked into her with deep, rolling thrusts of his hips.

He liked taking her this way until she climaxed—the first time—as the angle afforded far deeper penetration. Once he had reduced her to a babbling, incoherent wreck he would usually roll her onto her back so he could watch her face while he took her again, but slower and more torturously the second time, working her as close to the edge as he dared take her, without pushing her over.

Over and over, he would tease her, denying her at the last minute and feasting on her needy frustration. Winifred, normally so cool and self-possessed, forgot herself when she did not get the sexual release she wanted. She would often beg and sometimes even hector him.

Once, the week before, she had even used a very naughty word he had taught her.

Plimpton had no idea why he enjoyed controlling her pleasure and denying his own orgasm in the process. Perhaps it was just a natural male urge to dominate. But he had never felt such an urge with any other woman.

Maybe it was because Winifred was *his* that he wanted to possess and explore and master every part of her.

Well, regardless of the reason, he could not get enough of teasing her.

"Wyndham, please," she begged.

Desire shot straight to his already aching bollocks; the pleasure he got from hearing her beg was near orgiastic in itself. There was probably something wrong with him for enjoying it so much. But he decided it felt too good for him to care.

She squirmed beneath him, trying to urge him to fuck her faster. Some nights he punished her for such wanton behavior by denying her even longer. Some nights he rewarded her. The trick to toying with her was to always keep her guessing.

Right now, he could feel that she was well on her way to a second orgasm.

"I need—"

"I know what you need." He slid his forefinger and thumb around his shaft, right where they were joined. "I love to feel you stretched around me." He caressed her slick, sensitive skin, his hips pumping harder. "I adore the way your tight, wet body takes me so very—"

"Wyndham!" she shuddered, beginning to come undone.

"Take what you need, darling," he said, deciding not to tease her any longer.

This time, he did not stop when her body convulsed around his but kept going, fucking her through her climax into what might have been a third one, or perhaps just an extension of the second.

The Etiquette of Love

Only when she was lost to bliss did he give in to his need and flood her with heat as he joined her in mindless ecstasy.

When their pulses had both slowed to a canter, he rolled off her delectable body and turned on his side to face her.

She had worn her hair loose to please him and it was a wild, blonde storm around her head. She stared at him through pupils that were still dilated with passion. "I love you, Wyndham."

The words were as thrilling the twentieth time as they had been the first. Plimpton smoothed the silky curls away from her face, marveling that this woman was his. Would he ever stop feeling that jolt of wonder that struck him whenever he looked at her? He hoped not. He set a hand on her barely swelling belly, a surge of protective love filling him. "Have you decided whether or not you will tell your friends that you are expecting an interesting event?"

She smiled. "As almost everyone else seems to be expecting similarly interesting events, it only seems fair. And I daresay you would like to tell your family."

"I would, but not until you are ready."

"I am ready."

"Good." Plimpton would write to his mother first thing in the morning. He knew she was itching to meet his new wife, but she had agreed that it would be best to come directly from Sweet Clover to Granton Castle. Especially as this would be Winifred's last chance to spend time with Piers for a while.

Plimpton knew his mother would be over the moon to learn there was another grandchild on the way. It had been the dowager who had told him that childbirth was a very different event if a woman actually wanted a baby.

"You have suffered enough for your youthful infatuation with Cecily. And she certainly had an unhappy life, the poor thing," his mother had said after Cecily's death. *"You are a loving man, Wyndham. You should marry again. This time, to a wife of your own choosing."*

Plimpton stared at the wife of his choosing and could not resist giving her another kiss—a deep, searching one that left them both out of breath.

"What was that for?" she asked. "Not that I am complaining."

"No reason. Although I *did* want to thank you again for my wonderful wedding present." Winifred had stitched an astoundingly lifelike picture of Sweet Clover, compete with bees so real looking that he swore he could hear them buzzing. Plimpton had had it framed and it would hang in his library at Whitcombe, in a place of honor.

She laughed. "If you like my needlework, it will all be yours from now on."

"I certainly won't allow you to sell any of it," he assured her.

"Do you think you will enjoy this party, Plimpton?"

"Why wouldn't I?"

"I worry that you will feel left out given that the rest of us know each other so well."

"I like seeing you enjoy time with your friends, Winifred." Even if he *had* briefly wanted to throttle Avington for kissing her the day before. "And I am looking forward to becoming acquainted with both your friends and their spouses. Already I've had some interesting conversations with Lady Avington, Gareth Lockheart, and Lord Broughton." He paused and then added, "The Countess of Avington is a fascinating and somewhat intimidating woman."

Winifred chuckled. "Mary is very clever, and she also has a big heart—although she tries to hide it behind her businesslike façade. I am so delighted that she and Miles have made more of their marriage than just a convenient union." Her lips twitched. "I must admit at the beginning I thought one of us might have to strangle Mary for being so cruel to poor Miles."

It was clear that Winifred and her female friends considered *poor Miles* something of a pet, a role the handsome earl reveled in. Well, Plimpton could not blame the man for enjoying his special position; the women from the Stefani Academy were an impressive group.

"What did you think of Portia's husband and Mr. Lockheart?"

"Lord Broughton possesses the sort of business experience that I find fascinating but know nothing about. Lockheart is a bit…odd, but it is clear that he is brilliant. I think he is also a bit obsessed with his missing friend—er, McElroy, is it?" His wife nodded. "Lockheart said he might go looking for the man himself if he has no word from him by tomorrow." Plimpton had rarely met a man as...*intense,* for lack of a better word, as Gareth Lockheart.

"Serena says Mr. McElroy is not well."

"Why is he coming to a house party if he is ill?"

"Not that sort of *not well.*" She gave him a speaking look.

"A dipsomaniac?" Plimpton guessed.

"It sounds that way. Evidently Lockheart and McElroy are very attached—as close as brothers—and have been friends ever since they were boys. They grew up in an orphanage—a horrible place according to Serena."

Plimpton grimaced. "It is difficult to imagine having such a beginning in life. It makes Lockheart's achievements all the more admirable."

"He and McElroy are a team when it comes to acquiring new businesses.

"Interesting," he said, distracted by her breasts, which were still faintly passion mottled. He cupped one and thumbed the nipple. It immediately began to harden.

His wife's body shook with laughter, causing her breasts to jiggle enticingly. "Something tells me you are finished talking about poor Mr. Lockheart's missing friend."

"I have to admit I find other matters"—he lightly pinched her nipple, earning a hiss— "far more compelling."

"I never would have guessed you had such a short attention span."

"Not for everything." He captured the dark pink nub with his lips and sucked hard.

"*Ohhh.* No, not for everything," she agreed as he slid a hand down her belly to her mound. "Some things you apply your entire—*uh,* Wyndham."

"Such a good wife," he praised when her thighs parted for his touch.

"I try to be."

He chuckled at her prim, breathy voice, reveling in the way her hips tilted to give him better access.

"I love your laugh, Wyndham."

"What else do you love? This?" He pushed a finger inside her wet heat and worked her until she was vibrating like a finely tuned instrument which only *Plimpton* was allowed to play and master.

"Yes. *That*," she said, shivering with delight.

"*Hmm*. What about this?" Plimpton circled the source of her pleasure, teasing her little nub until it was engorged and throbbing.

Her eyelashes fluttered. "Yes...yes. I *love* that."

"Then I had better give you plenty more of it." Plimpton spread her thighs wider as he settled down between them and lowered his mouth to her sex.

She groaned. "That feels so *good*."

Plimpton preened at her praise, applying himself even more diligently.

She slid her fingers into his hair and gently but firmly lifted his head.

He raised an eyebrow.

"I am so greedy, Wyndham. You should allow me to—"

He growled and glanced down to where his fingers kept her spread and vulnerable. "You are not nearly as greedy as I am, Winifred." He thumbed the bundle of nerves in *precisely* the right place. "You should not thwart your husband's will."

Winifred groaned. "I surrender," she said, her hands going limp and releasing him.

"Such a good wife," he praised, and then returned to what he loved best. As tempting as it was to make her pay for her momentary disobedience, he could not resist making her come apart.

It did not take long before her entire body stiffened and arched off the bed. "Wyndham!" she cried, shaking as she gave in to bliss.

The Etiquette of Love

Watching her come undone was truly Plimpton's part of the day.

The last tremors had not yet fled before she again exerted pressure on his hair. "Come up here."

"As my duchess commands." He pushed up onto his hands and knees and prowled up her limp, sated body until he could lay down alongside her, face-to-face.

She gave him a tremulous smile. "You like to render me witless."

"Yes."

She gave an adorable gurgle of laughter. "Am I the only person in the world who knows what a wonderful, generous, funny person you are?"

"Just you, darling." He kissed her nose.

"How can I make you as happy as I am?"

Plimpton kissed her again, lingeringly this time. "I am already so happy that I feel guilty."

"Tell me this happiness will last, Wyndham. Tell me you will not stop loving me."

"I am not going to stop. In fact, I'm going to love you more, until you are quite fed up with me."

"You promise?"

"I promise with all my heart, darling."

Winifred took his face in her hands and looked not just into his eyes, but into his soul. "For always and forever?"

"For always and forever." Plimpton kissed her. "And that, my love, is a promise I look forward to keeping."

The End

Minerva Spencer & S.M. LaViolette

Dearest Reader:

I know what you are wondering… WHERE THE HELL IS DECLAN?

If you would like to enjoy a free teaser chapter (which I initially included here and called a Second Epilogue, but changed that when it became a bit too long and unconnected to be an *epilogue*) you can go to minervaspencer.com, find the blog post titled: SNEAK PEEK AT DECLAN'S STORY and enter the password: WICKED all upper case.

Enjoy!

Why is the password *wicked*? Because as I finished Declan's teaser the words of the immortal Katrina Van Tassel (a la Christina Ricci) came to me: "Was that wicked of me?"

Yes, throwing Declan into the mix WAS wicked. Well, I get at least one email a week from a reader asking about the guy, so I thought, "What the heck?"

When will I give you the rest of it?

I am afraid you will have to wait a year for it (insert author dodging rotten fruit, rocks, harsh language, etc.) but at least it is underway, right?

Putting Declan aside for the moment, let's talk about Freddie and Plimpton!

My husband, who is always my beta reader, said, "Why do you keep calling him Plimpton instead of Wyndham?"

That was a good question. The reason I kept Plimpton just a bit more formal than usual is because it seemed to fit with the kind of guy he is. For me, writing dukes is not something I do all the time (I think this is my 4th duke out of I don't know how many—30? 40?—books). I know dukes are EVERYWHERE these days. In fact, it seems like the

The Etiquette of Love

humble baronet or baron is far rarer than dukes in historical romance, lol.

Anyhow, if I'm going to write a duke then I feel like he should different because in the real world they are very different, indeed. And there are only about a dozen of them in England.

So, instead of turning Plimpton into the Regency equivalent of a casual, back-slapping frat boy, it seemed fitting to make him aloof, reserved, standoffish, and all those other words I used to describe him.

So that was fun for me.

Freddie was a bit of a surprise for me. For years now I've suspected that she was hiding something behind that repressed façade of hers. And boy was I right. She has been the grown up throughout the previous 6 books, so it was great to let her cut loose.

Okay, I have an embarrassing secret to share…

I wrote about 50 or 60 pages of this book before noticing a HUGE freaking problem. In the original story I had Mr. Gregg as Freddie's legitimate brother who had been done out of his title and wealth by a super devious series of events (you know how I like to do things) but at the back of my overcrowded brain a voice kept whispering, "*Psssst*, Minerva…something is very, very wrong here…."

Because I am a BAD, disorganized author who doesn't keep what is commonly referred to as a "story bible" I had to comb through the prior books looking for what sort of stuff I'd shared about Freddie over the last 5 years. Sure enough, I found her legitimate and very much alive and kicking brother, the Earl of Wareham, mentioned in **DANCING WITH LOVE**.

Whoops.

I had to scrap the entire story I had planned—and it was a doozy, too—and I apologized profusely to my muse, Mr. Spencer, who'd helped me talk out a bunch of tricky plot points that now went into the trash. And then I tried to open my mind to something completely new.

That…took a while. Hence the reason for pushing this story.

Anyhow, this story—I FEEL—was a very low angst love story. Wasn't it? I thought it was. At least that is how I wanted it to be. Right now, I am just reading stuff that doesn't rock my boat too much, so I wanted to share something that was gentle in the best of ways, like a warm fuzzy blanket. I think this is the second time I've opted for warm and fuzzy in the past year. Never fear, I'm sure I'll get all angsty again sooner rather than later.

I really grew to love Freddie. She clung to her public mask fiercely—after all, being the grownup was her identity among her small group of friends—but I loved the way all her reserve went flying whenever Plimpton came around.

I know some people like to imagine what the characters look like, but then others ask me what I envisioned.

If the book were made into a movie, Freddie would be played by January Jones—in her MAD MEN phase. Until she rips off her mask and then she is definitely Emma Frost from X-MEN: cold, but so hot.

Plimpton would FOR SURE be played by Rufus Sewell. *Uhngnh*, Rufus (only this guy could make that name sound good, lol).

I mean, he has to be one of the sexiest men alive, but he really *shouldn't* be because he is always such a bad guy. Anyhow, Plimpton IS Rufus—during his A KNIGHT'S TALE phase. Or any phase, really.

So, there you have it.

As usual, I cut tons from this story, especially since I really got carried away with the friend-reunion at the end of the book. It seemed like *everyone* wanted to get a bit of stage time. Soon it got out of hand, lol. So I had to get brutal with the red pen.

A character who came dangerously close to hijacking the story at times was Piers. I think he might need a book. I wrote a couple chapters that went into a lot of detail about how he was snooping around looking for clues. In one chapter I had him taking a job as a servant in one of the suspect's houses. Hijinks ensued with a frigid governess who had *her* own secrets and I was writing like a madwoman when I recalled that story was: *for later, Minerva.*

The Etiquette of Love

Out came my red pen. Again.

Anyhow, back to Freddie.

I knew she was hiding something in her life, but Miranda really surprised me.

Here is a bit of commentary on writing a character like Miranda. It's a real tightrope because until quite recently people used objectionable terms for those who are intellectually disabled—the currently "acceptable" term as far as I can tell. Even so, I'm sure it doesn't make everyone happy.

I don't use words like "idiot" or "simple minded" because I want to offend people. I use them because those are probably the *least* obnoxious terms most people would have used to describe somebody like Miranda in 1819. As an author, it feels weird and ahistorical to use the term "intellectually disabled" in a story set during this period. I feel strongly that we as readers should never forget there was a time in the not so distant past when it was perfectly okay to use such cruel language. Heck, some people still think it is okay, today. Anyhow, by covering it up or hiding the unpleasantness of the past, I worry we will raise a generation of people who think that the way things are *now* is how they always were.

Okay, I will climb down off my soapbox now.

So, what else is new? Well, I have stepped away from social media. I'm not sure if it will be forever, or just for now, but it was really messing with my tiny brain. I cancelled my IG account and was in the process of doing the same with Facebook when a friend mentioned that I might not want to give up my name on social media platforms, even if I wasn't using them. Well, dang. I hadn't thought about that. So, there is still a FB account, but I have not looked at it in a while and have no plans to. Someday, maybe.

Although I don't like the current vibes on IG and FB, I DO like keeping in touch with readers. So, I decided to take out my blog and dust it off. I have made a few posts and am slowly getting back into the groove of blogging, which seemed to disappear from everywhere except food blogger sites about 4 or 5 years ago.

The comments are open on my posts, and I encourage people to pop in and chat if they like.

What am I working on right now?

As usual, I am writing at least 5 things. I have hundreds and hundreds of stories I've begun and then put on ice. When I am stuck writing a work in progress, I find it useful to cut my imagination loose and just write whatever my fingers dictate.

This time, my fingers have been typing a lot about Kathryn—which just so happens to be my next book. Yay! I have also started stories for both Doddy and Lucy, who are the 2 books afterward. I am really loving their stories, especially since Katie and Doddy are the siblings who benefited from their sisters' "sacrifices" and now they are left sitting in whipped cream through no effort of their own. Which naturally bothers them and causes some interesting conflicts. We authors thrive on conflict.

As for Lucy, I am going to have so much fun with her! But that's for later…

After that is **ARES: THE RAKE**, which is book 3 in **THE HALE FAMILY**. I've not started Ares's book yet, but I already know who his heroine is. It's tough for me to say who might come after Ares as all 3 remaining Hale siblings are jostling for their turn in the spotlight.

As I mentioned above, I've already started Doddy's—or Dauntry if you want to be formal—book and it is up for preorder if you'd like to grab a copy. Yes, that is a goose standing beside Dauntry on the cover, and her name is Gherkin. She *might* be modeled on a real-life goose named Pickles. Maybe.

And then the book after that will be Declan's story, which is titled THE SPIRIT OF LOVE, which will come out in February 2026.

People frequently ask about the next Victorian Decadence installment. *Argh*. I dunno. But I have a freaking DOOZY of a story that I've been working on. I am dying to get it out into the world, but that will only happen if I get all my other ducks in a row. If you know anything about ducks, you will know why that is not always so easy…

Okay, that about wraps it up for now. Ooh, wait—there is one more thing… HOW could I forget this?!

In honor of Jane Austen's 250th birthday I hid an Austen Easter egg in this book. By that, I mean there is a single line in the book that comes from a Jane Austen book—you just have to find it…

The first five folks to find it and then post the answer on my blog on the post titled: EASTER EGG CONTEST FOR THE ETIQUETTE OF LOVE will get a lovely surprise from ME! What sort of surprise? If I told you, it wouldn't be a surprise, would it? But it will be something bookish, of course.

And it will be something I will send out in the mail because I love snail mail.

So, the surprise will go to the first five people to put the correct sentence I am looking for in a comment.

Other people will not see the comments, but I will. If I don't hit the "approve" button, the comments will be only visible to me, that way nobody can see anyone else's answers and cheat. Not that my readers would be cheaters!

Anyhow, don't worry that I never approve your post—I will have seen it.

The contest will close March 6, 2025.at 24:00 MST and I will contact the winners for their mailing details within a few days.

So, that is it for now!

As usual, I love to get (kind) emails from readers so please do reach out to me any time at: minerva@minervaspencer.com.

And if you find any typos or errors you'd like to share, I am always appreciative.

I hope you are safe and warm wherever you are and have plenty of good books to curl up with.

Happy reading,

Minerva/S.M.

The Etiquette of Love

Who are Minerva Spencer & S.M. LaViolette?

Here I am with Mr. Spencer and Lucille (on my lap) trying to wrangle Eva and Winston for a Christmas photo.

Minerva is S.M.'s pen name (that's short for Shantal Marie) S.M. has been a criminal prosecutor, college history teacher, B&B operator, dock worker, ice cream manufacturer, reader for the blind, motel maid, and bounty hunter. Okay, so the part about being a bounty hunter is a lie. S.M. does, however, know how to hypnotize a Dungeness crab, sew her own Regency Era clothing, knit a frog hat, juggle, rebuild a 1959

Minerva Spencer & S.M. LaViolette

American Rambler, and gain control of Asia (and hold on to it) in the game of RISK.

Read more about S.M. at: www.MinervaSpencer.com

Follow 'us' on Bookbub:

Minerva's BookBub

S.M.'s Bookbub

On Goodreads

Minerva's OUTCASTS SERIES

DANGEROUS

BARBAROUS

SCANDALOUS

THE REBELS OF THE *TON*:

NOTORIOUS

OUTRAGEOUS

INFAMOUS

AUDACIOUS (NOVELLA)

THE SEDUCERS:

MELISSA AND THE VICAR

JOSS AND THE COUNTESS

The Etiquette of Love

HUGO AND THE MAIDEN

VICTORIAN DECADENCE: (HISTORICAL EROTIC ROMANCE—SUPER STEAMY!)

HIS HARLOT

HIS VALET

HIS COUNTESS

HER BEAST

THEIR MASTER

HER VILLAIN

THE ACADEMY OF LOVE:

THE MUSIC OF LOVE

A FIGURE OF LOVE

A PORTRAIT OF LOVE

THE LANGUAGE OF LOVE

DANCING WITH LOVE

A STORY OF LOVE

THE ETIQUETTE OF LOVE

THE SPIRIT OF LOVE*

THE MASQUERADERS:

THE FOOTMAN

Minerva Spencer & S.M. LaViolette

THE POSTILION

THE BASTARD

THE BELLAMY SISTERS

PHOEBE

HYACINTH

SELINA

AURELIA

A VERY BELLAMY CHRISTMAS

KATHRYN*

DAUNTRY*

THE HALE SAGA SERIES: AMERICANS IN LONDON

BALTHAZAR: THE SPARE

IO: THE SHREW

ARES: THE RAKE*

THE WICKED WOMEN OF WHITECHAPEL:

THE BOXING BARONESS

THE DUELING DUCHESS

THE CUTTHROAT COUNTESS

THE BACHELORS OF BOND STREET:

The Etiquette of Love

A SECOND CHANCE FOR LOVE (A NOVELLA)

THE ARRANGEMENT